WE'LL MEET AGAIN

It is April 1939 and, unaware that the German war machine is heading towards the Channel Islands, seventeen-year-old Meg Colivet and her sisters are enjoying a holiday in Oxford with their aunt. Here Meg meets charismatic German undergraduate Rayner Weiss and the couple fall passionately in love. But all too soon Britain is at war with Germany and Guernsey occupied. Meg insists on remaining with her family determined to save her beloved island from the ravages of war. And then she meets Rayner, now a German officer. Torn between her love for Rayner and her duty to her family, heartbroken Meg has a terrible choice to make...

WE'LL MEET AGAIN

WE'LL MEET AGAIN

by

Lily Baxter

Magna Large Print Books
Long Preston, North Yorkshire,
BD23 4ND, England.

British Library Cataloguing in Publication Data.

Baxter, Lily
  We'll meet again.

    A catalogue record of this book is
    available from the British Library

    ISBN   978-0-7505-3522-9

First published in Great Britain in 2011 by Arrow Books

Copyright © Lily Baxter 2011

Cover illustration © Colin Thomas

Lily Baxter has asserted her right under the Copyright, Designs and Patents Act, 1988 to be identified as the author of this work

Published in Large Print 2012 by arrangement with Arrow, one of the publishers in the Random House Group Ltd.

Magna Large Print is an imprint of Library Magna Books Ltd.

Printed and bound in Great Britain by
T.J. (International) Ltd., Cornwall, PL28 8RW

For Pat and John Langlois OBE

CHAPTER ONE

April 1939

The stormy deck of the cross-Channel paddle steamer was deserted except for a single figure leaning over the ship's rail, his outline blurred by mist and spray. For a moment Meg thought she was seeing a ghost; a phantom passenger doomed to travel the sea forever like the Flying Dutchman, but then he sneezed and reached into his pocket for a handkerchief. Vaguely disappointed that she had been robbed of a spiffing yarn with which to amuse her sister, Adele, she hesitated at the top of the companionway taking deep breaths of the damp salt-laden air. The weather had been fine when they left St Peter Port harbour, but the wind had strengthened as the vessel negotiated the turbulent currents of the Alderney race. The sea was now the colour of gunmetal and it was impossible to tell where the water ended and the sky began. It was not the sort of day to promenade on deck, but if she had remained in the cramped confines of the cabin ministering to Addie for a moment longer she too might have succumbed to the rigours of seasickness. Her reluctant patient had eventually begged to be left alone for a while and Meg had promised to be back soon. She had considered stopping in the saloon for a cup of tea and a bite to eat, but the snatches of conversations

11

she overheard as she passed between the tables were fraught with anxiety regarding the political situation in Europe. The threat of war with Germany was something she would rather forget for the time being at least. This journey was the start of a fortnight's holiday for herself and Adele. They would be staying with their favourite aunt and uncle in Oxford, and one of the highlights of the trip was an invitation to the May Ball with their elder brother, David. Meg had been looking forward to it for weeks.

A particularly spiteful gust of wind whipped her long blonde hair into a tangled mass, and she brushed a strand from her eyes. She knew that the sensible course was retreat to the comfort of the saloon, but the hint of danger offered by the stormy sea was a definite challenge and she was not about to admit defeat. Clinging to the handrail, she could not resist a second look at the mysterious stranger who seemed oblivious to the fact that he was getting soaked by the clouds of spray. He appeared to be staring into the bow waves lost in a world of his own. He must, Meg thought, have something extremely pressing on his mind, or he would have realised that this was not the safest place to be. She took a tentative step forward just as the vessel hit a trough between the waves. Her feet skidded on the wet planking, and she found herself flying across the deck. 'Look out,' she cried in an attempt to warn the man for whom she was heading helplessly and at breakneck speed.

He turned just in time to catch her before she pitched headlong over the railings into the turbulent water. He set her back on her feet. 'That was a near one. Are you okay?'

'Yes. I think so. Or at least I will be when my heart stops pounding. I didn't realise it was so rough or I'd have stayed below.' She eyed him curiously. 'I know you, don't I? You're Gerald LeFevre.'

He met her gaze with a smile of slowly dawning recognition. 'Meg Colivet? Good Lord. It must be four years or more since I last saw you. You were just a kid then with pigtails and freckles.'

She pulled a face. 'Don't remind me. You and David were always teasing me. You were really mean to me then, but I forgive you.'

'How is David? I haven't seen him for ages.'

'Well, I think. He's not the best correspondent in the world, but I'm on my way to see him now.'

'Remember me to him. We had some great times when we were younger.'

'You were both mean to me,' Meg said, smiling. 'You wouldn't let me join in your games. You said I was a little pest.'

He grinned. 'I wouldn't say that now. You're a very attractive young lady, but one with suicidal tendencies, I suspect. Coming out on deck in this weather wasn't perhaps the most sensible thing to do.'

Another large wave combined with a cross-current made the ship yaw and Meg had to clutch his arm in order to save herself from falling. 'I needed some fresh air.' She was forced to shout in order to make herself heard above the din of the water plashing from the paddle wheel and the throbbing of the engines. 'But I think I've had

13

enough of it for today.'

He slipped her hand through the crook of his arm. 'We'd better go below. I don't know about you but I could do with a nice hot cup of tea.'

Clinging on to him, Meg nodded wordlessly and they made their way slowly and with difficulty towards the companionway.

The saloon was packed with disconsolate passengers, some of them looking decidedly green, others deep in conversation apparently oblivious to their surroundings. Gerald found them a table and Meg slid onto the banquette, waiting for him to return with their order of tea and cakes. She was finding it hard to equate the tall, dark-haired young man with the tousled-headed boy whose parents had worked for her family ever since she could remember. His mother, Marie, was the cook at Colivet Manor, and his father, Eric, was officially her father's chauffeur, but Advocate Charles Colivet spent long hours in his office or in court and over the years Eric had taken on more and more responsibility for running the estate and the home farm. Meg often wondered what her family would do if the LeFevres ever decided to leave their employ, although she would never have dared mention such a thing in front of her mother. Muriel Colivet's ideas regarding class and society were positively Victorian and set in stone. As far as Mother was concerned everyone had their place in the social order of things, and there they must stay.

Meg shifted on her seat, craning her neck to see how far Gerald had got in the queue at the food counter. He turned his head and smiled at her as

14

if he had sensed that she was staring at him and she looked away, feeling the blood rush to her cheeks. He was attractive rather than classically good-looking, but she liked the way his eyes crinkled at the corners when he was amused. She decided that she approved of this new and mature version of the boy who had been her brother's friend and playmate during the school holidays. His younger sister, Simone, had never been Meg's favourite person but she had only occasionally accompanied her parents to work, preferring to stay in St Peter Port with an elderly aunt who undoubtedly pandered to her every whim, which was why she was so demanding and spoilt.

Eventually, and to everyone's surprise, Gerald had been packed off to boarding school on the mainland. David had attended a public school in England, as had most of the sons of well-to-do island families, but it was unheard of for a boy from a relatively poor background to have a private education. Where the LeFevres had obtained the money for his school fees had always been a bit of a mystery as far as the young Colivets were concerned. David had been convinced that Eric had won the football pools, and Adele had suggested that a rich relation had stumped up the cash. Meg had been thought too young to have any opinion of her own.

Being the youngest in the family was definitely a disadvantage. David was the son and heir who was supposed to be studying law in order to qualify him to join the family firm, although Meg was convinced that he spent most of his spare time taking flying lessons. He had always fancied himself as Guernsey's answer to the Red Baron, and a career in law came a very poor second. Adele's ambition was to marry a rich man before she was twenty. She had it fixed in her pretty head that if she was not at least engaged by then she would never live down the disgrace. Estelle Plummer, who had been head girl when Addie was in the fifth form at Whitefields Academy, and Meg a humble second former, had enjoyed the grandest white wedding ever seen on the island when she had only just turned nineteen. Estelle now drove round in her very own sports car and lived with her husband in a French-style chateau overlooking Vazon Bay.

Meg's ambitions were simpler. She wanted to leave home and earn her own living, but unfortunately she had never particularly shone at school and the only sport at which she excelled was riding. She had sometimes fancied herself as the first female jockey to win the Grand National, or an Olympic champion show jumper, but she knew in her heart that this was wishful thinking. She longed to travel and see the world outside the confines of a small island. She loved Guernsey and she loved her family, but she had always had a vague feeling that she ought to earn the privileges that her brother and sister took so much for granted. There must, she thought, be more to life than simply waiting for Mr Right to come along, which was what her mother expected of both her daughters. Addie was happy to comply and eager to settle down, but Meg felt a restless spirit urging her on to do something out of the ordinary. If only she knew what that was.

16

She looked up and smiled as Gerald placed a tray on the table in front of her.

'Tea and cream cakes.' He offered her the plate. 'Or are you one of those girls who never eat anything but lettuce leaves?'

She selected a particularly delicious-looking éclair oozing with cream. 'Not me. I love my food. Anyway, sit down and tell me what you've been doing since you left school. Are you still working in London? I seem to remember Marie saying something about it. She's terribly proud of you.'

He took a seat opposite her. 'Yes, I know. But mothers always think their offspring are remarkable. I'm sure that Mrs Colivet is the same.'

'Not with me. I'm the black sheep of the family, according to Mother. Addie's the golden girl, and David's the white-hot hope for the future. I've yet to find what my place is in the grand scheme of things. I was born too late to be a suffragette and I'm not clever enough to have discovered something like radium. But I am good with horses.'

Gerald chuckled and his dark eyes glinted with golden lights: like sun pennies on the surface of the waves, Meg thought, dropping her gaze in sudden confusion.

'I'm sure there's a great future for you written in the stars,' he said, pouring tea and handing her a cup. 'As for me, I'm a humble clerk in a law firm in the City of London.'

Meg leaned her elbows on the table, facing him earnestly. 'I envy you, Gerald.'

He was about to sip his tea but he hesitated. 'Why is that?'

'Because you've got the chance to make

something of yourself. I'd give my eye teeth to be able to get a job, but my parents won't hear of it. I can't leave home without their permission until I'm twenty-one and I'm not qualified to do anything other than pick tomatoes or work in the stables, although I'd do that if they'd let me.'

'But you have a lovely life, don't you? Most girls I know would envy you.'

'I feel such a fraud, Gerald. Idle people like me are no use to anybody. I want to make a difference in the world.'

'You could go to university and get a degree.'

Meg almost choked on a mouthful of éclair. 'Me? I failed almost all my exams, apart from art and English. I'd love to work in my father's office, even if it was only filing things and making tea, but he says that's out of the question. No, as I said, I think you're very lucky. At least you're able to do something worthwhile.'

He shrugged his shoulders. 'I'm supposed to be training to be an articled clerk, but I don't think there's going to be much chance of that happening now.'

'Why not?' Meg stared at him, surprised by his serious expression.

'We all know that there's going to be a war. I've joined the Territorials and I'll be one of the first to be called up if push comes to shove with the Germans. That's why I spent last weekend with my folks. I needed to visit them while I had the chance. I might never see them again.'

Meg swallowed convulsively. 'Don't say that, Gerald. You mustn't even think that way. Mr Chamberlain is going to sort everything out.

18

Mother said so.'

'Well, if Mrs Colivet thinks that, it must be right.' Gerald's wry smile faded into a frown. 'I'm afraid that your mother never thought much of me. She didn't approve of my friendship with David.'

'Now you know what I'm up against. Mother doesn't approve of anything I do either. She says I should have been born a boy, and sometimes I wish I had.'

'That would have been a terrible waste.'

She shot him a glance beneath her lashes. 'Are you flirting with me?'

'You've grown up to be quite a girl, Meg, and a very pretty one too. But I expect all the fellows tell you that.'

Honest to the last, Meg shook her head. 'No. You're the first, as it happens. Mother would have us girls shackled to a chaperone if she had her way. This is the first time that Addie and I have been allowed to leave home without someone watching our every movement. I'm trying to be calm and sophisticated but inside I'm bubbling with excitement. We're staying with Aunt Josie and Uncle Paul for two whole glorious weeks, and David is going to take Addie and me to the May Ball. It may sound nothing to you, but to me it's a huge adventure.'

'I love your enthusiasm for life. You're like a breath of fresh air and I hope you never change.'

She covered her confusion by selecting a chocolate cup cake. She was on foreign ground where young men were concerned, particularly ones as attractive as Gerald LeFevre. It was embarrassing to be approaching her seventeenth birthday without having had a boyfriend. Addie had managed to slip through the net quite literally by joining the tennis club, which their mother considered to be socially acceptable. What she did not know was that Adele attended parties at her friend Pearl Tostevin's house where they drank exotic cocktails, smoked cigarettes and danced to gramophone records playing jazz music. She realised suddenly that Gerald was speaking to her. 'Sorry, I was miles away. What did you say?'

'I said I wish we had more time together. I'd love to get to know you better, Meg.'

'Oh.' She studied his expression in case he was teasing, but it was clear that he was deadly serious. She crumbled the cake between her fingers. 'Really?' She bit her lip. That was a feeble thing to say, but she was suddenly at a loss for words.

He seemed to understand her confusion and he reached across the table to hold her hand. 'Yes, really, Meg. I like you a lot and I'm kicking myself for not coming home more often. We might have met up in very different circumstances.'

She swallowed hard, staring at their intertwined fingers. Gerald's were long and slim, pale and slightly ink-stained from constant use of a fountain pen; hers were smaller, square-tipped and suntanned. She raised her eyes to his face and her heart did a funny little hop inside her chest. She opened her mouth to speak but closed it again as she saw a familiar figure teetering towards them on high heels. 'Oh dear. Adele's come to find me. I said I wouldn't be long.'

Gerald rose from his seat as Adele reached the table. 'Miss Colivet, I must take full responsibility

20

for keeping Meg talking. Won't you join us?'

Adele acknowledged him with a curt nod of her head. 'No, thank you. I came to find my sister.'

Meg patted the seat beside her. 'Sit down, Addie. Do you know who this is? It's Gerald. I didn't recognise him either.'

Adele cast him an appraising glance. 'Hello, Gerald. I'm sorry, I didn't recognise you, but...' she clasped her hanky to her lips, 'I'm not feeling too good. You'll have to excuse us.' She eyed Meg with a meaningful frown. 'Are you coming?'

'If it's all the same to you, I'd rather stay here and finish my cup of tea.' Meg met her sister's imperative gaze with a lift of her chin. She loved Addie, but she was tired of being treated like an irresponsible juvenile. No one in the family seemed to take her seriously, and Gerald had treated her like a grown-up and an attractive one too.

'It's not seemly,' Adele said stiffly. 'Mother wouldn't approve of your being seen in the company of a young man.'

'That's so old-fashioned.'

'Yes, it is, but I don't make the rules.' Adele turned to Gerald. 'You understand, don't you? It's nothing personal.'

'Yes, Miss Adele.'

His expression was carefully controlled but Meg wished that the deck would open up and send her shooting down to the hold with the cargo for the rest of the journey. She felt Gerald's humiliation as keenly as if it were her own, but anything she said now would only make matters worse. She rose to her feet. 'Thanks for the tea and cake, Gerald. Good luck with everything.'

She held out her hand.

He held it for a second or two longer than was strictly necessary. 'I hope we meet again soon, Meg.'

'Yes, I hope so too.' Meg was surprised to find that she meant what she said. It was not merely a platitude. She would have loved to stay and chat, but she knew better than to make a fuss. Reluctantly, she followed Adele back to their cabin. 'Why did you do that?' she demanded once they were out of earshot. 'We weren't doing anything wrong.'

Adele glanced over her shoulder. 'I know that, but at least half those people in the lounge know you if only by sight. What would Mother say if she heard you were consorting with Gerald LeFevre?'

'We weren't consorting. We were talking about old times.'

'I expect you were, but Mother put me in charge and I'll be the one to get it in the neck if she finds out I wasn't doing my bit to keep the wretched family name as pure as the driven snow. I know it's crazy, but while we live at home we have to obey Mother's rules.' Adele quickened her pace as they neared their cabin. 'Oh, heavens, I think I'm going to sick up again.'

Meg thrust the door open and Adele made a dash for the hand basin. 'Is that why you're so eager to get married, Addie? I mean, is it a husband you want or a reason to leave home?'

Resting her forehead on the china lip of the basin, Adele groaned. 'Both, I think. Pass me a clean hanky, please. And stay with me until we get to Weymouth. I don't want to fall asleep on the ferry and end up back in Guernsey.'

'All right. I won't leave you alone again. Try to get some sleep.'

It was early evening when the taxi pulled up outside the Shelmerdines' large Victorian house in a well-to-do area of Oxford. A soft pearly dusk gave the wide avenue a magical look and the street lamps cast a hazy orange glow on the pavements. Scatterings of cherry blossom lay like confetti in the gutters and a breeze rustled the tight green leaf buds on the plane trees which lined the street. The houses in Danbury Avenue were all of the period when the emerging professional and merchant classes vied with the academics for their place in the city of dreaming spires. Solid red brick and slightly Gothic in appearance the villas had been designed to house large families and a small army of servants to attend to their needs.

Meg climbed out of the cab, stiff and tired from the long journey, but her physical discomfort did nothing to allay the excitement that bubbled up inside her. She felt like a bottle of lemonade that had been shaken up and was about to explode. The prospect of a holiday with Aunt Josie was thrilling. Still young and beautiful, and more than twenty years younger than her half-brothers, Charles and Bertrand, Josie was the over-indulged only child of their father's second marriage. This, she often said, was virtually guaranteed to turn her into a rebel, and at the age of nineteen, while staying with an old school friend and her family in Kensington, Josie had met Paul Shelmerdine, a newly qualified lawyer. Their whirlwind romance had culminated in a dash to Gretna Green where they married against the wishes of both families. Meg never tired of hearing the story told and retold with Josie's inevitable dramatic embellishments. She often said that she had missed her vocation. She could have acted Merle Oberon and Vivien Leigh off the silver screen had she not fallen in love and devoted herself to helping her husband build his career.

Meg waited impatiently for Adele to find the right amount of change to tip the cabby, but his expression when she dropped the coins into his outstretched palm was not one of overwhelming gratitude. Meg shifted uncomfortably from one foot to the other. She had intended to wait for their luggage to be disgorged from the boot, but at that moment Josie's maid, Freda, came hurrying down the garden path, relieving her of that necessity. Meg turned and saw her aunt silhouetted in the doorway with light pooling around her.

Josie Shelmerdine could have been posing for a fashion shoot. Her figure was arrow slim and her dark hair hung about her shoulders in a pageboy style that complemented her oval face and classic features. In Meg's opinion Disney's Snow White might have been modelled on Aunt Josie, and, of course, Uncle Paul was the handsome prince.

'Darling, how lovely to see you again.' Josie enveloped her in an affectionate hug and a cloud of Mitsouko perfume. 'Come inside, Meg. It's still chilly in the evenings.'

'Addie's just insulted the taxi driver by under-tipping him.'

'No matter, darling. Freda will sort it out. Go and warm yourself by the fire in the sitting room

24

and I'll wait for Adele.'

Shrugging off her linen blazer, which was stiff with salt and probably ruined after her excursion on deck, Meg hung it on the coat stand. She wandered into the sitting room, which was furnished in an ultra-modern style. It was, she thought, just like the illustrations in the expensive magazines that Mother bought and left lying on the occasional tables when she was entertaining ladies from the various committees of which she was a member.

The carpet was cream with a geometric design in black, and the fawn leather sofa and armchairs were art deco in style. Although, if Meg were to be entirely honest, perhaps the rather theatrical decor might seem a little at odds with the high Victorian ceiling, the ornate plasterwork on the cornices and ceiling rose, and at variance with the black marble fireplace inset with tiles decorated with flowers and seashells. She moved closer to the hearth and flopped down on one of the armchairs. The leather expelled air like a sigh, or something slightly more embarrassing.

Josie ushered Adele into the room. 'Make yourselves comfortable, girls. You can tell me all the latest gossip from home while I pour the drinks.' She moved with the grace of a ballet dancer to the Japanese lacquered cocktail cabinet.

'Where's Uncle Paul?' Adele glanced round the room as if half expecting him to materialise from thin air.

'Unfortunately he's had to work late at the office, so it's just us for dinner tonight. It's such a bore and he works far too hard, poor sweet.'

'When will we see David?' Meg asked eagerly.

'We'll meet him in town for lunch tomorrow, but before that I'm going to take you shopping. Muriel has given me the task of finding you gowns for the May Ball. Isn't that exciting? Now what will you have to drink? You first, Adele. Gin and tonic, darling?'

Adele sank down on the sofa. 'Might I have a gin and It, Aunt Josie?'

'Of course. I keep forgetting that you're a young lady almost out of your teens now, Addie. No doubt you're the belle of the ball in St Peter Port.'

'Oh, I don't know about that,' Adele murmured modestly. 'But we do have quite a lot of parties, especially at Pearl's house. You must know the Tostevins, Aunt Josie. They live on the Grange.'

'I vaguely remember them,' Josie said, pouring a measure of gin into a cocktail shaker and adding a generous amount of Italian vermouth. 'It's many years since I was part of that particular scene, Addie.' She gave it a couple of shakes before pouring the contents into a glass. Impaling a maraschino cherry on a cocktail stick, she balanced it precariously on the edge of the glass. 'There, you won't get better than that at the Ritz. Now what about you, Meg? Are you allowed anything stronger than ginger beer these days?'

'I'd like a brandy Alexander, please.'

Josie raised her pencilled eyebrows. 'Darling, how chic. Is that what you drink at home?'

She could not lie, and anyway Addie was sending her a warning look. 'No, I've never tasted one. It just sounds nice.'

Josie's laughter tinkled round the room like

26

fairy bells. 'I think a weak G and T might be more suitable, Meg.' She poured a small amount of gin over some ice cubes and topped it up with tonic. 'Try that.' She watched critically while Meg took a sip. 'And don't wrinkle your nose. It's not considered the done thing.'

'It's very bitter,' Meg protested.

'That's the idea, darling. You'll get used to it. Now, where was I? Oh yes, I know. You were going to tell me everything that's been going on at home. How is my dear brother Charlie? And what about Muriel? Is she still ruling the roost like Catherine the Great?'

Meg and Adele exchanged wary glances.

'Mother asked to be remembered to you,' Adele said tactfully. 'Pa sends his love, of course.'

'Dear old Charlie. I do miss him. And how is my brother Bertie and maddening Maud? They had to get married you know,' Josie said with a giggle. 'Still in their teens, and then their ghastly daughter, my dear niece Jane, repeats history aged eighteen.'

'They're all well,' Meg volunteered. 'We don't see too much of them since Uncle Bertie gave up work for health reasons.'

'Health reasons, my foot. Charles was heroic to take him on, in the first place.' Josie sipped the gin and tonic she had mixed for herself. 'I love Bertie, of course, but he always seemed to think that the world owed him a living. As to Jane, we're so unalike that I can't believe we came from the same root stock, and that boy of hers is a freak.'

'We don't see her very often either, or Pip. He might be our second cousin but I feel the same

27

way about him as you do about Aunt Jane.' Adele twirled the cherry around in her glass. 'Could we change the subject, Aunt Josie? We came here to get away from the family for a while.'

'Of course, darling. It's just morbid curiosity on my part. Let's talk about something much more interesting.' Josie perched on the arm of Meg's chair. 'What sort of ball gowns had you in mind? You first, Addie.'

Next morning, after an exhaustive tour of the dress shops in Oxford, even Josie was beginning to flag a little. 'We've left it so late,' she said, shaking her head. 'There's only one tiny boutique that I can think of where we might find something suitable for both of you. It's not far from here and it's our last chance, but if all else fails we'll take the train to London tomorrow and scour the stores in Oxford Street and the whole of Mayfair if necessary.'

'I never realised it would be such hard work,' Meg said, frowning. 'We must have tried on dozens of frocks. If another sales assistant tells me I look lovely in something that makes me look like a marshmallow or a Christmas cracker, I think I'll scream.'

'Well, I'm enjoying it,' Adele said stoutly. 'I could have chosen several of those I tried on, but Aunt Josie knows best.'

'That I do.' Josie stopped outside a shop window with a single gown artistically draped on a headless mannequin. 'Madame Elizabeth's is where the top people go, so no funny remarks, Meg. This is serious and with the ball only two days away I'd

28

say it's critical. Follow me.'

She entered the salon with a determined twitch of her slender shoulders. By this time, Meg had lost all her enthusiasm for shopping. Her feet were sore and she wished that she had eaten something more substantial than a bowl of cornflakes first thing that morning. Josie did not believe in cooked breakfasts, but then she ate sparingly of every-thing, as Meg had noticed at dinner the previous evening. The food had been excellent but Josie picked at hers, confessing that the thought of gaining an extra pound or two was terrifying in the extreme. Paul, she said with a wry smile, did not like plump women. Meg thought privately that if she married a man who made her starve in order to keep her figure she would divorce him and find someone else.

'Madame Elizabeth,' Josie said with a charming smile. 'We need your help desperately.'

Meg took a seat on one of the spindly gilt and red plush chairs set out for prospective customers, and allowed her thoughts to drift in the direction of lunch. They were to meet David at the Mitre Hotel, which luckily was only a couple of streets away. She hoped there would be something deli-cious and substantial on the menu. Her stomach growled and she shot an apologetic glance at Mad-ame Elizabeth, who had somehow managed to pour Adele into a shimmering oyster-satin sheath of a gown that flared out in a fishtail around the ankles. A bit like one of the carp that lived in the lake at home, Meg thought inconsequentially.

Adele hitched the low-cut top a little higher. 'It's very tight. I can hardly breathe.'

Madame frowned. 'It is meant to hug the figure, mademoiselle. Otherwise it might not remain in situ.'

'It's really lovely,' Josie said enthusiastically. 'That shade is very flattering for someone with your ivory complexion, Addie.'

'Perhaps Mademoiselle would like to try the green silk organza, madame?'

Thankfully from Meg's point of view, the green organza received a thumbs down and the oyster satin was sent off to be wrapped in tissue paper by a bored-looking assistant.

'I'll take this one,' Meg said in desperation as she tried on the third gown. By this time she was past caring. Number three was a sickly shade of pink like melted strawberry ice cream, but it was marginally better than the lilac chiffon with a skirt the consisted of frills from waist to ankle and made her look like a bell tent.

'I don't think so,' Josie said, shaking her head. 'Is that all you have in Meg's size, madame?'

'My clientele are usually ladies of a certain age and sophistication,' Madame said, pursing her lips. 'There is just one other, but I am not certain that Madame will approve of that either.'

'Let me have this one,' Meg begged. She felt light-headed and was certain she would faint if she did not eat something very soon. 'Who's going to look at me anyway?' She hesitated, realising that she had said the wrong thing. 'I mean, no one will give me a second look when Addie's in the room.'

Adele blushed and pulled a face. 'That's not true.'

'We'll see the last gown,' Josie said firmly. 'Then

30

I'm afraid we must hurry, madame, as we have a luncheon appointment.'

Madame seized Meg's arm in a vice-like grip, and her lips stretched over her teeth in a caricature of a smile. 'Very well, madame. Come with me, mademoiselle. My assistant will look after you.'

Bearing an armful of gold shot-silk taffeta, the young girl gave Meg a shy smile. 'Perhaps you'd like to try this one?'

'Oh, I love that colour,' Meg said sincerely. She held her arms above her head and shivered with pleasure as the cool silky material embraced her flesh. It was a tight fit. And she had to hold her breath while the assistant struggled with the zip, but the result was stunning. The boned bodice fitted like a second skin and quite suddenly Meg had a figure that, if not exactly hourglass, was what could be described as shapely without fear of exaggeration. 'I've got a bust,' Meg said happily. 'And a waist too.' She did a twirl and the material swirled around her like the petals of a tea rose. 'It's beautiful.' She bundled up the skirts and emerged into the salon like a butterfly bursting from its chrysalis. 'What d'you think, Aunt Josie? Isn't it gorgeous, Addie?'

Madame folded her thin hands in front of her. 'In view of Mademoiselle's tender years, perhaps it is not quite suitable, madame? The colour is not quite right for an ingénue.'

Josie rose to her feet, taking her cheque book from her handbag. 'It's certainly eye-catching, and if Meg feels good in it then that's the one for her. Shall we get down to the vulgar business of the price, madame?'

31

'Pa will have a fit when he gets the bill,' Adele said in a low voice as they left the shop. 'That's my allowance gone for the next twenty years.'

'Nonsense,' Josie said, chuckling. 'The ball gowns are my present to you both. I've no children of my own to spoil so I think I might be allowed to indulge my beautiful nieces once in a while. You'll both look absolutely stunning, and David's friends will fall at your feet.'

'His friends?' Adele was suddenly alert. 'Are they joining us for lunch?'

Josie smiled and nodded. 'We're meeting your escorts for the ball at lunch. David will introduce you but I've already met Walter. He's a charming young man who's studying medicine, and there's Frank Barton.' She shot a mischievous look in Adele's direction. 'You'll like him, Addie. He's good-looking and frightfully well off. He could have been ordered for you straight from Harrods.'

Adele blushed and frowned. 'Don't be mean, Aunt Josie. You make me sound like a gold-digger.'

'Not at all, darling. I know you for a sweet girl and I'm sure Frank will see that too.' She turned to Meg, her expression serious for once. 'Now, Meg, I know you're inclined to speak your mind, so I want you to be very careful what you say. David's other friend is everything that Walter is and Frank too, so I've heard, but there's a subtle difference. I want you to think before you speak and treat him exactly the same as the others.'

Meg stared at her in surprise. 'What's wrong with him? Has he got two heads or something?'

CHAPTER TWO

As she left the bright sunshine and entered the cool interior of the Mitre Hotel it took Meg several seconds to grow accustomed to the dim light in the oak-beamed vestibule. 'It's really old,' she murmured, gazing around in awe.

'It was a coaching inn until 1926,' Josie said with a knowledgeable smile. 'There, girls, that's your history lesson for today. My darling husband would be proud of me. He always says I have the attention span of a goldfish and this proves him wrong. Anyway, let's go and find the boys. I believe I've worked up quite an appetite for lunch.' She led the way through the reception area to the restaurant, giving her name to the maître d'hôtel. With a courtly bow, he escorted them to a table at the far end of the room.

On seeing them David rose to his feet, and forgetting decorum Meg rushed over to fling her arms around him. 'It seems ages since you were last at home. I've really missed you.'

Laughing, he slipped his arm around her shoulders. 'I've missed you too, Meg.' He held his hand out to Adele. 'You're not going to make a show of me in front of everyone, are you, Addie?'

She smiled. 'No, of course not, but it's lovely to see you looking so well, David.'

'My turn,' Josie said, moving forward to kiss his cheek. 'Aren't you going to introduce the girls to

33

your friends? I know Walter, of course.'

There was a hint of coquetry in the smile that Josie directed at him. Meg was quick to notice that her aunt's charm was not lost on Walter or his two companions who had leapt to their feet and were waiting their turn to be introduced.

'It's good to see you again, Mrs Shelmerdine,' Walter said, blushing.

'Josie, please. None of this Mrs Shelmerdine nonsense.' Her attention wandered to a broad-shouldered young man. To Meg's eyes he looked the type who would be captain of the cricket eleven or one of the oarsmen in the annual university boat race.

'This is my good friend, Frank Barton, Aunt Josie,' David said, standing aside to allow Frank to shake her proffered hand. 'Frank, my aunt, Josie Shelmerdine, and my sisters Adele and Meg.'

'How do you do?' Frank shook hands rather too heartily, Meg thought, as he pumped her arm up and down. She noticed that his gaze rested rather longer on Adele than it did on either her or her aunt, but then that was only to be expected. Addie turned heads wherever she went.

David did not seem to be aware that anything out of the ordinary had occurred, or maybe he had grown accustomed to his friends falling head over heels for his pretty sister. Meg was used to taking second place, and catching Walter's eye she thought she saw a hint of sympathy in his smile. He was nice, she decided, warming to him. He looked like an overgrown schoolboy with a fresh face and smiling grey eyes. If Frank was the all round good egg and sportsman, then Walter was the sensitive, kind-to-animals type of person; someone to whom you could turn in a crisis. Walter was definitely all right in her book.

'This, as you've already gathered, girls, if you were paying attention, is Walter Howe,' David said somewhat unnecessarily.

'I'm delighted to meet you both at last,' Walter said, shaking their hands in turn. 'David's told me so much about you and your home in Guernsey.'

Adele flashed him a smile but Meg could see that her sister was far more interested in Frank. Aunt Josie, it seemed, had hit the nail on the head as far as Frank Barton was concerned.

'Last, but not least, is my good friend, Rayner.' David turned to a tall, blond young man. 'Aunt Josie, Addie, Meg, may I present Rayner Weiss who has come all the way from Dresden to study English.'

Rayner bowed from the waist. 'How do you do?' He spoke with only a trace of an accent.

Meg angled her head. So this was the mystery man. For almost as long as she could remember she had heard her father speak disparagingly of the Teutonic race, but this young man did not look like anyone's enemy. He had been standing quietly behind David but as he stepped forward she thought he looked surprisingly ordinary. He was a little above average in height and he had the straight features and fair complexion of any one of the Nordic peoples. What she had expected a German to look like she did not know, but Rayner Weiss looked as wholesome as an advert for breakfast cereal or toothpaste. She jumped as Adele nudged her in the ribs and she

35

held out her hand. 'How do you do, Mr Weiss?'

'How do you do, Miss Colivet?'

There was a hint of a smile in his blue eyes that reminded Meg of the sea on a summer's day. She felt herself blushing and looked away. Once again she wished that she had had more practice in dealing with the opposite sex. Addie was a natural; she made it all look so effortless.

'Everyone sit down, please,' David said, holding out a chair for Josie. 'I'm starving. I don't know about the rest of you, although I expect that Meg is more than ready for her lunch.'

She was about to retaliate when Rayner moved swiftly to her side. 'Allow me, Miss Colivet.'

'Meg,' she murmured as she took her seat. 'It's Meg, short for Marguerite.'

He smiled. 'That is a beautiful name.'

'Don't encourage her,' David said, sitting down next to Josie. 'Meg is still just a kid.'

'I am not,' Meg said fiercely. 'I'll be seventeen in June. You know that jolly well.'

He leaned across the table to pat her on the head. 'Now, now, little sister, don't get in a pet. I was joking.'

'It's such a pity that Paul couldn't join us for lunch, but the poor dear is snowed under with work,' Josie said swiftly before Meg could retaliate. She glanced at the waiter who was hovering at a discreet distance from the table. 'I think we should order now, don't you, David?'

The meal passed pleasantly with Josie encouraging the young men to talk about themselves, their studies and their ambitions for the future. Meg could only sit back and admire her aunt's ability to draw people into conversation, even the shy ones like Walter, who with a little gentle probing from Josie became quite animated as he talked about his desire to practise medicine in a rural area. Frank needed no persuasion in order to bring him out of his shell, if he had one, Meg thought wryly, when he talked at length about his father's business, which turned out to be a shipping line. Adele listened with rapt attention, hanging on his every word. Meg could almost hear the wedding bells ringing in her ears as she watched her sister being seduced by the world of wealth and privilege.

Rayner was less forthcoming and Meg admired him for that. He talked fondly about his parents and his home in Dresden, but said little about the toy factory owned by his family, and then changed the subject to include David and their shared passion for flying. Taking his cue, David was only too pleased to talk about their exploits in the air. Meg could not help wondering what their father would make of the fact that his son and heir spent more time flying aeroplanes than he did attending lectures. She did not blame David one bit, but she decided that this would be one piece of news that she would not pass on to her parents when she returned home. As she listened to her brother she could not help casting covert glances at Rayner. His calm expression and self-contained manner fascinated her. He did not seem to need to push himself forward like Frank, nor was he self-effacing like Walter. His reserve seemed to be based in the quiet confidence of a man who knew where he was going and what he wanted from life.

He might be of a similar age, but in her opinion he made David and the others look like callow youths. Rayner Weiss was someone she would like to know better. She realised suddenly that David had stopped talking. She looked up to find him frowning at her. 'You haven't heard a word I said, have you, Meg?'

Everyone was staring at her.

'I'm sorry,' she murmured apologetically. 'What were you saying?'

He shrugged his shoulders. 'Since you couldn't be bothered to listen, I don't suppose you'd be interested. We'll go without you tomorrow.'

'You were ogling Rayner Weiss all through lunch,' Adele said, chuckling. 'You were in a dream world all of your own, as usual. If Rayner hadn't stood up for you I think David really would have made you stay at home and miss the river trip tomorrow.'

Sitting cross-legged on her bed in the room they had shared as children and still elected to use now, even though the Shelmerdines' house boasted seven bedrooms, Meg tossed her slipper at her sister. 'I didn't ogle him. Anyway, you only had eyes for Frank so you wouldn't have noticed if I'd got up and danced on the table.'

Adele stopped brushing her hair for a moment to glance over her shoulder. 'I think I might.' She twisted round on the dressing table stool to face Meg. 'But Frank is absolutely super, isn't he? He's so good-looking, and charming too.'

'And rich. I don't suppose that has anything to do with your crush on him?'

'Of course not. Well, if I'm being perfectly honest, I suppose it does add a teensy bit to his attractiveness, but I'd like him even if his father didn't own a shipping line or two.'

'Well, good luck,' Meg said sincerely. 'He seems a decent enough chap and if you like him, that's all that matters.'

'I don't suppose it will come to anything. We'll be going home in less than a fortnight and I may never see him again.' Adele turned back to gaze soulfully at her reflection in the mirror.

'Then you'd best work fast if you want him,' Meg said, uncurling her legs to sit on the edge of the bed. 'You'll have a chance to get to know him better on the river trip tomorrow, and then there's the May Ball. I expect he'll dance you off your feet, and there'll be wine and moonlight and music...'

'Meggie, you're turning into a real romantic,' Adele said, smiling. 'You must be in love with the handsome German.'

Meg lobbed the other slipper, narrowly missing Adele and knocking a cut-glass perfume atomiser off the dressing table.

Frank and Walter arrived punctually at one o'clock the next day. Encouraged by Meg to make the most of her charms, Adele drifted across the gravelled drive in her ankle length rose-print chiffon dress. In one hand she carried a small white handbag little bigger than a purse, and in the other a wide-brimmed straw hat. Her high-heeled sandals were not designed for walking on rough ground, but Meg's master plan seemed to have worked as Frank helped Adele into his Riley tourer as if she were too fragile to get in unaided. Meg watched them with a satisfied smile; so far so good. Frank Barton would have to be made of concrete if he could not see what a lovely girl Adele was beneath the frills and furbelows. Her sister might aggravate her sometimes, but she would go to any lengths to see her happy.

'Hello, Meg. You look smashing,' Walter said, smiling shyly.

'Thanks, Walter.' She looked him up and down and was impressed by his smart, if conservative, appearance in a black blazer and grey flannels. 'You look pretty good yourself.' As she climbed into the back of the car Meg was glad that she had worn plain navy blue slacks, a striped sweater and deck shoes. She might not look a picture of feminine elegance like Addie, but at least she would be comfortable. Some girls were born to be pampered, and others to be a jolly good sport. She suspected that she was the latter.

David and Rayner were waiting for them on the towpath below Folly Bridge. The punt was moored alongside, complete with velvet cushions and a large wicker picnic hamper.

'This is lovely,' Meg said enthusiastically.

David ruffled her hair. 'Glad you think so, but don't forget, one peep out of you, kid, and it'll be man overboard.'

'Surely that should be woman overboard?' Rayner said with a wry smile.

David slapped him on the back. 'Pedantic as usual, you old Kraut.'

'Well, I am here to brush up my English. At least you might try to get it right for me.'

40

Meg pulled a face at her brother. 'David hasn't learned to speak English properly himself.'

'Get into the punt, Meg, and don't be cheeky to your elders.' David pulled the punt closer to the shore, and Walter caught her as she leapt aboard. Adele was already seated in the stern with her skirts spread out around her and Frank had placed himself next to her. The pair were deep in conversation, and determined not to play gooseberry Meg sat as far away from them as was possible. Walter and Rayner manhandled the picnic basket into position and took their seats while David untied the mooring rope and leapt onto the punt. He balanced expertly and poled it into midstream. Meg was secretly impressed by his efforts, but it was obvious that this was not his first time on the water. Again, she wondered what their parents would say if they knew of their son's extracurricular activities. 'It looks quite easy. Can I have a go?' she said after a while, as the punt skimmed silently downriver.

David shook his head. 'Not now, Meg. I want to find a quiet spot where we can have lunch. You can have a go later.'

She turned to Walter who had settled himself on a cushion beside her. 'This is fun. What a pity Aunt Josie couldn't come with us.'

He nodded his head. 'She's a wonderful woman. I've never known anyone quite like her.'

'She is rather special, isn't she?' Meg eyed him curiously, sensing a deeper emotion than simple admiration. 'Do you see very much of her?'

'She's very kind and invites us poor undergrads to supper at least once a week.' He trailed his

41

fingers in the water. 'That husband of hers never seems to be at home.'

'Uncle Paul's a busy man. He works terribly hard.'

Walter shot her a wary look. 'I didn't mean to criticise him. It's just that I don't understand how he can leave a lovely vibrant person like Mrs Shelmerdine so much on her own.'

Meg digested this in silence. She had seen her uncle briefly at breakfast the morning after their arrival, and he had apologised profusely for not being there to greet them when they arrived, but his place at table had again been empty last evening at dinner. Meg knew from the long hours her father spent at the office and in the law courts that the life of a lawyer was not necessarily his own, but she had never thought of Aunt Josie as a neglected wife. She pushed the disturbing vision to the back of her mind. It was becoming obvious that Walter had a crush on her aunt, but she was at least ten years his senior, maybe even twelve. Even if Aunt Josie were free, she would never consider allying herself to a much younger man. That would not be the accepted thing at all. Mother would have forty fits and even Pa might raise an eyebrow.

Meg leaned back against the cushions. Frank and Adele were nattering away as if they had known each other for years, and Rayner had pulled his straw boater down over his eyes as he lounged in the bows. She wondered if he was asleep or merely wanted to remain aloof from the party. She was not quite sure how to treat him, but she was keen to know him better. She found him enigmatic and fascinating. He was unlike

42

anyone else she had ever met, but he seemed to have set up an invisible barrier, excluding everyone except David. It was quite obvious that they were the best of friends and totally at ease in each other's company. Meg was mystified and intrigued. She relaxed and breathed in the scent of the river. The smell of mud and rotting vegetation mingled with the honey fragrance of clover from the fields on either side of the weeping willows that lined the banks. It was quiet and peaceful with just the plashing of the water against the hull of the punt. Adele and Frank were silent now, but a quick glance over her shoulder revealed them holding hands and gazing at each other. Meg smiled to herself. Things were going well for Addie. She could not have been happier.

When they were a little further downriver, David steered the punt towards the bank declaring that he had done enough hard work for now and needed a rest. 'Wake up, Rayner, you lazy dog. Look lively there. Hop ashore like a good chap and tie the painter to a tree or something.'

Rayner raised himself quickly for someone who was supposed to have been dozing and he leapt onto the bank to secure the rope to the branch of a stunted hazel. Walter undertook to heft the heavy hamper onto dry ground, and it was Rayner who held his hand out to help Meg ashore.

His fingers felt strong and cool, and she was vaguely disappointed when he released his hold and strolled off to assist David, who had selected a suitable place for their picnic in the shade of a willow tree. Frank had gallantly lifted Adele onto dry land, and taking off his blazer he laid it on

43

the ground for her. Like a modern-day Sir Walter Raleigh, Meg thought, sighing. How terribly romantic.

Walter was attending to the practicality of unpacking the hamper. He brought out several packets of sandwiches wrapped in greaseproof paper, a fruitcake and two bottles of champagne.

The food was consumed rapidly and the second bottle of champagne was opened and drunk with the same speed as the first. Adele said she would like to walk along the towpath and Frank scrambled to his feet saying that he also would like to stretch his legs. Walter had fallen asleep leaning against the trunk of the willow, snoring gently with his chin resting on his chest. David and Rayner sat smoking cigarettes and chatting about the flying club, which precluded Meg from the conversation. Bored and feeling slightly lightheaded after the champagne, she scrambled to her feet. 'I'd like to have a go at punting, David.'

'Not now, Meg. Sit down like a good girl or go for a walk. We're busy.'

'David, you promised.'

'I'll show you.' Rayner tossed his cigarette butt into the river and stood up, brushing the grass from his cream flannels.

Meg stared at him in surprise. 'Are you sure?'

'Come along. There's nothing to it.'

'If she falls in you can save her,' David said, leaning back against the cushions and closing his eyes.

Meg soon found out that it was not as easy as it looked. Rayner gave her a brief demonstration and then they changed places. To her intense embarrassment the first thing she did was get the pole stuck in the mud. She wobbled dangerously but with Rayner's calm guidance she managed to right her mistake. "This is lovely,' she said gleefully as the punt moved out into midstream. 'I can do it. Look at me, David. I can do it.'

'Mind the overhanging bough.'

Rayner's warning came too late. The branch caught her head a glancing blow and she leaned too hard on the pole. Once again it stuck in the mud but this time she could not regain her balance. She teetered for a few seconds but the punt had gained momentum and it continued downstream leaving her clinging to the slippery pole. Slowly and inexorably she slid into the turgid green water. The last thing she heard as the river engulfed her was Rayner's voice shouting to David. The shock of icy cold water numbed her brain and she forgot everything as panic overtook her. She struggled to reach the surface but she was hampered by her wet clothes. The current was strong and the undertow was dragging her down. She thrashed about with her arms but the weeds on the river bed clutched at her ankles. Water filled her ears and was trying to force its way up her nose and into her mouth. She could see the sunlight above the ripples but she could not surface. She could not breathe. She was going to die.

Suddenly a figure sliced though the water and came up beside her. Strong arms held her in a close embrace. She could feel the warmth of his body through the thin cotton of his shirt. Entwined, they twirled for a brief moment like partners in a macabre dance of death, and then

45

with a powerful kick of his legs Rayner thrust upwards and they surfaced together.

Coughing and spluttering, Meg gulped air into her lungs.

'It's all right. You're safe now. Relax.'

Rayner's voice in her ear was the most welcome sound she had ever heard. She clung to him, dazed and shivering from cold and shock as he swam her to the bank where helping hands dragged her from the water.

That evening they were all assembled in the Shelmerdines' drawing room for pre-dinner drinks. Paul had come home early from the office for once, and was dispensing champagne while Josie sat close to Meg on the sofa.

'You should have seen her, Aunt Josie,' David said, leaning back in his chair and stretching his long limbs. 'We pulled Meg out of the river looking like a mermaid. She had water weed in her hair and green slime all over her face.'

Josie frowned. 'That's not funny, David.' She squeezed Meg's hand. 'But she's safe and sound now, that's all that matters.'

Meg smiled wearily. She had never thought to see Aunt Josie's drawing room again, and she could still taste the muddy water of the River Thames. She could still feel the pressure on her lungs as she sank into its murky depths. 'I really thought I was going to drown.'

Paul topped up Rayner's glass with champagne. 'If it hadn't been for your prompt action, the outcome could have been very serious indeed. Meg could have died today but for you.'

46

Rayner accepted the accolade with a nod of his head. 'It was nothing, sir. We were very close to the bank.'

'You saved my life,' Meg said, smiling shyly. 'I can never thank you enough.'

'I expect someone would have fished you out further downstream,' David said casually. 'It was your fault you fell in anyway. You should have been paying attention to Rayner's instructions.'

Meg opened her mouth to argue but Josie, seeming to sense an impending squabble, turned to Rayner. 'I think you were terribly brave, and I'm so pleased you were able to come to dinner this evening.'

His serious expression melted into a smile. 'It was kind of you to invite me, Mrs Shelmerdine. Not everyone in Oxford is so broad-minded about Germans these days.'

'Oh, surely not?' Josie's eyes widened. 'I can't believe that anyone would hold someone like you responsible for the political situation.'

'Most people think that war is inevitable,' Paul said, pouring a large measure of whisky into his glass and adding just a dash of soda. 'What is your opinion, Rayner?'

'I wish it was not so, but I think you may be right, sir.'

'Don't spoil the evening by talking about war,' Josie said hastily. 'I'd like to know more about Rayner's home in Dresden, and his family.'

'Stop interrogating the boy, Josie,' Paul said sharply.

Meg looked up, startled. She had never heard him speak so harshly to Josie. She glanced at

Adele, who had been sitting on the window seat with Frank and had shown little interest in the general conversation so far, but now she too was staring at their uncle in astonishment.

Walter, who so far had taken little part in the proceedings, cleared his throat noisily. 'This is very good champagne, Mr Shelmerdine. It was kind of you to include us all in your invitation to dine tonight.'

'You have my wife to thank for that, Walter. I leave everything to her.' Paul raised his glass to Josie, but Meg was quick to note the mocking gleam in his dark eyes. Momentarily forgetting her traumatic experience, she wondered if all was well with the Shelmerdines' marriage. They had always seemed the perfect couple, ideally suited, and it was hard to believe that anything could have come between them.

She cast a sideways glance at Rayner, and as their eyes met she was certain that he too had sensed the tension between husband and wife. He turned to Josie with a smile. 'I'm happy to tell you anything you want to know, Mrs Shelmerdine.'

The warmth in his voice was a sharp contrast to Paul's cutting tone and Meg felt a surge of gratitude. It was the second time that day he had come to the rescue. She could have kissed him, but she managed to restrain herself. That was the sort of thing she would have done when she was thirteen or fourteen, but not now.

'Thank you, Rayner,' Josie said gently. She looked up as Freda entered the room. 'Perhaps we'll continue our conversation after dinner.'

'Dinner is served, ma'am.'

Josie rose to her feet. 'I'm sure you're all starving.' She held her hand out to Walter. 'We'll lead the way, shall we, Walter?'

Frank had already tucked Adele's hand through the crook of his arm and David strolled out of the room with his hands in his pockets.

'May I?' Rayner proffered his arm to Meg.

She smiled up at him. 'I think I read that in some cultures if you save a person's life then that life belongs to you.'

Paul downed the last of his drink. 'I'd say that was utter nonsense, Meg.' He ushered them out of the room.

Rayner's eyes were warm as they met Meg's anxious glance. 'I think it is an idea that has some merit. You have my word, that if you are in danger at any time I will do my best to save you.'

Unusually for her, Meg could think of nothing to say.

It was almost time to leave for the May Ball. The bedroom had all but disappeared beneath piles of undies and discarded clothes. The dressing table was littered with makeup, curlers, combs and bottles of nail polish. Meg took one last look in the mirror surveying the work of Josie's hairdresser who had performed a minor miracle on her thick, straight hair. She had cut it and styled it so that it hung in a shining honey-blonde pageboy. Josie had supervised her makeup and the result was a stranger staring back at her from the triple mirrors. Meg blinked and looked again. I look almost pretty, she thought. She twirled around several times, admiring the way the bias-cut skirt flared out in a swirl of gold and rose shot silk. She knew that Mother would not approve of the colour and she would say that the low-cut gown was too grown-up, but then Mother was not here and she would never know. Meg had already decided that the golden gown might be best left in Oxford when she returned home. She could always wear it again when they came on holiday.

'You look super,' Adele conceded, blowing on her freshly varnished fingernails.

'You look smashing, Addie. You'll knock Frank's socks off.'

'Don't be vulgar, Meg.'

'If he doesn't propose to you after the ball, I'm a monkey's uncle.'

'Where do you get these dreadful sayings?'

'I don't know. I think Cary Grant said it in a film, or it might have been the Marx Brothers. Anyway, I meant it, Addie, you look beautiful. If Frank's got any sense he'll snap you up before someone else does.'

Adele leaned back against the quilted satin pillow shams. 'I've always dreamed of being engaged before I was twenty. And Frank's father is terribly well off, not that that means anything of course. But the Bartons have got a flat in Mayfair and a country house in Hampshire.'

'And a rich husband is preferable to a poor one, as Mother would say,' Meg said, chuckling. 'And a handsome one is better still.'

'You're dreadful, Meg. But Frank is good-looking, isn't he? And he's so nice to talk to. I feel as if I've known him for years instead of a few days.'

The sound of car wheels grinding to a halt on

50

the gravel drive and a loud honking of a motor
horn made Meg rush to the window. A white
Rolls-Royce was parked in front of the house.
Meg flung the window open, leaning dangerously
over the sill as she watched David climb out of
the car, followed by Walter and Frank.

'Hello, there.' She waved to attract their attention.

'Meg, for goodness' sake behave like a young
lady,' Adele said plaintively. 'Shut the window
too. The breeze is ruining my hair-do.'

'The boys look splendid in their dress suits,
Addie.' Meg closed the casement. 'I'm going
downstairs to join them. Are you ready?'

'I'll be down in a moment. I don't want to
smudge my nail polish.'

'Okay. I'll make them wait in the hall so that
you can make a grand entrance.'

As Meg rounded the curve of the staircase she
saw Josie in the hall talking animatedly to David,
Walter and Frank.

Walter was the first to spot her. He stared at her
open-mouthed. 'By golly, you look marvellous.'

'Don't look so surprised, Walter,' Meg said,
negotiating the stairs with care. Long skirts might
look splendid, but she did not intend to spoil the
effect by tripping over the hem.

'I can't believe it.' David gave her a brotherly
hug. 'Who is this gorgeous creature? What have
you done with my scruffy little sister?'

Josie clapped her hands. 'Darling, you look a
picture.'

'Wait until you see Addie. She looks like a film
star.'

51

'I claim the first dance, Meg,' Walter said, stepping forward and handing her a corsage of clove-scented pink carnations tied with a silver ribbon.

'Thank you, Walter. No one has ever given me flowers before. They're lovely.'

He grinned shyly and his face reddened. Josie hurried forward to pin the flowers to Meg's shoulder strap. 'There, darling, you look like a princess.'

Meg was about to respond when she realised that Frank was gazing over her shoulder as if he had seen a heavenly vision. She knew without looking that Adele was making her way down the stairs. He leapt forward to present her with a delicate spray of orchids.

'Are you sure you won't come with us, Mrs Shelmerdine?' Walter asked tentatively. 'It seems unfair to leave you here on your own.'

'I'm going to curl up with a book,' Josie said, smiling wistfully. 'Now off you go and have a wonderful evening. I trust you to keep an eye on your sisters, David.'

'Don't worry, Aunt Josie. We'll have them back safe and sound before dawn.' He kissed her on the cheek. 'You could come, you know. I suppose Uncle Paul is working late as usual?'

'He's a busy man these days, darling. You can tell me all about it in the morning.' She opened the front door and held it while they filed past her.

Meg hesitated on the threshold. 'Is everything all right, Aunt Josie?' She thought she saw a shadow of doubt in her aunt's almond-shaped eyes but it was gone in a second. 'Are you okay?'

'Of course I am. Whatever put such thoughts into your head?' Josie patted her on the shoulder.

'Off you go. Your handsome German is waiting to drive you in style.'

Meg felt the blood rush to her face. 'He's not my escort. We're going as a party.'

Josie smiled. 'Yes, darling. I understand.'

Despite her denial, Meg's heart did a little flip when she saw Rayner leaning against the bonnet of the Rolls.

'Hop in, girls, and let's get going,' David said, opening the rear door. 'We want to arrive at the ball before midnight.'

Frank handed Adele into the back seat. She smiled up at him. 'Sit beside me, Frank.'

Walter helped Meg to arrange her full skirts as she climbed in beside Frank, and Walter squeezed in after her. David sat in the front seat next to Rayner, who had elected to drive. The engine purred into life and the Rolls moved forward.

'I'd love to drive this car,' Meg said dreamily. 'I can't imagine what it feels like to be behind the wheel of something so powerful.'

'You'd crash it before you reached the gates,' David said, laughing. 'I don't think driving the farm truck around the fields qualifies you to be in charge of an expensive motor like this.'

'I would like to bet that Meg could handle this machine,' Rayner said, braking slowly as they reached the main road.

'I'm sure I could,' Meg said confidently. 'If I can handle the rotten old truck I think this would be easy.'

'Yes,' David said, turning to look at her with a wide grin. 'Like you could manage the punt, only you nearly drowned.'

'I'll lay odds on Meg,' Frank said, reaching out to hold Adele's hand. 'How much are you willing to bet, David?'

'I don't think this is a good idea,' Walter said cautiously.

'Stop it. All of you,' Adele cried angrily. 'This is absolute madness. Meg really would kill herself if she tried to drive on proper roads and in a car like this. I don't want to hear another word said about it.'

Meg could see Rayner's face as he glanced in the rear view mirror. 'I could do it,' she muttered. 'I could, if I had the chance.'

CHAPTER THREE

There were three large marquees in the college grounds. Chinese lanterns hung from the branches of the trees, creating pools of light in the lengthening shadows. The strains of dance music filled the air together with the chatter of voices and the sound of laughter. It was, Meg thought, like fairyland, or a scene from a glamorous Hollywood film. The men looked dashing in their evening suits, even the ones she might normally have thought of as being dull and boring. The girls in their ball gowns seem to glide over the lawns like flowers that had been gifted the power of movement by a playful Greek god. Meg felt slightly envious as she witnessed the apparent ease with which they conversed with their partners. Not for

54

them the torments of shyness or the secret fear that they might trip over their skirts or make a social gaffe.

She clutched Walter's arm as David led them into the largest marquee, where he found a table close to the dance floor. Fairy lights twinkled above them and there were candles amongst the flower arrangements on the tables. The scent of warm crushed grass mingled with the heady aroma of Pimm's combined with subtle hints of strawberries, citrus fruit, cucumber and mint. Champagne corks were popping all round them and the orchestra was playing a Viennese waltz. Meg was entranced by it all. This was like nothing she had ever experienced in her life. There had been the annual school dance, where the boys from the boarding school on the other side of the island were allowed to mix with the girls from Meg's college, but the dances then had consisted of the veleta, the military two-step and the St Bernard waltz, with the occasional polka thrown in which often became a bit too rowdy for the harassed female teachers and the record on the gramophone was quickly changed to something less energetic.

Walter pulled out a chair for her and Meg sat down. At least she could come to no harm if she remained seated. She had been coerced into dancing lessons by her mother, but the teacher had admitted defeat after the first fortnight, declaring that very few people had the proverbial two left feet but she was the exception. She gazed around committing every last detail to memory. She felt quite inebriated already, although she had drunk

55

nothing stronger that day than tea. She realised with a start that Walter was asking her to dance. She hesitated, but she did not want to embarrass him by a refusal.

'I'm not much good at this,' Walter said, as they bumped into another couple.

Meg hastened to reassure him. 'I'm no expert myself, so don't worry. The very worst you can do is tread on my toes or I on yours.'

'That's true. You are a splendid girl, Meg.'

'Thanks, I like you too, Walter.'

They managed to shuffle round the dance floor a couple more times, but by then Meg was hot and thirsty. As they edged their way to the bar, she had the feeling that Walter was quite happy to be released from the onerous duty of attempting the foxtrot. She opted for lemonade and Walter ordered half a pint of bitter for himself. When they returned to their table they found it deserted. Frank and Adele were dancing cheek to cheek, and Rayner was partnering a rather plump girl in an off the shoulder green satin gown that was a size too small for her ample frame. She looked, to Meg's critical eye, like a peapod about to burst. David's partner was quite the opposite: tall and skinny with braces on her teeth and a rather bad case of acne. He could definitely have done better, Meg thought, and was then ashamed of herself for being uncharitable. David was doing the right thing in partnering a plain girl. Perhaps she had not given him enough credit for sensitivity in the past. She turned to Walter. 'Who are those girls dancing with my brother and Rayner?'

Walter glanced over her shoulder. 'David's dancing with Lavinia Langley. She's reading history at Lady Margaret Hall, and her best friend, Thora Wyndham, is treading on poor old Rayner's toes. I've forgotten what her subject is but they're both supposed to be really brainy as well as frightfully rich.'

'David never mentions girls in his letters. Has he got a girlfriend?' Meg watched critically as David whirled his partner around the floor with more enthusiasm than expertise.

'All the girls go for David, but he likes to play the field a bit.'

'And Rayner? Is that Thora what's-her-name his girlfriend?'

'I don't think so. I can't ever remember seeing him out with a female of any sort. He's more interested in studying and taking flying lessons.' Walter hesitated, looking at her with a wistful expression that reminded her of Rex, the cocker spaniel she had owned and loved as a child.

'I haven't got a girlfriend, Meg.'

'That just goes to show that the girls in college aren't all that bright,' she said, patting his hand. It was on the tip of her tongue to ask him about his feelings for her aunt, but she stopped herself just in time. It would be awful to embarrass someone as nice and kind as Walter, and it was probably just a crush anyway. Although, on the other hand, Walter was a bit old for something that people usually put behind them when they left school. She shot him a speculative glance but he was busy straightening his bow tie, and to her surprise he was blushing.

'Do you really think so, Meg? I mean, I've never

thought of myself as being attractive to women. Not like David and Frank.'

'You're a really nice chap,' she said, hoping that faint praise was better than none at all. 'You're very likeable, Walter. I like you, and so does...' she paused. She had been going to say that Josie was fond of him, but that would probably make matters worse. 'And so does everybody,' she ended lamely. She picked up her glass and gulped a mouthful of lemonade.

The music stopped and the couples drifted off to their tables. Meg craned her neck to see if Rayner escorted the rich and brainy Thora whatever-her-name-was back to her seat. She held her breath when he did, and smothered a sigh of relief when he left her almost immediately and began making his way back to their table.

Frank and Adele returned, holding hands and laughing. 'Let's get some champagne,' Frank said, pulling out a chair for Adele. 'We need to liven things up a bit.'

David strolled over to join them. 'Did I hear you mention champagne, old boy?'

'You did indeed. I was thinking that three bottles might do for a start.'

'Good idea,' David agreed enthusiastically. 'I'll give you a hand.'

Frank leaned over to brush his fingertips across Adele's shoulder. 'I'll be as quick as I can.'

She smiled up at him and Meg stifled a sigh. Their feelings for each other were transparent as glass. She had never seen two people falling head over heels in love, and it was an awe-inspiring experience. She was happy for Adele and only the tiniest bit jealous.

The orchestra struck up a quickstep and Meg's mouth suddenly went dry as she realised that Rayner was standing at her side, holding out his hand. 'May I have the pleasure of this dance, Meg?'

She stood up reluctantly. She had been willing him to ask her to partner him, and now her knees had turned to jelly. 'I'm not terribly good at this one.'

'I'll teach you.'

Held in his light but firm grasp, she found herself whisked expertly around the floor.

'You dance very well, Meg.'

She relaxed against him, breathing deeply and thinking that he smelt nice; a spicy mixture of sandalwood and vetiver together with a scent that was all his own. She could feel his warm breath on the top of her head as he held her close on the turns. His hands were smooth-skinned, as if he had never done a day's manual work in his life, but as her fingers touched the back of his shoulder she could feel the ripple of muscles beneath the severe cut of his black evening suit. To her astonishment she seemed to be able to follow his steps without any trouble at all. Unlike poor Walter who had stepped on her toes more than once and she on his. Doing a foxtrot with him had been a painful chore, but she would have been happy to dance all night with Rayner, and she felt cheated when the music stopped and he led her back to their table.

'You didn't disgrace the family after all,' David said, raising his glass to them.

'Meg is a good dancer.' Rayner handed her a

glass of champagne. 'I think you've earned this.'

She eyed David doubtfully. 'Are you going to tell on me if I have a drop of bubbly?'

He shook his head. 'Enjoy yourself, Meggie. I'm not playing the big brother tonight.'

She sipped the champagne, eyeing Rayner over the rim of her glass. She had not thought him particularly handsome when they first met, but now she was seeing him in a different light. His features might not be classic like Michelangelo's David, but his eyes shone with intelligence and his firm jaw suggested strength of character. Never one to analyse her own feelings, Meg was astonished to find herself inexorably drawn to him. It was a strange and curiously thrilling experience. He glanced at her and she realised that she had been staring. She looked away quickly and covered her confusion by smiling at Walter.

He rose from his chair. 'They're playing a tango, Meg. May I have this dance?'

'You can do the tango?' She had not meant to speak so plainly, and she bit her lip as she saw his face fall.

'I won't know until I try.'

She hesitated, not wanting to hurt his feelings, but she could tell by the expression on his face that it was important for him to prove himself in front of his friends. 'I'll have a go, but don't expect too much, Walter.'

Within a few minutes her feet were bruised and he had almost dropped her on one of the turns. Even worse, he had barged into another couple and they had not been amused. 'It's no good,' Meg said breathlessly. 'I think we'd better call it a day,

Walter. Perhaps the tango is a dance step too far.'

His shoulders drooped and she felt dreadful, but her silk stockings were laddered and there were black marks on her satin shoes. She returned to the table with Walter trailing behind her.

'I'm sorry, Meg.' He subsided onto his chair and reached for his drink. 'It looks easy, but it isn't.'

'That's okay,' Meg said hastily. 'It's a silly old dance anyway. I can't think what all the fuss is about.'

Rising from his seat, Rayner moved swiftly to her side. 'Come, I'll show you how they do the tango in Buenos Aires.'

'Well, this should be fun,' David said, putting his glass down on the table and grinning. 'Show us how it's done, old fruit.'

Meg laid her hand on Rayner's outstretched palm and allowed him to lead her onto the floor. He held her close and within seconds they were immersed in the hypnotic sensuality of the dance. One by one the other couples stopped to watch Rayner and Meg moving as if they had partnered each other all their lives. The steps seemed to come naturally to her under his guidance. She allowed herself to relax and trust him implicitly. Looking deeply into his eyes, she was under the spell of the music and erotic rhythm of the dance. Soon they were alone on the floor and when the music finally came to an end, there was a thunderous round of applause. Rayner bowed and held out his hand to Meg. He twirled her round so that she had her back to him and he clasped her to his chest. She could feel his heart beating, or perhaps it was hers? She could not tell which. She was

61

drunk with elation. There were cries of encore, but Rayner led her back to their table.

Adele gazed at her with open admiration. 'That was quite amazing, Meg.'

David rose to his feet and shook Rayner's hand. 'Didn't think you had it in you. You're a man full of surprises, you old Kraut. Where did you learn to trip the light fantastic?'

Rayner accepted a glass of champagne from Frank. 'I visited Buenos Aires when I was staying with my uncle and his family on their coffee plantation in Brazil. On that trip I learned how to grow coffee and to do the tango. I've never found either much use, until now.'

'Well, you realise you've set a precedent and now I'm going to have to prove myself on the dance floor, or I'll never live it down.' David cast his gaze around the marquee. 'There's Sheila Faulkner. I must go and impress her with my blinding quick-step.' He strolled off, making his way through the crowd to a table on the far side of the marquee.

Frank rose from his seat. 'May I have this dance, Adele? It seems that we all have something to live up to thanks to Rayner.'

She gave him her hand, smiling up at him as they made their way onto the floor. Walter pushed back his chair. 'I'm going to the bar to get a proper drink. What about you, Rayner?'

He shook his head. 'No thanks. I'm fine.' He waited until Walter was out of earshot before turning to Meg. 'Let's get some fresh air. I find it very stuffy in here.'

Feeling as though she were in a dream, Meg allowed him to take her by the hand. She might have been imagining it, but she was convinced that she felt a tingle run up her spine as their fingers touched. She nodded wordlessly.

Outside in the college grounds the air was redolent with the perfume of roses and night scented stock. She breathed in deeply. 'Shall we go for a walk by the river?'

'I've got a better idea.'

He led her to where the white Rolls-Royce was parked. Meg studied his face in the moonlight. She was certain that he must be able to hear her heart pounding as she waited for him to say something, anything. He had chosen to be alone with her, ignoring all the attractive and clever girls of his acquaintance. She could hardly believe that something as romantic and unexpected was happening to her. She was alone in the night with a young man she hardly knew, and he wanted to take her for a drive. She dreaded to think what her mother would say if she ever found out. Covering her nervousness with an attempt at levity, she smiled up at him. 'I hope your intentions are honourable, Herr Weiss?'

He opened the car door. 'I don't seduce young girls, Meg. Especially one who is the sister of my good friend.'

'I'm not sure whether I should be relieved or offended.'

'You said that you wanted to drive a Rolls-Royce.'

'I wasn't really serious. I mean, I was just teasing David.'

'I think you meant it. Now you can show me what you can do.'

She gazed at the dashboard, which was infinitely more complicated than the one on the farm truck. 'I've just drunk two glasses of champagne.'

'All the better. It will make you more relaxed. But if you're scared...'

It was a definite challenge, but she was still wary. 'I'm not scared, but what if I prang the car? Whose is it?'

'It's mine for the night. I hired it so it's insured. Get in, Meg. Let me see what you can do.'

She picked up her skirts and slid onto the driver's seat. She studied the control panel while she waited for Rayner to get in beside her.

He closed the door. 'Off you go then. Just think of it as driving the vehicle at home.'

The huge expanse of white bonnet seemed to stretch into infinity. She was scared, but she was determined to conquer her fear, and her nervousness began to dissipate as she manoeuvred the Rolls out of the car park and into the street. She drove slowly at first but she gained confidence as they left the city streets and headed north on the Woodstock Road.

She cast a quick glance at Rayner to see if he was suitably impressed, but he seemed disappointingly calm and unruffled. 'Where shall we go?'

'Wherever you like. Go faster. Enjoy yourself.'

'You're mad, you know that.' She pressed her foot gently on the accelerator and felt the power of the engine as the vehicle surged forward. She gripped the wheel with perspiring hands, keeping her eyes fixed on the road ahead. When they reached the wide main street of Woodstock, she pulled in to the kerb.

'Why have we stopped?'

'Because this is crazy. I've just driven over ten miles and I think we should go back to the ball before they send out a search party.'

'And I thought you wanted to prove a point.'

She eyed him curiously. 'What do you mean by that?'

'David and Adele treat you like a baby. I thought you wanted to show them that they are wrong.'

He was right, of course, but it came as a shock to hear the truth from someone else's lips. She stared at her hands clenched round the steering wheel. 'That makes me sound very childish.'

'No. That isn't so.'

She turned her head to give him a direct look, but his face was in shadow and she could not read his expression. 'Why did you ask me to come with you? Was it just to annoy David?'

'No. I wouldn't do anything to upset my friend.'

'Then why?' She felt she had to know. Was he just amusing himself, or was there something more behind his mask of reserve?

He shifted in his seat and she could see his face clearly in the lamplight. He was smiling. 'Don't forget that your life belongs to me now, Meg. That was what you said, wasn't it?'

The humour in his eyes drew an immediate response from her and she chuckled. 'I think I might live to regret that remark.'

He laid his hand on his heart. 'Never. But perhaps we'd better get you back to the ball now. I think you've proved yourself. Shall I drive?'

'No,' she said firmly. 'I'm just beginning to

enjoy myself.' She started the engine, turning the car easily in one large sweep outside the Bear Hotel. As soon as they were clear of the village she gunned the accelerator and they skimmed along the A44 back to Oxford. 'This is something you can never do in Guernsey,' she said happily. 'The roads at home are so narrow and twisting. I love my home, but sometimes I think I would like to live on the mainland.'

'You can do anything you want if you put your mind to it.'

'Like driving a Rolls-Royce, I suppose.'

'Exactly so.'

She drove a little faster just for the satisfaction of doing something dangerous and out of the ordinary. She glanced at him to see if he was alarmed by her daring, but whatever he was feeling, he maintained his outward calm. 'My mother would say you're a bad influence, Rayner.'

'I would be honoured to meet her and prove her wrong.'

The vision that this conjured up in Meg's mind was disconcerting. She wondered what her mother would make of the self-possessed young German, and she found herself hoping that both her parents would like him. They lapsed into companionable silence as she concentrated on the road ahead and the exhilaration of controlling a powerful motor car. When they reached the college she drove into the parking place that they had vacated less than an hour previously.

'I've done it,' she said proudly. 'And not a scratch on the paintwork.'

Before he had a chance to respond, the car door

66

was wrenched open. 'Bloody hell. This is worse than I thought.' David's eyes glittered strangely and Meg could smell the alcohol on his breath. 'I can't believe he allowed you to drive.'

Rayner stepped out of the car and rounded the bonnet to face him. 'Calm down, David. It wasn't Meg's fault.'

Struggling with her full skirts, Meg climbed out onto the tarmac. 'Please don't make a fuss.' Her heart sank as she saw Adele, Frank and Walter standing behind David. She could tell by their expressions that they were at once anxious and angry.

'What were you thinking of?' Adele said in a voice that shook with emotion. 'You might have been killed.'

David's face was ashen in the light of the street lamp. 'Are you completely out of your mind allowing my sister to drive a powerful machine like this, and at night? She's only ever driven a truck and that was on private land. You could have had a terrible accident.'

'There was no danger,' Rayner said calmly. 'She drove well.'

'You're insane,' David muttered through clenched teeth. 'Didn't it occur to you that we would be worried sick because we didn't know where you'd gone? What would I have told our parents if anything had happened to Meg?'

Walter stepped forward and clutched David's arm. 'Come on, old chap. This isn't the time or place. I think we should get the girls home and sort everything out in the morning.'

'Quite right,' Frank said quietly. 'There's no

real harm done, David.'

He shook off Walter's restraining hand. 'No real harm?' he repeated angrily. 'My sister has been gallivanting about alone with him.' He rounded on Rayner, clenching his fists. 'I thought you were a better man than this.'

To Meg's horror he swung a punch at Rayner but due to his unsteady state the blow missed its mark and David fell against the bonnet of the Rolls. Frank rushed forward to hold him back as he staggered to his feet. 'That's enough. This sort of behaviour won't help anyone.'

Rayner held out his hand. 'I'm sorry, David. I was in the wrong and I apologise.'

But Meg could see that her brother was too far gone in drink to be reasonable. He was struggling to free himself from Frank's grasp when a warning from Walter came too late.

'My God, it's the Dean. He's coming this way. Now we really are in trouble.'

Meg finished her packing with a sigh. Her punishment for risking life and limb, not to mention the possibility of damaging an extremely expensive motor car, was the curtailment of her holiday in Oxford. The matter might have been hushed up but for the untimely appearance of the Dean, who had threatened to send both David and Rayner down for brawling in public. He had not carried out that threat, but next morning had reported the sorry affair to Paul Shelmerdine. Meg was shocked to discover that this was not the first time her brother had been reprimanded for his misdemeanours, which included missing lectures and

68

failing his exams. Uncle Paul had not been amused, particularly as the Dean was an old friend, and David's indiscretions reflected badly on the family. Then, of course, the finger of blame had been pointed at Meg herself, and their uncle had decided that she was as much at fault as her brother. Unfortunately, and Meg thought unfairly, Adele was to accompany her on the journey back to the island, and of course she was extremely upset.

Meg shot a wary glance at her sister who was flinging clothes into her battered leather suitcase without bothering to fold them. This in itself was a bad sign, as normally Adele was obsessively neat and tidy. Eventually the heavy silence became too much for Meg. 'Look, Addie. How many more times have I got to say sorry for what I did? There's no need for you to cut your holiday short because of me.'

'Uncle Paul doesn't trust you to travel on your own. There's no chance that he'll let me stay.' She tossed her best silk dress on top of the jumble in her case. 'Frank and I were getting on so well. Everything was unutterably wonderful.' Her voice broke on a sob. 'And now we've got to go home tomorrow and I'll probably never see him again.'

'If he's half the man I think he is he won't let something like that put him off.'

Adele sank onto the bed, covering her face with her hands. 'I – I think I love him, Meg. What am I going to do?'

Stricken with remorse, Meg struggled to find words of comfort. 'I didn't mean it to end like this. I'm truly sorry for what I did. I didn't think...'

69

Adele dropped her hands to her lap. 'No, that's your trouble. You don't think before you do things. You've ruined my life, Meg.' She bent her head and her shoulders shook.

Meg gazed at her helplessly. She had apologised until her throat was sore and her head ached. She knew that she had behaved foolishly and she did not blame them all for being angry, but she was at a loss to know how to make things right.

The sound of the doorbell echoing round the entrance hall brought her back to the present, and she hurried from the room. Perhaps, she thought wistfully, it might be Rayner arriving like a knight in shining armour to carry her off on a white charger, although the white Rolls-Royce would be more comfortable and a lot quicker. It was two days now since the ball and she had been confined to the house in disgrace. She had not been allowed to contact Rayner and, as far as she knew, he had not called at the house.

If Uncle Paul had been draconian in his handling of the matter, Aunt Josie had been utterly splendid. She had admitted that she had done much worse things when she was a girl, although she said in a whisper it would be better if they did not mention that to anyone, especially her husband. She had tried her best to comfort Adele, but her words fell on deaf ears. Adele was past reasoning.

Meg crossed the landing to lean over the highly polished oak banisters. She could hear familiar voices and she craned her neck in order to get a better view. Although she could only see the tops of their heads, she recognised Frank and Walter, but there was no sign of Rayner or David. She ran down the stairs to greet them. 'Have you come to say goodbye?'

'Well, we couldn't let you go home without seeing you first.' Walter stared at her anxiously. 'Are you all right, Meg?'

'Absolutely fine. They didn't beat me too much.' She could see from their shocked expressions that they actually believed her and she smiled ruefully. 'Just joking, but I'm in deep disgrace.'

'Rayner was more at fault than you, and David only made things worse,' Frank said, frowning. 'I've taken him to task and I believe your uncle has too.'

'Yes. You were not entirely to blame,' Walter added earnestly. 'I'm really sorry you're going away so soon.'

'I don't want to go, of course. But the worst thing is that Addie is being sent home too. I feel awful about spoiling her holiday.' Meg turned to Frank with a meaningful look. 'She's very upset.'

'I'd like to see her, Meg. I really need to talk to her in private.'

She breathed a sigh of relief. Perhaps all was not lost. 'If you'd like to wait in the conservatory, I'll fetch her.' She grabbed Walter by the arm as he started to follow Frank. 'Why don't you wait here, Walter? I'll be back in two ticks.'

She raced up the stairs and burst into the bedroom. 'Addie. Stop crying and fix your makeup. You look like a panda. Frank is downstairs in the conservatory and he wants to see you urgently.'

Adele reached for her hanky. 'I must look a perfect fright.'

'No you don't,' Meg said stoutly. 'At least, it's nothing that a touch of mascara and lipstick won't fix.' She pulled Adele to her feet. 'Wash your face and put on your war paint. I've a feeling that Frank is very serious, if you get my meaning.' She picked up a silver-backed hairbrush and thrust it into her sister's hand. 'Do your stuff, Addie. And good luck.'

Downstairs in the entrance hall, Meg kept Walter chatting while Adele went to find Frank. She was running out of conversation when Josie emerged from Paul's study. She looked pale beneath her makeup but her serious expression melted into a smile when she saw them. 'Hello, Walter, how nice of you to call. But why are you two skulking around out here?'

'Frank and Addie are having a heart to heart in the conservatory,' Meg said earnestly. 'We're giving them a bit of privacy.'

'Then I suggest we go into the drawing room and have a drink before dinner. You will stay, won't you, Walter? I'm sure Cook could stretch the meal for another two hungry undergraduates. David is supposed to be coming, but he's always late.'

Walter nodded eagerly. 'Thank you, Mrs Shelmerdine. I mean, Josie. That would be super.'

'Good, that's settled then.' She opened the drawing-room door and went straight to the cocktail cabinet. 'Would you like a glass of sherry or would you prefer beer, Walter?'

'I'd love a beer, please.'

'Meg, would you like a drink?'

'I'm surprised I'm allowed to.'

'It's all forgotten now, darling.' Josie selected a

72

cut-glass decanter and was about to pour the sherry when Adele entered the room with Frank.

Meg was quick to note that they were holding hands, and she could tell by the glow on Adele's cheeks and the sparkle in her dark eyes that something momentous had occurred amongst the potted palms and Boston ferns.

'Aunt Josie, Meg, Walter,' Adele said breathlessly. 'We've got something to tell you.'

'What's going on?' David demanded when he joined them in the drawing room moments later. 'Yesterday everyone was gloomy and now you're all grinning like idiots, except you, of course, Aunt Josie. You could never look anything but perfect. Have I missed something?'

'You're just in time,' Josie said happily. 'Adele and Frank have just become engaged – unofficially of course, my dear, until Frank has spoken to your father.'

Meg held her breath, willing David to say something nice. She watched warily as he strode across the floor towards the newly engaged couple, and she sighed with relief when he kissed Adele on both cheeks and shook Frank's hand. 'Congratulations, old boy. I'm very happy for you.'

Josie clapped her hands. 'This is a marvellous end to the girls' holiday, especially after the slight contretemps at the ball, but that's all forgotten now. We're having a small celebration, David. Freda's just gone to fetch the champagne.'

'Shouldn't we wait until Uncle Paul gets home?' Adele asked anxiously. 'He might be upset if we start without him.'

73

Josie's smile faded and Meg saw that her aunt's fingers shook slightly as she attempted to fix a cigarette into an onyx holder. 'Paul telephoned to say he'd be a little late. Pressure of work, you know. But there's no law against opening another bottle when he gets home, is there?'

They opened two more bottles of champagne when Paul arrived, and the events at the May Ball seemed to have been forgotten, but as Meg glanced at their happy faces she could not help thinking that no one seemed to care that Rayner was absent and excluded from the celebrations. The family had apparently written him off like a bad debt and he was forgotten. It seemed terribly unfair that she was not even allowed to say good-bye to him. She sipped her champagne but it tasted sour and the bubbles shot up her nose making her want to cry. Perhaps Rayner did not care that she was returning home in disgrace tomorrow; after all, he had made no attempt to see her. He had not even sent a message with Walter or Frank. Maybe he thought she was a tiresome young girl who was simply not worth bothering about, and that the attention he had paid her at the ball had merely been an attempt to while away a boring evening.

'Cheer up, Meg, it may never happen,' David said, refilling her glass.

David and Walter were quite drunk by the end of the evening, and they were waiting for Frank to drive them back to their lodgings, but he had taken Adele for a moonlit walk in the garden and they had been gone for a very long time. Meg stood in the doorway, hugging her arms about her chest and shivering in her thin cotton dress. Aunt Josie had gone to find Frank and Addie and Uncle Paul had retired to his study to make an important telephone call. Walter had managed to stagger down the front steps, but was now sitting with his head held in his hands, groaning.

'Goodbye, Meg,' David said, leaning casually against the door jamb. 'Try to behave yourself on the way home.'

She chose to ignore this unfair jibe. 'Have you seen Rayner since the other night, David? It really wasn't his fault.'

'I know that.' Suddenly sober, he put his arms round her. 'Listen to me. There's going to be a war whether we like it or not. Rayner knows that too, and he also knows that we'll be on different sides. He's going back to Germany at the end of term. Forget him, Meg. Go home and put all this behind you. You'll never see him again.'

CHAPTER FOUR

Meg paused by the gilt mirror in the oak-panelled hall of Colivet Manor, patting her hair in place. She had decided to forego her early morning ride in order to present herself at breakfast on time and neatly turned out. She had suffered a long lecture from both parents when they returned from the mainland. Aunt Josie had telephoned simply to tell them that the girls would be returning earlier than expected, but apparently Mother had dragged the truth out of her with the ruthless efficiency of Torquemada, the Spanish Grand Inquisitioner. If it had not been for Adele, who'd championed her valiantly, Meg was certain that she'd have been put in the metaphorical corner until she was at least twenty-one. Addie had put the blame squarely on Rayner's shoulders despite Meg's murmured protests. Their father had listened in silence, but had said judiciously that no real harm was done and the matter should be forgotten. Their mother was not so forgiving, but Adele's good news eclipsed the whole sorry affair at the May Ball and Meg found herself, as usual, pushed into the background, for which she was truly grateful.

It was almost a week since they had arrived back on the island and Meg was deeply disappointed by Rayner's apparent abandonment of her. She had told no one, not even Adele, that her reason for leaving the ball and driving into the night alone with Rayner was quite simple. She'd followed her heart. No one seemed to think it odd that Adele and Frank had fallen in love at first sight, but she knew if she were to claim that for her it had also been a coup de foudre, Mother would tell her that she was being ridiculous. She would say that it was a childish crush on a totally unsuitable young man, and Pa would warn her, just as David had done, that when the inevitable hostilities started Rayner Weiss would be on the opposing side.

Stretching the taut muscles of her face into a smile, Meg went slowly into the dining room, where her parents and Adele were seated at the table finishing their meal. As always, Muriel Colivet was immaculately turned out, in a paisley silk dress, complemented by a double row of pearls and matching earrings. With her flawless maquillage and her blonde hair piled high on her head in an elaborate coiffure, she would not have looked out of place at a state banquet. Meg sighed. She knew she could never live up to her mother's high standards.

Muriel glanced up from buttering a slice of toast. 'I hope you're going to do something other than mope around the house today, Meg. You've been in a mood ever since you returned from Oxford. You're lucky that you're too old to be punished for your outrageous behaviour. I don't know why you can't be more like your sister.'

'I'm sorry, Mother.' Helping herself to bacon and scrambled eggs from silver breakfast dishes on the gleaming mahogany sideboard, Meg took her plate and went to sit beside Adele.

'You look very nice this morning,' Adele said, making an obvious attempt to lighten the atmosphere. 'You should wear that shade of blue more often.'

'It makes a change to see her out of those dreadful jodhpurs for once,' Muriel said, frowning.

'I should be hearing from Frank any day now, Mother.' Adele smiled sympathetically at Meg as she skilfully changed the subject to something much dearer to their mother's heart. 'He said he would come here as soon as humanly possible.'

'That's splendid, darling.' Muriel cocked her head on one side. 'I think I just heard the rattle of the letter box. Perhaps you'll hear from him today.'

Adele leapt to her feet. 'I do hope so. I'll go and see.' She hurried from the room.

Charles Colivet peered at them from behind his copy of *The Times*. 'What's all the fuss about? Can't a fellow read his paper in peace at his own breakfast table?'

Muriel dabbed her lips with a cream damask table napkin. 'Adele has gone to fetch the post, dear. She's waiting to hear from Frank.'

He turned the page with an exasperated sigh. 'I dislike it intensely when people rush about at breakfast time.'

Adele walked slowly back into the dining room carefully sorting through the mail. She uttered a squeak. 'This one's for me.' Dropping the rest of the correspondence on the table in front of Meg, she studied the postmark. 'It must be from Frank. May I leave the table, Mother?'

Charles raised an eyebrow. 'It looks as if you have already.'

Muriel shot him one of her Medusa glances, as Meg and Adele had dubbed them, which would turn any ordinary mortal into stone. 'Of course, Addie. Don't take any notice of your father. He's as delighted about your engagement as I am.'

'You're forgetting that I haven't given my consent yet, Muriel.'

'But of course you will, dear.'

'That all depends on the young man. When I've met him and had an in-depth discussion about his prospects I'll decide then.' Charles held his hand out to Meg who was sorting the rest of the mail. 'Anything for me?'

She handed him a pile of envelopes, but realising she had missed one she picked it up, and was about to give it to her father when she saw that it was addressed to her. She stared at the unfamiliar writing and her heart did a funny little flip inside her chest.

'You wouldn't say no, would you, Pa?' Adele's bottom lip quivered ominously.

'I expect I shall like him, Adele, if you do. Now run along and read your letter, there's a good girl.'

'You shouldn't tease her, Charles,' Muriel said when Adele was out of earshot. 'You know that she's sensitive just like me.'

'Is she, my dear? I can't say I'd noticed.'

Muriel turned to Meg, frowning. 'Your breakfast is getting cold, Meg. I don't know who's writing to you, but put it away now and eat your food. It's very rude to read at table.'

Meg glanced at her father and he raised his eyebrows with a wry smile. It was obvious that he knew the barbed comment was aimed his way, but as usual he did not bother to retaliate. Meg laid the envelope on her lap out of her mother's range of vision and she studied it while she ate. The postmark was smudged and illegible, but the envelope was addressed in bold Gothic script. She hardly dared hope that it was from Rayner, and the food stuck in her throat, but she ate as quickly as she dared without incurring a lecture from her mother. She was about to ask permission to leave the table when the door burst open and Adele reappeared, waving a piece of paper. 'Frank is coming to Guernsey next week, Mother. He and Walter are going to stay in St Peter Port for a few days.'

'How lovely, dear. Isn't that good news, Charles?'

'What is?'

'Frank Barton is coming to the island next week.'

'Splendid. I'm going to my study, Muriel.' Charles folded his newspaper and picked up the post. He rose from his chair. 'I'm in court this afternoon, but this morning I'm working from home. I don't want to be disturbed.' He left the room unnoticed by Muriel and Adele, who were happily discussing Frank's forthcoming visit.

Meg seized the opportunity to follow him. She slipped out of the house and went straight to the stables. Sitting on a bale of straw she ripped the envelope and stared at the single sheet of paper.

Christ Church, Oxford
4 May, 1939

Dear Meg,

I feel I owe you an apology for the trouble caused by our midnight drive. I hope you did not get into 'hot water', as David calls it, when you arrived home in Guernsey. I wanted to apologise in person but as you did not come to Folly Bridge, I suppose you are still angry with me. David says he cannot remember if he gave you my note or not but I am assuming that he did. I hope we will meet again, although as things are at the moment I am afraid it looks unlikely. Whatever happens, I shall never forget Meg in her gold dress or with waterweed in her hair.

My best wishes to you and your sister,
Rayner Weiss.

80

Meg read and reread the letter. She could hardly believe that he had wanted to see her again or that David had forgotten to give her the note that might have changed her life. She had lain in bed every night since the May Ball reliving the terrifying, yet wonderful, feeling as Rayner had snatched her from the clutching fingers of the waterweed. If she closed her eyes she could recall the moment when his strong arms had enfolded her and propelled her to the surface of the greedy Thames. She could not forget the electric charge that she had felt as he held her close in the erotic rhythm of the tango, or the quiet intimacy of the drive through the night in the white Rolls-Royce. He had wanted to meet her on Folly Bridge where they had begun the fateful river trip that might have ended her life, and all this time he must have been thinking that she did not want to see him again. She wanted to laugh and cry at the same time.

Waiting at the ferry terminal for Frank and Walter, Meg tried hard not to begrudge Adele her happiness. If their roles had been reversed and she had been waiting for Rayner, Meg knew that she would have been hopping up and down with excitement. Even so, she wouldn't have changed her dress half a dozen times as Adele had done, very nearly causing them to arrive late. Now a picture of serenity, looking as though she had stepped off the cover of *Vogue*, Adele stood on the quay holding her pert little straw boater to prevent it from being tugged off by the boisterous breeze.

The full skirt of her cream shantung dress billowed about her slender figure like a spinnaker on a yacht, and Meg wished now that she had taken the trouble to change out of her jodhpurs and white cotton shirt. Looking down at her feet, she realised that her riding boots were still covered with mud and dust from the stables. Balancing on one leg at a time, she wiped the toe of each boot on the tough material that encased her calves.

'I think I can see Frank,' Adele cried excitedly.

Meg shielded her eyes from the sun. 'And there's Walter standing beside him. What a pity David couldn't come too.'

Adele shot her a knowing glance. 'And Rayner, maybe? You really liked him, didn't you, Meg?'

She shrugged her shoulders. 'I liked him, but it's okay. I'm not silly enough to think anything could come of it. Anyway, don't worry about me. You've got Frank now, and I'm happy for you.'

Adele reached out to squeeze her hand. 'You're not such a bad little sister. I'm sorry if I used to tease you and pull your plaits.'

'Oh, shut up,' Meg said, swallowing a lump in her throat. 'You'll have me crying in a moment. Go and get your man, Adele Colivet.'

They had to wait while the vessel moored alongside allowing the passengers to disembark and make their way through the customs hall, but eventually Frank emerged from the building looking immaculate in a striped blazer and Oxford bags. In his hand he carried a pigskin valise and an enormous bouquet of red roses. Walter followed close on his heels, holding a sorry-looking cardboard suitcase bound by a length of cord.

'Adele! You look beautiful.' Frank dropped his valise and presented her with the flowers. He lifted her hand to his lips and kissed it with old-fashioned gallantry.

Meg smiled. She would not have been surprised if he had swept Adele into his arms and kissed her passionately. Adele was blushing and seemed quite overcome with emotion.

Walter coughed delicately. 'Hello, Meg. It's good to see you again.'

She shook his hand. 'And you, Walter. Did you have a good crossing?'

'Excellent. The weather was perfect and the sea calm as a mill pond, which was a relief as I'm not a very good sailor.' He matched his steps to hers as they walked along White Rock towards the car park, with Adele and Frank strolling behind them, arm in arm.

Walter gave Meg a searching look. 'I was sorry you had to leave sooner than you'd planned. How are you really?'

'I'm fine, but wish I hadn't made a mess of things in Oxford.'

'It wasn't all your fault, Meg. Rayner should have known better.'

'I could have refused to drive the wretched car. Anyway, I'm just sorry I spoilt things for Addie.'

Walter glanced over his shoulder at Adele and Frank, who were deep in conversation and holding hands. 'They seem to have survived,' he said, grinning.

'Thank goodness for that.' Meg stopped as they reached the car park where Eric sat patiently behind the wheel of the old Bentley. She waved to him and he responded with a smile as he opened the door and stood up to take Walter's case and stow it in the boot.

'We're going to drop you off at your hotel,' Meg said as she took the front passenger seat while the others settled themselves in the back. 'Mother's invited you both to dinner this evening. Eric will pick you up at seven.'

It was a short drive to the hotel in town and they left Frank and Walter to check in at reception. Meg shot a sideways glance at Eric as he restarted the engine. 'Have you heard from Gerald lately?'

His weather-beaten features creased into a smile. 'We had a letter last week.'

'Did he tell you we met on the cross-Channel ferry?'

'He did.'

Meg relaxed against the leather seat. She was always completely at her ease with Eric, who had been more like a favourite uncle to her while she was growing up than one of her father's employees. 'D'you know, Eric, it was really strange, considering the fact that we live on a small island, but we realised that we hadn't seen each other to speak to for years. It's even odder because I can remember a time when he and David were always together.'

'Gerald did well at school, and now he works even harder at his job in London.'

'He's done very well for himself.'

Eric smiled and nodded. 'Yes. I'm proud of the boy.'

'He wouldn't thank you for calling him a boy.'

'He'll always be a boy to me. That's how it is when you're a parent, Meg. You always think of your children as being young, even when they're grown-up.'

'I'll have to take your word for that.' Meg turned in her seat to look at Adele, who was still clutching her bouquet of red roses. 'I hope Frank's prepared to face Father tonight, Addie. Mind you, it will be Mother who puts him through the third degree. I don't envy him that.'

'He'll be fine,' Adele said happily. 'He's a born diplomat. He'll have Mother eating out of his hand.'

Frank had been in the study with Charles for an agonising half-hour, during which time Adele paced up and down the Aubusson carpet in the drawing room until Muriel complained that she was wearing it out. Glancing at Walter, Meg realised that he was looking slightly uncomfortable. The tense atmosphere was affecting them all and she offered to give him a conducted tour of the house. He needed no second bidding.

They began in the tapestry room, where the hangings had been made in Flanders and were at least two hundred years old, maybe more. History was not Meg's strong point, but she made up for her lack of knowledge by revealing the dirty deeds of the Colivets' privateering ancestors on which the family fortune was based. Although, she hastened to add, there was not much left of it now as he could see by the sad state of the decoration in some of the rooms least used. When they reached the attics Meg showed him the damp patches on the walls where the roof leaked, and the ill-fitting windows that rattled and shook during storms, giving the impression that the house was haunted. No one used this floor nowadays, but years ago before the Great War it was where the servants had slept. They arrived back in the drawing room in time to hear that Charles had given Adele and Frank his blessing and they were now officially engaged.

Next morning Eric drove Adele and Frank into town to buy the ring. Meg took Walter to Fermain Bay where they swam in the crystal-clear water and dried off lazing on the beach in the sunshine. After a leisurely stroll back to the house they were reclining on steamer chairs on the terrace when Adele and Frank returned.

Adele waved her left hand beneath Meg's nose. 'What do you think?'

Meg pretended to shield her eyes. 'It's gorgeous, Addie, but it's blinding me.'

'It's smashing,' Walter said dutifully. 'Well done, Frank.'

'I'm going to show it to Mother,' Adele said happily. 'Are you coming, darling?'

With a benevolent smile, Frank tucked her hand into the crook of his arm. 'Of course, my love.'

Meg watched them go with a heartfelt sigh. She was pleased that Adele had found the man of her dreams, but their closeness only made her loss seem the greater. The stupid escapade at the May Ball and the threat of war had destroyed any chance she might have had of seeing Rayner again. She lay back on the cushions and closed her eyes. No matter how much she suffered in private, life would go on as usual. Nothing ever changed on the island.

As the days went by Meg found herself almost solely responsible for entertaining Walter. Frank seemed to have become Adele's latest fashion accessory to be exhibited at so many social functions that Meg began to suspect her mother had had the itinerary drawn up for months ahead, if not years. But good-natured Frank appeared to take everything in his stride, and did not seem to mind attending all the parties that were suddenly announced in his honour. Meg did not accompany them on any of these occasions. She had always been considered too young to join the smart set at the tennis club or the get-togethers where Addie's old school friend, Pearl Tostevin, entertained in style. According to Addie, these gatherings in the large drawing room of the house on the Grange owned by Pearl's parents were the height of sophistication. All the young women wore designer gowns, smoked Balkan Sobranie cocktail cigarettes and danced to records of jazz music played on the gramophone. Meg had always thought privately that it sounded boring in the extreme, but she never said so. In fact, now she was that bit older, she might have enjoyed taking Walter to one of their dos, but it seemed that she was still thought to be too juvenile to be invited.

As the visit drew to its end, Meg experienced a feeling of relief. It was not that she disliked Walter; on the contrary, he was sweet and kind and eager to please, but if she were to be completely honest she found him a bit dull. She had shown him all the places popular with visitors, treating it at first as a chore, but gradually she had come to realise that seeing Guernsey through a stranger's eyes had made her think differently about things she had taken so much for granted. Walter's unstinting delight in the narrow twisting lanes, the wide sweeps of pale golden sand, the pink rocks at Cobo and the pine forests above Marble Bay had touched a chord in her. She had not known it until now, but she loved the island with every fibre of her being.

In the end, Meg was quite sorry to wave goodbye to Walter at the ferry terminal. Adele sobbed on her shoulder as she fluttered her hanky at the departing vessel, but cheered up a little when Meg suggested that she ought to go home and begin compiling the guest list for her engagement party. Meg gave her a hug. 'Dry your eyes, Addie. Frank will be back when the summer term ends, and you've got an awful lot to do before then. There's the do to organise, and if you're planning to get married next spring you'll have your trousseau to buy, and endless fittings at the dressmaker's. You won't have time to miss Frank.'

Adele blew her nose into the tiny scrap of cotton edged with lace. 'Yes, you're right. I've got heaps to keep me occupied. Isn't life wonderful?'

The weeks might have passed quickly for Adele, as Meg had predicted, but for Meg herself the days seemed interminably long. She was not included in the shopping trips to St Peter Port. Muriel and Adele went on these forays together, and although Adele sometimes offered a half-hearted invitation to join them, Meg always declined. She might have been tempted, but her mother made it plain that she was more a hindrance than a help, and shopping for clothes was not her thing. Neither was attending the dressmaker's for fittings, which entailed standing for hours in a cold room semi-naked while Mrs Vaudin, with even colder fingers, stuck the occasional pin into her flesh.

Meg spent most of the long, hot summer days riding her horse about the countryside or going to the beach, where she swam and sunbathed until her skin was tanned to a golden brown and her hair bleached to silvery blonde. She was not needed on the farm as there were enough seasonal workers to help with the hay harvest and in the greenhouse. Eric had no need of her in the estate office and her time was her own. On occasions she was lonely and, more often than not, bored. She thought more and more about having a career of her own, but every time she raised the subject with her father he told her she was too young to leave home, and advised her to enjoy her freedom. Many, he said, would think she was an extremely fortunate young woman to have everything she wanted without having to work for her living.

The engagement party was arranged for the first week in July and eventually Meg was asked to help. She was allotted the task of picking and arranging a variety of flowers from the gardens. It was not an onerous chore, but she felt that it was just another ploy to keep her gainfully occupied and out of Mother's way. She was placing an arrangement of tall blue irises on the piano in the drawing room when Adele came through the door, flushed and obviously bursting with news.

'Guess what, Meg?'

'Mr Chamberlain has asked you to go to Germany and sort out Hitler.'

'No, of course not, silly.'

'Don't be facetious, Meg,' Muriel said, looking up from the escritoire where she had been checking off items on a list. 'What is it, Addie?'

'It's a letter from Angela Barton, Frank's mother. She's invited me to spend a whole month with them in their holiday home on the Devon coast, that's all.'

Muriel dropped her pen with a gasp of delight. 'How splendid! When?'

'Next week. After our engagement party. She says that Frank's father has an important business meeting in Paris and she regrets that they won't be able to attend, but Frank will be here of course, and then I'll travel back to Weymouth with him. We'll motor down to Devon in the Rolls.'

'Oh dear,' Muriel said, frowning. 'That doesn't give Mrs Vaudin much time to finish your new gowns. I'll phone her. No. On second thoughts we'd better go and see her this afternoon, and if there's any fitting to be done she can do it there and then.'

'And I must ring Pearl and tell her. She'll be so excited for me, and probably green with envy too. I'm afraid that boyfriend of hers is never going to pop the question.'

Realising that she was again excluded from this frenzy of activity, Meg made for the door.

'Not so fast, young lady.' Muriel rose from the desk, shaking out her silk skirts.

'Yes, Mother?'

'I have some errands I want you to run in St Peter Port. Eric can drop you off when he takes us to Mrs Vaudin's house.'

'Can't Marie do it, Mother? I haven't finished doing the flowers.'

'No. I can't spare Marie. She's busy in the kitchen baking cakes for the party on Saturday. Anyway, the rest of the blooms will be better picked in the morning before the sun makes them droop. I've written a list of things I need.' She waved a piece of paper at Meg.

'All right then.' Meg crossed the floor to take the list. 'If I must.'

It had not been too bad after all. Meg leaned over the railings gazing down at the craft moored in the marina. Sunlight danced on the water and seagulls made lazy circles in the sky above her head. She had left the shopping lists with the grocer, the greengrocer and the baker, and had purchased cotton thread and elastic from Creaseys. Now all she had to do was to wait for Eric to collect her and take her home.

'Hello, Meg.'

She spun round. 'Gerald. This is becoming a habit. It's good to see you again.'

'I thought I'd come home for the weekend and see my folks.'

'They'll be pleased.'

'They don't know I'm coming. I thought I'd give them a surprise.'

'You'll do that all right and sooner than you think,' Meg said, smiling as she spotted the Bentley gliding towards them.

It slid to a halt and Eric leapt out, his face almost split in two by a broad grin. 'Hello, son. What are you doing here?' His smile faded. 'You haven't had the sack, have you?'

'No, Dad. I just fancied a break from London. It gets hot and stuffy in the city at this time of year. I needed to come home and breathe the fresh air.'

'Your mum will be thrilled to bits to see you when she finishes work.' Eric opened the rear door. 'Get in, Miss Meg. I'll see you at home later, son.'

Meg hesitated with one foot on the running board. 'Why don't you come home with us, Gerald?'

He shook his head. 'I don't think Mrs Colivet would like that. I'll walk to Hauteville.'

'I've never heard anything so crazy in my whole life. Of course Mother wouldn't mind.' Meg climbed into the car and slithered across to the far side. She patted the seat beside her. 'Please come with us.'

Eric and Gerald exchanged worried glances. 'I don't know, Miss Meg,' Eric said slowly. 'Mrs Colivet has her rules.'

'I'm sure Mother wouldn't mind. Anyway, she's gone to the dressmaker's with Adele. Who's to know?'

Eric smiled reluctantly. 'I suppose it won't hurt this once. I can run Gerald home when I go to collect Madam and Miss Adele.' He picked up Gerald's suitcase and tossed it into the boot. 'Let's go then, son.'

Reluctantly, Gerald took his place beside Meg.

'Are you sure about this?'

'Of course I am. I really enjoyed our chat on the ferry, and I was sorry when Addie dragged me away.'

Eric climbed into the driver's seat and started the engine.

'I'm pleased to see you too, but I'm afraid you've put my father in an awkward position,' Gerald said in a low voice. 'Your mother has always made it perfectly clear that Simone and I were allowed to visit as a special favour to Mum and Dad. She wouldn't want you to know me now.'

Meg stared at him in disbelief. 'What absolute rot. You must be mistaken. In fact I'm sure both Mother and Pa would love to see you again, especially now that you're going to be a professional man.'

'I don't know about that,' Gerald said, shifting about on the seat. 'Mr Colivet was always very kind to me when I was a boy, but things are different now.'

'No. I don't believe that. My father is a very liberal man.' Meg eyed him thoughtfully. 'In fact, I think you should come to Adele's engagement party on Saturday, as my partner.'

'Miss Meg, that won't do at all,' Eric said, glancing at her reflection in the rear view mirror. 'Don't tease the boy.'

'I'm not teasing him. I'm quite serious.'

'It's not his place, Miss Meg. You'll only embarrass him.'

Meg turned to Gerald. 'That's not true, is it? Why would you feel awkward if you were with me?'

93

'That depends on your reasons for inviting me. Why would you do that?'

'Because I like you. Isn't that good enough?'

A slow smile lit his face. 'It's good enough for me. I'd like to come, very much.'

'You're making a big mistake, son,' Eric said uneasily. 'There are things you don't know and are best buried in the past. I'm begging you not to go.'

CHAPTER FIVE

There was less than an hour to go before the guests were due to arrive for the engagement party. Meg took one last critical look at herself in the dressing table mirror. She had not had the heart to leave the golden gown in Oxford, and it was just as gorgeous as it had been on the night of the May Ball, although wearing it brought a flood of bittersweet memories. She had not forgotten Rayner, but during the past few weeks she had forced his memory to the recesses of her mind. He had returned to Germany at the end of term. David had confirmed that in one of his rare telephone calls when he had also announced casually that he had left university and joined the RAF. He was now somewhere in Scotland doing his basic training. Their parents had been shocked and angry at first, but there was nothing they could do about it and Meg suspected that her father was secretly proud of his son.

She did one last twirl, hoping that her mother

would be too caught up in the thrill of Adele's engagement celebrations to notice that her décolletage might be considered by some as rather too daring for a girl of her age. Anyway, Gerald would be here soon and she must get to him before Mother had a chance to make him feel unwelcome. On hearing that the chauffeur's son had been invited to the party Muriel's reaction had been of the tight-lipped, raised-eyebrows kind that usually preceded a sharp put-down. If it had not been for Pa stepping in and declaring that it was a splendid gesture, Meg was certain that Mother would have put up a fight, but she had merely sighed heavily and walked away.

As Meg hurried downstairs she could hear the orchestra tuning up in the drawing room. As she passed the dining room she could see Marie and Cora putting the finishing touches to the mouth-watering array of dishes set out on the table. The centrepiece was an elaborate silver epergne laden with grapes, apricots and peaches. The glass phial at its top was filled with bright-eyed pansies. The scent of roses, lilies and jasmine, picked fresh that morning from the garden, filled the house with fragrance. Everything was perfect in Meg's eyes. This was going to be the grandest party at Colivet Manor for many years, and she felt a buzz of excitement as she heard the first car coming down the drive.

She looked up to see Adele and Frank as they descended the wide staircase. They were holding hands and laughing. Meg could not help but be touched by their obvious delight in each other's company. Mother and Pa followed at a more sedate pace, and Meg felt a sudden lump in her throat. She thought that her father had never looked so handsome and distinguished as he did now in his black evening suit and her heart swelled with pride. Of course, Mother looked elegant too, as always, and her diamond necklace sparkled in the last rays of the sunlight flooding through the open door of the main entrance.

Meg hung back a little as the first guests entered like a flock of exotic birds. The ladies wearing their most glamorous gowns were escorted by men looking dashing in white tie and tails, but there was no sign of Gerald. After a while she was beginning to think that he had decided not to come, but then she saw him entering the house behind a group of latecomers. She was agreeably surprised to see that he was well turned out in what was probably a rented evening suit, with his somewhat unruly dark hair smoothed to a satin sleekness. He looked almost handsome, she thought, making her way towards him through the crush. 'Hello, Gerald. I'm so glad you came.'

'I almost didn't, but I'm pleased now that I made the effort. You look absolutely smashing, Meg.'

'Thank you, Gerald. You look pretty good yourself.'

He cast a furtive look at the other guests. 'I feel a bit out of place to tell the truth.'

Meg could see her mother glaring at them and it was obvious from her expression that she thought the same. 'Nonsense. You're as welcome as anyone here. Let's get a drink.' She slipped her hand through his arm and guided him through to

96

the drawing room where waiters, hired for the evening, stood to attention balancing trays of champagne cocktails on their fingertips.

The carpet had been rolled back to reveal the highly polished oak floorboards and some of Adele's friends were performing an energetic quickstep. The grand piano had been moved to the far corner of the room where the orchestra was now playing, and Muriel's highly prized collection of Meissen statuettes and Dresden figurines had been removed to a place of safety.

Meg took two glasses of champagne from the nearest waiter and handed one to Gerald. There was a flutter amongst Adele's female friends who rushed forward to greet the engaged couple as they entered the room, with Pearl at the forefront.

'Your sister looks very happy,' Gerald said, sipping his drink. 'He's a lucky chap.'

'I seem to remember that you and Addie didn't get on at all well when we were children,' Meg said, smiling. 'You used to tease her too.'

'I must have been a little toad. I apologise for that, Meg.'

'There's no need. It's all in the past.' She held up her empty glass. 'Would you mind?'

He took it from her, allowing his fingers to touch hers for a second or two longer than was necessary. As she watched him thread his way between the chattering guests, Meg was aware that Adele was coming towards her with an ominous scowl marring her lovely face. 'Addie. Whatever's the matter?'

'Why did you invite him to my party?'

'It's only Gerald. What's wrong with that?'

97

'Mother is furious. You've put her in an embarrassing situation.'

'I can't think why.'

'I shouldn't have to spell it out to you, Meg. He's not one of us. I know it sounds snobbish, but its just as bad for Marie and Eric as it is for Mother. You really shouldn't have done it.' With a toss of her long, dark hair, Adele crossed the dance floor to join Frank, leaving Meg staring after her in amazement. She had known that Mother would disapprove, but it had not occurred to her that Addie would be of the same opinion. She was shocked and also disturbed at the thought that she had put Gerald in an embarrassing position. She gave him a brilliant smile as he brought her drink, but glancing over his shoulder she was suddenly aware that some of the other guests were staring at him. She took the glass from him and set it down on a wine table. 'Let's get some air. It's too hot in here.' She had hoped that he had not noticed the fact that Adele had walked away without acknowledging him, but she could tell by his expression that he was painfully aware of the situation. She led the way out through the French windows onto the terrace.

'I shouldn't have come,' Gerald said miserably. 'Your mother doesn't approve, and your sister is obvious mortified.'

'You mustn't mind them,' Meg said, squeezing his hand. 'They're living in the past.'

He glanced over his shoulder into the crowded room. 'Then so are the other people who know who I am and look down their noses. I knew this was a mistake.'

'Addie's set are the most brainless, idle lot of people you could ever wish to meet. They're rich and spoilt and have never done a day's work in their lives. You mustn't pay any attention to them.'

'I don't care about them,' Gerald said slowly. 'But I do care what you think of me.'

The afterglow of the sunset was fading into a purple dusk with the ancient oaks and beech trees casting long shadows on the lawn. Bats zoomed drunkenly overhead and the rapidly cooling air was more heady than the champagne. Meg stared curiously into Gerald's face but his eyes were in shadow. 'I can't think why.'

'Can't you?' His voice deepened and he drew her into his arms, kissing her tentatively but with growing desire. Too startled to protest, Meg made a feeble effort to push him away. It was the first time she had been kissed, other than pecks on the cheek from her father and brother, and the sensation was new and exciting. Gerald's lips were soft yet demanding. A shiver of pleasure ran down her spine as his hands caressed the bare skin of her neck and shoulders. He released her mouth to nuzzle the small hollow at the base of her throat. Her knees were trembling and her heart was thudding against her ribs as if she had just ridden Conker across L'Ancresse Common at a full gallop.

He raised her hand to his lips. 'I love you, Meg. I knew it the moment you hurtled into my arms on the cross-Channel ferry.'

She shook her head. 'Don't say that. We hardly know each other.'

'How long does it take to fall in love?'

His eyes were dark with desire and she drew

away, glancing round anxiously to see if anyone was watching. She smothered a sigh of relief when she realised that no one had witnessed their embrace. She managed a tremulous smile. 'I like you a lot, Gerald, but soon you'll be going back to London. Your life is there and mine is here.'

'And that's it, is it?' There was pain in his eyes and in his voice. 'You invite me here when you know it's not my place to come, you lead me on and then you tell me to go away. You were having fun with me just as they were inside.'

'No, that's simply not true.'

'You let me kiss you and you kissed me back.'

'I'm sorry. You caught me by surprise and the kiss was lovely. It really was.'

'You couldn't have kissed me like that if you hadn't had some feeling for me, Meg.'

'I didn't mean to give you the wrong impression.' She clasped her hands together, eyeing him warily. 'And I don't mean to sound horrid, but you can't be in love with me. You really don't know me, Gerald. Nor I you.'

'Don't you dare tell me how I feel, Meg Colivet. I've thought about you every day since we met on the ferry. I thought it meant something when you invited me here tonight, and for a moment just now, a stupid, mad moment, I thought you might have some tiny spark of feeling for me. Now I can see you're just as shallow and unfeeling as Adele.'

'Don't you dare say such horrid things, and leave my sister out of it. I asked you to come because I like you. That's all there was to it.'

He executed a mocking bow. 'Sorry, milady. I was forgetting that I'm the one from below stairs.

I'd better leave before you have me horsewhipped for my insolence.'

Driven beyond endurance, she raised her hand and slapped his face. The sound ricocheted like a pistol shot through the still night air. Gerald clutched his cheek, staring at her in disbelief.

'I'm not apologising,' she said angrily. 'You asked for that, Gerald LeFevre.' Turning her back on him she stalked off in the direction of the French doors, coming to a sudden halt as she almost cannoned into Adele and Frank who were standing inside talking to Pearl and her boyfriend, Teddy.

'Are you all right, Meg?' Frank looked at her closely, his pleasant features puckered into a worried frown as he glanced over her shoulder.

'Thanks, I'm fine.' Following Frank's gaze, Meg saw Gerald disappear into the gathering gloom.

'I warned you, Meg,' Adele said with a worried frown.

Pearl hooked her arm around Meg's shoulders. 'Never mind that now, Addie. Can't you see she's upset? What is it, dear? Did he take liberties?'

'I'll go and sort him out, shall I?' Teddy fingered his bow tie nervously.

Meg shook off Pearl's arm, blinking away the tears that stung her eyes. 'If you must know, I was beastly to poor Gerald. It wasn't his fault at all and now he's gone, so he won't embarrass you any more.'

Despite Adele's pleas for her to stay indoors, Meg hurried off in pursuit of Gerald, but there was no sign of him. She stood for a moment in the gathering gloom. Her fingernails dug painfully into her hands clenched at her sides. She hadn't intended that he should feel out of place or that Adele's snooty friends would snub him. She paced up and down with the silk taffeta skirts of her dress swishing around her ankles and her high-heeled sandals tapping out an agitated tattoo on the paving stones. She hadn't intended to lead Gerald on, as he had obviously thought she did. Why was life so complicated?

'Meg, dear girl. What are you doing out here on your own?'

Her father's voice from behind made Meg spin around. The scent of Havana cigar wafted in a cloud about him as he strolled up to her.

Meg flung her arms around his neck. 'Oh, Pa. I've made such a mess of things.'

Three weeks later it was Meg who opened the door to the telegram delivery boy. Asking him to wait in case there was a reply, she ran to the study where her father had taken refuge after breakfast.

'I hope it's not bad news.' She saw that his fingers trembled as he opened the envelope, and she shifted anxiously from one foot to another as he read the telegram. 'It's bad news, isn't it?'

He took off his reading glasses and polished them with his handkerchief. 'No, Meg. Although your mother might think it is. Read it for yourself.'

She scanned the lines of print and burst out laughing. 'Addie and Frank got married by special licence. You're right, Pa. Mother will be livid. But why would they do such a thing?'

'I suspect that Frank's father is in a position to know more about what's going on in Downing Street than we are. Anyway, what's done is done.

102

You'd better go and break the news to your mother.'

'The boy is waiting to see if there's an answer.'

'I suppose congratulations would be in order?' Charles said, smiling.

Meg had a nasty feeling that like the Greeks or the Romans, or whoever it was, she might be slaughtered for being the bearer of bad tidings. Before she went to find her mother, she searched for the bottle of smelling salts, slipping it into the pocket of her jodhpurs, just in case. Muriel read the telegram and collapsed on the sofa with a muffled groan. Meg rang the bell for Marie, who took in the situation with one glance and went off to fetch the decanter of brandy from the drawing room.

'Of all the ungrateful children,' Muriel sobbed, taking alternate sniffs of sal volatile and sips of brandy, 'mine are definitely the worst. David defies family tradition and goes off to join the RAF instead of the army, and now Adele ruins my plans for her wedding. It was going to be the social event of next year and she goes off and gets married in secret.'

'Hardly in secret. It was at Caxton Hall.'

'Be quiet, Meg. You don't know anything about it. Getting married in a register office is as good as doing it in secret. It's underhand and everyone will think that she was in the family way. I'll be a laughing stock.'

'Why don't you go upstairs for a lie down, madam? I'll bring you up a cup of camomile tea,' Marie said, with a meaningful nod of her head to Meg.

103

'That's a good idea, Mother,' Meg said, backing towards the door. 'Let Marie help you upstairs and I'll go and put the kettle on.'

'Next thing you'll be bringing home a German or something equally hateful,' Muriel said, holding out her glass to Marie. 'Just a drop more, please. For medicinal purposes.'

'I blame that awful man Hitler,' Muriel said bitterly as she spread the wedding photographs on the dining table. 'It's all his fault.'

'I don't think he knew that Adele was due to be married in the spring,' Charles said with a wry smile.

'There's no need to be facetious, Charles. You know what I mean. If it weren't for all this war-mongering Addie would have got married from home as she was meant to. And anyway, it's all right for Angela Barton to send smarmy letters after the event, but they could have invited us, however rushed the arrangements were. I can't think why we were excluded. It's too humiliating for words.'

'Yes, dear.'

'Don't patronise me, Charles. I'm not in the mood for your cutting remarks.' Muriel pushed the photographs away and marched out of the room.

He sighed, shaking his head. 'Be nice to your mother, Meg. She's taken it all far too much to heart.'

'I'll try, Pa. But at least I won't have to be a bridesmaid and wear the hideous frilly pink dress that Mother had lined up for me.'

After a long, hot day at the end of harvesting, Meg sat on the steps in front of the house examining the blisters on her hands. She had done a man's work simply because it took her mind off the nagging sense of loneliness that overcame her when she had nothing better to do. She had not heard from Gerald since the night of Adele's engagement party and she had not really expected to. The feelings of guilt had worn off, and now all she experienced was exasperation and a degree of puzzlement as to why he had thought he was in love with her. She came to the conclusion that it must have been the champagne talking, or the effect of the moonlight and the soft summer evening, which had made him maudlin and romantic.

She shifted to a more comfortable position on the stone step. Now that the harvest was over and done with she hoped that her parents might be persuaded to let her go and stay in Oxford with Aunt Josie. Walter was still studying medicine and she thought that he would be pleased to see her, even if it just gave him an opportunity to spend more time in Josie's company. She wondered what Uncle Paul would make of Walter's crush on her aunt, but was inclined to think that he would be unlikely to notice even if he caught them kissing on the sofa. Uncle Paul spent far too much time at work, in Meg's opinion. He did not seem to realise what a treasure he had in his wife. She would not blame Josie if she did occasionally take a walk up the primrose path.

The sound of the Bentley's engine made her

105

look up as Eric turned the car into the drive. Rising to her feet she walked slowly down the steps to meet her father as he stepped out of the car.

'How did the meeting go, Pa?'

He passed a thin hand across his forehead. 'The Lieutenant-Governor has issued an order that all ranks should be called up.'

'It's not looking good then?'

'There's no doubt in my mind that we'll soon be at war with Germany, Meg. Not that I think we're in any danger here on the island, we're too small and insignificant to be of any use to the Germans. But, my dear, it's obvious we're going to be marooned here indefinitely while hostilities are going on. I think that you and your mother ought to go and stay with Adele in England, at least until we know exactly what's happening.'

'Mother can go if she likes, but I'd rather be here with you. Running away wouldn't be the Colivet spirit, would it?'

To Meg's surprise her mother also refused to leave, although she was obviously dying to visit Adele and see her new home. 'It can wait,' she said firmly. 'I'm sure they'll come over for Christmas and then perhaps I'll arrange a visit to them in the spring. I'm not having it said that I left my home in a panic. We mustn't give in to the Germans or let them see that we're afraid.'

It had seemed liked a normal Sunday. The soft September mist hugged the tops of the trees and a thick coating of dew on the grass sparkled in the sunshine. Meg and her parents had breakfasted as usual, and had been preparing to leave for the short walk to church when the BBC newsreader announced that the Prime Minister would address the nation at eleven o'clock. There was no question of missing the morning service, but when they arrived at the church they found it packed to capacity and the vicar had brought his wireless from home. The congregation sat in silence, listening to Neville Chamberlain's grave tones.

'It's almost a relief to know the worst,' Muriel said as they made their way home.

Charles shook his head. 'This is a tragedy, my dear. We're at war.'

'After all this shilly-shallying about at least we know that something is going to be done about Hitler and those beastly Germans.'

Meg eyed her father anxiously. 'It won't last long, will it, Pa?'

'I don't know, Meg. I just don't know, but I hope for all our sakes that it will be over by Christmas at the latest.'

'I'm sure it will,' Muriel said confidently. 'Our boys will soon put the Germans in their place, and then we'll have all the family together at Christmas. If Angela Barton thinks I'm going to allow Adele and Frank to celebrate the festive season in Hampshire, she can think again. What a year it's been. First we miss our own daughter's wedding, and now there's going to be a war. Personally speaking, I'd like to shoot Angela Barton and Hitler.'

In spite of the declaration of war, it seemed to Meg as if nothing changed very much in the following few months. Every evening they listened to the BBC news but, chilling as it was, what was going on in Europe seemed far removed from their daily lives.

Muriel was in her element organising meetings and supervising jumble sales and whist drives to raise money for the Red Cross. Charles spent most of his time at more serious meetings in the States offices, but business with the mainland went on very much as before. Walter wrote to say that he had joined the Wiltshire Regiment and asked Meg to write back and enclose a photograph. She replied to one in three of his letters and sent him a very old snapshot of herself taken on L'Eree beach.

Even when hostilities continued long after Christmas, everyone said it could not last much longer and quite soon the Germans would be beaten and everything would return to normal. The occasional Stuka flew overhead causing enough concern for those who could afford it to construct air-raid shelters, and just in case of an air attack people stuck crosses of sticky tape on their windows to prevent flying glass. Gas masks were distributed and blackout regulations came into effect. Muriel was amongst the first to instruct Mrs Vaudin to make up blackout curtains for every window in Colivet Manor. Marie and Cora spent a week taking down and washing the existing curtains before attaching the newly made black linings and laboriously rehanging the heavy, inelegant results.

Despite the fact that ration books had been issued to the islanders, there was no shortage of food and the mail boats continued to operate as ever. Meg kept her worries about Rayner's safety to herself. She wished with all her heart that she could forget him, but she knew that that was impossible. She worried about David, of course, but on the odd occasions when he telephoned home he sounded cheerful and positive. He had qualified as a pilot and was now flying Spitfires from an aerodrome somewhere in East Anglia. Meg realised that he risked his life every time his plane was scrambled, but either David was a very good liar or he was genuinely enjoying the challenge. Adele on the other hand seemed to be blissfully happy in her new home. Frank had been declared medically unfit for military service and he continued to work in the Southampton office of his father's shipping company. Never a great correspondent, Adele limited herself to writing a few words on a postcard each week.

One morning at the beginning of May, Meg came down to breakfast but to her surprise there were no appetising smells emanating from the kitchen. She wondered what could be wrong. Eric and Marie were never late for work. She glanced out of the window to see if there was any sign of the Bentley entering the drive, but all she could see was the postman getting off his bike to post the mail through the letter box. Scooping the pile of envelopes off the doormat, she arranged them neatly on the console table. She fingered Adele's latest communication, which had been hastily scrawled on a card depicting New Forest ponies and as usual contained little more than a list of her social engagements and acquisitions for the home. Meg was wondering if she ought to take it upstairs to her mother, who was laid low by one of her bad headaches, when the front door opened and her father entered the house, pale-faced and moving like an old man.

Meg was alarmed. 'Pa, where've you been? I thought you were still in bed.'

'I've been at a meeting all night, Meg.'

'You look exhausted, Pa. Are you all right?'

'I need to talk to you and your mother.'

'Mother's got one of her heads. She isn't up yet.'

'This is extremely urgent, Meg. Fetch her now. There's no time to lose.'

CHAPTER SIX

'I've registered you both for evacuation,' Charles said solemnly. 'It's for the best, Muriel.'

'I've a dreadful headache.' She clutched her forehead, closing her eyes for a brief moment. 'Is it really that urgent?'

'I'm afraid so, my dear. The government has demilitarised the islands. The local defence forces and military will be disbanded and evacuated to the mainland. We'll be unprotected should the Germans decide to invade us. I want you and Meg to leave on the first available boat.'

Meg could hardly believe her own ears. 'Surely they won't bother with us, Pa? What good would it do them?'

Charles met her anxious gaze with an attempt

at a smile. 'They would have invaded part of the British Isles, thereby creating a stepping stone to the mainland.'

'Your father is right,' Muriel said, fanning herself with her hand. 'We must leave as soon as possible. We'll stay with Adele until all this silliness is at an end.'

Meg fixed her gaze on her father's serious face. 'But what about you, Pa? Will you come with us?"

'I'll stay here, Meg. I'm not leaving Colivet Manor for the Germans to loot and destroy. Besides which I have responsibilities to the tenants. But you and your mother must go.'

Meg shook her head. 'I said I'm not going and I meant it.'

'You'll do as you're told, young lady.' Galvanised into action and apparently forgetting her migraine attack, Muriel leapt up from her chair and hurried towards the door. 'Come along, Meg. We've got to pack.'

'I'm afraid you'll have to go on your own, Mother.'

'I don't know how anyone is supposed to manage with just one suitcase,' Muriel said, pulling on her white kid gloves as Eric hefted her bulging case into the Bentley.

'It will give you the opportunity to take Adele on a shopping trip to the West End, my dear.' Charles held the car door while Muriel settled herself on the back seat.

She leaned out of the open window. 'You should be coming with me, Meg. It's not too late to change your mind.'

'I'm staying, Mother. Give my love to Addie and Frank.'

'You're a stubborn, stubborn child. You're just like your father.'

'Yes, Mother.'

Muriel made an exasperated tut-tutting sound. 'Well, I think you're very silly.' She turned to Charles. 'Aren't you coming to see me off?'

'This isn't a pleasure trip, Muriel. Eric is going to collect Marie and Simone on the way to the harbour. There won't be room for all of us in the car.'

If the situation had not been so tense Meg might have laughed at her mother's horrified expression. No doubt the thought of sharing the family limousine with their cook and her daughter was only a little less upsetting than having her home overrun by Germans. 'I hope you have a smooth crossing, Mother.'

Muriel sank back against the leather squabs and turned her head away.

'Better not waste any more time,' Charles said, nodding to Eric. 'Make sure they get on board safely before you leave the dock.'

Eric touched the brim of his peaked cap and climbed into the driver's seat.

'Are you sure this is what you want, Meg?' Charles said urgently as Eric started the engine. 'You could still go with your mother.'

Meg shook her head. 'I'm not leaving you, Pa. You'd starve if you were left on your own. I'll bet you don't even know where the kitchen is, let alone how to make a meal.'

112

He raised his hand in an automatic response to a vague flapping of Muriel's gloved hand as the Bentley glided smoothly towards the road. 'I'm an old soldier. You'd be surprised what I can do if needs must, but now you mention it I am a bit peckish.'

'I'll see what I can do about breakfast then,' Meg said, squaring her shoulders. 'Don't worry, Pa. We'll be fine, you and I.'

In the kitchen, Meg stared at the expanse of scrubbed pine table that seemed to disappear into infinity. The huge black range glowered at one end of the rectangular room, spilling grey ash onto the red quarry tiles like a hungry monster waiting to be fed its daily ration of anthracite. It was Eric's job to bank it up last thing in the evening and then Marie would riddle the ashes and stoke it when she arrived early in the morning to begin preparations for breakfast.

Breakfast. It had been an idle boast that she knew how to cook, but surely it couldn't be that difficult? Meg looked helplessly around at the china-laden oak dressers and the blank-faced cupboards that lined the walls. If it'd been the stables, then she would have known exactly to the last oat where the feed was kept, but the kitchen was no-man's land, a strange uncharted territory, and she was hungry. She opened a few cupboards and came face to face with baking tins, mixing bowls and measuring jugs, but no food. She was beginning to lose patience when the door leading to the scullery opened and Marie bustled into the room.

'Marie! I thought you'd gone on one of the boats.'

'Me?' Marie rolled up her sleeves and whisked her white pinafore off its hook. 'Not me, Miss Meg. Eric wanted us to go but Simone and I said not likely. She's just started her nursing training at the hospital and we don't have any family in England. We'd be stuck in some billet with people we didn't know and no means of supporting ourselves. Anyway, I've no intention of leaving my little house and all my precious bits and pieces for bloody foreigners to smash up or steal. It'd take more than a pack of Germans to frighten me out of my home and that's for sure.'

Meg had never heard Marie say so much all at once. Wielding a brush and poker Marie mastered the range with the ease of long practice and coaxed it back to life. At once the room felt warmer, and the black kettle that lived permanently on the hot plate began to simmer. 'You go up to the dining room, Miss Meg. I'll have breakfast ready in two ticks.'

Meg could see that her presence would be more of a hindrance than a help and she was only too pleased to do what Marie asked. She joined her father in the dining room, and it gave her a warm feeling to see him in his customary place at the head of the table, hidden behind yesterday's copy of *The Times*.

'Marie is still here, Pa. She and Simone decided to stay.'

Charles lowered his newspaper. 'I'm pleased for our sakes, but she should have left with the rest of the women. And so should you if it comes to that, Meg. It was wrong of me to let you stay.'

She hurried to his side and gave him a hug.

114

'You didn't have any choice, Pa. There's no way I'm leaving you, and that's that.'

He smiled, brushing her cheek with his finger-tips. 'You're a good girl. I just hope you've made the right decision.'

Meg smiled confidently, but beneath her outward show of bravado she was extremely apprehensive. She took her seat at the table, gazing out of the window. It was a lovely morning with the promise of a fine day ahead. It was almost impossible to believe that all this could suddenly come to an end. She unfolded her table napkin and laid it across her lap, but when she realised that she was repeatedly folding the starched linen into pleats she made an effort to still her twitchy fingers. It would all come right in the end, she told herself as she glanced at Pa, whose calm seemed unruffled. All this fuss would blow over. Mother would return from the mainland and everything would be as it was before the rumours of invasion began.

She sniffed appreciatively as Marie entered the room carrying a tray laden with bacon and eggs, toast and coffee. Charles folded his paper and laid it neatly by the side of his plate. He gave Marie a beaming smile as she put the toast rack in front of him. 'I'm delighted you stayed for my own selfish sake, Marie. But I hope you won't regret it later.'

'I'm sure I won't, sir,' Marie replied calmly. 'Eric says it will all be over by Christmas, so it didn't seem worth the upheaval.'

'Let's hope that he's right,' Charles said as Marie left the room. 'Things aren't going to be

115

easy from now on, Meg.'

'With most of the women evacuated we're going to be short-staffed when it comes to tomato picking, Pa. We've already lost the younger men to the armed forces. It's going to be difficult to run the farm with just Eric, Billy and Joe.'

'I think we'll have to take each day as it comes,' he said vaguely. 'Pass the coffee pot, please, Meg.'

It was not the answer she wanted, but she managed to bite back a sharp response. Pa was a wonderful man, a brilliant advocate and a good lawyer, but she knew that he had little interest in agriculture, relying instead on Eric's keen business sense to manage the farm and keep the accounts. She made up her mind to speak to him as soon as he returned from the harbour. She ate quickly, deciding that her first task of the day would be to groom Conker and muck out the stables. Her father barely seemed to notice when she excused herself from the table, but as she left the dining room she was startled by a loud hammering on the doorknocker. 'All right,' she shouted, 'I'm coming. Don't break the door down.' She hurried to open the door.

'Meg, how are you, my dear?' Her father's younger brother, Bertrand, was standing on the doorstep, beaming at her. Despite the warm weather, he appeared to be wearing his entire wardrobe and he clutched a large suitcase in each hand. Beads of sweat stood out on his forehead and trickled down his nose to drip onto his badly tied cravat. Standing behind him, red-faced and perspiring in her ancient musquash coat, was his wife, Aunt Maud.

'Uncle Bertie. Aunt Maud. This is a surprise.'

He put one foot over the threshold. 'I hope this is not an inconvenient time to call?'

'No, of course not,' Meg said, making an effort to sound welcoming. 'Come in, please. My goodness, you both look so hot. Why don't you take off your coats and hang them on the hallstand?' She glanced over her shoulder as she heard her father's quick footsteps on the marble tiles. 'We've got visitors, Pa.'

Charles stared pointedly at the suitcases. 'It looks as though you're planning on a long visit, Bertie.'

'So good of you to take us in, Charles,' Maud said, launching herself at him and enveloping him in a fond embrace. 'Bertrand was sure that you wouldn't mind, under the circumstances.'

'Circumstances? I'm not sure I understand.' Charles looked from one to the other with a puzzled frown.

'Germans, dear boy,' Bertrand murmured, looking furtively over his shoulder as if he expected to see a whole Panzer division in the garden. 'I'm surprised to find young Meg still here. Shouldn't she have gone on the boats today?'

'I didn't want to, Uncle Bertie,' Meg said, helping him as he struggled to take off his overcoat. 'It was my decision to stay with Pa. But I could ask you the same question.'

Bertrand peeled off his scarf. 'Maud wouldn't go without me, and our little house is in a very vulnerable position. If the Germans invade, or start dropping bombs on the town, we thought we'd be safer here. I expect you've got one of those newfangled air-raid shelters, haven't you, Charlie?'

'We're so far from town that I didn't consider it necessary. Do you really intend to stay here?'

'If you'll have us, dear Charles.' Maud flopped down on a hall chair, fanning herself with her fur hat. 'We're too old to cope on our own in a situation like this.'

'I see.' He turned to Meg. 'In that case I suppose you'd better ask Marie to make up one of the spare rooms for Bertie and Maud.'

'Too kind, Charles,' Maud said with an arch smile. 'You were always the perfect gentleman. We'll try not to get in your way.'

He mumbled something unintelligible as he picked up the post and strode off towards his study.

Meg had a sudden vision of her mother's shocked expression when she discovered that her home had been invaded by the in-laws she so heartily disliked. 'Leave your cases, Uncle Bertie. I'll get Eric to take them upstairs.'

'I should lock the family silver away if I were you.' Maud jerked her head towards the dining room where the sideboard was clearly visible through the open door. 'Unless you want to see it all shipped straight back to Berlin.'

'Yes, I believe the German soldiers steal everything in their path,' Bertrand said, mopping his brow with a red paisley handkerchief. 'We've buried our valuables in the back garden.'

'And Muriel's collection of porcelain figures will be the first to go,' Maud said earnestly. 'They're German, you know, Meissen and Dresden. They'll have those as mementoes before you can

118

blink an eye. You should pack them up and hide them in the attics or down the old well, Meg.'

'I'll see to it directly,' Meg said, edging away towards the kitchen. 'If you'd like to wait in the drawing room, I'll go and find Eric and Marie.'

'You'd best ask her to make up three rooms, dear,' Maud said, coughing delicately. 'Jane will be bringing Pip along later. I told her you wouldn't want them to stay alone in that tiny cottage near the harbour.'

Meg opened her mouth and closed it again. She had always disliked Maud's daughter Jane and her dreadful son. The 'unspeakable Pip', as David called him, was too awful for words. Meg raced off to pass the bad news on to Marie, who took it in her usual unflappable way. With a sigh of relief, Meg left everything in her capable hands and she slipped out of the back door, making her escape to the stables.

Conker whinnied and pawed the ground as she approached his stall. 'Hold on, old boy. I'm coming.' She picked up a yard broom. 'I'll start with you today and when you've got a nice clean stable we'll go for a canter–'

She broke off with a cry of fright as a man leapt from the shadows and grabbed her wrist.

'Meg, it's me, Gerald.'

She stopped struggling but her heart was thudding noisily against her ribcage and the blood was pounding in her ears like the surf on the Grand Rocques. 'You stupid fool. You scared me half to death.'

'I'm sorry. I didn't mean to. I just didn't want anyone else to know I'm here.'

'Why are you here? I thought you were in the army.'

He sank down on a bale of hay and fumbled in his pocket, producing a packet of Woodbines. 'I am. We were stationed on the south coast and we had orders to ship out somewhere, we didn't know where, but I just couldn't go into active service without seeing you and making things right between us.'

She stared at him aghast. 'Gerald, you fool. You haven't gone absent without leave, have you?'

'No, of course not. I made up a tale about needing urgent compassionate leave. I've got to get back to the barracks tomorrow. I'll get one of the first boats out in the morning.'

'You're crazy. They've just started evacuating women and children.'

He lit a cigarette and tossed the spent match out onto the cobbled yard. 'I couldn't stop thinking about you, Meg. And the stupid row we had at your sister's engagement party has played on my mind ever since. I had to see you again, if only to say I'm sorry.'

She was silent for a moment, not knowing what to say, but as Gerald sat with his head bowed and the cigarette burning away to ash between his fingers, she felt a sudden rush of pity. She could hardly believe that he had risked everything just to see her again. 'I'm sorry too. I was hateful to you that night.'

'Really?' Gerald's dark eyes shone with hope. 'Do you mean it?'

She smiled, holding out her hand. 'I do. I put you in an impossible situation because I didn't

120

stop to think things through. If I gave you the wrong impression, I'm really sorry.'

Flicking the butt of his cigarette out into the yard, Gerald leapt to his feet. 'I love you, Meg,' he said, taking her in his arms and kissing her on the lips. 'Do you think you could ever love me?'

She pushed him away gently. Everything was total confusion. When he kissed her it was exciting and left her wanting more, but was that love? She had nothing to compare it with other than the emotions that Rayner had aroused in her, and sometimes she wondered if that had been simply a glorious dream. She shook her head. 'I don't know, Gerald. I really don't know.'

'I think that means you do have some feeling for me. It was worth coming here just to hear you say that.'

'To hear her say what?' Eric's stern voice from the doorway made them move guiltily apart.

Meg felt a blush rising from her throat to suffuse her face. 'Eric, it's not what you think.'

'I don't know what to think.' He gazed at Gerald with a mixture of pleasure and puzzlement. 'I hope you've got an explanation for this, son.'

Meg moved away tactfully and went to saddle Conker. What passed between father and son was really none of her business and at this moment she wanted to be on her own.

After riding round the estate and discovering that her fears had been justified as Billy and Joe were the only workers who had not left for the mainland, Meg had a brief chat with them. Satisfied that they were content to stay on and work the land, she took Conker for a long ride along

121

the cliff tops. She hoped that Eric would have talked some sense into Gerald and convinced him to return to the mainland while he had the chance. She would feel terribly guilty if he got himself into trouble with the army because of her.

When she returned home in time for the midday meal she found Uncle Bertie and Aunt Maud already seated at the dining table eating roast chicken and vegetables as if they had not had a square meal in weeks. Demolishing food at an equally alarming rate were her cousin Jane and the unspeakable. Pip. Although he was seventeen, Pip still behaved like a ten-year-old. Something had gone wrong at his birth, or so Meg had been led to believe, although sometimes she thought he just put it on to get attention. He giggled a lot, spoke with a stutter and held his large head slightly to one side, peering at people through the thick pebble lenses of his spectacles. Meg's feelings of sympathy towards him were usually short-lived, as he seemed to take a delight in annoying her. She groaned inwardly at the sight of him now.

Jane looked up with a forkful of chicken halfway to her mouth. 'Hello, Meg.'

'Cousin Jane, Pip.'

'When I heard that Mummy and Daddy were coming here, I thought this was the best place for Pip and me,' Jane said, staring at Meg with eyes that appeared twice their size behind thick lenses similar to her son's. She put Meg forcibly in mind of a goldfish she had won at a school summer fete and kept in a jam jar on her bedside table.

'Capital plan. The whole family safe together under one roof,' Bertrand said, completing the statement with a loud belch.

'Manners, Bertie,' Maud said primly.

'It's quite dreadful to see the houses deserted. Some people haven't even shut their front doors.' Jane wiped the gravy off her plate with the remains of her crusty roll. 'There are abandoned animals everywhere. There are cows in need of milking; dogs and cats running loose. Where will it all end, I ask myself?'

Meg had witnessed similar scenes during her ride but it had seemed like someone else's problem. She was only just beginning to realise the full impact of the mass evacuation. 'Someone has to do something about it,' she murmured, more to herself than to the others.

'Not your problem,' Pip said, scraping his plate and licking the gravy off his knife.

She watched him with disgust and suddenly her appetite left her.

Marie bustled into the room and began clearing the table. 'I'll bring your lunch before I fetch the pudding, shall I, Meg?'

'I think I'll just get a sandwich in the kitchen, thanks,' Meg said hastily. She could not stand the sight of Pip shovelling food into his mouth one moment longer. The sound of his irritating high-pitched giggle followed her as she left the room.

With the help of Joe and Billy, Meg and Eric rounded up a dozen or more soft-eyed Guernsey cows that were in desperate need of milking and lowing pitifully. They found a few goats tethered and in need of fresh pasture, and soon had a following of abandoned dogs with eagerly wagging tails and soulful eyes.

'Meg, you can't take them all. We won't have room or be able to feed them,' Eric said as she made a leash out of baler twine and secured it through the collar of a collie that was attempting to lick her face and hands.

'Well I'm not leaving them to starve.' She patted the dog and secured the lead to the back of the farm cart with half a dozen other distressed animals. 'We'll manage somehow.'

It was early evening by the time they had herded cows and goats into a field and tethered them safely. Meg settled the dogs in the tack room with food and water, all except one, a large black Labrador who refused to be parted from her. Every time she went to shut him in with the others, he somehow wriggled through the door and stood looking up at her with laughing eyes as if it were a huge game.

'You're impossible,' Meg said, grinning back at him.

He wagged his tail and his pink tongue lolled out of his mouth. He ambled off in the direction of the house, stopped and looked at Meg over his shoulder.

Meg threw back her head and laughed. 'All right, you win. I can see you've adopted me.' She walked on towards the scullery door with the dog following close on her heels, but she stopped and caught him by the collar before stepping inside. 'You'd better behave or you'll find yourself back with your friends in the tack room.'

Marie was just about to hang her apron on its hook when Meg strolled into the kitchen. 'What

124

in the name of heaven is that?'

'He seems to have adopted me.'

'You're not going to keep that animal in the house, are you?'

Meg nodded emphatically. 'I am, and as I don't know his real name I'm going to call him Buster because it suits his character.'

'Don't blame me if he brings fleas into the house. And there might come a time when we can't feed ourselves, let alone a big brute like him.'

'We'll meet that when we come to it. Buster is my dog now and he stays.'

Marie sniffed, and jamming her hat on her head she stomped out of the kitchen.

With Buster following her, Meg wandered into the drawing room to listen to the BBC news and found Bertie and Maud seated comfortably on one of the sofas while Jane and Pip sprawled on the other. An empty coffee pot and cups scattered on side tables bore witness to the fact that they had already dined, and Bertrand was snoring gently with a brandy glass clutched in his hand.

Meg opened her mouth to speak and was immediately hushed by Jane and Maud who were listening to a big band concert.

'I don't like dogs,' Maud said with an exaggerated shiver.

Pip curled his long legs up on to the sofa. 'Does he bite?'

'He only bites people I don't like,' Meg said, frowning. 'Where's my father?'

'He went to his room,' Jane said, eyeing Buster nervously. 'Please take it away, Meg. Can't you see it's frightening Mother and Pip?'

Without saying a word, Meg left the room. She felt the sudden need to be alone and she left the house through the front door. It was dusk and bats were already spinning about the darkening sky as the sun plummeted towards the horizon and starlings squabbled noisily in the stand of Spanish oaks at the end of the drive.

'Come on, Buster, let's go for a walk.' Meg walked slowly towards the pleasure gardens and the lake. The scent of roses and mock orange blossom filled the air. A soft breeze rippled the water, which seemed to boil mysteriously in the last feeble rays of the setting sun. Buster snuffled about amongst the reeds, startling a family of ducks that had settled down to roost, and their agitated quacking echoed across the water, shattering the eerie stillness. Meg turned as she heard footsteps approaching and was barely surprised to see Gerald striding towards her. The whole day had been strange, with a surreal quality that made her wonder for a moment if it was a dream and at any moment she might wake up and discover that things had returned to normal.

'I've been looking for you,' Gerald said breathlessly. 'My dad's still a bit upset with me so I've left him to tell Mum that I'm home.'

'But you will leave tomorrow? You must.'

'I will, but I'm still glad I came.'

She was silent for a moment. He was standing so close to her that she could feel the heat from his body. She did not pull away when he curled his fingers around her hand. Buster took a sudden dive into the water just a few feet away from them and emerged carrying a stick, which he dropped at Gerald's feet, grinning up at him and wagging his tail.

'Good boy.' Gerald patted the dog's head. 'Dad told me you rescued a lot of livestock, including dogs. I suppose this is one of them.'

'I couldn't leave them to starve or wait for some government official to decide their fate.' She smiled and squeezed his hand. Suddenly it felt good to have someone who understood and approved of her actions. Gerald moved closer and as their eyes met, Meg felt the tug of desire. She closed her eyes, parting her lips as his mouth seized hers in hard, greedy kisses that rendered her breathless.

'Meg, I love you. I really do love you.' His dark eyes reflected the fiery afterglow of the sunset and Meg felt she was drowning in their depths. There was no mistaking his sincerity. An odd detached part of her mind thought of Rayner, whose thoughts she could not even begin to guess. He had been a thrilling enigma but he had gone away and she would probably never see him again. The romantic dreams that she had built up suddenly burst like a soap bubble and vanished into the encroaching dusk. She could not tell if it was love she felt for Gerald but tomorrow he too would be going away. She could feel the intensity of his emotion overriding her doubts and scruples.

'Meg, do you love me?' He kissed her again, this time with mounting desire. 'Say you do, please.'

She drew away in an attempt to catch her breath and gather her scattered thoughts. 'I'm not sure. I can't think straight when you do that.'

He looked deeply into her eyes. 'Say you love

127

me, Meg. I'll be leaving in the morning, and this might be the last time I ever see you. Tell me you love me. Just say it once and I'll carry it with me forever.'

Waking early next morning, Meg knew that she would never forgive herself if she did not make the effort to see Gerald off. She was tiptoeing across the entrance hall hoping to leave the house without being seen when her father emerged from his study, briefcase in hand.

'You look like a sneak thief caught in the act, Meg. Where are you going this early in the morning?'

She hesitated, twisting a strand of hair round her fingers. 'For a walk.'

'You can't fool me that easily. You look just as you did when you were little and you'd done something really naughty.'

'It's Gerald, Pa. He came home to see his parents and he's leaving this morning for the mainland. I was just going to see him off.'

'The damned young idiot!' Charles strode to the hallstand and picked up his hat. 'What on earth was he thinking of? If he doesn't get on one of the boats he'll be in serious trouble.' He opened the front door. 'I'm picking up Eric on my way to the courthouse. I'll make sure the young fool gets away safely.'

Meg followed him out to the car. 'I'm coming too.'

Charles swung the big car easily round the tight bend into Havelet and up the winding street into

128

Hauteville; a narrow canyon between tall terraced houses. The street was silent and deserted, and it felt to Meg as though the whole town had taken flight.

'Wait here,' Charles said, as he drew up outside the LeFevres' house. He stepped out onto the pavement and went to hammer on the brass doorknocker.

Peering out of the window, Meg saw that it was Eric who opened the door, and she was alarmed by his appearance. His face was ashen and dark circles underlined his eyes. He looked like a man who had had very little sleep. She could not hear what was being said but Pa must have put forward a strong case as Eric disappeared into the house, returning moments later with Gerald.

'You don't look too good, old chap,' Charles said, as Eric stepped forward to open the passenger door.

'I'm fine, sir. Had a bit of a bad night, that's all. Indigestion, you know, but I feel a bit better now.'

Gerald had climbed in beside Meg, reaching out surreptitiously to hold her hand. His smile was heartfelt and she squeezed his fingers.

'Drop me off at the States offices,' Charles said, as Eric urged the Bentley forward. 'You'd better take young Gerald to the harbour and make sure he gets on one of the boats.'

'Yes, sir. Thank you.'

It was a short drive to the courthouse, and as the car slid to a halt Charles laid his hand on Eric's sleeve. 'Don't hang about, Eric. See the boy off and then I suggest you get yourself checked over by a doctor.' He glanced over his shoulder.

'Good luck, Gerald. Don't take any unnecessary chances. We don't want a dead hero.' He climbed out of the car, closing the door with a thud and motioning Eric to drive on.

The streets closest to the harbour were blocked with abandoned vehicles and Eric had to make several detours before they could get anywhere near the White Rock.

'It looks as if half the island is here,' Meg said, staring at the mass of people sitting on the ground, standing in family groups, leaning against walls or huddled together as they waited for a chance to board a ship bound for England. Several small vessels, packed with human cargo, were already edging their way out of the harbour and Meg could see the funnels of a larger boat waiting to come in. There was a flurry of activity as the word passed round the anxious evacuees.

Gerald slipped his arm around Meg's waist. 'It's finally goodbye then, Meg.'

'I'm sure it won't be for long, Gerald. Look after yourself, won't you.'

He answered her with a long and passionate embrace. Meg slid her arms around his neck and kissed him back regardless of the fact that Eric was standing just a few feet away. All around them there was noise. Seagulls shrieked overhead, ships' sirens wailed and whistled and the drone of voices was punctuated by sobs and cries of distress. With a last soft kiss Meg pushed him away. 'You must go or you'll never get on a boat.'

Gerald's eyes were suspiciously bright as they met hers in a long look. Still clutching her hand, he turned to his father. 'Goodbye then, Dad.'

Eric did not answer or even look up; he was bent double as if in terrible pain with one hand clutching at the car door, his knuckles showing white through his tanned skin, and the other clasped to his chest.

'Dad. What's wrong?' Gerald rushed to support him. 'What's the matter?'

Eric raised his head a little and Meg caught her breath at the sight of his grey face with beads of sweat standing out on his forehead.

'Bloody indigestion, son. I'll be fine in a minute or two.'

Gerald opened the car door and lowered his father onto the back seat. 'Take it easy, Dad. I'll get you to the hospital.'

'No, son. You – go.' Eric gasped as another obvious spasm of pain bent him double.

'You've got to get on the boat, Gerald,' Meg cried, tugging at his arm. 'Your father will be all right. I'll drive him to the hospital. Dr Gallienne will take care of him.'

'I'm not leaving him like this. Get in with him and I'll drive.'

Meg took one look at his set face and the arguments died on her lips. She climbed in beside Eric and held his hand. It felt cold and claw-like in her warm grasp.

'I'm dying, Meg,' Eric whispered.

She wrapped her arms around him. 'Don't be silly. Of course you're not dying. It's just a touch of indigestion. You said so yourself.' She caught Gerald's anguished gaze in the rear view mirror. 'Hurry,' she breathed. 'For God's sake, hurry.'

131

CHAPTER SEVEN

Meg sat in the hospital waiting room while Gerald went off to fetch his sister from the female surgical ward. She shifted anxiously on the hard wooden seat, praying silently that Eric would be all right. He was more than just an employee; he had been like a second father to her, or a much-loved uncle. It was Eric who had taught her how to ride; he had given her driving lessons in the farm truck, and had always been ready to lend an ear to her complaints about school or homework, or anything that had troubled her while she was growing up. She realised suddenly that she was biting her fingernails; a habit she thought she had long outgrown. She folded her arms and waited.

After what seemed like an eternity, Gerald returned with Simone. Meg had never particularly liked her and she knew that the feeling was mutual. On the infrequent occasions when Simone had accompanied her parents to the manor house, she had shown nothing but resentment towards Meg and the rest of the family. They were of a similar age, but the likeness ended there. Simone had the exotic looks of a Spanish flamenco dancer. Her smouldering dark eyes were set beneath slanting black eyebrows. Her thick, blue-black hair complemented her flawless olive complexion and she was as slender as a willow wand.

As their eyes met, Meg's first instinct was to

rush over and offer comfort, but the look on Simone's face was not encouraging. She turned her back on Meg and took a seat at the end of the row. With an apologetic smile, Gerald went to sit beside his sister. Meg realised that she had been excluded, and she settled down for the seemingly endless wait for news of Eric's progress.

After nearly an hour the door opened and Dr Gallienne walked into the waiting room. Meg leapt to her feet and took a step towards him but he met her eyes with a slight shake of his head. He laid his hand on Simone's shoulder. 'We did all we could for your father, but he suffered a massive heart attack. We did our best but I'm afraid that there was nothing we could do to save him. I'm so sorry.'

Meg felt as though the sterile walls were closing in, crushing them all with their silent force. Simone buried her face in her hands, and Gerald put his arm around her heaving shoulders. 'I don't understand, Dr Gallienne. Dad never had any trouble with his heart before.'

'It sometimes happens like that, Gerald. I'm sorry, my boy.'

'He was only forty-nine.'

Gerald's bewildered look went straight to Meg's heart and she rushed to his side, throwing herself down on her knees beside him. 'I'm so sorry.'

Dr Gallienne cleared his throat. 'I'll send a nurse in with some tea and I'll let the ward sister know you won't be returning to duty today, Simone.'

She raised her head, wiping her eyes on the back of her hand. 'No need. I've got work to do.'

Dr Gallienne took his spectacles off and wiped

them several times on the tail of his white coat. 'You're not in a fit state to go back to the ward, my dear. Go home and rest.'

'I haven't got a home now that my father's dead. My mother spends all her time looking after the damned Colivets. She doesn't care about me and never has. It's always been Gerald this and Gerald that. I'd rather stay in the nurses' home and take my chances with the Germans.'

Meg rose slowly to her feet. 'What has my family ever done to you, Simone?'

'Didn't your daddy tell you that he wanted my parents to move into the manor with you lot for the duration? He said it would be safer for them, but he's obviously thinking of his home comforts now that your snob of a mother has run away to the mainland.'

'Simone!' Gerald sprang to his feet. 'There's no need for this. Apologise to Meg.'

'Mum and Dad may have been happy to let the Colivets rule their lives but I'm different. If you want to end up like them that's your problem.' Simone stormed out of the room, slamming the door.

'She's in shock,' Dr Gallienne said, clearing his throat. 'She doesn't know what she's saying.'

'Why does she hate us so much?' Meg looked to Gerald but he had sunk back on his seat and was holding his head in his hands. She stared at him for a moment, too stunned to think straight, but suddenly the solution was obvious. She turned to Dr Gallienne. 'I'll go and telephone my father. He'll know what to do.'

There was no chance now of getting Gerald on a boat for the mainland, and even if there had been, he refused point blank to abandon his mother and sister at such a time. Despite Meg's pleas, he remained adamant that he would not leave the island until he had buried his father. When they arrived back at Colivet Manor, Charles took Marie and Gerald into his study and closed the door.

Meg was left in the hallway, not knowing quite which way to turn. Events had occurred so quickly that she had difficulty in believing that Eric was no longer with them. She half expected that any moment the door would open and he would walk in demanding to know why she wasn't feeding the animals they had rescued. There was a nightmare quality about everything that was going on around her, and for the first time she found herself wishing that her mother were here to take command of the situation. A cold wet nose pressed against her hand and Meg flung herself down on her knees to hug Buster. He licked her face and butted her with his head when she stopped stroking him. 'Good boy,' she murmured, rising to her feet. 'Come on, Buster, we'll go and do our jobs. Eric would have wanted that.' She hurried out of the house with the dog at her heels, and was about to head for the stables when she saw Maud and Bertrand sunning themselves on the terrace. They had to be told, of course. There was no point in putting it off. Meg braced her shoulders and went over to them.

Bertrand squinted up at her beneath the brim of his panama hat. 'That's dashed bad news. Poor old Derek.'

'Eric,' Meg said sharply. 'His name is Eric.'

'Was, dear,' Maud said, smiling. 'What time will lunch be ready? I'm ravenous.'

It had been a long and emotionally exhausting day spent comforting Gerald and Marie, and now she needed time on her own. The early evening was balmy and as she walked through the woods she revelled in the intoxicating scent of briar roses and honeysuckle. The pine needles crushed beneath her feet added a spicy resinous aroma to the fragrance of wild flowers, and the mournful keening of seagulls echoed her mood as she clambered down the steep cliffs to Marble Bay. Through the straight columns of the trees, she could see the metallic glint of the sea glowing ferrous red in the rays of the dying sun. She glanced down at the beach where the pebbles shone like precious jewels in the fading light. They had collected them as children, pretending they were pirate treasure. If she closed her eyes she could see twelve-year-old David with a hanky tied around his head and a wooden cutlass in his hand, with Gerald as his second in command and a reluctant Addie grumbling that she was always the captive Indian princess waiting to be rescued. At seven years old, Meg had been willing to play any part as long as she could tag along after the bigger children, but more often than not they made her stay at home. She could hear their childish laughter. The days had seemed endless and full of magic then.

She opened her eyes with a start and turned her head as an ominous droning sound coming from the south grew rapidly into a dull roar and filled her ears with the thunder of powerful aeroplane engines. A series of explosions shook the ground beneath her feet. The sky behind Castle Cornet was streaked crimson with flames and plumes of black smoke. More planes followed the bombers and the sound of machine gun fire reverberated around the cliffs in nightmare percussion. Numbed with shock and fear, Meg stared bemusedly at the appalling sight. Gradually her petrified limbs began to tremble back to life and she started to run, breaking through the undergrowth, tearing her clothes on brambles and cutting her face on snapping twigs. Deafened by the blood pounding in her ears, she raced for the safety of home.

'It's a tragedy,' Charles said, replacing the telephone receiver on its hook. His face was deathly pale as he turned to Meg. 'Twenty-nine people were killed in last night's air raid.'

'Why would the Germans bomb us when they must know the islands were demilitarised?'

He shook his head. 'It doesn't look good, I'm afraid. I have to go to a meeting of the emergency committee. Can you cope with the farm business, Meg?'

'Of course I can, Pa. But you will try to get Gerald to go to England on the next boat, won't you?'

'The mail boat yesterday was the last boat to leave, but if there's any way to get him to the mainland, I'll make sure it's done.' He kissed her on the cheek. Picking up his hat and briefcase he went to open the front door, pausing on the

137

threshold to give Meg an encouraging smile. 'We'll get through this somehow.'

Left alone in the entrance hall, Meg heard the sound of raised voices coming from the dining room. She could not face another family squabble and she decided to head for the comparative peace of the stables. She was grooming Conker when Joe appeared in the doorway.

'We've just about finished the milking, miss. What shall we do next?'

'Better get the rest of the potatoes in, Joe. We'll bag them up as usual and store them in the barn until we find out what's happening.'

'What about shipping them out, miss? Billy says there won't be any more boats going to the mainland.'

'We'll just have to wait and see. Anyway, we can't leave the crop to rot in the fields.'

He seemed reluctant to leave. 'Bad business about Eric.'

The slow realisation was beginning to dawn on her that Joe and Billy, who had always taken their orders from Eric, were now relying on her for guidance. She felt sick at the thought, but she forced herself to appear calm. 'We all miss Eric, but we've got to carry on.'

He nodded, seemingly reassured by her outward display of confidence. When he had gone, Meg returned to her task of grooming Conker. 'What will happen next, I wonder?' she said, speaking her thoughts. 'Will they realise that I'm just as much at sea as they are?' Buster, who had been lying in a patch of warm sunshine, raised his head from his paws and wagged his tail.

There was plenty to do around the farm and in the estate office but every little thing reminded Meg of Eric. She found herself listening for his familiar footsteps or waiting for him to tramp into the office, wiping his brow on his hanky and complaining about the heat. The sun beat down and the birds sang but she knew that nothing would ever be quite the same again; last night's bombing raid had brought the war to their doorstep.

Late in the afternoon she realised that she had not eaten since breakfast. She crept into the kitchen, peeking around the door first to make sure that none of her relations were there rifling through the cupboards for food. Marie had been complaining bitterly about their gargantuan appetites ever since they arrived, and had threatened to put a padlock on the larder door. Relieved to find the room empty, Meg put the kettle on the hob. She was warming the teapot when Gerald walked into the room. He was pale beneath his tan and his face was drawn. He made a brave attempt at a smile. 'Meg, I thought I might find you here.'

She struggled to maintain her composure, but seeing him like this made her want to cry. 'It's a sad time for all of us, but how is Marie coping today?'

'Badly. But I suppose that's only to be expected.'

She made tea and poured a cup for Gerald, lacing it with two spoonfuls of sugar. 'I am so sorry, Gerald. I just don't know what to say to you.'

He slumped down on a chair, resting his elbows on the table. 'I know. I can't believe it myself.'

'But you've got to return to your regiment. Eric would have wanted that above everything.'

'It's too late now,' he said tiredly. 'I've over-stayed my leave as it is.'

She reached across the table and squeezed his hand. 'You have to try. You'll be in terrible danger if you stay, and branded as a deserter if you don't get back to your unit.'

'I say. What's this, Meg? Hobnobbing with the servants again?' Pip had entered the kitchen un-noticed.

'Shut up, Pip,' Meg said automatically. She was too concerned for Gerald to pay much attention to her cousin's stupid remarks.

Pip stared pointedly at Gerald. 'Shouldn't you be off fighting for your country?'

'Shouldn't you?'

'Here, you can't talk to me like that, you're just the son of the hired help and he's dead, so you've no right here at all.' Pip stepped aside, giggling nervously, as Gerald pushed his chair back, send-ing it crashing onto the tiled floor.

'Ignore him, Gerald. Everyone else does.' Meg rounded the table swiftly and caught Gerald by the hand. 'Let's get out of here.'

Pip followed them through the scullery and into the stable yard. 'You're very brave when you've got a girl to stand up for you!'

Meg rounded on him furiously. 'That's enough of your idiotic remarks, Pip.'

'I'll tell Uncle Charles what you said.'

Gerald snatched his hand free and made a move towards Pip. 'You'll tell him what exactly?'

Meg slipped in between them, although she knew that if it came to a fight Pip would run away or scream out for his mother. 'Take no notice of him, Gerald. He's just a nasty little toad. Pa can't stand him any more than I can.'

Pip retreated into the house. 'I'll tell Uncle Charles you said that too.'

Meg slipped her hand through Gerald's arm and she could feel him trembling with anger. 'Let's get away from here. My bike's in the stables and you can use David's.'

Riding side by side with Gerald along the deserted Forest Road towards the airport, Meg had no particular destination in mind. She had simply headed in the opposite direction to town and all the earth-shattering recent events. Normally there would have been a few cars passing them in both directions, filled with families out for a Sunday drive, or young men on motorcycles with their girlfriends riding pillion. But today the only person they saw was an old farmer with a loaded hay wagon drawn by an equally elderly shire horse. Both kept their heads bent, staring gloomily at the ground. The rumble of the cartwheels and the steady clip clop of the horse's hooves gradually faded into the distance, but another low droning sound took its place, growing louder every second.

Meg braked hard, coming to a sudden halt, and Gerald pulled up beside her.

'What on earth was that?' Shielding her eyes, she squinted into the clear azure sky.

Seconds later a huge plane swooped down towards the airport. 'By God, Meg. It's a Junkers, and it's coming in to land.'

There was no mistaking the destination of the huge aircraft and Meg could only watch in silence, too horrified to speak.

'Bloody hell.' Gerald spun the bicycle round to face the way they had just come. 'The Germans have landed.'

'Come on,' she said, leaping onto the saddle and pedalling frantically. 'We've got to get home. Pa's on the controlling committee. He'll know what to do.'

Charles sat behind his desk steepling his fingers. 'There is nothing we can do. Resistance would be useless in the circumstances.'

'We can't just let them walk all over us, Pa.' Meg rested her hands on the desk, willing her father to say something that would give them hope, but his expression remained impassive.

'We will do what we have to in order to survive.' Charles turned to Gerald, frowning. 'But matters are more serious for you, I'm afraid.'

'I won't run away from danger, sir.'

'This isn't a question of bravery or cowardice, Gerald. It's a matter of common sense. If you give yourself up to the Germans, they'll make you a prisoner of war and you'll be sent to France or Germany to one of their camps. If you don't give yourself up and they catch you, you'll be shot as a spy.'

Meg sat down suddenly, gasping as if the air had been sucked from her lungs. 'They wouldn't, would they?'

'Yes, my dear, they most certainly would. Gerald is a British soldier and as of today we're an occupied country.'

'There must be someone with a boat who would take me to England, sir.'

'Even if it were possible, it's too risky. You wouldn't stand a chance,' Charles said gravely. 'As far as I can see, there's only one answer.'

'I'll do anything you say.'

'You're roughly the same age, height and colouring as David. You must take his identity. We'll make up a story as to why an able-bodied young man like you has stayed on the island.'

Meg leapt to her feet. 'That's ridiculous, Pa. He'd never get away with it.'

'It won't work,' Gerald said slowly. 'I don't look anything like David.'

'The Germans won't know that.' Charles pushed back his chair and opened one of the desk drawers. He took out a sheaf of papers. 'I had a ration book made out in David's name and I have a copy of his birth certificate. We'll say that you are unfit for military service.'

'I don't want to put you all in danger.'

'I'm afraid you did that when you came home this time, my boy.' Charles replaced the documents and turned the key in the lock. 'Your only hope is to do as I say. Perhaps later on there will be a chance for you to escape from the island, but until then I can't see any other way of keeping us all safe.'

Meg was forced to agree. She laid her hand on Gerald's arm. 'I think you must do as Pa says. You haven't any choice.'

Eric's funeral passed with quiet dignity, uninterrupted by any military presence, although Meg had heard that German troops marched down the main street in St Peter Port. The Union

143

flags had disappeared from all the public buildings and had been replaced by swastikas, and the rumble of heavy vehicles and tanks travelling along the main road from the airport had been audible in the house, but so far she had not seen one German uniform.

In the church of St Martin de la Bellouse, Meg had felt too numb to shed a tear for her old friend, and oddly distanced from the loud grief of Marie and Simone. Afterwards, when everyone had dispersed in respectful silence, Meg had taken little comfort from the service. It was just words, and however eloquent the speakers might have been, their rhetoric did nothing to alleviate the pain of losing her old friend.

Later that afternoon, after the mourners had left the house and Colivet Manor seemed to slumber in the warm sunshine, Meg cycled back to the cemetery to lay a posy of garden roses on the grave and say her own personal goodbye to Eric. At the churchyard gate, Meg patted the head of the prehistoric stone figure of la Gran'mere du Chimquiere and she broke off a small pink rose-bud, laying it on the weather-worn head, following the local custom as she had done many times since she was a small child.

'Good morning, miss.' A voice close behind her made her spin round, coming face to face with a German officer. Petrified by the sight of the smoke grey uniform, Meg stared at him dumbly, but he did not move any closer and stood clutching his peaked cap in his hands. He had spoken with barely a trace of an accent and he was young, probably the same age as David and Rayner. For

144

a wild moment she could almost imagine it was Rayner standing gravely before her, and her heartbeats quickened leaving her quite breathless.

'I did not mean to startle you.' He clicked his heels together and nodded his head in a formal salute and a shy smile flickered across his clean-shaven face.

She squared her shoulders and looked him in the eyes; intelligent dark blue eyes with a darker rim around the iris. 'It's all right. You didn't.'

'Excuse me. I came only to see the church.' He glanced at the flowers clutched in her hand. 'I did not mean to intrude.'

'The church is open to everyone.' Meg turned away. There was something agonisingly familiar in the way he spoke and the smile that trans-formed his serious features. Memories of Rayner came flooding back and almost overwhelmed her; but this was not the carefree summer of just over a year ago, it was another time and another place and this young man was her enemy.

She left him and hurried to the spot beneath the trees where Eric's new grave lay hidden beneath a carpet of flowers. She placed the roses on top of the floral tributes, but out of the corner of her eye she watched the soldier. He disappeared into the church and even as she murmured her last good-bye to Eric she was uncomfortably aware of an alien presence. An army lorry rattled past the church gate, shattering the tranquillity of the graveyard, and in spite of the hot sun a cold shiver ran down Meg's spine. She hurried to retrieve her bike from behind the stone wall.

Returning home, she had left her bicycle in the

stables and was making her way to the house when Pip scuttled out of the tack room. 'You're brave, aren't you?' he said, grinning. 'I wouldn't go outside the gates with the enemy lurking behind every tree and bush.'

'There's no need to exaggerate.' She went to open the scullery door but Pip moved with surprising speed and barred her way.

'Don't think you're kidding anyone, Meg.'

She stared at him, wondering if he had finally lost his wits completely. 'What are you talking about?'

'I'm referring to having your boyfriend living under the same roof, and pretending to be your brother. I can see what's going on even if Uncle Charles can't.'

'You're crazy.'

'But I'm not stupid.' Pip leaned closer. 'I know all about it. I could report him to the Germans.'

She pushed him away, catching him off balance so that he staggered against the brick wall. 'You're talking nonsense, as usual. But if I catch you saying anything along those lines to anyone I'll make your life hell. Do you understand me, Pip?'

He backed into the scullery, rubbing his bruised shoulder. 'Bitch.'

'What was all that about?' Gerald strode across the yard carrying a basket filled with freshly picked peas and beans.

She shrugged her shoulders. 'Just Pip being Pip.'

He followed her into the kitchen. 'Want to tell me about it?'

'No, I don't.'

Marie dropped the potato that she had been

146

peeling and gave them an anxious glance. 'Haven't we got enough trouble on our hands without you two squabbling like kids? I can't cope if there's going to be an atmosphere in the house.'

'We weren't fighting, Mum.'

'No,' Meg said. 'It was all Pip's fault, as usual.'

Marie wiped her hands on her apron. 'Forget Pip. Mr Colivet wants us all in the drawing room. I was to tell you when you came in. It's very urgent.'

'Now we're all here,' Charles said, reaching for his reading glasses, 'it's my unpleasant duty to tell you about the German orders. These were given to me at the Bailiff's office this morning and came straight from Colonel Graf von Schmettow of the German High Command. So I'm afraid we must take them very seriously. There's an immediate curfew; everyone must be indoors between eleven p.m. and six a.m. All British servicemen have to report to the police.' He paused here and looked at Gerald over the top of his spectacles. 'Just as well we took the decision to loan you David's identity, my boy. And I must remind all of you not to let the truth slip out. There are very severe penalties for a deception of this nature so we must all keep our mouths firmly shut. Do you understand, Pip?'

'I say, Uncle Charles, that's not fair.' Pip moved closer to his mother.

Jane's faced flushed a dull brick red. 'Yes, Charles, don't pick on Pip.'

'I have to make certain that everyone grasps the seriousness of the situation. Anyway, to continue,

147

and I'll make it as brief as possible. Of course you all realise that communications have been cut off to the mainland and wireless sets are being confiscated. All weapons have to be given up, including shotguns, and there's an embargo on every type of boat, including fishing boats, without an order from the military.'

'No hope of smuggling you off the island that way, then, Gerald,' Meg whispered behind her hand.

'Shh...' Bertrand nudged her in the ribs. 'Be quiet and listen.'

'The sale of petrol is banned, as is the use of all private transport, except for essential services. So I suppose we can still use the farm truck when we need to. Blackout restrictions are already in force, but they've got to be strictly observed – so I'm asking each one of you to be responsible for your own rooms and keep an eye on the reception room windows at night.' Charles consulted his notes. 'All alcohol sales are forbidden. That means no more after dinner-brandy, Bertie.'

'Steady on, Charles,' Bertrand protested feebly.

'I never thought I should live to see the day.' Maud sniffed and tears trickled down her cheeks creating runnels in her face powder.

'Don't take on so, old girl,' Bertrand said, handing her his hanky. 'Don't cry or you'll start me off.'

Charles cleared his throat. 'And now I must give you the last and probably the worst news as far as this family is concerned. The Germans have already taken over most of the hotels and a good few private houses to billet their officers and men.'

148

Meg was suddenly alert. She knew by her father's tone of voice that this was going to be dire. 'Not here, Pa? Please tell me it's not true.'

CHAPTER EIGHT

'I'm afraid it is, Meg. Hauptmann Dressler informed me that he intends to billet some of his officers here from tomorrow, and there's nothing I can do about it.'

A murmur of consternation rippled round the room.

'We'll be murdered in our beds, or worse,' Maud muttered into the folds of Bertrand's hanky.

'I don't think so,' Charles said, shaking his head. 'But it's even more important now for everyone to remember Gerald's new identity.'

'See the danger you've put us in, young man. I hope you're satisfied.' Jane's face puckered up as if she had been sucking a very sour lemon.

Marie tapped her on the shoulder. 'Begging your pardon, Miss Jane, but you leave my boy alone. I'm sick of hearing you and that son of yours sniping at him.'

There was a momentary silence as everyone turned to stare at Marie.

'Well, the impudence.' Maud heaved her portly body out of her chair. 'You'd do well to remember your place, Mrs LeFevre.'

'That's enough,' Charles said, raising his voice for the first time that day. 'There's no difference

149

between any of us at this moment. We're all prisoners on the island and that makes us equals. I don't want to hear any talk of that kind or any hint of it. Understood?'

'We understand,' Meg said, glaring at Jane. 'We do, don't we?'

There was a mutter of assent and Jane sprang to her feet. 'You're the head of the family, Charles. I expect you to take extra special care of my boy. After all, he is your blood, unlike some.' She jerked her head in Gerald's direction.

Marie opened her mouth as if to protest, but Charles silenced her with a look. 'I'll do everything in my power to protect all of you, but I won't stand for petty jealousies and bickering. Take the boy away, Jane, and try to impress some common sense into his head before tomorrow morning, if that is possible.'

'Well, really!' Jane stormed out of the room dragging Pip along in her wake. Maud and Bertrand followed, casting malicious glances at Gerald as if the situation were entirely his fault.

'Are you all right, Marie?' Charles asked anxiously. 'You're as white as a sheet.'

'I'm worried about Simone. She's still at the hospital and she doesn't know about any of this. She might let it slip that her brother is still on the island.'

Gerald hooked his arm around his mother's shoulders. 'I'll go and see her. You mustn't worry.'

'You really should stay within these grounds,' Charles said, frowning thoughtfully. 'But I take your point, Marie.'

'There are tomatoes boxed and ready to deliver

to the docks and there are still ships going to France,' Gerald said, after a moment. 'I can drive to St Peter Port this afternoon and stop at the hospital on the way back.'

Meg shook her head. 'I won't supply the German army with tomatoes. They can bloody well starve.'

'And so will we if we don't trade,' Charles said gently. 'We have no choice, my dear. Whether we like it or not these people are here and if we want to survive then we have to do as they say. It's as simple as that.'

'Well I don't have to like it.'

'No, Meg. You don't have to like it. Neither do I.'

Gerald squeezed the truck in between two German armoured cars in the hospital car park. They had dropped the boxes of tomatoes off at the depot and Meg had spent a good half hour filling in the necessary documentation supplied by a German soldier who only had two or three words of English. Now, with her nerves almost at breaking point, she leapt to the ground and slammed the door with such a degree of pent-up fury that the old vehicle shuddered, sending flakes of rust fluttering to the ground. 'I'll go and find Simone. You'd better stay in the truck, Ger – I mean, David.'

'Yes, sis,' Gerald said, winking at her.

'I'm glad you think it's funny.' Hunching her shoulders, she strode off towards the main entrance. No matter how hard she tried, she was finding it difficult to remember that Gerald was now supposed to be David, and if it was hard for

151

her it must be almost impossible for his mother. What Simone would make of the deception she could not begin to imagine.

The hospital receptionist seemed tense and nervous, but she gave Meg a wan smile and said she would phone around the wards to see if she could locate Nurse LeFevre. Looking around, Meg was unnerved by the number of grey German uniforms that seemed to be everywhere. She took a seat by the window, and picking up a dog-eared magazine from the table she flipped through its pages even though the recipes, household hints and the inevitable short story held little interest for her. She looked up as a shadow fell across the page.

'Good afternoon, miss.'

She found herself staring into the face of the young German officer she had encountered in the churchyard.

'You are here to visit someone sick?' His smile was tentative and it was almost as if he were expecting a sharp put-down.

She hesitated, not knowing quite how to react. She wanted nothing to do with the enemy, but it was impossible to ignore a young man who was so heart-wrenchingly like Rayner. He seemed anxious to be acknowledged and for a brief moment she felt almost sorry for him. 'Hello.'

His face lit up with a smile. 'Lieutenant Dieter Brandt. Miss...?'

Meg stood up as she saw Simone coming towards them. 'Marguerite Colivet,' she said hastily. 'Excuse me, I see my friend coming.'

'You wanted to see me?' Simone brushed past

152

Dieter, casting him a sideways glance beneath her thick black lashes.

'Can you spare me a few minutes?' Meg said urgently.

'I'm on duty. Can't it wait?'

'No it can't. It's family business.'

'Aren't you going to introduce me to your friend?' Simone said archly.

Meg gritted her teeth. She was beginning to feel as though she were caught up in some surreal nightmare. She could hardly believe that Simone was not only ogling a German solder but was actually demanding an introduction. 'Simone, this is Lieutenant Dieter Brandt. We bumped into each other in the churchyard when I was laying some flowers on your father's grave. Lieutenant Brandt, Simone LeFevre.'

Simone held out her hand. 'Please to meet you.'

Dieter shook hands and bowed. 'Fräulein LeFevre.'

Meg grabbed Simone by the arm. 'I really do need to talk to you now, please. Let's go for a walk outside. It won't take a minute.'

'Oh, all right,' Simone said reluctantly. 'Good-bye, Lieutenant Brandt.'

'How could you?' Meg hissed as she propelled Simone towards the glass doors. 'You were flirting with him. They're the enemy, for God's sake.'

Outside the air was warm with summer scents and free from the hospital smell of strong disinfectant.

Simone wrenched her arm free. 'That hurt, you spiteful cow.'

'Gerald is in the truck. He's got something

important to tell you, so please just try to look casual as we walk across the car park.'

'All right, but don't touch me again.'

Meg leaned against the tailgate and waited. After a few minutes, Simone strutted off in the direction of the main entrance without a backwards glance. Gerald opened the cab door and beckoned. 'I've put her in the picture,' he said as Meg climbed in beside him.

'She didn't look too happy about it.'

'No. Simone thinks I've sold out to the Colivets.'

'Perhaps she'd rather see you deported to a prisoner of war camp or worse. I'm sorry to say it but your sister is a pain in the neck.'

Gerald started up the old engine, which coughed and spluttered and threatened to stall. He gave it some more choke and it finally wheezed into life. 'She can't help it.'

'Well, hopefully she'll keep her mouth shut. Let's get home before one of those damn Germans starts asking questions.'

As they drove from the car park Meg caught sight of Simone inside the glass doors and she was talking animatedly to Dieter Brandt. Meg said nothing.

Early next morning Charles waited at the top of the stone steps with Meg standing resolutely just a little way behind him. They watched in silence as the convoy of army vehicles came slowly up the drive. Meg made an effort to appear calm, but her mouth was so dry that her tongue felt hard and cracked like an old leather shoe. She could feel a trickle of cold sweat running down between her

154

shoulder blades and she was inwardly quaking. She slipped her hand into her father's and the pressure of his fingers on hers was comforting until she realised that he was trembling convulsively. Brakes squealed, tyres spun on the gravel and doors were flung open as the German officers climbed out of their transport. Their jackboots crunched on the gravel drive.

Hauptmann Dressler announced himself formally with a curt bow and named Major Jaeger and Captain Grulich as his next in command. Charles led the way to the drawing room and Hauptmann Dressler tossed his peaked cap and gloves onto Muriel's escritoire sending a small ormolu clock crashing to the ground; the glass face splintered into tiny shards. Meg clenched her fists at her sides as a feeling of helpless rage welled up inside her. The Hauptmann's obvious unconcern for this small accident made the fact that he had destroyed one of her mother's treasured belongings even harder to bear, and she blamed herself to some extent. Last night, with Marie's help, she had packed her mother's valuable ornaments in newspaper and stowed the boxes under the eaves in one of the attics, but she had overlooked the clock.

Not for the first time, Meg wondered what sort of men these were beneath the harsh grey uniforms. Hauptmann Dressler looked like a clean-shaven Santa Claus but one glance from his steel-plated eyes was enough to convince Meg that he was a man to be feared and avoided at all costs. He paced the drawing room while he stated his demands coldly and impersonally.

155

'Major Jaeger, Captain Grulich and myself will need rooms on the first floor away from the rest of your household. Captain Grulich you will go now and make sure this is done.'

Grulich clicked his heels and saluted as he left the room. Hauptmann Dressler continued to pace the floor, which was already becoming scuffed and in desperate need of a good polish. Meg could only be thankful that they had thought to store her mother's beloved Aubusson carpet under the eaves. It was a small matter, but she would not wish to see it ruined by the careless pounding of jackboots.

'This room will be used as my office.' Dressler pointed to the door at the far end of the room. 'What is through there?'

'The dining room,' Charles said, in a low voice.

'That will do as well. Your family will not enter these rooms, Herr Colivet. Is that understood?'

'Perfectly.'

'My cooks will take over the kitchen to prepare our meals and my men will make use of whichever of your outbuildings they need in order to make camp.' He came to a standstill at last and made himself comfortable in Charles' favourite chair by the Adam fireplace. He took out a gold cigarette case and Major Jaeger stepped forward to light the cigarette. Dressler inhaled deeply and then exhaled slowly, all the time keeping his gaze fixed on Charles' face. 'The occupation of your island is to be a model of its kind, Herr Colivet, and as long as your family obey the rules they will be treated well. I am not a patient man and I will not tolerate insubordination. I want to make that clear.'

'One question, Hauptmann Dressler?'

'Well?'

'My family has to be fed. We will need to use the kitchen at some time.'

'Captain Grulich will make the necessary arrangements.' With a dismissive wave of his hand, Dressler turned his head away.

Major Jaeger gave a deprecating cough and opened the door. Meg gave him a sideways glance as she followed her father out of the room. Had she imagined it, or had Major Jaeger looked just a little discomforted by the arbitrary way that Dressler had treated her father? His expression was impassive now, but she thought she had seen just a flicker of sympathy in his grey eyes.

As they emerged from the drawing room they heard the sound of raised voices coming from upstairs followed by what sounded like someone's fist crashing against the wood panelling of a door. Charles ascended the staircase, taking two steps at a time, closely followed by Meg and the major.

Captain Grulich was standing outside Maud and Bertrand's room with his fist raised, ready to pound again. 'Open. Open, I say.'

'Go away,' Bertrand shouted in a voice that shook with terror. 'Leave us alone.'

'Open the door.'

Maud began to scream hysterically.

'What's going on?' Charles demanded breathlessly.

Major Jaeger rattled off a string of orders in German and Captain Grulich stood back, his face expressionless.

'Who are these people?' Jaeger demanded.

'My brother, Bertrand Colivet, and his wife Maud. Do they have to be distressed like this?'

Major Jaeger spoke once more to the captain, raising his voice in order to make himself heard above the noise from the bedroom. Maud continued to sob and Bertrand, protected by two inches of solid oak, was shouting obscenities.

'Hauptmann Dressler is very particular about his accommodation but in the circumstances perhaps we can leave your relations where they are. Have your family remove their belongings immediately and let them know that the bathroom is for Hauptmann Dressler's use only. They must make other arrangements.'

Meg opened her mouth to protest and was silenced by a stern look from her father. 'Very well, Major. Come along, Meg.'

'There are more rooms upstairs?' Major Jaeger pointed to the staircase leading up to the second floor.

'They were once used as guest rooms and the nursery. The attics housed the servants in the past,' Charles said gravely. 'But they have not been in use for many years.'

'Nonetheless, they will be needed. Captain Grulich and I will inspect them. You don't need to accompany us.'

'Pa, you can't let them do this to us,' Meg whispered.

'My dear, we have no choice. You heard what the Hauptmann said, they want this to be a model occupation, but that doesn't alter the fact that we are virtually prisoners and completely at their mercy. If we comply with their rules we

158

stand a chance of surviving this ordeal; if not, I can't bear to think of the consequences.'

'But, Pa...'

'If you want to do something, go and find Gerald and send him to me. And you'd better get Marie and Jane to help you move everything out of our rooms before the Germans do it for us. I'll be in my study. It's far too small to be of any use to our unwelcome guests. I suppose I should be grateful for that.'

He brushed Meg's cheek with a kiss. His lips were soft and dry like the touch of a moth's wings and Meg flung her arms around him in response. 'I'll do anything you tell me, Pa.'

'That will be a first,' Charles said with a hint of the dry humour that Meg had always loved.

In the kitchen she found herself in the centre of another bitter confrontation, this time between Marie and a nuggety German corporal who stood with his arms folded across his chest while Marie brandished a saucepan at him.

'I can't cook the lunch with you in my way, you heathen brute.'

Meg did not have to understand German to know that the string of guttural words which flowed from the corporal's mouth was peppered with expletives, and the grinning faces of two young privates hovering in the background confirmed her suspicions. In any case, Marie had lapsed into patois and was screaming at him so loudly that it would have been impossible for her to hear what he said, even had she understood. The noise must have filtered through the corridors to the main hall as Grulich erupted into the kitchen and silenced the corporal by bellowing the loudest of all. He seized Marie by the arm and dragged her out of the room. Horrified and frightened, Meg ran after them. Grulich came to a halt in front of Major Jaeger and thrust Marie at him so roughly that she stumbled and would have fallen if the major had not caught her and set her back on her feet.

'Madame,' Jaeger said, having listened to Grulich's explanation. 'Corporal Klein has his orders and he is now in charge of the kitchen. You may use it to prepare food when he says you may. Captain Grulich will prepare a roster and you will please obey this.'

Marie opened her mouth and then closed it again.

Jaeger turned to Meg. 'We can't have this behaviour from your household, Miss Colivet. Hauptmann Dressler will not stand for it, and if any of these matters come to his ears he won't take them lightly. Do I make myself clear?'

Meg nodded. 'Perfectly, Major Jaeger.'

'Then I suggest you call your people together and tell them what is expected of them. You may use the rooms designated to you, and the curfew must be strictly observed. Any other matters you will refer direct to me.'

'I understand.'

'I have observed a young man of military age. Why is he not in the British forces? You understand that we have strict orders regarding any British servicemen found on the island.'

Meg met his gaze squarely. Suddenly she was calm and cool as if her veins pulsed with iced water instead of blood. 'That is my brother, David. He is unfit for military service.

'Hmmn.' Jaeger tapped his forefinger on his chin. 'He looked healthy enough to me.'

'David had rheumatic fever when he was a child,' Meg said, improvising. 'He has a heart condition.'

'Nevertheless, he will be expected to work. Your land must be cultivated to feed my men. I shall speak to your father.'

'You'll find that I know more about running the estate,' Meg said, drawing herself up to her full height. 'My father has enough to do without worrying about the farm.'

'Then tomorrow you will accompany me on an inspection of your land, and I will tell you what to do.'

Meg met his gaze stare for stare, drawing on the stubborn streak that had often got her into trouble when she was younger. She was determined not to let him see that deep down she was shaken and terrified. After all he was just a man, a grey ghost of a man, she thought, with his close-cropped hair and his slate-coloured eyes that seemed to reflect the exact shade of his uniform. But to be fair, he had shown some slight consideration towards them and for that she was grateful.

Major Jaeger's stern features relaxed for a brief moment into what was almost a smile and then he turned and walked away. As the drawing room doors closed behind him Meg realised with a start that she had begun to attribute human qualities to the invaders. She must be mad to imagine that a German would show compassion

161

for their captives. They were the enemy. She made up her mind to hate them all.

The family ate their dinner late that evening, Marie having had to wait until Corporal Klein had vacated the kitchen before she could commence her own preparations. Gerald had discovered Pip hiding in his makeshift workshop above the tack room, and having enlisted his somewhat unwilling help they had carried the old nursery table downstairs to the morning parlour. It was a far cry from the elegant dining room where Hauptmann Dressler and his officers ate their meal off the best Wedgwood dinner service. Captain Grulich had demanded the keys to the wine cellar, and Meg had been forced to stand by helplessly as her father's carefully laid down vintage claret was brought up to complement the Hauptmann's meal.

After supper, Charles called for quiet. 'We must all be extremely careful and remember that these men literally have the power of life and death over us. One false move and they can order deportation or any other punishment they choose.'

'They frighten me,' Jane said, with a theatrical shudder. 'I shall sleep with my door locked and a chair pushed against it too.'

'Wishful thinking,' Meg whispered, grinning at Gerald.

Maud shot a warning glance at her as she leaned across the table to pat Jane's hand. 'I shall never sleep again, not while the enemy is under our roof.'

'Then I'm afraid you're going to get very tired,

162

Maud,' Charles said drily.

'Surely it will all be over by Christmas?' Bertrand gazed regretfully at his empty wineglass. They had drunk the last of the cooking wine that Marie had hidden in a sack of potatoes.

'We can but hope.' Charles raised himself from one of the bentwood chairs that Gerald had found in the attic. 'And now, I don't know about the rest of you, but I'm going to bed.'

'I'm not going upstairs on my own with that man standing by the front door,' Jane muttered, rolling her eyes.

'I'm afraid you don't have much choice,' Meg said, making an effort to sound sympathetic. 'If you're scared then perhaps Pip ought to go upstairs with you.'

'We'll all go up together,' Bertrand said, rising slowly to his feet. 'Come along, Maud. We'll go first. The brutes won't attack an elderly gentleman and his lady. Jane, you and Pip follow on behind.' He slipped Maud's hand through the crook of his arm and led them out into the hallway.

Jane seized Pip by the hand. 'Come along, my precious. Mother won't let those beastly Germans hurt her boy.'

Marie had been quietly clearing the table and she picked up the tray of dirty dishes. 'I'll just see to these, if that oaf's finished with my kitchen for the night, and then I'm going to my room.'

Gerald stood up to open the door for her. He kissed her on the cheek. 'Goodnight, Mother. Leave the dishes. I'll do them later.'

'I won't say no. Thanks, love.' She gave him a tired smile as she left the room.

They were now alone except for Buster. He had been sleeping quietly on the rug by the fire but he leapt up suddenly, wagging his tail and looking expectantly at Meg.

'Poor old boy,' she said, leaning down to pat his head. 'I should have taken you for a walk earlier. I'm afraid you've had it until morning now.' She stood up and stretched. 'I think I'll turn in too. It's been a long day.'

Gerald reached out and caught her by the hand, pulling her down onto his lap. 'I thought they'd never give us a moment alone.'

'Are you mad?' She leapt to her feet. 'We're supposed to be brother and sister. You'd better start acting like it or we're all in trouble.'

'I'm going crazy living close to you like this but not allowed to touch you or tell you how I feel about you.'

'You mustn't talk like that, Gerald. We can't afford to make mistakes.'

'It's not easy for me.'

His dark eyes were filled with pain and longing, but she knew she had to be strong for both of them. 'You've got to let it go, Gerald. I don't know how long the Germans are going to be here in this house, but the slightest slip could be fatal. You know it's true.'

'First I lose Dad and now you. Perhaps we could meet in secret.'

'Absolutely not. It would be madness.' The pleading look in his eyes made her feel guilty. She should never have allowed him to hope. 'Please don't look at me like that.'

'Why not? Or are you sorry that you let me kiss

164

you and make a fool of myself? Perhaps you're glad that the Germans are here and you don't have to pretend that you love me.'

She gazed at him in dismay. 'Where is all this bitterness coming from? I never actually said I loved you. I said I didn't know how I felt, and I suppose that's still true.'

'Admit it, Meg. You can't allow yourself to have feelings for someone like me. That's the truth of it, isn't it?'

'Why are you being like this? Haven't we got enough to bear without you making things worse?'

He took a step towards her, hands outstretched. 'I'm sorry. Oh God, I'm sorry, Meg. I'd no right to say that.'

'No, you hadn't, and anyway you're wrong. I don't see you as being any different from the rest of my family, but this has got to stop, Gerald.'

He bowed his head. 'I suppose you're right.'

'You know I am. We've got to do what my father says and take one day at a time.' She stroked Buster's head as he licked her hand.

'I didn't intend to hurt you, but I meant what I said. I do love you.'

'I believe you, Gerald. But I just don't know how I feel about anything at the moment. It seems as though the whole world has gone mad and we're caught up in the middle.'

'I'd die for you, Meg.'

'Don't,' she said, frowning. 'You mustn't even think like that now. Who knows what will happen in the future, but for the present we're brother and sister, and if we don't believe it then we can't expect the Germans to believe it either.'

Overnight Colivet Manor changed from Meg's dearly beloved home into a billet for German officers and a barracks for their subordinates. Military vehicles churned up the gravel drive and booted feet trampled the pleasure gardens, turning them into a sea of mud. Muriel's scented shrubbery was dug over for latrines and the stable block and outbuildings were turned into living quarters for an entire platoon. Even Pip's little cubbyhole above the tack room was discovered and he was made to clear it out and dispose of the rubbish it contained. He scuttled about for a whole morning with his arms full of cardboard boxes containing bits of electrical appliances that had long since been discarded, carrying them to his attic room like a demented worker ant. Meg had seen the soldiers watching him and laughing openly at his ungainly walk and odd appearance and her own dislike of Pip was temporarily forgotten in a blaze of righteous indignation. It was easy to hate the common soldiers with their arrogant attitude and their leering glances. She could guess at what they said as she walked past them when there was no officer to snap them to attention like malignant puppets.

Meg had found herself locked out of the estate office and her status now was on a par with that of Billy and Joe. She toiled alongside them in the fields, doing physical labour that left her with cracked and bleeding hands and muscles that screamed out in protest. If her lot was hard, it was preferable to being cooped up in the house and forced to listen to the bitter complaints of Jane and

Maud. For the first time in their lives they had to dirty their hands with housework, cleaning and polishing to Major Jaeger's exacting standards.

Meg aimed to avoid the kitchen whenever possible. There seemed to be a private war going on between Marie and Corporal Klein, with bitter altercations in German and patois that stopped only when a superior officer entered the room. Meg never ceased to wonder how the soft-eyed, gentle-voiced Marie could have changed over-night into a shrill harpy who treated Corporal Klein with fearless contempt. It was as if the old Marie had gone away after Eric's sudden death, leaving a hard-faced stranger in their midst.

There were occasions when Meg would have given anything she possessed for her mother to return home and take control of their daily lives. She was safe and well on the mainland, according to the brief messages that they received through the Red Cross. For that at least Meg had to be thankful, but she worried constantly about her father, who seemed to have aged by ten years at least since the Germans billeted themselves at Colivet Manor. He spent many long hours in St Peter Port at meetings of the controlling commit-tee, and came home looking ashen and exhausted. He ate with the family, such food as there was, and then every evening he retreated to his study and shut himself in with his books and papers. The closed door haunted Meg. She longed to burst through it and tell him about the burdens that the family laid on her slender shoulders. She had never felt so helpless or so alone.

CHAPTER NINE

It was October, and the nights were rapidly drawing in. The family had already begun their evening meal when Charles arrived home late from a meeting at the States offices.

'You look tired, Pa.' Meg left her place at the kitchen table to ladle out a plateful of the stew simmering in a pan on the range. Marie had worked hard to make a tasty meal from potatoes and cabbage by adding a handful of herbs and a couple of beef bones that Corporal Klein had discarded.

'What news?' Bertrand asked, mopping up what was left on his plate with a slice of dry bread. 'Is there any progress in the fight against the Hun?'

Maud glared at him. 'Do we always have to talk about war?'

'I just asked. You'd be interested enough if it was all over.'

Charles sat down, staring at his plate. Meg thought he was going to push it away and she wouldn't have blamed him if he did, but it was food and it was reasonably hot. She fretted miserably when Pa refused to eat. They had all lost weight but Pa looked positively skeletal and so frail that she was afraid he might not survive the rigours of a harsh winter.

'I did hear some news, as it happens.' Charles

lifted his spoon and sipped some of the thin broth. 'Dreadful news. London has been bombed night after night, killing thousands and reducing whole streets to rubble. They're calling it the Blitz.'

Meg shuddered. 'How awful. I suppose we're lucky that we don't live in fear of attacks from the air.'

'Lucky!' Jane ladled more potatoes onto Pip's plate. 'We're almost starving and being treated like slaves and you call it lucky. I don't.'

Meg was about to change the subject, but the sight of Pip shovelling food into his mouth and grunting like a pig sickened her, and suddenly she could bear it no longer. 'Your manners are disgusting, Pip.'

He licked the thin trickle of gravy from his chin and gave her a sly smile. 'You'll change your tune when you know what I've got.'

'Something painful and preferably fatal, I hope.' The sharp words tumbled from her lips and were instantly regretted. The war was doing dreadful things to people. She would never have said anything so harsh in the old days.

'Just you wait and see.' Apparently unabashed, Pip seized the last slice of bread and stuffed it into his mouth.

Meg glanced at Jane to see if she would reprimand her son, but she was smiling indulgently. 'What is it, Pip, darling?'

Charles pushed his half-eaten meal away with an apologetic smile. 'Thank you, Marie. That was good, but I haven't much appetite today.'

'What I wouldn't give for a nice juicy steak,' Bertrand said, leaning back in his chair and closing his eyes. 'And a glass of claret to wash it down.'

Maud dug him in the ribs with her elbow. 'I thought we'd agreed not to talk about food in that way.'

'You can't blame a chap for dreaming.'

Meg sighed. She could hardly blame anyone for making comparisons between the meals they used to enjoy and the things they were forced to eat now. Salt, like most things, was in short supply and had to be used sparingly. It was amazing how little things they had taken for granted before the war were now suddenly more precious than gold. She cast an anxious glance at her father as he pushed his plate away. 'Are you all right, Pa?'

'Just a bit tired, my dear. It's been a long day. I think I'll just go to my study and read for a while before I go to bed.'

'You can't go yet.' Pip jumped to his feet. 'Just wait. I've got something to show you all. Something very clever.'

'Not now, Pip,' Charles said tiredly.

'Don't go away. I'll be really quick.' Pip raced from the room, leaving a trail of breadcrumbs in his wake. Minutes later he returned clutching a cardboard shoebox.

Jane beamed at him. 'What clever thing have you done? Show us, dear.'

Pip lifted out a strange-looking piece of equipment with wires sticking out of it at odd angles. He began to fiddle with switches and a round dial and suddenly the thing began to make high-pitched noises and then crackles and finally they heard a voice. 'This is London calling.'

'For God's sake,' Charles said, glancing nervously at the closed door. 'Turn it down,'

'It's a crystal set! By golly, well done, Pip.' Gerald leapt up and slapped Pip on the back.

'Do you mean we can actually listen to the BBC?' Meg craned her neck so that she could see the small object in Pip's hands. It didn't seem possible that this odd-looking thing could be a radio receiver.

'Yes. I made it all by myself.'

'I told you all he's a genius with electrical things,' Jane said triumphantly.

Meg was genuinely impressed. 'That's terrific, Pip. Well done. Now we'll know what's going on first hand.'

Charles reached across the table and snatched the radio from Pip's hands. He switched it off. 'Do you realise just how dangerous this is? Men have been executed for sending carrier pigeons to the mainland and for cutting telephone lines. What do you think the Germans would do if they found a radio in your possession?'

'Then they mustn't find it, Pa,' Meg said, taking it gently from him. 'Pip's been clever enough to make it. Surely we can find a safe place to hide it in a house this size?'

'I agree.' Bertrand nodded emphatically. 'We can't go on like this day in and day out without knowing what is happening in the rest of the world.'

'All right,' Charles said slowly. 'If that's how you all feel, I'll leave it to you to find a safe hiding place, but make certain it is absolutely secure.'

Meg replaced the crystal set in the shoebox and gave it back to Pip. 'I don't think they'll bother

Pip. The Germans seem to think he's the Guernsey joke, so let's keep it that way.'

Pip clutched it to his chest. 'They think I'm stupid, but I'm not.'

'You're very, very clever, Pip. I always knew you were,' Jane said, throwing her arms around him and giving him a kiss. Pip pulled a face and wiped his cheek.

'It was clever of you,' Charles said, rising stiffly to his feet. 'Clever but dangerous and don't forget it. Now, if you'll excuse me, I'm going to my study.'

When the door closed on him Meg nodded to Pip. 'Get the BBC again if you can, but keep the volume down low in case Grulich is snooping around outside.'

Although the family was never told what was going on, it seemed as though Hauptmann Dressler's troops were engaged in some sort of engineering or surveying work. Every morning they left in convoy and came back at dusk. In the daytime there were just the normal guards at the entrance checking everyone who went in and out. Meg had kept Buster close by her side when she was out in the fields and never let him roam round the house, ever since the day he had wandered into the kitchen and Corporal Klein had threatened to shoot him. When she complained to Major Jaeger his face had assumed the shuttered, blank expression that he adopted when repeating Dressler's orders. 'If the animal gets out of control once more, Miss Colivet, he will be shot. Do not let it happen again.'

After that, Buster always slept at the foot of Meg's bed and when she took him out in the morning she kept him on his leash.

Winter closed in and Christmas came and went with no sign of a let-up in the fighting abroad. If anything, Charles told Meg in one of their rare quiet moments alone, the way that the Germans were building defences around the coastline made it look as if they were planning a long stay. Dangerous minutes spent listening to the BBC on Pip's crystal set brought news of the terrible blitz on London and the major cities on the mainland and of the intense fighting in North Africa.

Dressler's rules and regulations became stricter and more difficult to follow. It was almost impossible to go through a day without someone accidentally doing something that Captain Grulich was only too pleased to report to the Hauptmann. Punishment usually came in the form of something physical such as labouring in the fields, cleaning the stable yard or forfeiting their meagre bread ration for a day or even several days. Meg rebelled inwardly but her stubborn streak grew tougher with every passing day. She struggled to keep a calm and passive outward appearance, but the humiliations, injustices and hardships thrust upon the family raged inside her. She despised Dressler and had a sneaking respect for the gentlemanly Major Jaeger, but she loathed and detested Grulich. Humourless, ambitious and cunning he watched every move, trying to find fault and eager to report the smallest misdemeanours direct to Dressler rather than Major Jaeger.

173

His pet victim was Gerald and Meg observed with growing unease that Grulich followed his movements with the persistence of a bloodhound.

On a pearly June morning before the cooks had risen to start preparing breakfast for the men, Meg crept out of the house to take Buster for his morning walk. The early mist had not yet burnt off and the cobbled stable yard glistened beneath the filtered rays of the sun. Meg could feel the warmth bouncing back from the cool stones as she trod softly, not wanting to attract attention to herself.

The pleasure gardens had been totally destroyed and the flowerbeds had been turned into vegetable plots. The latrines stank where once mock orange and buddleia had scented the air with their sweetness, and her mother's favourite magnolias had been felled and used for firewood. Even so, the morning was glorious and the birds sang their hearts out in the surrounding trees, creating an illusion that everything was right with the world. When she was far enough away from the house, Meg let Buster off his lead and he ran down to the lake barking excitedly as a moorhen flew up with a distressed cry to lead the intruder away from her nest.

Meg stopped and shielded her eyes, gazing across the water. The summerhouse had been one of the first casualties of the occupation. The soldiers had knocked it down to build their first campfires and all that remained now was a rectangular concrete base almost concealed by nettles and ivy. She breathed in deeply, filling her lungs with the fresh summer air. All too soon the peace would be shattered by reveille and the thump of heavy boots as the troops began yet another day.

She called Buster to heel, and reluctant to give up the precious moment of freedom she retraced her steps to the house. With an eerie feeling that she was being watched, Meg looked up at the windows gleaming in the sunlight. A curtain fluttered at an open first floor window but she could not see anyone. It must have been her imagination, she thought, but the uncomfortable feeling persisted even after she had gone indoors and locked Buster safely in her room. As she made her way to the kitchen, hoping that she would get there before Corporal Klein, she remembered that it was market day and it was her turn to go with her father in the official car. She would have the morning to do her shopping, taking their ration books into the few shops that remained open, but even then there was unlikely to be much on the shelves. At least it gave her a chance to get away from the house and perhaps see a few familiar faces in town.

She finished her shopping earlier than planned. Even after purchasing their rations of meat, tea, sugar and butter her basket was not over full, and it was hard to feel optimistic when passing the long queues for bread and skimmed milk. She realised with a pang of guilt that these anxious people, who waited so patiently for so little, had to make do with what they could find in the shops. However much Meg hated the German invaders, she had to admit that the amount of farm produce that Major Jaeger authorised for their own consumption was adequate if not generous in the circumstances. She also knew that the common soldiers still ate well and the officers fared even better. She passed yet another queue of hungry-looking islanders and a bitter taste flooded her mouth. She was hungry and thirsty. Breakfast had been a bowl of thin porridge and a cup of weak tea, and that had been hours ago; she had to eat something soon or she would faint.

She walked up the High Street towards the Pantry, a café that had managed to keep going, mainly because German officers chose to go there for their morning coffee. She had a little money left in her purse and she decided to treat herself to a cup of coffee and a bun. The sight of German uniforms had become normal and it was no surprise to find the café crowded. She edged her way between the crowded tables, apologising automatically as she bumped the chair of a young woman sitting with a German officer.

'Look where you're going.'

'Simone!'

'Oh, it's you.' Simone smiled grudgingly as her companion leapt to his feet. 'I think you know my friend, Lieutenant Brandt. After all you did introduce us.'

Dieter bowed from the waist. 'It is nice to meet you again.'

Meg forced a smile.

Simone's dark eyes sparkled with malicious humour. 'Cat got your tongue, Meg?'

'Won't you join us, Miss Colivet?' Dieter pulled out a chair.

Meg looked around desperately. The café was crowded; either she would have to share with

Simone and Dieter Brandt or she must leave. She opened her mouth to refuse but someone seated at a table in the window called her name.

'Meg, over here.' Adele's friend, Pearl, was waving enthusiastically.

'Thank you, but I'm meeting a friend,' Meg said with an apologetic smile. She made her way to Pearl's table and sank down with a sigh of relief. 'Pearl, I thought you'd be in England.'

'I thought you would be too. No, my silly old appendix flared up the day before everyone was evacuated and I spent three weeks in hospital. You might say I missed the boat.'

Meg ordered coffee and a bun from the waitress who appeared suddenly at her elbow. 'Did your parents go to England without you then? And what about Teddy?'

'He joined the navy. I pray for him every night, Meg. That's a laugh in itself isn't it? Pearl, the atheist, devoutly praying to God.' She took a mouthful of coffee and swallowed hard, her eyes suddenly bright with tears. 'Wouldn't Addie and the others have a good giggle at that?'

Meg shook her head. She knew what it was to worry about a loved one risking his life for his country, whether it was for Britain or Germany. 'No one would laugh.'

'You're very sweet, Meg.' Pearl blew her nose on a lace hanky. 'Anyway, Mummy and Daddy decided they couldn't leave their one and only offspring on the island and so we all stayed. Why didn't you go when you had the chance?'

'It's a long story.' Meg was uncomfortably aware of the two German officers sitting at the

177

next table, but the timely arrival of the waitress with her coffee and bun saved her from having to go into details. 'I'll tell you later.'

'I'll keep you to that. Just tell me who that girl is you were speaking to when you came into the café.' Pearl shot a curious glance at Simone. 'The dark-haired girl dressed like a tart, who's flirting with a German officer.'

'That's Simone LeFevre, Gerald's sister.'

'The handsome young chap who caused a stir at Addie's engagement party?'

Meg broke the bun into tiny pieces and found that her appetite had deserted her. 'Pearl, I've got to tell you something and you must keep it secret from everyone, including your parents.'

'This sounds exciting. I've been so bored.'

Meg pushed her plate away. 'Not here.' She drained her coffee cup and carefully wrapped the pieces of bun in a paper napkin, shoving it in her pocket. 'Let's go.'

Pearl scanned the bill left by the waitress and tipped a few coins from her purse onto the saucer. 'I'm coming.'

Meg walked briskly back down the High Street towards the town church where she had arranged to meet her father, with Pearl teetering along behind on her ridiculously high heels.

'Right then,' Pearl said, catching Meg by the arm and dragging her into a quiet corner by the iron railings. 'Now tell all.'

Glancing warily around to make sure no one could overhear, Meg gave a brief account of the events that had led up to Gerald switching identity with David.

Pearl stared at her wide-eyed. 'You've all taken a terrible risk!'

'You won't breathe a word of it? Promise?'

'Of course not. But what about Simone and her German boyfriend?'

'Simone may be a trollop but she wouldn't do anything to harm Gerald.'

Pearl screwed her face up. 'You know what they call girls who associate with the Germans, don't you?'

'Simone can do as she pleases; it's nothing to do with me.'

'Jerrybags, that's what they call them, and quite right too, if you ask me.' Pearl glanced across Meg's shoulder and waved. 'There's Daddy coming out of the library. Sorry, darling, I must go, I promised to carry his books for him and, poor old dear, he's getting even more short-sighted these days. He'll never see me.'

'You'd better run then.'

'Do keep in touch somehow, Meg. I'm going dotty for want of someone nearer my age than a hundred and one.' She kissed Meg on the cheek. 'And good luck,' she called over her shoulder as she hurried off towards the library.

Almost immediately the chauffeur-driven official car pulled up alongside the pavement and Charles leaned across to fling the door open. 'Who was that girl in the ridiculous hat?'

'Pearl Tostevin, Pa. One of Addie's old friends.'

Charles went back to reading the *Guernsey Press*. 'I recognise the type.'

Meg leaned back in the seat and watched the familiar streets pass by the window. They were going at a snail's pace stuck behind a lumbering German tank when, out of the corner of her eye, she spotted a young German officer who was so like Rayner that her heart gave a great leap. She twisted her head, craning her neck in an effort to get a better view, but he was walking away from them and she could not see his face. The tank turned into Fountain Street and their car picked up speed along the Esplanade towards Le Val des Terres and then he was out of sight. It couldn't have been Rayner, she thought, as they continued towards St Martin's. The laws of coincidence surely couldn't have brought him here to Guernsey when he could have been sent anywhere in the war zones. She wound the window down and gulped a deep breath of fresh air.

That night she dreamt about the May Ball; she was dancing with Rayner but he was wearing German uniform and Hauptmann Dressler and Captain Grulich were sitting at their table. Captain Grulich jumped up and dragged her away from Rayner saying that this was his dance. He held her very close and he began to kiss her – Meg woke up in a cold sweat to find Buster licking her cheek, his big brown eyes shining in the moonlight. She stroked his dark coat and let him nuzzle her face. Wagging his tail, he leapt onto the bed, curving his warm body against hers.

Grulich continued to haunt Meg, both in her dreams and during her waking hours. His malignant presence seemed to follow her whether she was working in the fields or in the greenhouses, and the feeling of being constantly under surveillance was beginning to make her nervous. Buster

180

was her shadow and her protector; his hackles rose and he growled deep in his throat whenever he sensed that Grulich was near. Although Meg was grateful for this, it also terrified her when she saw the way Grulich looked at the dog. She feared for Buster almost as much as she feared for Gerald.

Meg was in the kitchen helping Marie peel vegetables one warm afternoon late in September when Gerald burst into the room, grinning from ear to ear and holding up a basket of wild mushrooms.

'Look what I've found, Mother.'

'Mother?' Grulich stood in the doorway, a triumphant smile spreading across his face.

Meg stared at him in horror. She opened her mouth to speak but her tongue seemed to have stuck to her palate.

'I didn't say that,' Gerald blustered. 'I said Marie.'

'I know what you said, and if this woman is your mother then you are not David Colivet. I have suspected there is something not quite right for a long time.'

'No, you misheard him. He said my name.' Gripping the paring knife in her hand, Marie squared up to Grulich, but Gerald caught her by the wrist.

'This is between me and Captain Grulich.'

'You are mistaken,' Grulich said tersely. 'This is a matter for Hauptmann Dressler.'

'This is simple a misunderstanding,' Meg said earnestly. 'David is my brother.'

Grulich's lip curled in disbelief. 'Tell that to

Hauptmann Dressler.'

'I demand to see Major Jaeger,' Meg said, defiantly.

'This has nothing to do with Meg.' Gerald stepped in between them as Grulich took a step towards her. 'Leave my sister alone.'

Marie whipped off her apron. 'We will all go and see the major.'

For a moment Meg thought Grulich was going to refuse, but he turned on his heel and marched out of the kitchen uttering a curt order to follow him.

Fortunately for them all it was Major Jaeger who was working alone at Hauptmann Dressler's desk. He listened to Grulich with an impassive expression on his face before turning to Gerald, who said that he sometimes referred to Marie as 'mother' but it was simply a family joke. He lied so competently that Meg eyed him with newfound respect. Major Jaeger dismissed the whole episode as nothing but a trivial misunderstanding, and Meg realised that the major disliked Grulich almost as much as she did. But the flash of cold hostility in Grulich's eyes as he grudgingly stood aside to let them pass sent icy fingers of fear to clutch her at her heart.

Although he could not prove anything, Grulich made it obvious that he still suspected Gerald. He was compelled to clean the latrines and muck out the stables every morning. He was given all the filthy back-breaking work, which included clearing up the mess left behind when the soldiers went off to carry out their daily duties at Jerbourg Point. Meg continued to do a man's work in the fields, and at least this was something of an escape from the leering glances and innuendo to which Grulich now treated her. He had improved his English enough to make himself understood and she shivered with unease every time he came near her. He would brush against her, insinuating his face close to hers, if they happened to come across each other in the house. She suspected that he lay in wait for her, but however vigilant she was there was barely a day that passed without some incident between them.

She dared not tell Gerald in case he lost his temper and physically attacked Grulich. Telling her father was not an option either. She worried constantly as she watched his physical condition gradually worsening beneath the strain of working on the controlling committee and the nightmare of living with the enemy. He looked so frail these days. His veins stood out like blue ropes beneath a parchment-like skin and he seemed to be retreating into an inner world where Meg could no longer reach him.

As winter set in early and the days grew shorter, Captain Grulich only allowed the family enough wood to light a small fire in the morning room. The house was always cold and everyone began to suffer from chilblains and bronchitis. Charles' chest condition worsened and he spent weeks in bed with a recurring low-grade fever that left him weak and listless when it had run its course. During a particularly bad bout of fever, Major Jaeger gave permission for Dr Gallienne to visit him. At the end of the consultation Meg took him into the parlour and gave him a cup of roasted barley coffee. It was nothing like the real thing, but tasted better than the version made from acorns. 'He will be all right, won't he, doctor?'

'Your father needs complete rest and a nourishing diet, but I'm afraid that's a luxury we've all been deprived of, and he's working too hard for a man of his age. I've advised him to stand down from the controlling committee, certainly while the bad weather lasts. Perhaps he can think about it again in the spring.'

Meg stared at him in horror. 'Do you really think the war is going to go on that long?'

Dr Gallienne squeezed her hand. 'I hope not, Meg. But I can't see a quick end to it. We get snippets of information from people who have managed to keep their radio receivers but it's a dangerous game. The Germans put spies in the food queues to listen to conversations, and if anyone appears to have outside information they are arrested on suspicion of owning a receiver. What with that and house to house searches, as I said it's a dangerous game.'

Meg was silent for a moment, thinking how tired he looked and how, since she had last seen him, the lines seemed to have been etched on his face as if someone had drawn them with a sharp pencil. They had all changed so drastically during the last sixteen months; she had only to look at herself in the mirror to realise that. The young carefree Meg no longer grinned impudently out at her. She barely recognised her reflection nowadays; it was a thin stranger who stared back with serious blue eyes that looked too large for her pale face.

'You look exhausted, my dear.' Dr Gallienne laid his hand on her arm and his red-rimmed eyes behind the thick lenses of his spectacles shone with sympathy. 'You must take care of yourself too. I know that Charles depends upon you entirely.'

She nodded and swallowed hard. She had grown used to hiding her feelings behind a tough façade that fed on hatred for the Germans, but this unexpected sympathy made her want to cry. She longed to confide her worries in someone, but she dared not tell Dr Gallienne that Pip's crystal set had put them all in mortal danger, or that she suspected Gerald of having joined the group of saboteurs who were rumoured to be causing a great deal of annoyance to the German High Command. Before she had a chance to speak, the door burst open and Grulich strode into the room.

'The staff car is waiting to take you back to the hospital, Herr Doctor, but Major Jaeger wishes to see you in the office before you leave.'

Dr Gallienne handed his empty cup back to Meg with an encouraging smile. 'Goodbye, my dear. Take care of yourself.'

She watched helplessly as he left the room. Grulich closed the door slowly, giving Meg a look that seemed to strip her naked.

That night, finding sleep impossible, Meg sat on her bed, staring out of the window at the moonlit garden. Miraculously the Germans had not touched the sweep of lawn at the front of the house, confining their activities to the land at the rear. In the cold silver moonlight it was almost possible to imagine that everything was as it had been before they invaded the island, but out of the corner of her eye she thought she saw a movement. Peering into the shadows she became aware of a male figure creeping stealthily through the bushes. Instinctively she knew that it was Gerald. It was certainly not Pip, and whoever it was knew exactly where the guards were posted and how to leave the grounds without using the main entrance. She slid off her bed and crept out of her room, pausing on the landing to listen for sounds of movement downstairs, but the house was darkly silent. She tiptoed to the foot of the staircase that led up to the old nursery and the servants' rooms and, avoiding the stair that creaked, she crept to the upper floor where Gerald had a small room next to Pip's. As she had suspected, the room was empty and his bed neatly made up. With her heart thudding uncomfortably inside her ribcage, she made her way back to her own room. Buster leapt up, wagging his tail enthusiastically. She climbed into bed, allowing him to jump up beside her. She whispered soothing words until he was calm again and he slept, snoring gently. She kept watch until just before dawn when she saw a grey ghost of a figure heading towards the house. Minutes later she heard the creaking of a floorboard, and opening her door just a crack, she saw the back of a man disappearing up the stairs that led to Gerald's room.

It was not until much later that day that she found Gerald alone in one of the greenhouses scrubbing down the staging ready for planting next year's crop of tomatoes. She glanced over her shoulder but there was no one in sight, and the soldiers were unlikely to return from Jerbourg Point until evening.

'Meg.' Gerald's face creased into a pleased smile.

'Well, are you going to tell me what you've been up to?'

'What?'

Weary from lack of sleep and bristling with nervous tension, she gave him a straight look. 'Don't act all innocent with me, Gerald LeFevre. I saw you last night. I want to know where you've been going.'

'You don't need to know, Meg. It's safer if you don't.'

'You're involved in something dangerous. I know that much.'

'I can't tell you what it is. If we're caught then you'd be in danger too.'

'You're doing some sort of resistance work. That's got to be it.'

'Leave it at that, Meg,' Gerald said, scrubbing viciously at the wooden staging.

'Please tell me what's going on. Maybe I can help. I'm sick of being cooped up here and having to kowtow to the bloody Germans.'

He threw down the scrubbing brush and seized her in his arms. Caught off guard, Meg allowed herself to give way momentarily, opening her lips and sliding her arms around his neck as he almost devoured her with the intensity of his kisses. Even as she abandoned herself to the heat of his mouth on hers, his tongue teasing, tasting, probing until she was faint with desire and the hardness of his body almost crushing the breath from her, a small

187

voice somewhere in her head screamed at the madness of what they were doing. She wrenched herself free, struggling to regain control of her drowning senses.

'We can't do this.'

'Meg, I love you, I always have. I can't go on pretending to be your brother when every moment I'm with you is torture.'

His eyes burnt into hers and she almost weakened. She had felt so alone and his arms wrapped around her had been wonderfully strong. His need for her had been absolute and the temptation to give in was almost unbearable. One word from her, one half-smile, one tender look and she knew they would both be lost; there would be no turning back. Her traitorous knees trembled and her heart pumped wildly; she could smell him, taste him, and her body screamed out with desperate need. His breath was sweet on her face, his eyes opaque with desire as his hands slid down her buttocks.

'No.' She pushed him away. 'You're going to get us all shot, you idiot.' Even to her ears her voice sounded harsh, but fear of discovery and its consequences forced her to be cruel. 'I've told you I don't love you and this time you'd better believe it.'

He shook his head slowly. 'You're lying.'

'And you're a stubborn fool.' She folded her arms across her chest, hugging herself protectively. 'I care about you, of course I do, but I don't love you. I've never loved you.'

'You wanted me as much as I want you.'

'Stop it, Gerald. I shouldn't even be here talking

to you now. If Grulich finds out he'll have it in for you even more.'

'Why did you come then?'

'I wanted to know where you've been going in the middle of the night and what you've been doing.'

'I can't tell you.'

'I just hope you know what you're about, that's all.' Unable to bear the reproach in his eyes, she turned her back on him and walked away. She heard him call her name but she strode on with Buster racing on ahead. She picked up a stick and tossed it into the middle of the newly ploughed field. He tore after it barking joyfully. A sudden staccato crack of gunshot rang out, and Buster dropped to the ground.

CHAPTER TEN

With a scream of pain as if the bullet had torn into her own flesh, Meg raced across the field and threw herself down on the dark earth beside Buster. Crying and calling his name she ran her hands over his silky black coat and felt the hot sticky trickle of blood, but at her touch he lifted his head and his pink tongue lolled out as if he was attempting to smile and reassure her. Staunching the flow with her cotton headscarf, Meg saw with a sob of relief that the wound was superficial and the bullet had merely grazed the flesh. It was a nasty gash but not fatal. As Buster

189

struggled to get up, she raised her head and saw Grulich standing on the edge of the field, holding a gun in his hand. He saluted her casually, turned his back and walked towards the house. A red mist fogged her vision. She forgot everything except her loathing for the man who had been making their lives hell. He had tried to kill her beloved pet and she was beside herself. Leaping to her feet she raced after him. He had reached the stable yard before she caught up with him. 'You bastard,' she cried. 'I could kill you.'

He seized her round the waist, pinning her arms to her sides. His eyes pierced hers like shards of glass. 'I warned you what I would do if the animal was let loose.'

'Let me go. You shouldn't be here at this time of day. I'll report you to Major Jaeger.'

She struggled desperately but he held her with surprising strength. His breath was foul, and, even as she attempted to fight him off, Meg saw with revulsion that his teeth were yellow and his gums were bleeding.

'No, I shouldn't be here. But lucky for me I had the aching tooth. I had to visit the dental surgeon or I would not have caught you out. I think Major Jaeger will be most interested to hear the truth from your lips.'

'I don't know what you mean,' Meg said, struggling against a wave of nausea that swept over her.

'I think Hauptmann Dressler will be interested to know that you and your father have been harbouring a British serviceman.'

'That's a lie.'

Grulich pushed his face closer. 'The lie is yours

and that of the young man you pretend is your brother.'

'David is my brother.'

'I've seen you together, Fräulein. I saw him kiss you just now. Not very brotherly behaviour, would you say? And that woman, the cook, she is his mother. I know that too, so don't pretend any more.'

She cried out as he twisted her arm behind her back, but just as the pain became so unbearable that she was close to fainting, he released her. She stumbled forwards, pitching against the wall of the outhouse. Winded and barely able to grasp what had happened, she stared stupidly at Grulich who lay senseless on the cobbled yard with Pip standing over him, grinning and giggling.

'Oh, my God. Pip, what have you done?'

He brandished a wooden pick handle. 'I hit him. I hope he's dead.'

Fighting to regain control of her erratic breathing, Meg looked up to see Gerald hurrying across the yard, carrying Buster in his arms. 'What the hell happened here?'

'I hit him,' Pip said gleefully. 'Shall I do it again?'

Setting Buster down on the ground, Gerald knelt beside Grulich and felt for the pulse in his neck. 'That was some knock-out blow.'

'Is he dead? I want to hit him again.' Pip danced up and down on the spot, waving the stick about his head.

Meg made a grab for it. 'You'd better pray he's not. Can you imagine what would happen to us all if you had killed him?'

'He isn't dead, but we've got to get rid of him

somehow,' Gerald said, rising to his feet. 'I don't think Dressler will think there's much difference between assault and murder when it comes to one of his own.'

'Throw him in the lake.' Pip gave Grulich a spiteful kick.

'Don't be silly, Pip,' Meg said without thinking. 'What do we do now, Gerald?'

'We'll fetch Sapphire from the pasture and harness her to the farm cart. We can hide Grulich under some hay and I'll make out that I'm taking it to feed the cattle.'

'You're not going to finish him off, are you?' Meg stared down at the unconscious Grulich. She could have killed him herself a few minutes ago, but now she was desperately afraid of the consequences if he were to die. Buster raised himself and licked her hand. She stroked his head and her hatred for Grulich hardened into a ball inside her stomach. She looked up and met Gerald's eyes. 'Do what you have to.'

He nodded. His face was deathly pale but his jaw was set in the stubborn line that put Meg in mind of the real David. 'Pip, fetch Sapphire,' Gerald said firmly. 'And Meg, you'd better lock Buster in the house while I clean up this mess.'

Between them, Gerald and Pip hitched Sapphire between the shafts, and it took all three of them to manhandle Grulich onto the wagon. He began to come round and before anyone could stop him Pip punched him on the jaw, knocking him senseless once again. Meg was certain that he would have continued battering his victim if Gerald had not stopped him. For once she was in complete

192

sympathy with Pip.

'Leave him,' Gerald said urgently. 'Captain Grulich is going to meet with an accident but it's got to look real enough to convince the Germans. Don't leave any marks on him.'

Meg tossed armfuls of hay over Grulich's insensible body. 'You'd better get a move on before he comes round.'

Gerald leapt up onto the driver's seat. 'Get back to work, you two. I'll see to this my way.' He flicked the reins. 'Giddy-up, Sapphire, old girl.'

Having cleaned Buster's wound, Meg locked him in her bedroom and hurried out of the house. She went about her tasks outside barely noticing the cold wind, spiked with sharp pellets of rain, that slapped her face. It was almost impossible to keep her mind off Grulich, and the unthinkable repercussions if his superiors discovered the truth about his death. She had no doubt that by now he would be well on his way to meet his maker, but she felt no remorse for his inevitable demise. She was party to a murder, but she did not feel the slightest twinge of conscience. This was war, and war was hateful.

Gerald did not return until just before curfew, and by then there was no way she could get him on his own. She did her best to hide her feelings, struggling to appear outwardly calm while inwardly she was seething with anxiety. She froze with fear every time she saw a German officer, waiting for the accusations to begin, but so far no one seemed to have noticed that Grulich was missing. She had expected that if anyone gave the game away, it would be Pip, but astonishingly he seemed to have forgotten all about Grulich and was more interested in tuning his crystal set in order to listen to the BBC news.

Charles had stayed in bed all day with one of his more virulent attacks of bronchitis, cared for devotedly by Marie. After supper that evening, Maud, Bertrand and Jane were huddled around the radio receiver listening to the reports of the bombing of Coventry and the continued devastation of the East End of London. There had even been a direct hit on Buckingham Palace. It seemed to Meg that the world had gone mad. She tried to concentrate on the sock that she had been darning and pricked her finger. Her eyes filled with tears of pain and exhaustion as she sucked her finger. Across the room she met Gerald's eyes. He grinned and winked at her and she had to be content with that.

'What can have happened?' Maud said, spooning barley porridge into her mouth next morning at breakfast.

'Perhaps the Allies have landed.' Bertrand licked his spoon. 'Any porridge left?'

'We'd all like more, Daddy,' Jane said, handing the remains of her porridge to Pip. 'He's a growing boy,' she said defensively, looking round at their disapproving faces.

Maud sipped her coffee and pulled a face. 'Is this roasted acorn or barley, Marie? Whatever it is it's disgusting.'

'Something is going on,' Marie said, ignoring this last remark. 'They've been riding their motorbikes up and down the drive since before dawn. I hardly had any sleep.'

'Perhaps it's an army exercise.' Meg pushed her plate away and rose from the table. 'Whatever they're doing is not our business. Come on, Gerald, we'd better get to work.'

When they were far enough from the house she clutched his arm. 'What did you do with Grulich? I lay awake all night worrying about it.'

'We made it look like an accident. The patrols will find him soon enough and there's nothing to lead them back to us.'

'You mean he really is dead?'

'Dead as a doornail!'

'But how? And who are "we"? What have you got yourself into?'

He quickened his pace and she had to run in order to keep up with him. They crossed the muddy waste that had once been the pleasure gardens and skirted the lake to the open fields beyond the woods. The sun gleamed feebly in the watercolour sky and there was silence except for the mewing of a few seagulls wheeling hopefully overhead. Gerald searched under a bare hawthorn hedge for a rusty garden fork and began to dig the hard ground.

'For God's sake, Gerald. Tell me!'

'A few of us have got together to cause the Germans a bit of grief. Anyway, we soaked Grulich's clothes in some alcohol, which was a damn waste, and we made it look as if one of their staff cars had knocked him down while he was staggering back to the house after a drinking binge. As far as they know he'd gone absent without leave since he

195

didn't report for duty after his dental appointment.'

Frowning thoughtfully, Meg watched him dig. 'Do you think Major Jaeger will buy that?'

'We'll soon find out.' He uttered a triumphant cry as he dug up a small stash of carrots and turnips. 'Marvellous. Let's get these back to Mother. It's meat ration day so we'll have a decent meal tonight.'

'You've just killed a man and all you can talk about is food?'

'I didn't kill him, although I would have done if I had to. Pip's knock on the head must have fractured his skull. He was dead by the time I got him to the north field. I just left him there under the hay until it was dark. My friends came along later and helped with the rest.'

'What friends? And if you tell me it's safer for me not to know I'll hit you with the fork and bury you with the potatoes.'

'So you do care what happens to me?'

'I care what happens to all of us, you idiot. If you get caught doing heroic things with the saboteurs we'll all suffer for it.'

'We won't get caught, I promise you, Meg. And you can't bully me into telling you any details so you'd better give up.' He hitched the sack over his shoulder and trudged back across the field towards the house.

In the middle of the afternoon a motorcycle messenger arrived with the news that Captain Grulich's body had been found in a quiet lane between St Martin's Church and the road to the

Jerbourg peninsula. It was Corporal Klein, having negotiated a truce with Marie in exchange for English lessons, who passed on the news. The story that buzzed around the soldiers' quarters and filtered back through the kitchen was that Grulich had been drinking, and in the blackout had stumbled into the path of a vehicle that had not bothered to stop. There did not seem to be much sympathy amongst his compatriots, or any visible signs of grief at his passing. Meg knew that she ought to feel some degree of sorrow for the untimely death of another human being, but she could not. She was glad that Grulich's hateful personality no longer haunted her life, and relieved beyond belief that no one had suspected foul play.

Two days later, after the meagre breakfast rations had been eaten and cleared away, Jane was in the morning room trying to coax the fire into life, but the damp twigs merely smouldered and belched smoke into the room. Marie and Gerald had taken the plates back to the kitchen and Charles, as usual nowadays, had stayed in bed. Meg folded the tablecloth while Bertrand fussed about setting the chairs straight and getting in everyone's way.

Maud perched on the window seat, staring idly at the rain-soaked garden. 'There's a staff car coming up the drive.'

'Can't you do something more useful than gawk out of the window, Maud old girl?' Bertrand glanced at the clock on the mantelpiece. 'Aren't you supposed to be dusting the staircase or something?'

'Not with Grulich out of the way,' Maud said smugly. 'I don't think Major Jaeger notices dust, and anyway he's more of a gentleman than Grulich. He knows better than to make a lady of my background and advanced years do menial work.'

'I wouldn't bet on it, Auntie.' Meg looked round to make sure she had put everything back in its place. 'Anyway, I've finished here and I'm going out to check on the livestock.'

'There's a man getting out of the car,' Maud said, craning her neck. 'I expect it's Grulich's replacement. My eyesight isn't what it used to be. You have a look, Meg.'

'I don't want to. They're all as bad as each other.'

'He looks quite young.'

'Don't let him see you, Mummy,' Jane said, working the bellows energetically.

'He's coming up the steps to the front door. Let's hope he's more pleasant than that last chap. I couldn't abide him.'

'I'm off then,' Meg said to no one in particular as she slipped out into the hallway. An ice-cold blast of wind whistled through the open door. She was tempted to glance over her shoulder to find out who had come to torment them further, but she resisted the temptation. She had taken a few short steps when the drawing room doors were flung open and she heard Major Jaeger's clear voice. 'Captain Weiss, come this way, please.'

She could not move. Her whole body seemed to be paralysed. Even before she turned her head, she knew who it was who had come to replace Grulich. For a split second their eyes met. There

198

was no flicker of recognition in his cool blue gaze and his features were as immobile as those of a stone statue. He knew that I would be here, she thought in a moment of near panic. What do I say? What shall I do? She had dreamed of meeting him again, but not like this. Never like this.

Abruptly, she turned on her heel and forced herself to walk at her normal pace towards the kitchen. Marie looked up from scrubbing the table. 'What's the matter, Meg? You look as though you've seen a ghost.'

'I'm going to see to the horses.' Taking her coat from its peg in the scullery, Meg shrugged it on. A gust of sleet-laden cold air greeted her as she opened the door leading into the stable yard. She stepped outside into a hail of icy pellets that slapped her cheeks and stung her eyes, but she was oblivious to physical discomfort. Shock was giving way to anger and bitter disappointment. The coldly handsome German officer might look like the dashing undergraduate who had made such an indelible impression upon her, but there the resemblance ended.

The sleet was turning into snow and the sky and ground had merged into a uniform gunmetal grey. Feathery white flakes spun in concentric circles, some of them floating upwards, giving Meg the odd impression that the whole world had turned upside down. An eerie silence enveloped her as she trudged through the fields, intent on bringing the horses into the shelter from the storm. She could just make out three shapes huddled together in the lee of a snow-covered hedge. She called their names and Conker was first to reach her. He whinnied with pleasure, rubbing his nose against her shoulder. The Germans had taken all the horses that she had rescued after the mass evacuation, but Conker had been overlooked because he was too highly strung to be of much use to them. Sapphire was needed to work on the farm and Caspar was too old to be of value to anyone. Meg led them to the relative shelter of the Dutch barn and gave them an extra ration of hay. She stayed with the horses longer than she would normally have done, making small jobs for herself and fussing around the animals, grateful for their undemanding company. She cracked the thin layer of ice on the trough and was filling the bucket with water when a sudden thought struck her. She dropped it with a stifled cry.

'Oh, my God,' she said out loud, startling the horses so that they stamped and whinnied, rolling their eyes. 'I've got to find Gerald before he runs into Rayner.'

She ran through the snowstorm that had now transformed the ugliness of the ruined gardens into a fairy-tale landscape. She burst into the kitchen kicking snow off her boots all over Marie's newly scrubbed floor. 'Where's Gerald?'

Marie looked up in surprised as she was about to empty a bucket of filthy water into the sink. 'What's wrong?'

'Never mind that now. I've got to find Gerald. It's urgent.'

'He went that way just a minute ago.' Marie nodded her head towards the doorway. Without stopping to take off her outer garments, Meg ran through the kitchen and along the passage that led to the entrance hall. She could hear voices as she turned the corner and she skidded to a halt in front of Major Jaeger and Rayner. Gerald was standing stiffly to attention outside the morning room.

'Is the house on fire, Miss Colivet?' Major Jaeger asked with barely a trace of humour.

'No, I – no.'

'You are just in time to meet Captain Weiss, the replacement for Captain Grulich. He will take over the captain's duties and you will report to him. Captain Weiss, may I introduce Miss Colivet and her brother, David.'

Meg held her breath waiting for him to say something, but Rayner inclined his head towards Gerald and to herself with a convincing lack of interest before following Major Jaeger into the drawing room. Breathing a sigh of relief, she leaned against the wall for support as her knees threatened to give way beneath her.

'What's the matter with you?' Gerald demanded anxiously. 'You look terrible.'

'My God, that was a close one.'

'I don't understand.'

'Come into the morning room. We can't talk out here.' She waited until he closed the door. 'Grulich's replacement,' she said urgently: 'I know him. He's an old friend of David's.'

'Bloody hell.' Gerald sank down on the nearest chair. 'What do we do now?'

'Nothing at all. If Rayner had been going to give the game away he'd have done it when he met you. I've got to get him alone and explain things.'

'I must make an effort to get to the mainland,

201

Meg. I'm endangering all your lives by staying here.'

'You'd never make it, and if you were caught then we would be in even worse trouble. No, leave it to me. Let me do it my way.'

The snowfall had been unusually heavy but by evening the thaw had set in and the glistening white covering that purified the landscape was corrupting into black slush.

Meg fretted all day as she waited for a chance to speak to Rayner alone. After the family had gone to bed she lingered in the comparative warmth of the morning parlour, standing by the door which she had left ajar. It had taken hours for the miserable fire of damp twigs and green logs to take the chill off the room, but now it was time to go upstairs to the icy bedrooms the room was tantalisingly cosy. She could hear the sounds of merriment as Hauptmann Dressler and his officers finished their brandy and cigars. The faint hint of fragrant Havana seeped into the hall and there was the occasional burst of laughter as if someone had just told a joke. Meg stiffened as the door opened and some of the more junior officers strolled out, chatting, laughing and looking relaxed as they made their way up the staircase towards their quarters on the second floor. She was afraid that Rayner might leave at the same time as Major Jaeger, but after a few minutes he emerged and to her intense relief he was alone. He stood in the hallway, looking about him. Opening the door wider, she beckoned.

Casually, he strolled across the hall to join her,

closing the door behind him. 'Hello, Meg.'

'Is that all you can say? You're here as part of the occupying force and all you can say is hello, Meg?'

He eyed her warily, his smile fading. 'I was posted here. For me there was no choice.'

'You must have realised that this was my family's home.'

'Yes, of course, although I didn't expect to find you here. I thought you would have been sent to your aunt's house in Oxford.'

The logic of this was undeniable, but still she was not satisfied. 'You could have refused to be billeted here.'

'I obey orders, Meg. But you're right; I could have asked to be sent elsewhere.'

'Then why didn't you?' Her voice broke on a sob and she turned away, unable to meet his earnest gaze. 'Stop looking at me like that.'

'There is nothing I can tell you that would make this easier for either of us. Perhaps I thought I could make a terrible situation a bit better by being here. I knew that your father was an important man on the island, and I hoped I might make things a little easier for him.' He reached out to take her hand in his. 'I am sorry we had to meet like this, Meg. Truly sorry.'

In the face of such heartfelt sincerity she felt herself weakening, but she snatched her hand away. 'Whichever way you look at it, you've come here as the enemy. Don't expect me to treat you as anything else.'

'If I was your enemy I would have informed Major Jaeger that the man who claims to be David is an impostor.' He moved to the fireplace, and

203

leaning his arm against the mantelpiece he kicked at the dying embers of the fire so that they burst into a feeble show of sparks and small flames.

Meg allowed herself to relax just a little. 'I'm grateful for that.'

'Who is this person who makes you risk so much?'

'He is Gerald LeFevre. His father and mother have worked for my family for years. He was supposed to return to his regiment but his father had a heart attack and died. Then it was too late for him to escape from the island.'

'He should have given himself up. He would have been treated as a prisoner of war. Don't you realise what danger he's put you all in by staying here?'

She shrugged her shoulders. 'What's done is done. I'm begging you, as David's friend, to say nothing.'

'He would be furious if he knew that you were risking your life in this way.'

'David would think as I do.'

'I know that he would want his family to be safe.'

She met his gaze with a defiant toss of her head. He looked strange and alien in the severe German uniform, so unlike her golden memories of their first meeting that it hurt her to look at him. 'You call this safe? Prisoners in our own home, subjected daily to humiliation and harsh treatment.'

He frowned. 'How have you been treated badly? Major Jaeger is a good officer and he told me that your family have been treated well.'

'Major Jaeger put Grulich in charge of us.' She dropped her gaze. To say anything else might make him suspicious and there was no way of knowing how far she could trust him.

He was silent for a moment and Meg could feel his gaze upon her but she would not raise her head. She stared down at her hands clasped tightly in front of her.

'We are not all like that,' he said softly. 'No one knows the connection between us. You can trust me, Meg.'

She wanted desperately to believe him, but she knew that she must be strong. If she allowed herself once again to fall under his spell, all would be lost. One slip, one careless word and the whole family would be in terrible danger. She raised her chin to look him in the eyes. 'I don't know you. You're not the man I knew in Oxford. Whatever you say you're part of the German war machine and that means we can never be friends.' She left the room without giving him a chance to respond.

Meg kept Rayner's identity a secret from the rest of the family, but under his command there were subtle improvements in their daily lives. Corporal Klein relaxed the stringent rules regarding the times that the family were allowed to use the kitchen, and occasionally Marie found small amounts of extra rations in the larder. The back-breaking duties that Grulich had imposed as punishments were a thing of the past, and if Captain Weiss found any of his fellow officers tor-menting Pip, they were severely reprimanded. Despite all this, Meg avoided Rayner. She was too resentful of his uniform to be grateful for the small but important privileges they were allowed, and too afraid of her own emotions to let down her guard. She could not bear to admit, even to herself, that the old attraction was simmering beneath the surface like a monster preparing to pounce and devour her heart and soul. She avoided Rayner as much as was humanly possible.

Christmas was only a few days away and the snow had melted leaving the island under a pall of grey cloud and fine drizzle. It was Meg's turn to go to market and she rode her bicycle into town. She chained it to the railings of the town church and made certain that the padlock was secure, well aware that left unattended it would be stolen as soon as she was out of sight. She joined the dismal people queuing in the rain for their rations and finally, chilled and tired, she made her way up the High Street to the Pantry, where she hoped that she might meet Pearl, as it was the day she usually accompanied her father to the library.

Meg felt a degree of relief when she saw Pearl sitting at a table near the window. She looked thinner, and pale without makeup, which was now unobtainable except on the black market, but her face lit up when she saw Meg.

'Meg, darling. Lovely to see you. Happy Christmas.'

'Happy Christmas, Pearl. But I'm afraid it's not going to be much of a festive season.'

'Don't. I can't bear to think of all those parties with lashings of food and drink. It's too depressing.'

A waitress appeared at the table and Meg ordered coffee and a bun. 'How are your parents?'

'All right, I suppose. Daddy has a terrible cough and Mummy gets a bit depressed now and then. She sleeps rather a lot these days. I wish my so-and-so appendix had waited until we'd been evacuated to England. It's so quiet and lonely at home that I sometimes think I'll go mad.'

'I've got a few dozen Germans you can have,' Meg said, grinning. 'They'd liven things up for you.'

Pearl shuddered theatrically. 'I don't know how you can joke about it. I'd die of fright with all those jackboots trampling round the place. Unlike some, who actually seem to like their company.'

Meg turned her head to follow Pearl's gaze, and was dismayed to see that Simone had just walked in accompanied by Lieutenant Brandt. Although she wore a new winter coat, her condition was immediately obvious.

'See what I mean?'

Meg stared aghast at the heavily pregnant Simone. What would Marie and Gerald say when they found out? A cold shiver shot down her spine. The looks of disgust on the faces of the locals were indicative of the general view of girls who fraternised with the enemy. They were known as Jerrybags and publicly shunned. It had not occurred to Meg until now, but this would be the path she would be forced to tread if she allowed herself to fall in love with Rayner for a second time. She caught Simone's eye and smiled, but Simone ignored her and made her way to a vacant table. She sat down, glaring around the room as if daring anyone to approach her.

Meg sat without listening to Pearl's chatter,

interjecting the right noises here and there, but every now and then she found herself casting covert glances at Simone and Dieter. They did not look as though they were enjoying themselves. Simone's restless fingers toyed with the cutlery on the gingham tablecloth. Dieter was speaking to her but she remained impassive, saying nothing. Just as the waitress appeared with their order, Simone pushed back her chair, struggled to her feet and stormed out of the café.

Dieter made no attempt to follow her. He remained seated, stirring his ersatz coffee and staring into space.

Meg threw some coins onto the table and gathered up her scarf and gloves. 'I've got to go, Pearl. Sorry.'

'Don't waste your time on that slut, Meg,' Pearl said, shaking her head. 'She's not worth it.'

CHAPTER ELEVEN

Outside the café, Meg was just in time to see Simone hurrying off towards the town church. Running, Meg caught up with her. 'Simone, are you all right?'

'Don't ask bloody silly questions. Do I look all right?'

'I can see you're pregnant, if that's what you mean.'

'I'm not a tart.' Simone quickened her pace.

'For God's sake stop and talk to me.' Meg

dragged her into the doorway of a shop that had used to sell luxury goods but was now closed and shuttered. Cold sleety rain had begun to fall from a cast-iron sky. Although it was only three o'clock in the afternoon darkness was already engulfing the island.

'You want to lecture me, I suppose. Well you can keep your opinions to yourself, Meg Colivet.'

'I don't care what you've done or what happens to you, but I do care about your mother and your brother, and if you're in trouble they'll want to help.'

'I don't need them, and I don't want anyone poking their noses into my business.'

'Is Dieter going to stand by you and the baby?'

'He's being posted to France.' Simone spat on the pavement. 'They know how to look after their own, the German bastards.'

'What about your job at the hospital?'

'They sacked me two weeks ago.'

'So how are you managing? Where are you living?'

'I've been staying with a friend, but she wants me out as soon as I've found somewhere else.'

'Right, that settles it. Get the bus to St Martin's and come straight to the house. If the guard on the gate challenges you, just tell him you're Marie's daughter and you're visiting.'

'Why would I want to do that? Why lay myself open to a lecture from Mum?'

'You can't avoid her forever, and you might find that she's more open-minded than you think. You can stay with us, Simone. At least you'll have a roof over your head and you'll be safe from the self-righteous busybodies in town.'

Simone hesitated as if weighing up the odds against her. 'I haven't much choice, have I?' she said slowly.

'Not really. Look, if you hurry you'll catch the bus. If you miss it you'll have to wait a couple of hours or walk all the way. Suit yourself.'

Simone's shoulders hunched and she stared down at the ground. 'All right, you win.' She set off towards the bus station.

Meg went to collect her bicycle and pedalled home as if the devil were on her heels. She arrived at the house just as Simone was stepping off the bus. The guard on the gate accepted Meg's explanation for Simone's visit with a curt nod of his head, and waved them in. As they made their way towards the servants' entrance a sudden downpour drenched them both. Rainwater dripped off their clothes onto the flagstone floor as they entered the scullery.

'Wait here,' Meg whispered. 'We don't want Corporal Klein asking awkward questions.'

'Who's he?' Simone's teeth were chattering audibly and her face was pale and pinched with cold.

'You'll find out soon enough.' Meg hurried into the kitchen and was relieved to find that Marie was on her own. 'I've brought someone to see you.'

A spark of hope lit Marie's eyes. 'Simone?'

'Wait, there's something you must know before you see her.'

'She's ill, isn't she?'

'She's pregnant.'

'I don't believe it, not my Simone.'

'That's the least of it. She'll tell you all the ins and outs herself, but I wanted to warn you because she's in a delicate state. If you go on at her she might take off and do something stupid.'

'For God's sake, tell me what's going on.'

'She's been going with a German officer and he's being transferred to France. You know what the locals will make of that if it gets out.'

Marie sat down suddenly as if her legs had given way beneath her. 'That's terrible, Meg. What will we do?'

'She must stay here. There's no question about that.'

'Yes, that's the only solution, but we must keep quiet about the baby's father.'

'I knew you'd say that, Mum.' Simone stood in the doorway, shivering but defiant. 'I suppose you want to throw me out on the street.'

'You know me better than that.' Marie leapt to her feet and opened her arms. Slowly, Simone crossed the floor and laid her head on her mother's shoulder.

Meg backed towards the door. 'This is a family matter. I'll go and find Gerald.' She hurried along the narrow passageway that led to the main entrance, and hearing footsteps on the marble tiles in the entrance hall she broke into a run. Her wet hair hung limply about her shoulders but her appearance was the last thing on her mind. As she turned the corner into the entrance hall she came to a sudden halt as a man stepped out of the drawing room. Rayner took in her dishevelled appearance with a ghost of a smile. 'You look as you did when I fished you out of the

Thames. Is something wrong?'

'No, of course not.'

'You usually run about the house in that state, I suppose?'

'I got wet. I was going to my room to change.'

'I need to speak to you in private, Meg.' He opened the door.

It was not an order, but she could hardly refuse without some sort of explanation, and she did not want to tell him about Simone's fall from grace. It was a personal matter and best kept from the attention of Hauptmann Dressler. Reluctantly she followed him into the drawing room.

It was the first time she had been invited into Dressler's inner sanctum since the day that he had commandeered it for his own purposes, and she was shocked to see it in its current state. A large desk stood in the middle of the room, surrounded by chairs taken from the dining room. The bare floorboards were badly marked and showing signs of neglect. The Louis Quinze chairs were almost threadbare from constant use, and the lingering odour of stale tobacco smoke and sour wine filled the air. Metal filing cabinets had replaced the Sheraton side tables, and the credenza was piled high with wicker baskets overflowing with documents. Meg shuddered to think what her mother would say if she could see the room now. She looked up to find that Rayner was regarding her with a look of concern in his blue eyes. He motioned her to sit down, but instead of taking a seat at the desk he perched casually on the edge. His fair hair glinted in the light from the chandelier. 'You can tell me anything, Meg. I'm not a monster just because I wear a foreign uniform.'

'You made your choice. That puts you on the other side. I have nothing to say.'

'Very well. I can't force you to confide in me, but I want you to know that I've done everything I can to make your family's life a little easier. I don't like this any more than you do. You must believe that.'

She looked away quickly as the old familiar pull of attraction tugged at her heartstrings and she felt the blood rush to her cheeks. She hesitated, but in the end she knew she must put her trust in him. 'I suppose I'd better tell you before one of your men says anything and Major Jaeger finds out. Gerald's sister has been seeing a German officer and she's pregnant. You know what my fellow countrymen think of girls who fraternise with the enemy.'

He nodded.

'I've brought her here so that her mother can take care of her. Simone has lost her job and she's been thrown out of her digs.'

'The father, does he know?'

'He knows all right, and very conveniently he's being posted to France.'

'I see.'

'It's a difficult situation, but I can't abandon her.'

He nodded. 'I understand. Leave it with me, but keep her out of the way for now. If you let me have her papers, I'll see what I can do.'

'Thank you. And thank you for keeping quiet about Gerald.'

'Even Krauts have their Achilles heels, Meg,' he said, smiling.

She met his gaze and it was as if nothing had

changed since that day on the river. The warmth in his eyes made her catch her breath. She could not think and she could barely breathe. She was in danger of drowning but this time it was in a maelstrom of emotion. 'I must go.' She hurried from the room, not daring to look back.

Christmas Day dawned clear and cold. Hoar frost lay like icing sugar on the bare branches of the oak trees and the green fingers of the pines looked as though they had been sprinkled with glitter. Meg was up early as usual, milking the cows on her own, having given Billy and Joe the time off to be with their families. As she leaned against the warm flank of the cow she thought of Christmases before the war and suddenly her eyes filled with tears. Those comfortable, carefree days seemed like another lifetime. Her stomach growled and nowadays hunger was a physical pain. She had become used to going to bed on an empty stomach and waking up famished. The thought of a bowl of hot mushed barley with a dusting of their precious sugar ration was all that kept her going.

The last drop of rich milk poured into the pail and Meg patted the cow, telling her what a clever girl she was. The animal turned its head, lowing softly, and her liquid brown eyes seemed to smile. Meg stood up and stretched. She carried the pail to the churn and, with a surreptitious glance over her shoulder to make sure there was no one about, she scooped a panful of the thick cream from the top. She knew she was taking a risk and the punishment for stealing would be severe if she were caught, but High Command had provided a generous beer ration to the troops, apparently hoping to raise the morale of men absent from their families at Christmas. She had heard the sounds of revelry emanating from the stable block into the small hours, and she hoped that they were sleeping off last night's excesses. She hummed 'Good King Wenceslas' on her way back to the house.

Marie had made a special effort with their breakfast and had thrown a handful of carefully hoarded dried fruit into the porridge as a special treat. The addition of fresh cream was an un-imaginable luxury. The barley and acorn coffee was hot and bitter but Charles gazed at the thick cream floating on the top of his cup and sipped it with a blissful expression on his face. 'This is wonderful, almost like pre-war.'

'What's that, Charles? Can't even remember that far back,' Bertrand said with his mouth full.

'Manners, Bertie. We've got to keep up our standards.' Maud wiped her lips on one of Muriel's second best damask napkins.

'Is there any more porridge?' Pip had cleaned his plate and was looking hopefully at Marie.

Meg laid her hand on Marie's arm as she was about to rise from her seat. 'I'll go. Sit down and finish your breakfast.'

'Let the boy get his own,' Charles said, frowning.

'I don't think so, Pa. He'd gobble the last drop and no one else would get a look-in.'

'That's not true,' Pip said, scowling. 'You always pick on me.' He looked to his mother, but Jane said nothing.

Meg smiled to herself as she left the room.

Perhaps Jane had realised at long last that her son behaved like a spoiled brat. Maybe there was hope for him yet, although somehow she doubted it. She went to the kitchen and found a big black saucepan had been left to keep warm on the hob. She was searching for the ladle when the door opened and to her astonishment it was Rayner who entered the room. To her knowledge the officers never came near this part of the house. She shot him a curious glance.

'Happy Christmas, Meg.'

'You're joking, of course.'

'I wasn't, but I remember the days when you used to enjoy a joke. You were bold, beautiful and, as I remember, fearless.'

'Perhaps because I had nothing to fear then.'

'You know that I would do nothing to harm you or your family.'

'Yes, I do and I'm sorry. You've treated us as well as we can expect.' She placed the ladle in the saucepan. 'Did you want something?'

He came slowly towards her, holding her gaze so that she could not look away. 'Whatever you think of me, it's still Christmas and I have something for you.'

She shook her head. 'This is madness. I think you'd better leave. Corporal Klein might come in at any moment.'

He silenced her with a kiss. It was the most fleeting of embraces but she could still feel his lips on hers after he drew away. He took her hand and closed her fingers over a small box. She shook her head. 'Whatever it is, it wouldn't be right to accept. Not as things are now. Can't you understand that?'

'You don't know what it is. You might be pleased.'

His smile was infectious and she struggled with her conscience. In the end curiosity won and she opened the oblong jeweller's case. Inside on a bed of black velvet was a single strand of tiny, irregularly shaped pearls. She held it up, allowing the necklace to hang from her fingertips.

'Marguerite means pearl,' he said anxiously. 'I'm no expert but I was told these are river pearls. I thought it was appropriate.'

She looked up and met his worried gaze and she realised that he was watching her reactions with a degree of nervousness that she had not seen in him before. He had always appeared confident and in command of every situation. Now he looked like a schoolboy in need of reassurance. She could not have rejected his gift even if she had wanted to. 'It's very appropriate,' she murmured, smiling. 'It's quite beautiful.'

'It is very important to me that you like it.' He leaned towards her but the sound of approaching footsteps made them draw apart. Corporal Klein ambled into the kitchen, snapping to attention and saluting when he saw his superior officer.

Rayner returned the salute. 'You're late on duty, Corporal. Hauptmann Dressler wants his coffee, now.'

Meg thrust the necklace into her pocket, and without saying a word she seized the saucepan and hurried from the kitchen. She clutched the hot handle, barely noticing that it was burning her fingers as she carried the pan to the morning

217

parlour. Rayner's gift had thrown her off balance and she was in a state of utter confusion. She smacked Pip's hand as he attempted to grab the saucepan. 'Simone first,' she said sharply. 'She's eating for two.' She helped Simone to the porridge. 'Anyone else, apart from Pip?'

Bertrand gazed longingly at the pan and then at his empty plate but a sharp nudge in the ribs from Maud made him shake his head. Meg could easily have eaten more, but as Pip was the only one who was holding out his plate she pushed the pan towards him. 'It's all yours.' She sat down to finish her coffee.

As soon as the meal was over, Meg and Gerald handed out the small presents they had tied to the branch of a fir tree that they had lopped off and stuck in a pot. They had painstakingly decorated it with some of the family hoard of baubles and tinsel that had graced the huge Christmas trees in the past, and it made a bright splash of colour in the drab room. Meg had searched around amongst her belongings and had managed to find something for everyone. She had wrapped them carefully in white tissue paper tied with scraps of ribbon from her mother's work basket.

Simone stared at the Sarkstone brooch that had been one of Meg's favourites when she was younger. She mumbled a thank you but her dark eyes were resentful and she made an excuse to go to her room. Marie turned to Meg, her face puckered with concern. 'You mustn't mind Simone. It's her condition. She doesn't mean it. She really appreciates what you've done for her.'

'So she should, Mother,' Gerald said, frowning.

'Simone would probably have ended up in a German brothel if Meg hadn't brought her home.'

'And you'd be in a prisoner of war camp if we didn't risk our lives covering up for you.' Pip tapped the side of his nose, grinning.

'That's enough of that,' Charles said angrily. 'Remember that it's Christmas Day and we all depend on each other. I expect everybody to be ready for morning service at eleven o'clock sharp.' He caught his breath as a paroxysm of coughing rendered him temporarily speechless. He took a sip of cold coffee. 'Don't forget, eleven o'clock and no excuses.'

The church was freezing and the sermon was long but the islanders sang loudly and defiantly, casting resentful glances at the German officers seated with the non-commissioned men. Meg could hear their voices, loud and strident, singing in broken English. It was ironical, she thought, that the men who were at war with her country were singing Christmas carols and joining in a service of worship with the very people they were oppressing. As the congregation filed out of the front pews Meg saw Rayner standing amongst the group of officers. She avoided meeting his gaze as she walked out of the church with her father leaning heavily on her arm.

The feeble rays of the winter sun had filtered through the skeletal branches of the trees, melting the early morning frost. A few traces of snow remained in the deep shade but otherwise it could almost have been a spring morning. Snowdrops poked their heads above the soil and a blackbird warbled his song from the branches of a yew tree nearby. Charles stopped to listen courteously as two of his elderly tenants claimed his attention and Meg hovered by his side. She knew that Rayner was somewhere close behind her but she forced herself to stare straight ahead. She slipped her hand through her father's arm and waited for him to finish his conversation.

Strolling home behind the Germans in a straggling procession with neither side acknowledging the presence of the other, Meg was struck once again by the incongruity of it all. When they reached the comparative warmth of the manor house, Hauptmann Dressler and Major Jaeger took the officers into the drawing room and Meg settled her father in a chair by the meagre fire in his study.

'Are you all right, Pa?'

He smiled weakly. 'I'd love a brandy, my dear, but as that is out of the question do you think I could have a hot drink?'

'Of course.' Meg dropped a kiss on his forehead and tucked a blanket around his knees. 'I'll be as quick as I can, Pa.'

In the kitchen she found Marie and Simone standing at the table staring at a basket filled with food.

'Where on earth did that come from?' Meg touched the handle gingerly, half expecting it to be a mirage brought about by hunger.

Marie eyed it warily. 'It might be a German trick. I don't want to touch it and then find myself shot for pilfering their rations.'

'I never did believe in Santa Claus,' Simone

said, sniffing. 'But I could eat the lot and still be hungry.'

Meg unpacked the basket, laying the items on the table one by one. 'I haven't seen this much food since the war started. Chicken, ham, apples, cheese, wine – we'll have a feast.'

'You're sure it's all right then?' Marie asked anxiously.

'Perhaps it's a Christmas present from Hauptmann Dressler,' Meg said, chuckling. 'Don't ask – just cook it. I'll take the blame if it turns out to be a gift for Major Jaeger from an admirer.'

Simone seized the plucked chicken by its neck. 'Come on, Mum. Meg's right for once. We'll have the best meal we've ever had, even if they put us against the wall and shoot us for it.'

Marie held the chicken at arm's length, as if it might at any moment explode. 'If you're sure...'

'I am,' Meg said firmly. 'And I'm going right now to tell Pa that tonight we'll have a proper Christmas dinner.'

Meg burst into the study and froze in surprise when she saw Rayner sitting in a leather armchair by the fire, looking relaxed and at ease.

Charles turned to her with a delighted smile transforming his worn features. 'Meg, Captain Weiss has just informed me that he knew David in Oxford. Why didn't you tell me?'

She hesitated, trying to think of an adequate explanation when really there was none.

'That was my fault, sir,' Rayner said hastily. 'I thought it would be safest if no one knew, apart from Meg of course.'

The ease with which he came up with such a

glib answer only added to Meg's discomfort. 'So what has changed suddenly?'

'Meg!' Charles stared at her over the top of his reading glasses. 'That was very rude of you.'

'I'm sorry.' Meg met Rayner's gaze with a frown. She could see a dangerous situation evolving both for her family and for Rayner should Dressler discover their friendship. 'I don't think that the Hauptmann would approve of your fraternising with any of us. Whatever we might wish to believe, you can't alter the fact that we're on opposite sides.'

Charles shook his head. 'My dear, we are all caught up in something that we haven't the power to change.' He began to cough uncontrollably.

Meg filled a glass with water from a carafe on the desk, and held it to his lips. 'You'd better go,' she said, casting a worried look in Rayner's direction. 'My father isn't well.'

'We'll talk again,' Charles murmured breathlessly.

Rayner rose from his seat. 'I can't acknowledge you in front of my fellow officers, sir; I'm sure you appreciate that. But I'll try to make your lives a little easier if I can.'

As they shook hands, Charles managed a weak smile. 'Thank you, Captain. I feel much happier knowing that there is someone looking out for my family.'

Rayner smiled. 'Goodnight, sir.'

Meg followed him out into the deserted entrance hall. 'That wasn't very wise, was it?'

He took her hand in his, but his expression was grave. 'This war is going to drag on longer than anyone ever thought. I respect your father and I wanted him to know that he has one ally in the house.'

'And the basket of food – was that from you? Did you steal it from the quartermaster's stores? I certainly hope you didn't do anything so risky.'

'No. I bought it with my own money. I can't bear to see you and your family suffer. You must allow me to help in any way I can.'

The warmth in his eyes elicited a reluctant smile from Meg. 'It doesn't go with the uniform, Captain.'

'The man beneath it is the same. I haven't changed since we first met in Oxford.'

'Are you saying that I have?'

He put his head on one side, his lips twitched and his eyes teased. 'You used to laugh more often.'

She had done her best to convince herself that he was her enemy, but just as she felt the last of her defences crumbling a burst of raucous laughter emanating from the drawing room brought her back to reality. 'You Germans have every reason to laugh. We have none.'

'We celebrate Christmas too,' he said gently. 'Can't we be friends again, if only for today?'

'We have to keep up the fiction that we're on different sides.' She laid her hand on his arm. 'It's not what I want, Rayner, but it's dangerous for you as well as for us.'

His smile warmed her heart. 'Does that mean you will wear my gift of river pearls, Marguerite?'

She took the box from her skirt pocket and opened it. 'It's beautiful, but I thought that all the jewellers' shops on the island had been looted. How did you come by it?'

'Look at the name inside the lid.'

'Mabb and Sons, Jewellers and Silversmiths, High Street – Oxford?' She shot him a questioning look. 'Oxford?'

'I bought it for you the day after the May Ball. It was a little gift to make up for the trouble I caused you by suggesting that midnight drive.'

'But you didn't come to see me.'

'I was going to give it to you when we met on Folly Bridge, but you never came.'

'I didn't get the message. David forgot to give it to me.'

'I waited for two hours.'

'I didn't know that.' She felt suddenly light-headed and confused. He was looking at her with a light in his eyes that was disturbing, and the slightly lopsided curve of his lips made her weak with desire.

'Would you have come?'

'I don't know.'

'The Meg that I knew then would have come, I'm certain of it.'

The hard shell that she had been building around her heart splintered into shards, but she was afraid to let go completely. 'Perhaps, but I was very young. It's probably just as well Uncle Paul sent me home and saved me from making a fool of myself.'

'Will you wear it for me now?' He took the pearls from her and fastened the necklace around her neck. He was standing so close to her that she could feel the warmth of his body. The achingly

224

familiar scent of him filled her senses. The tiny pearls instantly absorbed the warmth from her flesh but she shivered with anticipation as his hands slid down her arms. He twisted her round to face him, gazing deeply into her eyes. 'Meg, I–' He broke off as the doors opened and Major Jaeger strolled out of the drawing room.

Rayner dropped his hands to his sides and Meg took a step backwards, but if Major Jaeger had noticed anything he kept his thoughts to himself.

'May I wish you and your family the compliments of the season, Miss Colivet?'

'Thank you, Major Jaeger.'

'Captain Weiss, you are going to join us, are you not?'

'At once, Herr Major.' Rayner followed him into the drawing room and Meg stood alone in the echoing hallway, her fingers caressing the necklace of river pearls that nestled so comfortably at the base of her throat.

She did not see Rayner again that day but she wore the pearls, touching them occasionally and reliving the sensation of his fingers brushing against her skin as he fastened it around her neck. She had not considered the risk of flaunting such an expensive gift until Simone drew everyone's attention to it during dinner. Meg felt herself blushing uncontrollably as she tried to pass it off as an old piece of jewellery given to her long ago by her parents. Pa, of course, would never remember anything like that and Mother was not there to contradict her. Meg hoped that the incident had passed unnoticed but she had seen

Gerald looking at her curiously and Simone met her explanation with a cynical stare.

When the meal was over Meg was carrying a tray laden with dirty dishes to the kitchen when Simone caught up with her in the narrow passageway. 'Don't think you're fooling me, Meg Colivet. I've seen the way you look at each other. I'm not the only Jerrybag in this house, am I?'

CHAPTER TWELVE

New Year began with a Red Cross message from Muriel, proudly announcing the birth of twin daughters to Adele and Frank. Meg was delighted at the thought of being an aunt, but it was difficult to get excited over an event that was so far removed from the drudgery and the rigours of their daily lives that it seemed almost unreal. She sat at her father's bedside while they composed the few precious lines allotted to them for a reply, although it would, of course, be heavily censored. They sent congratulations to Adele and Frank, adding that they were all in good health and being well treated. Meg hoped that her mother would not read between the lines.

She lived in constant fear that David would break the habit of a lifetime and communicate with them, but thankfully he remained his usual unreliable self. It would have been difficult to explain to the authorities how David Colivet could be in two places at the same time, and Meg could only be grateful to her brother for being thoughtless and utterly self-centred. She could imagine him blissfully unaware of his family's plight while he lived day to day, playing the hero, which he undoubtedly was. She said a prayer for him every night, and hoped that he never changed.

The bitter January days dragged on and the increasing scarcity of food and fuel simplified their existence to a daily struggle for survival. Meg saw very little of Rayner and they were never alone for long enough to do more than exchange a brusque greeting. Sometimes she thought she had imagined their conversation on Christmas Day and she would fall asleep at night with the pearls around her neck, waking early to tuck the necklace safely away in its box beneath the mattress at the start of another backbreaking day.

Pip's crystal set kept them in touch with news of the German surrender in Stalingrad and at the end of January they heard of the first daylight bombing of Berlin by the RAF, but it was becoming increasingly dangerous to use the radio and Pip was almost caught with it on several occasions.

At the beginning of February it was as if Grulich's ghost had come to haunt them in the shape of Lieutenant Nordhausen, who had been sent as a replacement for an officer who had become ill and been repatriated to Germany. Rayner was kept busy with duties overseeing the construction of gun emplacements at Jerbourg Point, and Nordhausen seemed determined to earn his promotion by spying on the family and finding fault with everything they said or did.

One bitterly cold evening in late February, Meg had just come in from the fields where she had been helping Gerald to bring the cows into the barn. The constant threat of escaped slave workers stealing food and even milking the cows made it necessary to lock the animals in at night. It had been a long, gruelling day and she had had almost nothing to eat; she was cold, exhausted and faint from hunger.

'Oh, it's you.' Simone, far advanced in her pregnancy now, waddled into the kitchen clutching a pile of empty plates. She crashed them down on the wooden draining board.

Meg was in no mood to tolerate Simone's tantrums. 'Just what is your problem?'

'Oh, sorry, Miss Colivet. I forgot my place for a moment.'

Meg's hand shook as she attempted to pour what was left of the acorn coffee into a cup and some of it slopped onto the table. 'I wish you'd stop behaving like a spoilt brat, and grow up.'

'What's going on?' Gerald stood in the scullery doorway, shrugging off his damp coat.

'Ask Simone. I'm sick to death of her snide remarks.'

Gerald eyed his sister warily. 'What have you been saying to Meg?'

Simone's mouth drooped at the corners. 'Whatever I do or say is wrong. Tell her to leave me alone.'

He tossed his coat onto a chair and went to stand by the rapidly cooling range, warming his hands in front of the iron bars. 'Look, I don't understand what's going on between you two, but we can't fall out like this. Simone, say sorry to Meg.'

'Like hell I will.' She stamped out of the kitchen.

Gerald sighed. 'What has she said this time?'

'Your sister hates me for some reason,' Meg said, frowning. 'I don't know why she's being like this when all I've ever done was try to help her.'

He moved to her side and wrapped his arms around her. 'Of course she doesn't hate you. God knows she should be on her knees thanking you and your father for taking us all in. But Simone's a bit too fiery for her own good. It's all an act; she's not a bad girl at heart.'

'You would say that, and I do try to ignore her moods. She just caught me on the raw today.' In spite of herself, Meg leaned her head on his shoulder. The warmth of his arms and the sympathy in his voice was comforting and welcome.

He rubbed his cheek against her damp hair. 'One day you'll admit you love me, Meg.'

'You never give up, do you? You're a stubborn fool, Gerald,' she said, smiling.

A sudden movement in the doorway made them leap apart as Lieutenant Nordhausen strode into the room. It was impossible to tell from the set of his thin, bird-like features what he had heard or seen, but he said nothing, merely giving them a calculating look before helping himself to the remainder of the coffee.

Simone's baby was born in the spring just as the daffodils and narcissi engulfed the lawn with their golden trumpets. Marie and Jane had been up all night, doing what was necessary, with Meg running errands and making tea from leaves that had been used and reused until the pale straw-coloured infusion was more like hot water than a restorative beverage. Meg had finally dozed off in an armchair by the window when the last loud moan from Simone was followed by the wailing cry of her son.

'Jeremy Eric LeFevre,' Marie said, smiling proudly as she showed the baby to Meg. 'Isn't he just beautiful?'

Meg looked at the crumpled red face and tiny flailing fists and nodded, wondering how anyone could be so besotted as to think this monkey-faced infant was anything but ugly.

'He is so gorgeous,' Marie said, cuddling Jeremy and kissing his bald head.

'At least he looks more like the LeFevres than his father,' Meg said, speaking her thoughts out loud and instantly wishing she had kept her mouth shut.

Marie clutched the baby to her. 'Hush, Meg. Someone will hear you.'

Instinctively Meg glanced over her shoulder but the ubiquitous Nordhausen was, for once, not lurking in the shadows. 'Don't worry. No one outside the family knows about Brandt,' she said, stroking the baby's cheek. 'And I'm sure he'll grow into a lovely little boy.'

'I heard that,' Simone said, from the bed where Jane was making her comfortable. 'Give him to me, Mum. Don't let Meg hold him.'

Meg was about to protest but Simone's drawn face and sickly pallor brought back memories of the long painful night when her screams had shattered the silence. 'He's a fine baby, Simone. You should be proud of him.'

'Hadn't you better get about your business, Meg?' Jane said, plumping up the pillows behind Simone as Marie placed the baby in his mother's arm. She jerked her head in the direction of the door.

Meg met her eyes and understood the unspoken message. 'Yes, I'm going or Nordhausen will be waiting to pounce on me for being late on duty.'

'That man is almost as bad as Grulich,' Jane said. 'He makes my flesh creep.'

Meg glanced at her watch as she left Simone's tiny room, which had once been the place where a seamstress had found full-time employment mending the family linen. The house was already alive with sounds of movement and she would have to creep out of the side door if she wanted to avoid bumping into Nordhausen or one of his spies. Using the servants' staircase Meg had reached the ground floor without seeing anyone, when suddenly a grey figure loomed out of the shadows. She stifled a cry of alarm.

'Meg, it's me.'

'Rayner, you scared me half to death. I thought it was Nordhausen.'

'That's only the second time you've used my name since Oxford.'

He smiled and Meg felt the mysterious chemistry begin to work, but lack of sleep and the shock of meeting him unexpectedly made her edgy. She glanced nervously over her shoulder. 'Sorry. Perhaps I should say Captain Weiss.'

'You're afraid of something or someone. Has

Nordhausen been bothering you?'

'No more than the rest of your compatriots. I can handle him.'

'You must tell me if he has been abusing his position. Neither Major Jaeger nor myself will tolerate that kind of behaviour.'

'Thank you, but as I said I can look after myself. And if I don't get to the milking parlour on time I'll be in trouble, and neither you nor Major Jaeger will be able to do anything about it.'

'I know you're worried that we might be found out, but it doesn't have to be like this, Meg.' He took a step away from her as the door that led to the stable yard opened and a soldier trudged in carrying a sack of potatoes.

'I think that proves my point, Captain.' She slipped past Rayner, avoiding the curious stare of the soldier as she hurried out into the stable yard. 'Bloody war,' she muttered. 'And bloody Germans, I hate them all.' But she knew that was a lie. Whatever happened now or in the future, she could never hate Rayner.

Nordhausen was in the kitchen when later that morning Meg came through from the scullery carrying a jug containing the family's meagre milk ration. He sat with his booted feet on the kitchen table watching Marie kneading the grey sticky bread dough, consisting mainly of potato flour.

Nordhausen turned his head to look Meg up and down. 'Captain Weiss is a good friend. No?'

'I don't know what you mean.'

He slid his feet off the table and stood up. 'You address me as Lieutenant Nordhausen. You are not the lady of the manor now.'

'I don't know what you mean, Lieutenant Nordhausen.'

'Be very careful, Fräulein. I'm watching every move you make. You won't get rid of me as easily. as you did Captain Grulich.'

'I don't understand.' Meg forced herself to appear calm but her mind was racing.

'I think you do. I believe that you and your brother know a lot more about Captain Grulich's accident than you care to admit.'

'You are mistaken, Lieutenant.'

'We shall see. Don't rely on your friend Captain Weiss to save you when I have proof.' He strolled out of the kitchen and slammed the door.

'He knows something.' Marie's face had paled to the colour of the dough she was kneading.

'He's just trying to trick us.'

'If he finds out about Gerald and how he disposed of Grulich, there'll be hell to pay.' Marie met Meg's startled gaze with a wry smile. 'My son tells me everything.'

'Then let's hope that Nordhausen was bluffing.'

'I don't like this,' Marie said, sighing. 'I wish we could get Gerald to the mainland.'

'So do I, but it's out of the question. We've just got to go on as we are and not let a bully like Nordhausen trick us into giving anything away.'

After a week of summer storms and heavy rain, Meg's birthday dawned clear and fine. Her father gave her a diamond brooch that had once belonged to her grandmother, and Gerald presented her with a wicker basket filled with wild

233

strawberries. He had risked breaking the curfew to search for them in the woods and they were still pearled with dew. Jane presented her with one of her few remaining handkerchiefs wrapped in a yellowing copy of the *Guernsey Press*, and Maud had painstakingly unpicked one of Bertie's old pullovers and had knitted the wool into a scarf. It was slightly wider at one end than the other, but Meg said it was beautiful and just what she needed for the winter. Marie's contribution was a boiled egg and soldiers for her breakfast. Only two hens and the old rooster were left now, the others having ended up in Corporal Klein's cooking pot, and the eggs were earmarked for Hauptmann Dressler only, but one of the hens had found a secret laying place and Marie had come across it by accident. With everyone looking on, Meg could only imagine their thoughts as she carefully sliced off the top. Spoon poised, she was about to eat the egg, but suddenly her appetite deserted her and she pushed the plate towards Simone.

'Here, give this to the baby. He needs it more than I do.'

Birthday or not, there was no getting away from the drudgery of the work roster that Nordhausen had laid down for them. Meg went straight to the greenhouses after breakfast. She began by filling heavy cans from the butt and watering the growing plants. The first tomatoes were ripening nicely and it was tempting to pick and eat one ruby red globe, warm from the sun and sweet as honey. She hesitated, instinctively looking over her shoulder in case Nordhausen was lurking outside. She was hardly surprised when she saw him standing quietly by the open door.

'It's your birthday, Fräulein.'

'How did you know that?'

'I know everything that happens in the house.'

'Good for you.'

'I understand sarcasm. You would be wise not to annoy me.'

'Heaven forbid.' Meg carried on with the watering.

'Look at your hands.' Nordhausen leaned against the greenhouse door, watching Meg heave the heavy cans of water. 'Not the hands of a young lady now, are they? Before the war you would have scorned to do such work.'

Meg tried to ignore his jibes, but she had of necessity to squeeze past him in order to refill the cans.

'My good friend Captain Grulich knew that there was something not right here. He suspected but he couldn't prove anything. I think you or your brother know more about his so-called accident than you have said.' Nordhausen stretched his booted foot across the doorway and Meg stopped suddenly, spilling a can of cold water down his leg.

'Oh dear, how clumsy of me.'

'You bitch.' Nordhausen caught her by the wrist and twisted her arm behind her back.

She bit her lip so that she would not give him the satisfaction of hearing her cry out. He twisted her arm a little harder and this time she yelped.

'Don't play games with me.' He emphasised his words with a savage jerk. 'Do not cry out, Fräulein. Your brother is digging potatoes far away in the north field where I sent him this morning and he cannot come to your aid. But you and I need to talk.'

'I have nothing to say,' she gasped, wincing and biting her lip as he increased the pressure on her arm. His fingers dug into her flesh and through the red mist of pain she thought vaguely that one more move on Nordhausen's part and her bones would snap.

'You have plenty to say to Captain Weiss, but he won't be able to save you if I can prove what my friend Grulich told me.'

Meg closed her eyes and felt the cold sweat trickling down her face as the pain intensified. Nordhausen's breath was warm and sour on her face.

'Very convenient for you that poor Grulich died in the accident and strange that he appeared drunk when I have never known him take more than a glass of wine to toast the Führer.' He punctuated his words with sharp savage jerks on Meg's arm and she cried out in agony. 'So tell me, Fräulein Colivet, how exactly did my friend die?'

'I – I don't know.'

His fingers tightened on her wrist. 'Such small bones and so little flesh. If you don't tell me the truth it will be so easy to break them.'

'Lieutenant Nordhausen!'

Rayner's voice rang out bringing Meg back from the brink of unconsciousness. Nordhausen released her so suddenly that she stumbled and would have fallen if Rayner had not caught her.

'Fräulein Colivet deliberately threw water over me, Captain.'

'It was an accident,' Meg said, leaning against Rayner's shoulder as her legs threatened to buckle beneath her.

'It was an accident,' Rayner said, eyeing Nordhausen with barely concealed dislike. 'She has said so. You may go, Lieutenant. I'll deal with this.'

Nordhausen cast a vicious look at Meg as he leapt to attention and saluted. He marched towards the house, his whole body quivering with affront.

'Are you all right, Meg?' Rayner's voice was deep with concern.

She nodded even though the pain was still intense. 'I think so.'

He examined her arm and wrist with gentle fingers. 'At least it's not broken.' He kissed the red weals left by Nordhausen's fingers.

She wrenched her arm free. 'Don't. He might be watching.'

'Even Nordhausen can't see round corners, my darling Meg.'

The warmth in his voice brought a rush of scalding tears to her eyes and she turned away. 'Don't be nice to me, I can't stand it.' She stumbled into the greenhouse and leaned against the wooden staging, trembling violently, more shaken by Nordhausen's terrifyingly accurate guesses at what had happened to Grulich than the physical pain he had inflicted on her.

'If he touches you again, I'll kill him,' Rayner said, twisting her round to face him. His eyes glittered with suppressed rage, but Meg knew that his anger was for Nordhausen and not for herself. He pulled her roughly to him and kissed

237

her on the mouth, softly at first but with mounting fervour. She knew that she should resist but instead she slid her arms around his neck, closing her eyes and parting her lips. She relaxed against his hard body, giving herself up to the sensuous delight that made her heart feel light and caused her head to spin. He held her so that it was impossible to push him away but that was the last thing on her mind. The long-denied feelings she had tried so assiduously to crush burst to the surface like the bubbles of air trapped beneath the murky waters of the Thames when Rayner had saved her from the clutching fronds of the weeds. She was beyond reckless.

'I've wanted to do that for so long, Meg. You'll never know how much I've wanted to hold you and kiss you and tell you that I fell in love with you from the first moment I saw you in Oxford.'

'I can't believe it. You were always so aloof and so – so grown-up. I felt like an awkward schoolgirl.'

He kissed her temples, her eyelids and her cheeks, running his fingers up and down the bones of her spine beneath the soft cotton folds of her shirt. 'My poor girl, you're so thin, but even more beautiful. I loved you as you were then but I adore you now and it hurts me to see you living like this, a prisoner in your own home, forced to work in the fields like a common labourer.'

'This is crazy.' She clung to him, knowing that what they were doing was close to insanity but reluctant to end the magic. 'If we're caught, God knows what they'll do to us.'

'You mean Nordhausen?' Rayner smiled grimly.

'I'm still his superior officer. I think I can handle him.'

'He suspects Gerald, and he thinks that Grulich's death wasn't an accident.'

'He is just trying to frighten you and I won't stand for it. I'll speak to Major Jaeger and get him transferred to another unit.'

'You could do that?'

'I can do anything now, my darling.' Rayner brushed her lips with his and his stern features dissolved into the boyish smile that made Meg's heart contract with desire. 'But I must go before someone sees us together. We must find some-where else to meet.'

'I've told you before, Rayner. It's too dangerous.'

'Do you think I could walk way from you now pretending that nothing has changed between us?'

'It's impossible.'

With a swift movement he wrapped his arms around her, burying his face in her hair, which had come loose from the confines of her headscarf. 'Nothing is impossible. I love you, Meg. Nothing will ever change the way I feel about you.'

'I love you, too.'

'Say that again.' He held her away just far enough to study her face, a smile of delight making his eyes dance.

She threw back her head and laughed. Suddenly nothing mattered. The world began and ended here amongst the pungent tomato plants that they had accidentally crushed. 'I love you, Rayner Weiss. I love you.'

When finally they drew apart, Rayner brushed her tangled hair back from her face. 'I have to leave you now, sweetheart, but we must find a safe place to meet.'

Gazing deeply into his eyes, Meg knew she had fought and lost the battle to stop loving him. Nothing mattered now except being with him and no risk was too great. 'It's my turn to go to market this week. I always go to the café in the High Street to meet Pearl. I'll be there at eleven o'clock tomorrow.'

'Can you trust this woman?'

'Of course, or I wouldn't suggest it.'

'Then we might meet by chance tomorrow morning.'

Pearl almost choked on the sawdust-dry cake that was all that the café could offer that day. She swallowed convulsively. 'Meg, are you crazy?'

'I think I must be.'

Pearl leaned across the table, lowering her voice to a whisper. 'If you start an affair with a German officer you'll be in the same position as Simone LeFevre.'

'We're not having an affair.' Meg felt herself blushing furiously and she glanced over her shoulder to see if anyone had heard, but the other occupants of the café were too busy with their own conversations to take any notice of them.

Pearl curled her lips in a cynical smile. 'Come off it, Meg. You mean you're just going to hold hands and go for moonlight walks amongst the barbed wire and gun emplacements?'

'I know it's dangerous and I know it's foolish, but I have to see him alone. Will you help me or not?'

Pearl crumbled the remains of her cake into small pieces and she avoided Meg's eyes. 'I shouldn't condone such madness. If you get caught it will be serious. And if you get...'

'I won't,' Meg said, feeling her cheeks flaming. 'It's not going to go that far. I just want to see him alone and be able to talk and get to know him again. I had a schoolgirl crush on him in Oxford but it's different now.'

'I'll say it is. I'm afraid for you, Meg.'

'Then you'll do it? You'll let us meet at your house?'

Pearl smiled reluctantly. 'I must be mad but yes, you can tell your father you're visiting me and I'll fix it with my folks. As long as it's within the curfew.'

'Oh, it will be, Pearl. And I'll be in your debt forever.' Meg had been glancing nervously out of the café window but when she saw Rayner's familiar figure striding up the Pollet on the other side of the street she barely suppressed a cry of delight. 'There he is. Isn't he handsome?'

Pearl craned her neck to look. 'Well, he's certainly tall and he walks with a swagger like a buccaneer, but does he always look that stern?'

'He looks quite different when he smiles.' Meg leapt to her feet and made a grab for her shopping basket. 'Quick, give me a day and time to come to your house.'

'Saturday afternoon. I usually take Mother to the pictures on Saturday afternoons and Daddy has a nap.'

'You're an angel. I love you, Pearl.' Meg leaned across and kissed Pearl on her cheek and ran out

241

of the café, leaving the door to swing on its hinges.

Meg arrived at Pearl's house at exactly two o'clock on Saturday afternoon. She hid her bicycle beneath the shrubs in the back garden and entered the drawing room through the French windows. As promised, Pearl had taken her mother to see a Cary Grant film and her father was taking his afternoon nap. The only other person who remained in the household that had once boasted a staff of living-in servants was Hannah, the housekeeper, who had been with the family since she left school. Pearl had assured Meg that Hannah was getting on in years and very deaf. She also had the habit of sleeping the afternoons away in her tiny room on the top floor. Meg paused, listening for signs of movement, but the whole house slumbered quietly in the heat of the afternoon as if it too were having a siesta. The only sound was the ticking of the long-case clock in the hall and the gentle flap of the lace curtains as the summer breeze wafted in from the garden.

The drawing room looked sad and faded like an old photograph. Dust gathered on the baby grand piano and the Spanish shawl that had draped it so stylishly now hung in limp folds, lacy with moth-holes. The gramophone that had once blared out dance music for Pearl, Adele and their friends now stood in a corner mute and neglected beside a pile of records in tattered brown sleeves. Meg had been too young to be invited to Pearl's parties but she had often listened to Addie's accounts of what sounded to her young ears to be highly sophisticated behaviour.

'Meg.'

She spun round to see Rayner entering through the French windows.

CHAPTER THIRTEEN

She turned in the circle of his arms and their lips met in a kiss that made time stand still. The clock on the mantelpiece struck four and Meg broke away from him.

'That can't be the time. We must leave now.'

'We must meet again soon. I can't bear to lose you again.'

She picked up her cardigan and draped it around her shoulders. 'We'll find a way to be together, but you must go before Pearl and her mother get back. God knows what Mrs Tostevin would say if she found a German officer in her drawing room.'

Rayner grinned reluctantly and brushed his lips against her cheek. 'It's going to be even harder to keep up pretences now.'

'I know, but we must. Nordhausen already suspects and so does Gerald. Anyway, never mind them. Please go now, and I'll follow in a minute or two. We mustn't be seen together.'

He was gone and Meg stared at herself in the mirror. The young woman with luminous eyes and tenderly curved lips smiling back at her was almost a stranger, so different from the thin-faced, hollow-eyed reflection that Meg had grown used to seeing every morning when she brushed her hair that she hardly recognised herself. She had thought that the carefree, fun-loving Meg had gone forever; she knew now that was not true. She lingered in the room, telling herself that she was making sure they had left no telltale signs to alert Mrs Tostevin, but in reality she could not bear to relinquish the memory of the precious moments they had shared. In two wonderful hours they had talked about so many things. She could scarcely remember all that had been said, but in between passionate embraces they had explored each other's hearts and minds.

With a contented sigh and a last glance around the room, which was haunted now by yet another memory, she picked up her handbag and went outside to find her bicycle. She rode home feeling happier than she had done for a long time. The soft breeze caressed her cheeks and the sun warmed her back as she pedalled with renewed vigour. She felt she was flying and nothing, simply nothing, could mar her joy. She knew now that she had always loved him, and to discover the depth of his feelings for her had made a heaven from the present hell.

Colivet Manor was bathed in sunlight as she rode down the drive towards the house. Outwardly the Queen Anne façade looked exactly the same as always. In her present state of euphoria, Meg could imagine that nothing had changed and that the occupation had never happened. She had regained her youth and she felt free.

'Where the hell have you been?' Gerald caught hold of the bicycle handlebars, almost unseating her as she rode into the cobbled stable yard. Saving herself by putting both feet firmly on the ground, Meg met his angry eyes and her stolen moments of happiness vanished like smoke in the wind.

'It's none of your business. How dare you speak to me like that?'

Gerald's knuckles whitened as he tightened his grip. 'I saw him leave the house after you did and he came back twenty minutes ago looking very pleased with himself. You've been with the German. Don't try to deny it.'

'Let go of my bike and stop acting like a fool.'

He took a step backwards, scowling angrily. 'I'm not the fool this time, Meg. I know you're in love with him and I know that you've been together. It's mad and it's dangerous.'

She leapt off the bike and thrust it at him. 'You're the one leading us into danger. You have been all along so don't you dare lecture me.' She began to walk away but Gerald flung the bicycle to the ground and ran after her, catching hold of her arm in a grip that made her wince with pain.

'Tell me that you haven't been with him and I'll believe you.'

'You're a jealous idiot and I don't have to explain my movements to you or anyone else.'

He released her with a look of revulsion. 'What is it with you women? Can't you be satisfied with your own kind?'

'What do you mean by that?'

'The bloody Germans, you can't resist them. First Simone and now you.'

'You're mad. Simone made a mistake, but that's

all in the past.'

Gerald shook his head. 'That's all you know. She's been seeing Nordhausen for months. Creeping out after curfew and meeting him. She's a slut and a Jerrybag and that's what you are too. A bloody, stinking Jerrybag.'

Simone made no secret of her relationship with Nordhausen; rather she seemed proud of the fact that the young lieutenant was taking an interest in her. Meg saw them walking together in the grounds whenever he was off duty, and sometimes they went off on his motorcycle with Simone riding pillion. If anyone dared to raise an objection they received a hostile reaction from her which made them think twice before approaching her a second time. Meg said nothing. After all, how could she criticise Simone for having a relationship with a German soldier? It would have been both hypocritical and unfair, and, on a different level, it was a relief to have Nordhausen's attention diverted from spying on the rest of the family.

Maud and Bertrand made it clear that they disapproved and would not speak to Simone, but Jane stoically refused to be drawn into the argument. She quite obviously adored little Jeremy, and as Simone's initial enthusiasm for motherhood soon wore off Jane was always on the spot and more than willing to take care of him. Meg found that she was actually beginning to like Jane, in spite of her caustic tongue and brusque manners. Even Pip annoyed her less these days, or perhaps it was simply that the world seemed a much better place now that she and Rayner had admitted their true feelings for each other. Every morning when she awakened, Meg had to remind herself not to appear too happy in front of the family, not to sing while she worked and above all not to seek out Rayner's company.

Pearl was a reluctant but good-natured ally and she made her parents' house available whenever possible. Sometimes she took her mother to visit relations living in Cobo Bay and on other occasions she took her to the pictures, leaving Meg and Rayner free to snatch an hour or two together. They were always very careful to arrive and leave separately, but Meg was painfully aware that Gerald watched her every movement, and no matter how carefully she contrived her absences from the house he always seemed to know when she had been with Rayner. He rarely said anything to her but the hostile look in his eyes was hurtful, and Meg missed his friendship more than she would have thought possible.

The warm days lengthened into a gloriously long, hot summer. Despite everything, Meg managed to be with Rayner at least once a week, and she had Buster to thank for giving her an excuse to visit the Tostevins' house on the Grange. It had become more and more difficult to keep him confined to the house while she was out working in the fields and Nordhausen disliked dogs even more than Grulich. The scarcity of food for everyone, including the Germans, made it difficult to justify feeding an animal that did not work for its living, and when Nordhausen complained to Major Jaeger, she was told that the dog must go. In desperation, Meg had walked Buster all the way to the Tostevins' house, prepared to do anything if only they would keep him safe until she could claim him again. Pearl's parents had dithered at first. She realised that they were too kind to say outright that they would not help, but they were obviously not very keen on the idea. It was only when Meg promised to come once a week bringing vegetables, fruit and milk that they finally gave in and allowed Buster to stay.

'Is there anything wrong, sweetheart?' Rayner's long, slim fingers played with the strands of hair that had come loose from her snood during their first hungry embrace. Meg nestled into the curve of his body as they sat on the Tostevins' sofa with Buster sleeping at their feet.

'Of course not.'

He lifted her chin with the tip of his finger, searching her eyes with a worried frown. 'I know that's not true, my love. There is something.'

She sighed and cuddled closer to him. 'Gerald knows about us, and Nordhausen is suspicious even though he's more interested in Simone than anything else, but it's all getting so complicated.'

He twisted a lock of her hair around his forefinger. 'It's never going to be easy, Meg. Let's just be thankful for the brief time we have together.'

'I know. You're quite right. It's just that I get this awful feeling that something dreadful is about to happen. It's so perfect here with you and I'm terrified it's all going to end.'

'I'll speak to Major Jaeger and see if I can get Nordhausen transferred to another unit. As for Gerald, of course he's jealous. It's obvious he's in love with you, and who could blame him?'

Unable to resist the warmth in his voice, Meg giggled. 'Naturally, because I am so adorable.'

'And so you are, my dearest Meg.' He kissed her with growing urgency, short hard kisses that persuaded her lips to part and blotted out thought and fear.

The grandfather clock in the hall struck the half-hour and Meg realised that their time together was growing short. 'Tell me about your home town again,' she said, kissing him playfully on the tip of his nose. 'Tell me about the little house on Linden Strasse where we're going to live happily ever after.'

He leaned back against the silk cushions. 'Ah yes. The house! It belonged to my grandfather, who left it to me.'

'Were you the only grandchild?'

'No, my father has a brother who has two children, a boy and a girl, but they emigrated to Brazil in 1920.'

'The uncle who has the coffee plantation. You told us about him.'

'Yes, I am very fond of Uncle Wilhelm. He always wanted me to join them in the family business.'

'But I thought you wanted to take over your father's factory.'

Rayner tightened his arms around her. 'Of course. That is what I promised my father, and whatever my personal desires I would never let him down. I take over the factory when he retires and you and I, my darling, will have lots of children to fill the old nursery at the top of the house.'

249

'At least they will have plenty of toys,' said Meg, chuckling.

'You don't know how good it is to see you laugh again.' He drew her into his arms and kissed her.

Meg sang as she entered the house through the scullery door. She chuckled to herself as she recalled the narrow escape they had had when Pearl and her mother returned from the cinema earlier than expected. Actually, Meg thought, feeling her face flushing at the memory, it was more that Rayner was late leaving. If it had not been for Buster leaping up suddenly and barking, Pearl and her mother might have come into the drawing room and caught them in a passionate embrace. As it was, Rayner had slipped out of the French windows just as the door opened, and Meg had bent over Buster and fussed over him to hide her blushes. Mrs Tostevin had lowered herself into her chair by the fireplace and had begun to chatter happily about the film they had just seen. Pearl had raised her eyebrows and shaken her head.

'You've been with him again. I can tell by the silly smile on your face,' Gerald said, jumping to his feet as Meg entered the kitchen. He slammed his mug of mint tea on the table so violently that it spilled over, leaving pools on the scrubbed pine.

'Can't you let it drop?'

'No, I bloody can't. You're risking everything for a man who's our sworn enemy.'

'I'm not going to argue with you, Gerald. Can't we be friends again?'

'Friends?' His voice broke with emotion. 'I don't want us to be friends, you know that.'

She walked slowly towards him with her hands outstretched. 'I know I've hurt you and for that I'm truly sorry, but we have to stick together.'

'Not while you're having an affair with that Kraut.'

Meg stared at him, her patience suddenly evaporating as he used David's old nickname for Rayner, making it sound somehow obscene. 'What I do is my business. Perhaps you should worry more about what your sister is doing.'

'My sister is a slut. I thought better of you.'

'Interesting,' said Nordhausen, sauntering into the room. 'And just how many sisters have you, Herr Colivet, or should I say Herr LeFevre?'

Meg stared at him, struck dumb with fear, but Gerald leapt to his feet, knocking his chair over as he turned to face Nordhausen. 'You're talking rot.'

Nordhausen smirked. 'Well, I really seem to have hit on the truth at last.'

'You don't know what you're saying.'

'Don't I?' Nordhausen leaned nonchalantly against the door post.

'You've got it all wrong,' Gerald said hastily. 'I am David Colivet.'

'Ask Simone,' Meg found her voice at last. 'You're so friendly with her. Ask her if this is David Colivet or her brother Gerald.'

'I think I can prove that this man is Gerald LeFevre without involving his sister any further. She's already told me more than she realises. And as for you, Fräulein Meg, I think Hauptmann Dressler will be very interested in what I have to tell him about a certain captain.'

'This is nonsense,' Meg said, putting on a show

251

of bravado despite the fact that she was quaking inwardly. 'You can't prove a thing.'

'I don't have to. We shall see what Hauptmann Dressler has to say.'

Nordhausen turned and walked away, slowly and deliberately, his footsteps echoing on the stone-flagged floor and then fading into a deathly silence. Meg could hear a rasping sound and realised it was her own harsh breathing. She spun round to face Gerald. 'You stupid, jealous fool. You've ruined everything.'

'If you hadn't gone off with that Kraut–'

'Don't you dare blame me. If your little tart of a sister hadn't slept with half the German army we might have had a chance.' Meg ran to the door with some vague idea of stopping Nordhausen and begging him to reconsider, but the sound of Major Jaeger shouting for someone to find Captain Weiss made her stop and clutch at the door frame for support. 'Oh, my God! Now see what you've done.'

'I'm going to find your father. We need his help to settle this.' Gerald pushed past her and strode off in the direction of the study.

Meg followed him but the sound of Hauptmann Dressler's voice raised in anger made her hesitate outside the drawing room. Unable to grasp more than a few words of his rapid German, she strained her ears to catch the sound of Rayner's voice, but it was obvious that Dressler was not giving him a chance to defend himself. She could hear Major Jaeger's calm tones, but he was being out-shouted by his superior. Nordhausen's higher-pitched voice only seemed to add to the Hauptmann's fury. Tears of desperation ran down her cheeks. She was on the point of rushing into the room, regardless of anything other than the desperate need to be with Rayner, when Gerald emerged from the study and beckoned furiously. She hesitated, as common sense battled with her instinct to fight for the man she loved. Reluctantly she joined Gerald and her father in the study. Charles was seated behind his desk but he rose to his feet as she entered the room. 'My dear, Gerald has told me what's happened.'

'Please, Pa. You must do something to help Rayner.'

He shook his head. 'I'm afraid there's nothing I can do or say that will make any difference.'

'They'll send him to the Russian front and that's what he deserves,' Gerald said, scowling.

Meg turned on him like a fury. 'And what do you think they'll do to you when Nordhausen tells them who you really are?'

He paled visibly and cast an appealing look at Charles. 'Sir?'

'We're not going to get anywhere by fighting each other. We must stick together.'

'It's a bit late for that, Pa,' Meg said tiredly. 'Nordhausen has wheedled the truth out of Simone and Gerald all but admitted it just a few minutes ago.'

Gerald eyed her coldly. 'None of this would have come out if you hadn't fallen for a bloody Kraut bastard.'

Charles held up his hand. 'That's enough. I won't have that kind of language in my house.'

'Well, it's true.' Gerald turned away and began

253

to pace the floor.

'You're just jealous,' Meg said bitterly. 'The real blame lies with you because you can't control your temper.'

'Stop it, both of you. This has gone far enough.' Charles sank back on his seat, holding his head in his hands, and Meg hurried round the desk to put her arm around his shoulders.

'I'm sorry, Pa. I never meant it to end like this.' She shot an angry glance at Gerald. 'See what you've done.'

He bowed his head, clenching his hands at his sides. 'I love you, Meg. You know I love you. I thought you loved me too.'

'Meg, is this true?' Charles gazed up at her with an agonised look. 'Were you leading the boy on?'

'I told Gerald then that it was a mistake. I'm very fond of him but I don't love him and I never could.'

'It's worse than I could ever have imagined.' Charles gazed at Gerald, shaking his head. 'What have I done by allowing you to remain here, my boy? I knew it was a risk but I'd no idea it would turn out this way.'

'I never intended all this to happen, sir.' Gerald glanced anxiously at Meg. 'I'm sorry for the way I've been treating you.'

'It wasn't all your fault,' Meg said with an attempt at a smile.

'I need to see your mother, Gerald,' Charles said in a hoarse whisper. 'I can't do anything to help Captain Weiss, but I may be able to save you.'

'I don't understand, sir.'

'You will. Now do as I say and hurry.' Charles

254

leaned back in his chair and closed his eyes.

Gerald opened the door and the sound of angry voices filtered into the room. Meg clenched her fists, digging her fingernails into her palms as she strained her ears to hear Rayner's measured tones as he defended his actions.

'Hurry,' Charles said, motioning Gerald to leave. 'Fetch Marie quickly, boy.'

Gerald left the room, closing the door behind him.

Meg studied her father's ashen face and was overcome by the need to unburden herself. 'I'm so sorry about this, Pa. I tried not to fall in love with Rayner but I couldn't help myself. It all started in Oxford at the May Ball, but we could never have imagined it would end like this.'

Charles gave her a half-smile. 'I understand, believe me. More than you think.'

She laid her hand on his and a shiver ran down her spine. He looked ill and frail and she felt a surge of panic rising in her throat. If only Mother were here, she would know what to do. 'You should rest, Pa. Let me help you to your room.'

'No, I need to speak to Marie. You go, my dear. I'll be all right. Marie will look after me.'

There was nothing Meg could do or say to make him change his mind, and she went out into the hall, almost colliding with Nordhausen.

'You will not be seeing Captain Weiss again, I think.' He smiled triumphantly.

'What have you told Hauptmann Dressler?'

'Simply the truth, Fräulein Meg.'

He was obviously enjoying himself and it took all her self-control to remain calm. 'And what was that, may I ask?'

'Hauptmann Dressler does not approve of officers defiling the daughters of prominent States officials.'

'And does that include your relationship with Simone?'

'Simone is nothing to me. You on the other hand are the daughter of an important man in the eyes of the natives. But even your father's influence won't save the fellow who pretends to be your brother.'

'You can't prove anything.'

'Don't be too sure of that. There is also the matter of my friend Grulich's supposed accident. Don't think I have forgotten my comrade.'

'I know nothing about that.' Meg looked him in the eye. She was trembling, but she would not give him the satisfaction of knowing that she was desperately afraid.

He leaned closer. 'You had better be nice to me, Fräulein. I control everything that happens to you and your family now that your lover Captain Weiss has been ordered to the Russian front. He cannot save you. No one can, except yourself.'

Meg hardly slept at all that night. She drifted off just before dawn but soon after the first rays of sun filtered through the early morning haze she was awakened by the sound of an approaching motor vehicle. She peered out of the window as a German staff car drew up outside and the driver leapt out, saluting the officers waiting on the steps. From above Meg could only see the tops of their peaked caps but she would have known Rayner anywhere. She watched helplessly as he climbed into the staff car, followed by Major Jaeger. One of the privates slammed the door and stood to attention while the driver started the engine and the vehicle drove off. She watched it until it was out of sight. He had gone, taking the most vital part of her with him. Rayner held her heart in his hands and she was left an empty shell.

She dressed hurriedly and crept downstairs to the kitchen. Corporal Klein had just finished preparing breakfast for the officers. He poured coffee into a tin mug and handed it silently to Meg. She gave him a tired smile.

'Better drink up and keep out of the way this morning, Fräulein,'

'What's going on, Corporal?'

'Captain Weiss has been transferred to another unit. I don't know where. I think Major Jaeger has gone too. There's talk about the Russian front, but you know how soldiers love to gossip.'

Two days later, Nordhausen was promoted to the rank of captain and soon after that Major von Eschenberg arrived to take Major Jaeger's place. Meg found it almost impossible to sleep and her appetite deserted her. She blamed herself for Rayner's fate. If she had kept him at arm's length instead of allowing her emotions to overrule common sense, he would not have been sent away. Then there was Nordhausen who had the power of life and death over Gerald, but seemed to be enjoying a cat and mouse game with them. Days passed and then weeks without the dreaded summons from Dressler's office.

Von Eschenberg appeared to be coldly indifferent to the family, and the small privileges they had enjoyed under Major Jaeger, and interpreted liberally by Rayner, vanished overnight. Nordhausen was left in charge of the day to day running of the manor and he did not bother to hide the fact that he enjoyed making their lives hell. He was too clever to force himself on Meg, but he waged a private war of attrition by constantly shadowing her, making lewd suggestions when no one could hear, and barring her way in the narrow corridors, fumbling her breasts or buttocks and then pretending it was purely accidental. She knew that it was only a matter of time before he carried out the threats of sexual violence that he whispered in her ears. If she had known fear before, she knew now what real terror was and it stalked her by day and night.

CHAPTER FOURTEEN

Nordhausen had ruthlessly abandoned Simone. Meg might have felt sorry for her had she not taken out her spite on the rest of the family and made everyone suffer with her constant bad moods and tantrums.

It would have helped if Meg had been able to confide in Gerald, but she knew that his hatred of the Germans simmered below the surface like magma beneath the earth's crust; one careless word, one hint of the torture she was enduring and he would erupt like a volcano, bringing disaster upon them all. She had to live with the knowledge that this was exactly what Nordhausen wanted. She would have liked to tell her father, but his health had begun to deteriorate again as the soft autumn mists were replaced by the chill wind from the Atlantic and October gales wrapped the island in a blanket of rain.

Charles took to his bed in the middle of the month, racked with bronchitis and bouts of fever. Lack of heating and food had worn them all down to thin shadows. Maud and Bertrand had lost so much weight that they reminded Meg of two old tortoises. Folds of skin hung from their throats and their hooded eyes stared bleakly at the miserable fires of wet twigs or sawdust and the inevitable bowls of cabbage soup.

Pip spent most of his time hiding in his tiny attic room, venturing downstairs only at mealtimes. The Germans had obviously decided that he was a simpleton and had grown so accustomed to his odd appearance and mannerisms that mostly they left him alone. Jane worked hard doing the extra laundry duties allocated to her by Nordhausen and complained very little nowadays. She seemed to have found a new purpose in life in looking after Jeremy and was all the better for it. Simone re-mained a problem. Meg was just about at her wits' end when Dr Gallienne suggested that Major von Eschenberg might allow Simone to return to work. There was, he said, a desperate shortage of trained nurses. Perhaps Simone's moody presence had even sunk into the consciousness of the aloof von Eschenberg as, to Meg's surprise and consid-erable relief, he signed the permit without raising any objections. Simone returned to the hospital, living in the nurses' quarters and visiting her son occasionally on her days off.

By November there was still no news of Rayner and no way of finding out what had happened to him. Meg still lived in constant fear of Nordhausen. He appeared when she was least expecting it, like an evil genie of the lamp, to taunt her with threats of exposing Gerald as an impostor. So far he had not seriously molested her, but the leering, lustful expression in his eyes was enough to sicken and terrify her. For her the nightmare lived on.

Adding to her misery, Nordhausen had commandeered her bicycle, making visits to see Pearl impossible unless she walked, and then von Eschenberg decided that everyone needed a pass if they wanted to leave the grounds. Meg suspected that Nordhausen had something to do with this sudden change of tactics, but all she could do was request a permit and then wait. It seemed like months before she was granted one, although it was only a matter of weeks, and she set out to walk to the Grange, eager to get away from the stultifying atmosphere of the manor house.

As she reached the outskirts of town she quickened her pace. It was bitterly cold and her mother's old coat would have gone round her twice. Catching sight of herself in the window of an empty shop Meg grimaced, wondering what Mother and Adele would have said if they could see her now. Strands of hair had escaped from the multicoloured cap that she had painstakingly knitted from scraps of wool. Old jumpers had been unpicked by Maud so that they could be made into gloves, scarves and hideous hats like the one Meg was now wearing. The soles of her shoes were riddled with holes and the uppers were scuffed and coming apart at the seams. Meg could barely remember what it was like to be warm and well dressed. The days when food was plentiful and her belly did not contract with hunger pains were so long gone it seemed like another world. She trudged on, passing people she knew but barely recognised as they went about their daily business looking like gaunt scarecrows.

When she finally reached the house in the Grange, Hannah ushered her into the drawing room and hobbled away to find Pearl. The cold winter light made the room appear like a scene from a black and white film. The shadowy shapes of the furniture were ghostly memories of the past. Meg felt a lump rising in her throat as she recalled the ecstatic moments that she and Rayner had shared in those scented summer days that seemed like part of her dream world now. Nothing had changed, although everything was just that little bit shabbier. The sofa was still there, bringing back memories of being held in Rayner's arms and the stolen moments of forbidden love that had made life worth living. Meg sighed. Dwelling on the past too much was surely the path to madness. She shivered, wrapping her coat even tighter around her body. A desultory fire burned in the grate, but it gave out little heat.

Moments later, Pearl rushed into the room followed by Buster, who jumped up at Meg and licked her face, wagging his tail and grinning. She bent down to make a fuss of him. 'He still

261

remembers me.'

'Of course he does, darling,' Pearl said, smiling. 'He's missed you and I have too.' A look of concern puckered her face. 'You look awful. Are you ill?'

'No, I'm fine,' Meg lied, rubbing Buster's ears and smiling down at him. 'I'm just cold, and I had to walk all the way. That swine Nordhausen has stolen my bike, blast him.'

'I've asked Hannah to bring coffee.' Pearl sat on the sofa, patting the empty space next to her. 'Sit down and tell me all about it. Has that brute hurt you?'

'No, he just mumbles obscenities in my ear and leers at me.' Meg stroked Buster's head as he settled down at her feet.

'You should report him to the Hauptmann.'

'I can't, Pearl. He knows too much about Gerald. One word against him and he'll go to Dressler with the truth.' She paused as Hannah entered the room carrying a tray of coffee, which she set on the low table in front of the sofa.

'Thank you, Hannah,' Pearl said, smiling. 'Hot coffee is just what Meg needs. She's frozen, poor thing.'

'It's that ersatz stuff, which isn't what I'd call coffee, but it's warm and wet. It's almost impossible to boil a kettle these days. The gas is so low that there's barely a flicker.'

'Thank you anyway, Hannah,' Pearl said hastily. 'I'm sure it will be lovely.' She passed a cup to Meg. 'Drink up, darling, and if it doesn't poison you, you'll feel better.'

Meg managed a smile at the feeble joke and

drank some of the bitter liquid; it was sweet and she realised that Hannah had used some of their precious sugar ration to sweeten it. 'Thank you. This is very good.'

Hannah nodded grimly. 'Well, I suppose it's better than nothing.'

'It's being so cheerful that keeps her going,' Pearl said with a chuckle as Hannah left the room. 'There now, you look a bit better. You've got some colour back in your cheeks.'

Meg put her coffee cup back on its saucer. She had a special reason for visiting Pearl but she did not quite know how to broach the subject. 'I know you do a lot of volunteer work for the Red Cross, Pearl.'

'Yes, I do. It stops me from going out of my mind with boredom. Why?'

'I just wondered if you'd heard anything about Rayner. I don't know if he's still on the island or if they sent him away.'

Pearl grasped Meg's hand and her lips curved in an excited smile. 'I was going to tell you after you'd had time to recover from your long walk. You won't believe this, darling, but I saw him yesterday.'

Meg closed her eyes as the room spun dizzily. 'You – you saw him?'

'Are you all right? You're not going to pass out or anything like that are you, Meg?'

The anxious note in Pearl's voice made Meg struggle for self-control and she nodded. 'I'm fine. But how did he look? Where did you see him?'

'I happened to be on the quay helping to load Red Cross parcels onto a farm cart and he was

263

standing in a line of men waiting to get on a ship. He must have heard Mrs Gallienne calling to me. She wanted me to run an errand for her, the lazy old cow...'

Meg raised an impatient hand. 'What happened then? Did you speak to him?'

'He asked me if I was Pearl Tostevin, and when I said I was he asked if I would give you a message.'

'Don't keep me in suspense. What did he say?'

'He said "Folly Bridge." Honestly, darling, that's all he said, and anyway there was a horrid-looking German sergeant poking him in the back and making him move on up the gangplank with the others.'

'Folly Bridge,' Meg repeated slowly.

'Does that mean something to you?'

'It means everything. Are you sure he didn't say anything else?'

'He didn't have a chance.'

'Where were they taking him?'

'Darling, if I knew that I'd be Mata blooming Hari. At least you know he's still alive.'

'Yes,' Meg murmured, as the reality of his situation hit her with full force. 'But for how long?'

Even though he was far away from her, the knowledge that Rayner was alive and well kept Meg going through the long, dark winter days. It gave her the courage to go on and helped her to be patient when the family looked to her for comfort and guidance. Life was simplified into a daily struggle to find enough food to eat and fuel of any kind to make the smallest amount of heat needed to survive. Charles was confined to bed and at times was so ill that Meg thought he was going to die, but somehow he managed to keep his tenacious hold on life and as the spring sunshine brought a fine mist of green to the trees he began a slow recovery that Meg thought little short of a miracle.

She had come to an unspoken truce with Gerald and it was a relief to have him as a friend and ally in their uncertain world. He seemed to have accepted the fact that there was not, and never could be, any chance of a romance between them. Meg never spoke about Rayner to anyone other than Pearl, but that didn't stop her thinking about him constantly. She wore his necklace like a talisman, never taking it off even at night.

As the tender green leaves unfurled and the cherry blossom opened in a cloudburst of pink, a surge of optimism filled the air as rumours circulated that the Allies were close to invading France. Pip's crystal set had kept them in touch with the outside world during the long winter and now, with the hope that the end of the war might be getting nearer, there was for the first time in four years a low-grade buzz of excitement rippling through the long food queues. Meg saw haggard faces beginning to smile again.

It was with renewed optimism that she set out one morning with the permit that allowed her to go into St Peter Port safely tucked in her handbag together with the shopping list that Marie had given her more in hope than expectation. Halfway down the drive she stopped to take off her shoe and shake out a piece of gravel. She grimaced as she slipped it back on. The leather was scuffed and not so long ago the shoes would have been consigned to the dustbin, but just when she had thought them past repair, Gerald had given them a new lease of life by sewing on soles cut from an old rubber tyre. Although each step felt odd and strangely springy, it was far more comfortable than walking on lumps of matted cardboard. She set off again and had just reached the gates when Nordhausen sprang out from the stand of Spanish oaks and caught her by the arm.

'Let me go.' Anger replaced fear as she attempted to free herself. 'How dare you jump out on me like that?'

He grinned. 'You have such spirit. I love a woman with fire.'

'Let me go, Captain Nordhausen. I have a permit to go into St Peter Port signed by Major von Eschenberg himself.'

He released her with a casual flick of his wrist. 'I find it very interesting that you spend so much time in town. Surely there is not much there for a lady like you. Now if it was Simone LeFevre then I could understand it, but you, Fräulein Meg, what do you do in St Peter Port all by yourself? Do you go there to meet someone? Perhaps your brother?'

'Don't be ridiculous.'

'I'm not a patient man and I tire of the games you play. Meet me tonight at eight o'clock, by the lake.'

'You're mad.' Meg's stomach contracted with fear. 'Why would I want to have anything to do with you?'

'Captain Weiss is no longer here to protect you, Fräulein. Either you do as I say or I tell the major that David Colivet is really Gerald LeFevre. As you know, I could have done that some time ago, but I enjoy seeing you both suffer.'

'I won't do it.'

'You have no choice. I was instrumental in sending Captain Weiss to the Russian front. Think what I might do for Herr LeFevre. Eight o'clock.' Nordhausen strolled away with his hands clasped behind his back.

Meg wished she had a weapon – a gun, anything. At this moment she could have committed murder in cold blood and not turned a hair.

After a meagre supper that barely satisfied her hunger, Meg sat on the window seat in the parlour staring out into the garden. All day Nordhausen's words had haunted her but she was no nearer to finding a solution to her problem. His intentions were perfectly clear, as was the threat to Gerald. If Nordhausen denounced him it would be a death sentence. She glanced around the room. Whatever she decided would inevitably have consequences for her family. They knew nothing of the turmoil within her or the choice that she was being forced to make. Maud sat at the table, darning one of Pip's socks. She had to hold the work close to her eyes as her sight had deteriorated, and she was in desperate need of new spectacles. Bertrand and Charles dozed in armchairs on either side of the fireplace, their chins resting on their chests and soft snores emanating from each one in turn. Gerald was in the kitchen helping his mother with the dishes and Jane had taken Jeremy upstairs to put him to bed in the cot that was now permanently in her room. Pip was off somewhere, probably listening to his crystal set.

'Care for a walk, Meg?'

She turned her head with a start. She had not realised that Gerald had returned and was standing at her side. 'Sorry. I was miles away.'

'Obviously. I've asked you the same question twice.'

'What did you want to know?'

'I asked you if you wanted to go for a walk before curfew. It's a lovely evening.'

She glanced at her watch and was shocked to see that it was almost eight o'clock. 'No. I mean, no thanks. I've just remembered I've got things to do.' She leapt to her feet and hurried from the room.

Gerald followed her. 'There's something you're not telling me. I know you too well, Meg. You can't hide anything from me.'

'It's my problem, not yours. I've got to do this on my own.'

'What have you got to do?' He grabbed her by the arm.

'Let me go. It's none of your business.'

'If you won't tell me then I'm coming with you.'

'Please don't.'

'It's Nordhausen, isn't it? He's been bothering you again?'

'I can handle him.'

'If you think that then you're a simpleton. He's ten times worse than Grulich. What has he said to you?'

'Leave me alone.'

'I'm coming with you.'

'Do as you please.' Meg shook off his restraining hand and hurried through the maze of passages to the kitchen, ignoring Marie's demand to know where they were going. Gerald was close behind her but she waited until they were out in the stable yard before turning to face him. 'Go back in the house. I'm begging you not to ask me any questions, just do as I ask and let me sort this thing out my way.'

He stared at her, his expressive eyes filled with anxiety. 'I can't let you do this, Meg. If you're going to meet Nordhausen at least let me go with you.'

'No. You've got to trust me. I know what I'm doing. If you insist on following me you'll put us all in danger.' She could see that this last desperate plea had struck home. She turned her back on him holding up her hand as she walked resolutely onwards. She dared not look over her shoulder, but she sensed that he was standing where she had left him, staring after her. She could feel his eyes on her back but she squared her shoulders and hurried on towards the lake.

The aquamarine sky was bruised with crimson and black as the sun plunged like a fireball towards the horizon. The sound of voices and laughter coming from the soldiers' quarters faded into the distance as she approached the ruins of the summerhouse. A faint smell of cigarette smoke was the only sign that Nordhausen was somewhere near and he stepped out from behind a clump of budding hydrangeas. His face was hidden in shadow and Meg felt a frisson of fear run down her spine, but she held her head high.

'You're late.' Nordhausen's voice cracked with ill-concealed excitement. 'Come here.'

Meg held her ground. 'No. I came to tell you that I'm not going to play your game.'

'What is this?'

'I'm not a servant girl or a whore. If you persist in propositioning me then I'll have no alternative but to go straight to Hauptmann Dressler.'

'Do you think he'll listen to you? He knows that you have already consorted with one of his officers.' Nordhausen came towards her, swaggering and arrogant.

She wanted to run away but she forced herself to face him. 'Hauptmann Dressler disapproves of his officers fraternising with local women, but he would be even more furious if he knew you were forcing your attentions on me.'

'I will tell him that Gerald LeFevre is a British soldier who should have given himself up years ago. He will be shot and the rest of you will be deported to a labour camp. I don't think your father would survive very long in those conditions, do you?'

Meg opened her mouth to retaliate but Nordhausen seized her in his arms and clamped his mouth over hers. She struggled, but her strength was no match for his. He swept her off her feet, carrying her towards the bushes, but at that moment a figure appeared as if from nowhere and all three of them were sent crashing to the ground. Winded and gasping, Meg rolled away from the flailing arms and legs as Gerald fought with Nordhausen. He managed to land several punches on Nordhausen's jaw, but it was painfully obvious to Meg that Gerald's strength had been sapped by hard work and malnutrition, and the fight was unequal. With a swift movement Nordhausen gained the advantage and pinned Gerald down. He drew his service revolver from its holster.

Hauptmann Dressler sat behind his desk grim-faced as he listened to Nordhausen's account of what had happened that evening. He interrogated Meg and Gerald but it was obvious that nothing they could say was going to make the slightest bit of difference to the outcome. Major von Eschenberg was sent to fetch Charles, and, one by one, the rest of the family were brought into the room and questioned. Finally, after an hour of continuous interrogation, Dressler leaned his elbows on the desk.

'Since you are all obviously in this together, you must receive the same punishment. Captain Nordhausen has proved to me that you have harboured a British soldier when you should have reported his presence to the authorities, and that you all conspired to conceal his identity. Herr Colivet, you said that this man was your son. Do you deny this?' Dressler stared, stony-eyed, at Charles.

Charles raised himself from the chair that Major von Eschenberg had provided. His breathing was laboured and his skin had taken on a blue tinge as he fought to catch his breath. 'Hauptmann Dressler, I take full responsibility for what has happened in my household but Captain Nordhausen is only partly correct in his accusations.'

271

'Explain that statement, if you please.'

'This young man is not David Colivet, but he is my son and I can prove it.'

There was a stunned silence. Meg clapped her hand over her mouth to stifle a cry of shock and disbelief. She stared at her father, wondering if he had gone mad. His illness must have affected his brain for him to utter such an obvious lie. If Gerald was her half-brother – suddenly she felt sick with shame. She turned her head to look at Marie for confirmation that Pa was lying, but Marie had buried her face in her hands and was sobbing convulsively.

Dressler leaned forward, staring at Charles over the top of his steel-rimmed spectacles. 'You are telling me that this young man is not Gerald LeFevre?'

'He was brought up as Gerald LeFevre but I have his birth certificate in my possession. If you will permit me to get the document from my study it will prove that he is Gerald Colivet.'

Dressler nodded. 'Very well.'

Charles stood up slowly and hobbled from the room. Meg sat with her hands clenched tightly on her lap. Every muscle in her body was tensed as if for flight. She closed her eyes, unable to meet the curious stares from Maud, Bertrand and Jane. Pip muttered beneath his breath and giggled. No one told him to be quiet.

Agonising minutes passed until Charles returned clutching a document, which he handed to Hauptmann Dressler.

Dressler rearranged his spectacles and studied its contents. 'It would appear that this is a genuine birth certificate, Herr Colivet. You will tell everyone here in this room why you kept this man's identity a secret.'

'No.' Marie lifted her head, her face pale and streaked with tears. 'No, please.'

Dressler leaned across the desk. 'You will speak, Herr Colivet. We are all most interested to hear your story.'

Charles held himself upright, looking directly at Meg. 'I'm so sorry, my dear. This is not the way I wanted you to hear this sad tale of your father's selfishness and self-deception. Nor you, Gerald, this is not how I wished the truth to come out.'

'Herr Colivet, spare us the apologies, they are of no interest to anyone except you.' Dressler waved his hand impatiently. 'You realise, I am sure, that more than your own life is at stake here.'

Charles sat down suddenly as if his legs had given way beneath him and he nodded his head. 'The fault is all mine.'

'Leave him alone, can't you?' Meg leapt to her feet and moved swiftly to his side. She flung herself down on her knees, wrapping her arms around him. 'Can't you see he's a sick man?'

Dressler leaned across his desk, frowning. 'If you can't be silent I will have you removed from this room.'

'It's all right, Meg.' Charles patted her hand. 'I never meant to hurt you, or your mother or anyone. It was a long time ago. I was a young man and I fell in love.'

Marie's loud sobs echoed around the room.

'I fell in love,' Charles repeated, raising his voice. 'Marie Ozanne came to work as a kitchen maid here, in my father's house. She was little more than a schoolgirl then, and I was an up and coming barrister in the family law practice. My engagement to Muriel Brehaut was a long-standing arrangement between our families, and there was no honourable way out.' He turned to Meg with tears in his eyes. 'Your mother was and always has been a much better wife than I deserve, Meg. But I was desperately in love with Marie, and to my everlasting shame I allowed passion to override common sense and caution. We became lovers, even though I was much older than she, and soon to be married. Gerald, you were born a few months before David. If I had recognised you as my son then it would have ruined my career. I can't tell you how sorry I am.'

Gerald shook his head, saying nothing. Everyone was silent, even Dressler.

Charles cleared his throat. 'I can never undo the damage I've done to you or to your mother, Gerald. I've tried to look after you both in my own way. I saw to it that you had a good education and I arranged for you to train as an articled clerk in London. There is not much else I can add, except to apologise to my family and most of all to Marie. I hope she will forgive me for my cavalier treatment of her and our son, and I hope my children will try to understand, if they can.'

Gerald looked up, his face pale and drained of emotion. 'Eric LeFevre, the man I've always thought of as my father? Did he know?'

'He did, and it's true that I encouraged him to marry your mother because I knew that he loved her as much as I did and he was a good man. He loved you like a son, I know that.'

'You mean you paid him to marry my mother?'

'Money changed hands, but it was to ensure that you and your family had a good home and to pay for your education.'

'Enough of this.' Dressler lifted his hand for silence. 'I'm not interested in your recriminations or excuses. Herr Colivet, you utter tired old clichés that have been used as an excuse for a young man's irresponsible behaviour since time began. I find it very amusing, but boring. This hearing is at an end and you, Gerald Colivet, are under arrest. You may be the illegitimate son of Herr Colivet but you are still a British soldier and as such you should be in a prisoner of war camp. Major von Eschenberg, ensure that he is kept under lock and key until I can arrange for his deportation.'

Meg stood up, resting her hand on her father's shoulder. 'That's your idea of a fair trial, is it?'

Dressler glared at her, his eyes narrowed. 'I could have you all deported to camps in Germany and I'm still considering this action.'

Meg held her breath as Gerald was led away. He looked neither to left nor right but Nordhausen shot a look of triumph in her direction, as if to underline the fact that he had won. She dropped her gaze and waited her turn as the family shuffled out of the room. As they emerged into the hallway Charles was seized by a fit of coughing. Marie hooked his arm around her shoulders. 'You must rest,' she said gently. 'You should be in bed, Charles.'

Jane rushed forward and spat in Marie's face. 'Slut!'

Charles' eyes blazed with anger as he rounded on her. 'That's rich coming from you, Jane Colivet.'

She took a step backwards. 'I meant...'

'It seems like yesterday that you came to me weeping about your condition and the fiancé who abandoned you when he discovered that you were pregnant,' Charles said, eyeing her coldly.

She gasped and her hands flew to her face. 'That's cruel, uncle.'

'I've helped support you and your son for over twenty years. Don't you dare speak to Marie like that again, or judge us when you are just as culpable.'

'I was seduced, abandoned and betrayed.' Jane's voice broke on a sob. 'You carried on with a servant and still are as far as we know.'

'That's not true.' Marie faced her angrily. 'You'd best keep a civil tongue in your head when you speak to Charles. He's the kindest, sweetest man who ever lived and you're an ungrateful bitch.'

'Go and look after your son, Jane,' Charles said, lowering his voice. 'We've just lost ours. God knows what will happen to him now.'

Meg felt as though she were watching a dramatic scene in a play. Nothing was real and she seemed to have lost the power of speech and the ability to move as the shocking truth sank into her brain. She turned her head as Nordhausen strode into the hall through the open front door.

'That's the last you will see of your dear brother, Fräulein Meg. What a pity.'

Suddenly she knew exactly what she had to do. She pushed past him and burst into the drawing room. 'Hauptmann Dressler, I wish to make a formal complaint against Captain Nordhausen.'

Despite Meg's angry outpourings to Dressler and von Eschenberg, Nordhausen was not sent away as she had so recklessly demanded, but he was detailed off to duties that took him away from the manor all day. He chose to ignore her if their paths happened to cross and she could only surmise that he had been warned to stay away from her. Nevertheless, his continued presence made her feel uncomfortable.

After the shocking revelation by Charles and the admission of his illicit affair with Marie, a cloud seemed to envelop the whole family. Charles took to his bed, and Marie devoted every spare moment to caring for him. When she was not in the sick room she went about her work silently, pale and wraithlike, refusing to talk about the grief and shame that were obviously gnawing away inside her.

Meg could not bring herself to go and see her father. She tried in vain to convince herself that he was still the same person she had always adored and hero-worshipped, but she struggled to equate her vision of him with that of the unfaithful husband who had lived a lie for so long. She wondered if he realised the extent of the distress that his duplicity had caused her and Gerald, and for once her sympathies were with her mother. They had never achieved a loving mother-daughter relationship, but now she could understand the reason for her mother's attitude to Marie. Meg wondered how she had managed to live with her husband's past infidelity all these years, let alone having his onetime mistress there as a daily reminder of their affair. So many things fell into place. It explained why Gerald had never been welcomed into the house by her mother, and her father's stubborn championing of him. Meg's opinion of her mother had changed to one of admiration and awe.

Added to all this Meg was worried about what would happen to Gerald. Now that she understood their relationship she realised that what she had felt for him all along was sisterly affection. Her cheeks burned with shame as she recalled the ardour of his kisses that had been anything but brotherly, but eventually common sense forced her to push guilt to the back of her mind. Their blood relationship had been kept from them deliberately; what had happened afterwards was not their fault and Gerald was paying a high price for his love of the Colivets. Meg knew she had to do something to save him, but what? That was the question that tormented her day and night.

CHAPTER FIFTEEN

'How absolutely appalling!' Pearl's eyes widened in horror. 'And you mean to say you were in love with your own brother?'

'Half-brother.' Meg pushed her cup of ersatz coffee away from her in disgust. 'And I wasn't in love with him; it was the other way round.'

'Poor you. Poor Gerald.'

'That's just it, Pearl. Poor Gerald. He's been taken off God knows where by the Feldpolizei. Pa and Marie are going out of their minds with worry and so am I.'

Pearl stirred her coffee thoughtfully. 'How do you feel about your father and Marie?'

'At first I was furious, and hurt too. I couldn't bear to go and see him even though I knew he was ill.'

'And now?'

Meg shrugged her shoulders and stared out of the window at the rain-drenched street. The air in the café was thick with cigarette smoke, although it was only the higher-ranking German officers who seemed to be able to get hold of the commodity long denied to the islanders. 'I used to think that Pa was wonderful,' she said after a moment's pause. 'To me he was a sort of demigod who never did wrong, and I thought that everything he said was bound to be true. Now I know that he's human like the rest of us, and he's making his illness worse by fretting about Gerald. Pearl, I've got to do something. I can't go on day after day without knowing what's happened to him.'

'Have you told Simone?'

'No. To tell the truth I'd forgotten all about her.'

'I can understand that, but don't you think you ought to go and see her?'

Meg smiled reluctantly. 'You're right, of course. I suppose I just didn't know how to break it to her. She's always been so against us, and now she's got a real reason to hate the Colivets.'

Meg hesitated outside the hospital. She had not seen Simone since she walked out of the house and she did not particularly want to see her now, but Pearl had been correct in saying that Simone had the right to be told everything. Bracing her shoulders she entered the building. The smell of strong disinfectant brought back painful memories of Eric's sudden collapse, and the anxious hours spent in the waiting room before they were given the sad news. She was tempted to leave now, but she forced herself to walk up to the desk. The receptionist was a middle-aged woman with a mouth like a steel trap, who was obviously well acquainted with Simone. Disapproval was written all over her sharp features as she told Meg to take a seat. After what seemed like an eternity, Simone finally appeared. She did not look pleased. 'What do you want? I'm on duty.'

'I need to talk to you.' Meg rose to her feet. 'In private.'

'It had better be important.' Simone led the way along a corridor, coming to a halt outside a door marked *Sluice*. A few feet away a ward maid was languidly mopping the floor. 'Okay, say what you've got to say and then leave.'

Meg glanced at the cleaner. 'This isn't something you'd want anyone else to hear.'

Simone opened the door to the sluice. 'Is this private enough for you? Now get on with it.'

Meg wrinkled her nose in distaste at the mingled smells of carbolic, antiseptic and human excreta that assailed her nostrils as she entered the room. The slender thread of sympathy that bound her to Simone snapped and her patience with it. 'All right. You want the truth, then here it is.' In short succinct sentences she told Simone exactly what had happened on the fatal evening when Gerald had attacked Nordhausen, but she was shocked by Simone's impassive reaction to the fact that Gerald was only her half-brother. Slowly, the truth dawned on her. 'You knew, didn't you?'

Simone gave a curt nod. 'I've known for years. Why do you think I hated the Colivets so much? Once, when I was just a kid, Mum and Dad were having a row. I heard my dad call Mum all sorts of names, accusing her of staying on at the manor house because she was still in love with the boss. Dad was a mild man normally but that time he really let fly, calling Gerald the Colivet bastard. It was then that I understood why my brother had always been treated differently. He had the best of everything. He went to a posh private school in England. He always had new clothes and shoes and I had my cousin's hand-me-downs.'

'I'm so sorry.' Meg was shocked beyond belief. 'But it wasn't Gerald's fault.'

'I know that.'

'The Feldpolizei have taken him away, Simone. I must find out what's happened to him. Can you help?'

'Why do you think I should know any more than you do?'

'Because you're friendly with the Germans and because you must hear a lot of talk in the hospital.'

'How do I know that I can trust you?'

'Why would I want to hurt you, Simone? Gerald is our brother. Surely that gives us something in common?'

Simone eyed her warily. 'I don't know where he is,' she said slowly. 'But I do know the name of one of his contacts.'

'You mean the saboteurs?'

Simone's black brows snapped together. 'Keep your voice down, you fool.'

'Just tell me.'

'And you would risk your life to help Gerald?'

'Yes. Wouldn't you?'

'Maybe. But on the other hand probably not.' Simone pulled a pencil from her apron pocket. Tearing the corner off a paper towel, she scribbled something down and handed the scrap of paper to Meg. 'Destroy this when you've memorised the name and the place. They meet tonight after curfew.'

'I'll be there.'

'You know what will happen to you if you're caught?'

Meg nodded.

'I still think you're a fool, but good luck anyway.'

There was no moon that night, and the air was hot and humid as Meg slipped quietly out of the house. Dressler was so confident of the superior strength of the German force and the subservience of the islanders that he no longer posted guards at the front door, although a sentry still watched over the main gates. In the long hours spent waiting for Gerald to return from his secret missions, Meg had seen the guard cutting across the grass as he headed off in the direction of the stables. Whatever his reason for deserting his post, it had left the gate unmanned for at least ten minutes, and tonight was no exception.

The velvety blackness was stifling and, until her eyes became accustomed to the darkness, she could see almost nothing. She darted towards the safety of the trees, following the exact path that she had seen Gerald taking on one of his night missions. She stumbled over an exposed tree root and almost fell, suppressing a cry of pain as she twisted her ankle. She leaned against the trunk rubbing the aching joint, her ears pricked for the slightest sound. An owl screeched overhead and some unidentifiable small animal scuttled past her, rustling through the carpet of leaf mould. She clenched her teeth and moved on cautiously.

Once outside the grounds, Meg kept close to the shadow of the hedgerows. She reached the church gate and steadied herself on la Gran'mere. 'Wish me luck, *ma mère*,' she whispered, gently stroking the ancient stone head. The gravel path leading up to the church shone palely silver like a strip of satin ribbon. It appeared to wind on into infinity although it was only a matter of yards to the safety of the low door that led into the crypt. Meg had never been there before, and would not have gone there even in daylight but this was the place where she would meet Hugh Martel – unless Simone had led her into a trap. The thought had been at the back of her mind all along, but it was a chance she had to take.

She dodged between the headstones, avoiding the path as much as possible. Tapping three times on the door, she waited for five seconds and repeated the knocks. It opened like a mouth in a silent scream and Meg was unceremoniously yanked inside. The darkness was absolute for a few seconds until the door was closed and then someone lit a candle.

'Meg Colivet. What the hell are you doing here?' Hugh Martel's lean, weather-beaten face was so close to Meg's that she could feel his breath on her cheek.

'Simone told me you would help.'

Silently he guided her down a flight of stone steps to the buttock-clenching cold below the ground. Meg shivered convulsively, hugging her arms around her body in an attempt to keep warm. By candlelight, the vaulted crypt looked like the setting of a horror film. She half expected to see a vampire looming out of the shadows, but there were two ordinary-looking men sitting on upturned crates.

'Now sit down, and tell us why you came.' Taking her by the shoulders, Hugh gave her a gentle shove towards an upturned orange box.

The faces of the two other men were in shadow but Meg thought she recognised one as Tom de Gruchy, a farmer from Torteval. She cleared her throat and licked her dry lips. 'You must know that Gerald was taken by the Feldpolizei. I want to find him.'

Their laughter echoed eerily round the stone walls and was quickly subdued.

Hugh sat astride an empty wine keg. 'And if you knew, what good would it do you?'

'I'm afraid they will send him to a camp in Germany and we may never see him again.'

Tom de Gruchy leaned forward, his eyes searching Meg's face. 'And you think you could prevent that?'

'I might. If I knew where they are holding him at least I could try to get him out.'

'No chance.' Hugh shook his head. 'Too risky.'

'You mean you're afraid to help me?'

'You live with a house full of Germans. How do we know we can trust you?'

Meg faced Hugh with a defiant lift of her chin. 'You seem to trust Simone. She sleeps with the enemy.'

'Simone works with us and she has done from the first.'

Meg looked from one to the other and they each nodded in agreement.

'You can trust Meg.'

Meg recognised the voice of the second man instantly. 'Billy!'

He chuckled. 'Yes, it's me. Who would suspect old Billy?'

'I never did,' she said with feeling.

'We know that Gerald is still on the island,' Hugh said seriously. 'But to try to rescue him would be insanity.'

'For you maybe, but no one would suspect me, and even if they did they wouldn't connect me with you. Please tell me where he is.'

Hugh and Tom exchanged glances and Meg held her breath.

'We don't know, but we can find out,' Hugh said. 'After that you're on your own. We can't take the risk of being discovered, not with the Allies about to invade Normandy. We're needed to put a spoke in the works of the German war machine and make their rotten lives just a bit more unbearable until it's all over.'

'I understand. Just tell me what to do.'

'Go home now and act normally. Billy will pass a message on to you as soon as we have news.' Hugh stood up and held out his hand to Meg. 'Good luck.'

Next day Meg went straight to the largest greenhouse where Billy should have been working, but to her dismay he was not there. Joe met her in the doorway, hunched over and looking like an old man as he hefted two cans of water over to the tomato plants.

'Joe, have you seen Billy this morning?'

He shrugged his shoulders. 'No, Miss Meg.'

She was alarmed to see him looking so exhausted this early in the day, and so thin that his hands seemed too large for his skinny wrists. She hurried over to help him lift the cans. 'Do you know where he might be, Joe?'

'He should be here helping me, but I haven't seen him since yesterday tea time.'

Meg felt a cold iron hand grip at her heart as she feared the worst. She had left the men in the crypt and made her way home uneventfully, entering the house unseen. But supposing they had been discovered after she had left? The thought was too awful to contemplate. She helped Joe to water the plants, and leaving him munching his breakfast of a slice of dry bread she made her way to Billy's cottage on the edge of the estate. She knocked on the door and after a few moments it opened and

Billy's wife came out, wiping her hands on a scrap of cloth.

'Miss Meg. Sorry to keep you waiting, but I was doing the washing out the back.'

Meg forced a smile and tried to sound casual. 'Is Billy around?'

'No, miss, he's gone to the hospital. Cut his hand badly trying to chop up an old chair for firewood. I've never known him be so clumsy.'

'What a thing to happen.' Meg's mind whirled around the possibility of Billy having done it on purpose as an excuse to go into St Peter Port. She managed a sympathetic smile and backed away. 'Tell him I'm sorry and to come up to the house to see me when he feels up to it.'

That evening Meg was bringing the cows in when she heard someone calling her name. Looking over her shoulder she saw Billy hurrying across the field towards her.

'How is the hand?' Meg said, swishing a stick at a cow that had stopped to munch the grass.

'Worth a couple of stitches,' Billy said, grinning. 'I had to have an excuse to go into Peter Port.'

'Did you find out where he is?'

'He's in the prison with the rest of them that's going to be shipped off to France tomorrow. The ship is there in the harbour waiting to be loaded.'

'It could sail at any time; it might be too late to do anything.'

'Can't sail until the tide's right. That'll be six thirty tomorrow morning. They won't be going anywhere until then.'

Meg had just sunk into the deep sleep of sheer

exhaustion when a loud droning noise awakened her. She almost fell out of bed and threw up the sash window, sticking her head out into the cool, rose-scented air. Above her she could see strings of lights as planes flew overhead towing huge gliders. She listened to the throbbing of the engines with hope surging through her veins. When the Allies landed in France surely the war must come to an end soon and then they would be free? She cupped her chin on her hands and prayed for Rayner's safe delivery wherever he was.

She slept fitfully and woke up as the first light of dawn cracked the sky. There was no time to worry about the danger of breaking the curfew and Meg dressed hurriedly, slipping out of the house before the soldiers had begun to go about their daily routine. It was a strange and unnerving experience to walk the distance into St Peter Port in the cool morning light with the constant sound of aircraft engines droning overhead. By the time she reached the outskirts of the town people were coming out of their houses and looking skyward, their faces alight with hope for the first time in the long years of the occupation. Meg did not stop to chat. She knew exactly what she had to do and that was to wait outside the prison. What she would do if she saw Gerald she had no clear idea, but she had reasoned that there would be fewer guards than normal, as most of the soldiers would have been sent to man the fortifications. There was just a slim chance that she might be able to create a diversion, allowing Gerald to slip away from the other prisoners. She knew it was a feeble plan but it was worth a try.

The prison walls loomed dark and forbidding, vertical cliffs of impenetrable grey stone. Meg tried to make herself inconspicuous as she lolled against a tree trunk on the opposite side of the street. She glanced down at her faded cotton frock and skinny bare legs burned to a deep tan from long hours of working outdoors. Very few people seeing her now would recognise her as Marguerite Colivet of Colivet Manor, or even stop to wonder why she was loitering outside the prison gates at this ungodly hour of the morning. Her hand automatically flew to her hair. It felt like tow and the strands that blew across her face were bleached almost white by the sun. She had not been to a hairdresser for so long that she could barely remember what it felt like to be shampooed, set and pampered like a pet poodle. She grinned ruefully. What would Mother and Aunt Josie say if they could see her now?

The prison doors opened and Meg darted behind the tree. Her heart was pounding against her ribs as adrenalin coursed through her veins. She was ready for anything, although she did not have the slightest idea what lay before her.

But she realised that something was wrong, or at least things were not happening as she had thought they might. A German soldier came out first and stood back as a straggly line of prisoners trickled out through the gateway, shuffling, stumbling, blinking in the first rays of the morning sun and looking bewildered. The soldier became impatient and began to shove and push, shouting in rapid German. Meg's understanding of the language was fairly basic but it sounded as

289

if he was telling them to get on their way. She held her breath, biting her lip and digging her fingernails into the bark of the tree. Then, stifling a cry of relief, she saw him. 'Gerald.' She pushed her way through the crowd of confused men and seized him by the arm. He looked and smelled terrible. He had lost even more weight and obviously had not shaved for days. His clothes were crumpled and filthy and Meg suspected that he was running with fleas and probably lice too.

'Meg? What are you doing here?' He stared at her blankly with the dazed look of someone awakened suddenly from a deep sleep.

'Never mind that. I'm going to take you home.' She linked her arm through his and led him up the hill and away from the grim exterior of the prison. He swayed and almost fell at they reached St James's Church on the corner of College Street.

'I'm sorry,' Gerald said, wiping his eyes with the back of his hand. 'So stupid.'

'Don't worry; I'll soon have you home.'

He shook his head. 'It's no use, Meg. I wouldn't be able to make it that far.'

People were hurrying about their daily business and if they looked anywhere today it was upwards as the constant roar of aeroplane engines continued to fill the sky. What she needed now was some kind of transport or a safe place to leave Gerald until he was strong enough to walk home. The hospital was not far away but Meg abandoned that idea in case it put Simone in danger. There was only one place she could take him and she hoisted his arm around her shoulders.

'Come on, it's not too far to walk. We'll go to

the Tostevins' house on the Grange.'

Wrapped in her dressing gown with her hair set in snail-like curls fastened with kirby grips, Pearl stood in the open doorway, staring at them in amazement. 'My God! What's happened to you, Gerald?'

'Can we come in?'

'Of course,' Pearl said, stepping aside to let them into the house. She wrinkled her nose in disgust. 'What's that God-awful smell?'

'Don't ask,' Meg said, propping Gerald up against the wall. 'But it might be a good idea to stick him in the bath with some Lysol if you've got any.'

Pearl clutched her dressing gown to her throat, taking a step backwards. 'I'll get Hannah; she deals with that sort of thing. Better take him through to the kitchen and give him something to eat and drink.'

'There's no need to talk about me as if I wasn't here,' Gerald said, with a hint of his old humour. 'And I don't need you girls to bath me, thanks very much.'

Before Meg had a chance to reply, the kitchen door opened and a black shape hurled itself along the passage and skidded across the marble-tiled floor. Buster flung himself at her, jumping up and attempting to lick her face. It was impossible to remain serious with several stone of enthusiastic Labrador greeting her ecstatically and Meg laughed delightedly as she attempted to calm his exuberance. 'Good boy, good dog.'

Hannah appeared at the top of the stairs, her

291

long grey hair hanging in a plait and her spectacles balancing precariously on the tip of her nose. 'What's all this commotion?'

'Hannah, dear,' Pearl said, clasping her hands as if in prayer. 'We need your help.'

'I can see that.' Hannah came slowly down the stairs. She stopped in front of Gerald, looking him up and down. 'Yes, well I can see you're in a bit of a mess. Come with me, young man. You need a bath. Buster, you dratted dog – kitchen.'

Eyeing her warily, Buster turned and fled.

'He won't do that for me,' Pearl said, following him towards the kitchen. 'Come on, Meg. We'll have a cup of mint tea and you can tell me what's been going on.'

Leaving Gerald being ruthlessly ministered to by Hannah and Pearl, with Buster adding sympathetic licks and much tail wagging, Meg walked briskly home. She was too elated to feel tired but she was worried that Nordhausen might have noticed her absence. No doubt he would delight in bringing her before Dressler for ignoring the curfew. But as she approached the main gates of Colivet Manor she was surprised to see that there was no sentry. As she walked up the sweep of gravel drive the unusual silence was a sign that the soldiers were out on duty to a man. Even more surprising, she could see Pa, Uncle Bertie and Aunt Maud sitting in deck chairs on the terrace like holidaymakers on the beach. As she drew nearer she realised that they were watching the planes that continued to fly towards France.

Charles saw her first and waved. 'Isn't it a bit

292

early for a walk, Meg?'

She felt a hysterical laugh bubbling up inside her. She quelled it with a long draught of water from the carafe placed on a small camp table.

'You should have worn a sunhat, Meg,' Maud said, squinting at her. 'Your hair looks like straw. What would Muriel say if she could see you now?'

This time Meg did laugh, and seeing their astonished faces made it even harder to stop. She sank down on the warm stone step to sit beside her father.

'Are you all right, Meg?'

'Yes, Pa. I'm fine.'

'You were out before curfew. Marie told me so.'

'I know but it was worth it.' Meg clasped his hand in hers. 'Pa, I've got some good news for you.'

Even though the Germans had thrown the prisoners out on the streets, Charles thought that it would be too dangerous for Gerald to return to Colivet Manor just yet, and Meg had to agree. She had gradually come to terms with her father's youthful indiscretion. When he had tried to explain that his feelings for Marie had changed and matured over the years and that they in no way diminished his love for his wife, Meg was able to listen with a degree of empathy. Her complicated relationship with Gerald and her abiding love for Rayner made it easier for her to understand her father's predicament. It was possible to love two people equally, but differently. She felt pity for all three persons involved in the emotional triangle. In some ways she thought that the bonds between her father and Marie should have been severed years ago, but they had their son to consider and for good or ill Marie had taken the decision to stay on and work for the Colivets. Meg could only imagine how difficult this must have been for her, and she was filled with admiration for Eric, whose patience and devotion to his wife had enabled him to live with a situation that might have driven lesser men to madness. With all this knowledge came understanding and respect for her mother, whose undoubted strength of character had kept her family together.

The events of the past few years had changed them all, and Meg knew she had grown up. She was no longer a carefree girl. She was a young woman who had known hardship, loss and sorrow. She might never see Rayner again, but she knew in her heart that she would never love anyone else. The future stretched ahead of her, lonely and childless. She would face it somehow and she must get on with life as best she could. Her first task would be to pay another visit to Simone at the hospital and pass on the good news about Gerald.

'I'm glad,' Simone said, when Meg told her that Gerald was safe and well.

Meg had not expected Simone to leap about with joy but she might have tried to look happy. As it was she was frowning and kept glancing at the nurse's watch pinned to her breast pocket. 'Yes, well, I thought you'd want to know.' She was about to walk away when Simone caught hold of her sleeve. 'What is it, Simone?'

'I wasn't going to tell you, because I wanted you

to suffer as I did when Dieter finished with me.'

'Tell me what?'

'You thought I was a cold, unfeeling cow, I know you did, but I wasn't. I loved Dieter even though I knew all along that he was simply out for a good time. Pathetic, isn't it?'

'No,' Meg said, slowly. 'Not at all. Love is like that sometimes.'

'It was for me anyway. The bastard couldn't get away fast enough when he knew I was pregnant. If you hadn't taken me in I doubt if I'd be here today. I hate to think what might have happened to me because I simply didn't care, but your kindness made me even more resentful of the Colivets.'

Meg laid a hand on her shoulder. 'You don't have to say all this. It doesn't matter now.'

'It matters to me and that's why I've got to tell you something because I know you love him.'

Meg's heart missed a beat. 'What are you saying?'

'Your German. He's here in the hospital.'

'No. That's impossible. You must be mistaken. He was sent away from the island. Pearl saw him board the troop ship.'

'It was sunk by the RAF. The survivors were picked up by a German warship and brought back here. He was badly hurt and they didn't think he would live.'

'Oh my God,' Meg hardly dare frame the question. 'But he's all right now? He is, isn't he? Don't look at me like that, Simone. Tell me the truth.'

CHAPTER SIXTEEN

He was asleep. Meg stood looking down at his pale face, the skin drawn taut across his high cheekbones and thick crescents of corn gold eyelashes resting on bruised shadows beneath his closed eyes. The painful intensity of her relief almost suffocated her; she wanted to laugh and shout for joy, but at the same moment the urge to cry was almost overpowering. As if he sensed her presence Rayner's eyelids fluttered and opened. 'I knew you'd come.'

She held his hand. 'I didn't know you were here or I would have come sooner.'

'You're here now. I've dreamt of this moment.'

'You must go,' Simone said in a low voice, glancing nervously over her shoulder. 'If Matron catches you here there will be trouble.'

'Just a few moments longer.'

Simone shook her head emphatically. 'No. I've done my bit and now you must leave.'

'I'll be back soon,' Meg promised, bending down to kiss Rayner on the lips. 'Very soon, my darling.' Outside the ward, she turned on Simone. 'Why couldn't you have let me stay just a bit longer?'

Simone jerked her head in the direction of the matron steaming down the corridor at the head of a ward round. 'Keep walking and don't say anything.'

When they were out of earshot, Meg caught

Simone by the arm. 'Now then, tell me everything. Why is he here instead of the military hospital and what exactly is wrong with him?'

'There were so many casualties, the underground hospital was full and in the beginning the doctors didn't think he would survive his injuries.'

'You could have let me know that he was alive.'

'I've got to get back to the ward.' Simone quickened her pace.

Meg matched her step for step. 'What exactly were his injuries?'

'He had a broken leg and ribs, a punctured lung and pneumonia. He was in the water for hours before they picked up the survivors. Your German was lucky.' Simone came to a sudden halt outside the women's surgical ward. 'I'll be in trouble if I stay a minute longer.'

'Is he allowed visitors? I must see him again.'

'It's a closed ward. No visitors for the Germans, and I can't smuggle you in again.'

Simone slipped noiselessly into the ward, closing the door behind her.

That night, the sixth of June, they listened to the BBC newscaster informing them that the Allies had landed in France. Pip let out a whoop of joy that made everyone round on him angrily for fear that Nordhausen might be snooping about outside the morning parlour, but to their surprise and relief nothing happened.

'At last,' Charles said with a break in his voice. 'The war must be coming to an end soon.'

But as the days went by their optimism began to waver. The fighting, which had always seemed so very far away, suddenly came frighteningly close. The once quiet skies screamed with the engines of RAF bombers flying mission after mission to target St Malo. From the vantage point of her bedroom window Meg could see distant plumes of smoke. She could hear the muffled sounds of gunfire and feel the vibrations of the bombs falling. It was a tense time and the Germans appeared to be ill at ease.

Meg said nothing at home but secretly planned her next visit to town when she intended to do whatever it took in order to see Rayner again. As soon as the opportunity arose, she set off early and, having reached the hospital, she walked purposefully through the corridors as if she had every right to be there. She followed a ward maid carrying a mop and bucket and waited and watched as the woman deposited her cleaning tools and her overalls in a room little bigger than a cupboard. When she left, dressed in her faded cotton blouse and patched skirt, Meg slipped inside and put on the discarded cap and apron, tucking her long hair out of sight. She picked up a basket of dusters and cleaning cloths and marched boldly to the ward where she had last seen Rayner.

She could have cried with relief when she saw him. Her fears that he might have been moved were proved groundless. He turned his head as she entered the ward and she knew that he had recognised her, but she bowed her head and made a pretence of dusting the bedside locker of the patient nearest the door. Thankfully he lay sleeping, looking more like a schoolboy than an enemy soldier, and Meg flashed her duster around praying that he would not wake up. She moved on swiftly. There were just two beds separating them now. The soldier in the first bed grumbled at her for disturbing him, and the man in the next bed looked too ill to care what was going on around him. She moved casually to Rayner's bedside, flapping the piece of cloth ineffectively over the locker.

'You crazy girl,' Rayner whispered. 'You shouldn't be here.'

'I had to see you again.' Meg abandoned the duster and pretended to fuss with the sheets so that she could move closer. She closed her eyes and breathed in the achingly familiar scent of him. 'You're looking better.'

'Seeing you is the best medicine. But you must not come again, sweetheart. It's too dangerous.'

She brushed his hair back from his forehead. It had grown during his illness and the natural wave softened the chiselled outline of his face, giving him the look of a poet rather than a soldier. She smiled. 'You can't get rid of me that easily.'

At that moment the ward door opened and a staff nurse bustled into the room. She stopped at the first bed to examine the patient's temperature chart.

'Go,' Rayner said, squeezing Meg's hand. 'Go now.'

Picking up the basket of cleaning materials, she glanced over her shoulder to make certain that the nurse was still occupied with her patients, and blowing a kiss to Rayner she hurried from the ward. It was surprisingly easy to replace the overall, cap and basket in the maids' room and to stroll casually out of the hospital. Once outside

299

she found that she was trembling from head to foot, but she had done it; she had seen him and she would do it again. She had to force her legs to move, one step at a time until she was walking briskly, heading homeward.

After that day, Meg went to the hospital at least twice a week. She had only a matter of minutes with Rayner on each hazardous visit, but it was worth the risk just to see him, to speak to him and occasionally to touch his hand or on one occasion, when the nurse had left the curtains drawn around the bed, to snatch a kiss that was so full of longing that it physically hurt. She had the satisfaction of seeing his condition improve almost miraculously, so that after a few weeks he looked very much like his old self. She was almost caught out on several occasions when surprised by an early ward round or given a direct order by one of the nurses who took her for a genuine ward maid, but luck seemed to be always on her side. She existed only for her visits to the hospital. Afterwards, if there was time, she called in at the house on the Grange to see Pearl and Gerald, who had now recovered completely and was becoming bored, restless and grumpy.

'You'll have to speak to him, darling,' Pearl said, taking Meg aside. 'He's talking about coming back to the manor or trying to get to France so that he can join the British Army. I can't reason with him.'

'I don't suppose he'll listen to me,' Meg said, fondling Buster's silky ears.

'I'm afraid he'll do something rash. You must try.'

'Where is he now?'

'In the garden. He works out there all the day-light hours. He says it gives him something to do.'

'I'll try,' Meg said doubtfully. 'Come on, Buster, let's go and find him.'

Gerald was at the bottom of the Tostevins' large garden, hoeing weeds in between rows of straggly-looking cabbages and yellowing turnip tops. He looked up as Meg approached and grinned. 'Meg, it's good to see you.'

She eyed him speculatively. 'You look well, Gerald.'

'I am, but I'm dying from boredom stuck here in town. I wanted to come back home but Mr Tostevin thinks that Dressler would have me locked up again.'

Meg plucked a stray dandelion clock and twirled it between her fingers, watching the downy seeds float up into the still summer air. 'He's right. And Nordhausen is still around. He doesn't bother me too much but I hate to think how he would be if you turned up again.'

Gerald threw the hoe down onto the sun-baked soil, wiping his hands on the seat of his trousers. 'Then I'll have to think of something else.'

'You won't do anything silly?'

'Pearl told you?'

'Yes, and you mustn't even think of it. If the Germans don't get you the sea almost certainly will.'

'I can't stay on the island any longer. You know perfectly well why.'

'You didn't know we were brother and sister.'

'Feelings don't change overnight, Meg. At least when I was helping the saboteurs I was doing my

301

bit to fight the enemy. I must try to get back to my regiment if I can.'

'Is there nothing I can say that will stop you?'

'I know you've been seeing him again. Pearl told me.'

'I love him and I always have. But I love you too, just as I love David.'

'I don't want you to love me like a brother,' Gerald said, bitterly, shoving his hands deep into his pockets. 'That's why I must leave the island, whatever the risk.'

'How will you go?'

'Simone has arranged a meeting with Hugh and Tom. I'll know then.'

Meg bit her lip; she knew there was no dissuading Gerald. He had the mutinous, stubborn look in his eyes that she had seen so often in Simone's expression. 'I still think you're mad, but good luck anyway.' She held out her hand but he turned away.

'Goodbye, Meg.'

'Don't leave like this. Can't we at least be friends?'

'Not while you're with him.' Gerald hunched his shoulders and kicked a clod of earth so that it burst into a cloud of dust. He walked off in the direction of the house.

Summer storms prevented Meg from going to the hospital for a few days and she worked in the greenhouses picking and packing tomatoes, none of which would get to market but would all go to feed the desperately hungry German Army. When she was certain she was not being observed, she hid a few of the smaller or misshapen tomatoes in a hole dug just outside the greenhouse; later she would smuggle them into the house. Food was even scarcer now that the sea links with France had been cut and the whole island, including the Germans, was on the brink of starvation. Meg had heard horrific stories about pets being stolen and killed for food and she was glad that Buster was safe in the town house, never allowed out except in the garden and then only when Pearl or Gerald was there to watch him. Being separated from Rayner, even for a few days, left a gaping hole in her heart, but she comforted herself with the fact that he was safe in his hospital bed. She would go and see him as soon as the last tomato was picked, regardless of the weather.

News filtered through that the German garrison at St Malo had been captured by the Allied troops and the family celebrated quietly. The German officers were even more edgy these days and easily irritated. No one wanted to get on the wrong side of Nordhausen or von Eschenberg.

Meg set off for the hospital unchallenged. There were no sentries on the gate and no need for a permit to leave the grounds, but the starvation diet had sapped her energy and walking any distance took a great deal of effort. She found she tired easily, having to stop every so often and sit down to rest. She was late arriving, and having changed into the maid's uniform, she hurried to the ward but to her horror she found it empty and the beds stripped down to bare mattresses. For a moment, she stood dazed and uncomprehending. Only a few days ago this place had been a hive of activity with nurses attending the sick and injured.

'What are you doing here?'

She spun round to face a stern-looking ward sister with a faint shadow of a moustache on her long upper lip. 'This ward is closed.'

'Sorry, sister. My mistake.' Meg ducked her head and sidled past the irate nurse.

'I'll report this to your supervisor.'

Panicked and desperate to find Rayner, Meg broke into a run. More by luck than judgement she found Simone in a tiny ward kitchen making hot drinks for the patients.

'What are you doing here?' Simone demanded angrily. 'And why are you dressed like a ward maid? What have you done, you silly cow?'

Meg wrenched the mobcap off her head, allowing her hair to fall loose around her shoulders. 'He's gone. They've all gone,' she said breathlessly. 'Where have they taken Rayner?'

'There was a suspected case of typhoid. They've taken the lot of them back to the underground hospital.'

The white walls spun in dizzying circles and Meg grasped the edge of the table in an attempt to steady herself.

'Don't you dare pass out on me,' Simone hissed in her ear. She thrust the mug of hot milk into her hands. 'Here, drink this. Then you'd better get going, and keep away from here in future.'

The milk slid down Meg's throat. She could feel it warming her empty stomach and almost miraculously she began to feel better. 'Thanks. But I don't want to get you into trouble.'

'Never mind the apologies, just go.'

'I will, but first tell me if there's any way I can get a message to Rayner.'

Simone snorted with laughter. 'D'you think I'm a bloody miracle worker?'

'You have your contacts.'

'I can't help you.'

Meg put the mug down on the table. 'Then I'll just have to do something myself.'

'If you're caught hanging around the underground hospital you'll bring the Feldpolizei down on the lot of us.'

'I don't understand.'

'They'll make you talk. You won't be able to help yourself but they'll drag it from you.'

'What? I don't know anything.'

'You know about Gerald and his friends. That's enough.' Simone cocked her head on one side, holding her finger to her lips. 'Someone's coming,' she whispered. 'Get out of here now before they start asking questions.'

This was not the time to argue. Meg shot out of the kitchen, ignoring the outraged protests of the orderly who was about to enter the room and whose toe she trod on in her haste. She ran towards main reception, tearing off the overall and dropping it on the floor. Even when she was safely outside the hospital she kept running until she reached the Tostevins' house, collapsing over the threshold as Hannah opened the door.

The pungent odour of sal volatile brought her gasping to her senses.

'Take it easy, Meg.' Pearl's voice and face floated somewhere above her head.

Meg struggled to sit up but was thrust back into the chair. 'I must see Gerald.'

'Drink this.' Pearl pressed a glass of water into Meg's hands and helped her raise it to her lips. 'Take your time and then tell me what happened.'

Meg swallowed a mouthful of water and choked. 'They've taken Rayner to the underground hospital.'

'He'll be safe there.'

'I must speak to Gerald.'

'You can't. He's gone.'

'What do you mean?'

'Don't get upset again.' Pearl took the glass from Meg's nerveless hand and put it on the kitchen table. 'He's safe with his friends. They're going to help him.'

'Tell me everything,' Meg said urgently. 'I'm not leaving here until you do.'

'You shouldn't have made me bring you here, miss.' Billy's voice was muffled by the thick white fog that enveloped them both as they clambered down the steep wooden steps leading to the cove below. Meg could hear the soft sucking sound of the waves on the beach and breakers further out to sea as the swell encountered the jagged rocks. The cold salt air filled her lungs as she clung to the railings. She almost missed her footing on the slippery surface, and as she made a grab for anything that would save her from falling, her fingers tore at the rock face, breaking her nails and making her bite her lip to stop herself from crying out in pain. Catching hold of a slippery clump of thrift, she clung on desperately, and with a supreme effort she managed to conquer her nerves. Moving cautiously she found a foothold, and went down, down into the swirling, choking blanket of fog. By the time she reached the sandy cove her knees had turned to jelly.

'You all right?' Billy's large hand gripped her shoulder.

'Yes, yes. I'm fine but I can't see anything. Are they here?'

'Shh.' Billy clamped his hand over her mouth. 'Sound carries on a night like this. Stay here. I'll be back in a minute.'

Suddenly she was alone as Billy disappeared into the soup of fog and darkness. She could hear his feet squelching on the wet sand and then nothing but the rhythmic motion of the waves. Meg shivered as the dampness chilled her bones. It had been blisteringly hot for the last few days, punctuated with fierce thunderstorms followed by a sudden calm that had brought the fog sweeping across the island. Perfect conditions if an escape were to be made. Something rustled nearby and instinctively she moved forward, crashing into a warm human body. Her cry of alarm was instantly muffled by a man's hand.

'Meg, what the hell do you think you're doing here?'

Gerald's voice close to her ear made her want to cry with sheer relief. 'Thank God it's you.'

He wrapped his arms around her shivering body. 'You must go at once. Billy shouldn't have let you come.'

'He couldn't stop me. I had to come to try to make you see sense. You mustn't do this.'

307

'I can't stay. It's better this way.'

'You'll be killed.'

Gerald's arms held her like a vice. Meg could not see his face clearly but she felt his breath warmly caressing her cheek. His damp clothes smelt faintly of woodsmoke and pine and she could feel his heart beating beneath the coarse wool of his guernsey.

'If I die in the attempt it's better than living on here without you,' he said, tracing the contour of her face with his finger.

'It doesn't have to be like this.'

'I love you, Meg. I don't feel like your brother and I won't stand by and watch you give yourself to someone else, especially when he's the bloody enemy. It would be a slow death.'

'But think about your mother and Simone and our father, who loves you deeply, I understand that now. Think of them.'

'I am thinking of them. This is the best way out for all of us.'

'It's time. Come on.' Hugh's voice cut through the darkness.

Gerald released her, backing away. 'Goodbye, Meg.'

'Please don't go.' She ran after him, stumbling over small rocks and splashing through deep pools of ice-cold seawater, but just as she reached the water's edge strong arms held her back.

'Please be quiet, miss. You've got to let him do this.'

Leaning her head against Billy's shoulder, Meg struggled with guilt and grief. Gerald was leaving because of her and she was helpless to prevent him going to almost certain death. She could just make out the shape of the boat as it was launched into the waves, and it was frighteningly small.

She raised her hand in a feeble attempt to wave but the vessel was swallowed up by the fog and all she could hear was the gentle slicing of the oars as they cut through the waves.

'We've done all we can,' Billy said, hooking his sinewy arm around her shoulders. 'Best get away from here before the fog lifts.'

'Do you think they'll make it?'

'God willing, and only if the wind doesn't change.'

She was numb with cold and a deep sense of loss and foreboding as she allowed Billy to lead her back up the beach. At the bottom of the steps she turned for one last look, but suddenly the mouth of the cove was clearly visible and even more disturbingly she could see the outline of the small craft. She gripped Billy's arm. 'I can see the boat. The fog is lifting.'

'By God, so it is, but only from ground level. I don't think the lookouts could see them from the cliff tops.'

'Better pray that they can't,' Meg said, placing one foot on the first step. 'Please God, please don't let it clear until they're out to sea.'

Climbing upwards was much harder than climbing down and they had to stop frequently. Meg's legs trembled and her muscles screamed in pain as she forced herself to continue her ascent, glancing over her shoulder every now and then to peer anxiously out to sea.

'Go on,' Billy urged from below. 'Don't stop.'

They were about halfway up the cliff when the first shot rang out. Meg clung to the hand rail, praying for their deliverance. A volley of shots echoed round the cove, ricocheting off the cliffs. It seemed to Meg that all hell had been let loose. The air was thick with the smell of cordite.

'Go on. Go on.' Billy was on the step below, pushing her upwards.

Meg fell onto the grass at the top of the cliff, gasping for breath. She found herself staring at a pair of booted feet and the muzzle of a rifle was poked in her face with the abrupt command in German to put her hands up. Billy was seized by rough hands and dragged across the ground.

'Stop that,' Meg cried, struggling to her feet. 'Leave him alone. Can't you see he's an old man?'

The German soldier dug the rifle into her ribs. 'Silence. You don't speak.'

At this moment Meg didn't care if the whole German 319 Infantry Division was surrounding her. Her only concern was for Gerald, Hugh and Tom in their bid to escape from the island. In the time it had taken for them to climb the steps, the fog had lifted completely and a warm westerly breeze had parted the clouds, allowing a pale yellow moon to light up the scene. She made a move towards the edge of the cliff, desperate to catch a glimpse of the boat, but she was dragged backwards and her hands bound behind her with a length of rope. She looked helplessly across at Billy but he shook his head. They were forced to walk at gunpoint along the narrow cliff path, torn at by brambles and stumbling over stones, until

310

they came to the gun emplacement.

'Inside.'

Billy was thrown in head first and Meg tumbled in after him. It was dark and the air was stale with the rank smell of human sweat and gun oil, but the soldiers withdrew, leaving them on their own. Meg could hear their booted feet stamping up and down on the concrete as they kept watch outside.

Billy was coughing and his breathing was laboured.

'Are you all right, Billy?' Meg's eyes gradually became accustomed to the dark and she could see him doubled over and retching miserably.

'Winded, that's all.'

'I hope they got away.' She struggled to a sitting position and leaned against the cold, damp wall.

'Yeah, me too.'

They lapsed into silence, broken only by Billy's occasional cough and the sound of the sea crashing on the rocks a couple of hundred feet below. It was cold and dank and there was no way of escape. Meg did not much care what the Germans did to her at this moment; all her thoughts were with Gerald and the men who had been with him. Brave and gallant but misguided. If only he had listened to reason and stayed on the island. Guilt battled with grief. He was her brother and her friend and he had risked his life because of a situation that was not of their making. She choked on a suppressed sob.

'They did what they had to,' Billy said, almost as though he had read her thoughts. 'They were young and wanted to fight.'

'You talk as though they're dead.'

311

'Don't think they stood much of a chance, miss.'

Meg closed her eyes, and when she opened them again she realised that she must have fallen into the deep sleep of physical and mental exhaustion. Her head ached and the ropes cut into her wrists. Cramps shot through her arms and legs and the damp seemed to have permeated her whole body. A faint grey light shone through the slits in the concrete, and although she had lost all sense of time she realised that it must be daybreak. She glanced anxiously at Billy who was slumped on one side, his stertorous breathing the only sign that he was still alive.

A sudden burst of activity outside banished the last hazy remnants of sleep. A vehicle pulled up outside with the squeal of brakes, followed by the sound of brisk footsteps and curt orders given in German. Bolts were drawn back, the steel door screamed on its hinges and a man wearing the uniform of a high-ranking German officer stepped into the confined space, filling it with his presence. Sunlight flooded in behind him leaving his face in shadow.

CHAPTER SEVENTEEN

For a moment Meg clung to him, barely able to believe that this was not part of her dream, and then reality hit her like a slap across her cheek. The hows and whys of his being there were insignificant details. The wonderful truth was that he was here now, holding her so tightly that she could hardly breathe. The terrors of the last few hours were banished to the realms of a nightmare. 'Rayner.'

'Are you hurt, Meg?' His voice was deep with concern.

'I'm all right.' Safe in the circle of his arms, she leaned her head against his shoulder, giving herself up to the luxury of being held by the man she loved, but she knew in her heart that the danger was far from over. She forced herself to remain calm and objective. 'Please take a look at Billy. I'm really worried about him.'

'Of course.' Rayner set her back on her feet and with a deft movement untied the ropes that had cut into her wrists leaving them sore and chafed. He went to kneel beside Billy, raising him to a sitting position. 'It's all right, Meg. He's not injured, as far as I can see.'

Billy opened his eyes. 'It's you, Captain.'

Rayner helped him to stand and freed him from his bonds. 'We must get you both to safety. Don't say anything. Just follow me.'

He was about to open the door but Meg caught him by the arm. The question that she hardly dare ask tumbled from her dry lips. 'What happened to Gerald? Did he get away?'

He hesitated for a moment and then he shook his head slowly. 'It was a gallant attempt but they didn't stand a chance.'

'The fog must have protected them.'

'It had lifted.'

'Bugger!' Billy muttered. 'Begging your pardon, Miss Meg.'

'It could be a mistake? They were a long way from the guns.' Meg's eyes searched Rayner's face for an answer, but even as she spoke she knew that what he had said was the truth. She bent her head to hide the tears that flowed unchecked down her cheeks. 'Poor Gerald.'

'He knew the risks. He was a brave man.' Rayner's voice cut crisply through her misery. If he felt regret, he was not allowing it to show. 'You are more important now. I've got to get you two away from here. Keep calm, follow me and don't say a word.'

Meg gulped and wiped her eyes on her sleeve, hooking her arm around Billy's shoulders. She could feel him shaking and his weathered face had crumpled into a contour map of lines. She must be strong for both of them. 'We're ready. Open the door.'

Stepping outside into the pale early morning sunlight, Rayner strode off, motioning them to follow him. The soldiers snapped to attention as he passed, and suddenly he was just another German officer. Loving him as she did, Meg had managed to push their different loyalties to the back of her mind, but now they were painfully clear. Returning the salutes of his men, Rayner walked towards a parked staff car. The driver saluted smartly and opened the door, standing stiffly to attention. Ignoring Meg and Billy, Rayner slipped into the front seat leaving them to scramble into the back as the driver leapt in and started the engine. As the car sped through the narrow lanes Meg was beginning to feel anxious. 'Where are you taking us?'

'You'll find out soon enough. You are both

under arrest.' Rayner's curt reply startled her even though common sense told her that he was acting out a part. Within minutes they were driving through the gates of Colivet Manor and Meg suppressed a sigh of relief.

'Hauptmann Dressler will deal with you both,' Rayner said, as Meg and Billy climbed stiffly out of the staff car. He turned to the driver with a curt command in German.

'*Danke*, Herr Major.' The driver marched off towards the stable block at the back of the house.

With a ghost of his old familiar smile, Rayner turned to Meg. 'The promise of breakfast does wonders for morale.'

She stared at him, her tired mind struggling to come to terms with everything that had happened in the last few hours. 'You've been promoted to major?'

'It's just a title. It doesn't mean anything.'

Billy coughed and shuffled his feet. 'Can I go now?'

'Yes, and you should rest,' Rayner said, shaking Billy by the hand. 'Last night's activities won't be mentioned. I'll see to that.'

'Thanks,' Billy said gruffly and, with a weak attempt at a grin, he loped off towards his cottage.

'Poor Billy. He'd been Eric's friend for years and he was fond of Gerald. Now he's lost them both.'

'I understand. I'm truly sorry.'

He sounded sincere but Meg could not help feeling that to him Gerald's death was just one of the misfortunes of war. He was eyeing her warily, his expression carefully controlled. Tense, nervous and exhausted, Meg felt an irrational wave of

315

anger wash over her. How dare he walk back into her life after disappearing from the hospital ward and not even attempting to get word to her? She thought of the anxious days and sleepless nights that she had spent worrying about him, and now he stood there calmly flaunting the rank of major. It had not taken him long to resume his position in the enemy ranks, and she, like a fool, had been overjoyed to see him. 'You're not sorry at all,' she said slowly. 'You hated Gerald.'

'That's not true. Of course I'm sorry that a brave man died. If I had any reservations about Gerald it was because he was putting you all in danger by being here and pretending that he was your brother.'

'He was my brother, or rather my half-brother, although we didn't know it until recently. Now I've got to tell our father and his mother that he's dead. How do I do that?'

'He took his chance, Meg. He knew the risks.'

Shaken, exhausted and confused, Meg could not bring herself to look at him. 'That sounds so callous.'

'You've had a terrible experience,' he said gently. 'I am truly sorry about Gerald, but he knew what he was doing.'

She raised her eyes to his face. 'You disappeared from the ward. You didn't even try to contact me and I thought you were dead. Now you've turned up promoted to the rank of major and fit as a flea.'

'I apologise for not being dead.'

'Now you're laughing at me. How dare you make jokes at a time like this?'

'I'm not laughing, and you need to go home

and rest.'

She glared at him; his very reasonableness conspired to make her ever angrier. She wanted to lay the blame for what had happened on someone and he was wearing the right uniform. She had feared for his safety, longed for his presence and yearned for his embraces. She had fallen in love with the enemy and in doing so had unwittingly sent Gerald to his death. Whatever happened now, she knew that she would have to live with that fact for the rest of her life. Anger was replaced by deep sadness. 'We're on opposite sides and however much we pretend that it doesn't matter it will always come between us.'

Rayner stared at her, his face pale and drawn. His eyes had dulled from blue to grey, like the sea on a cloudy day. 'I love you, Meg. Nothing can alter that.'

She heard the words and knew they were heartfelt but she felt as though something had died within her. 'Maybe I've been living with a young girl's dream of romance. The war has changed everything.'

'I'm still the same person I was when we first met.'

She shook her head. 'No. We're both different. Your compatriots killed my brother. How can I live with that?'

He raised his hand and then let it fall to his side. 'Ironic, isn't it? Von Schmettow himself ordered my promotion for my part in helping to keep some of my fellow countrymen from drowning when our ship was sunk. It seems that the nearer you are to being killed the higher the promotion.'

'I can't cope with this now,' Meg said, turning away from him. 'Please go.'

He reached out and caught her by the wrist. 'You think I deserted you, but that isn't true. When the hospital ward was closed the medical officer decided I was fit to go back on duty. I was never sent to the underground hospital, but I had no way of getting a message to you without arousing suspicion and putting you in danger. I was in headquarters when the message came through that an escape attempt was being made. I had no idea it was Gerald and his friends.'

'And if you had?'

'I still couldn't have saved them.'

She shrugged her shoulders. 'It's not just the uniform. It's the conflicting loyalties that will always come between us. I can't love anyone who could stand by and watch innocent men murdered in cold blood.' Choked by tears, she ran up the steps, ignoring his pleas for her to stop. Wrenching the door open she burst into the entrance hall, coming face to face with Nordhausen.

'Have you been out during curfew, Fräulein Colivet? Hauptmann Dressler will be most interested to hear this.' He took a step backwards as Rayner followed Meg into the house.

'I will speak to Hauptmann Dressler.'

Nordhausen jumped to attention and saluted, his eyes starting from his head as he took in Rayner's new rank. 'Herr Major.'

Meg walked slowly towards the staircase. She would not let them see that she was close to breaking point and that one word would breach the dam that she had built up inside herself, releasing

318

a flood of uncontrollable tears and grief. She could feel Rayner's eyes on her as she mounted the stairs, counting each step as she went in an effort to concentrate her thoughts. She refused to glance back. She must not show any signs of weakness now or she would be lost forever.

Outside her father's bedroom, Meg hesitated, bracing herself for the awful task of passing on the terrible news. In those few silent moments she made up her mind that, no matter how long the war lasted, she would never again have anything to do with the enemy.

Grief settled in a heavy cumulus cloud over the whole household. Even little Jeremy seemed to sense that something was very wrong. Everyone, it seemed to Meg, had been fond of Gerald in their own way, but Marie's grieving was more dreadful in its heartbroken silence than any amount of weeping and wailing. Charles absented himself from home on the excuse of attending meetings of the controlling committee, and for once Maud and Bertrand hushed their argumentative voices. Even Nordhausen left them all alone.

Gerald's coffin was brought back to Colivet Manor on a gun carriage covered in a Union flag. Meg was certain that Rayner had ordered this outward demonstration of respect but she could not allow herself to weaken in her resolve. Loving the enemy had brought nothing but pain and suffering. Simone had already been down that path and Meg was determined not to follow.

The funeral took place quietly in the church at St Martin's where Gerald was to be, at Marie's request, buried alongside Eric instead of in the Colivet family plot. Charles had argued about this, urging Meg to back him in his wish for his son to be buried with his forebears, but Meg had sided with Marie. She knew that Eric had loved Gerald as dearly as if he had been his own son, and it seemed right that they should rest for eternity side by side. She was touched and surprised by the number of people who came to the simple ceremony. Billy and Joe and their wives were there, of course, but people came from cottages and farms all around to pay their respects. They were mostly elderly folk who shambled up the narrow path into the church, shabbily dressed but proud to honour one of their island men.

Pearl arrived in an ancient governess cart borrowed from a neighbour and drawn by an even more elderly donkey that looked as though it should have been put out to pasture long ago. She flung her arms around Meg, her face wet with unashamed tears.

'Meg, darling. I'm so very sorry. Mummy and Daddy send their deepest condolences. Oh God – what do you say on a bloody awful occasion like this?'

Meg, who up until then had remained dry-eyed, found tears coursing down her own cheeks. She hugged Pearl but she froze as she saw Rayner walking through the gate into the churchyard.

Pearl released her, looking puzzled. She turned her head, following Meg's gaze.

'How dare he come?' Meg muttered through clenched teeth. 'This is for friends and family only.'

Pearl gripped her hand tightly. 'Don't make a scene, darling. It's not his fault; you know that. It's grief talking. He's not a bad man.'

Meg turned her back on Rayner. 'He's a German, isn't he? They're all in it together.'

'Come inside,' Pearl said, guiding Meg towards the doorway. 'Your family need you now. Nothing else matters today.'

The family clustered around Meg like defeated soldiers rallying to the standard as she stood fighting back tears as Gerald's remains were lowered into the ground. Simone and Marie leaned on each other, sobbing. Meg held her father's cold hand, giving it an encouraging squeeze as she felt him tremble when the clods of earth fell on the cheap pine coffin. Maud wept softly behind a long black veil and Bertrand sniffled, blowing his nose loudly every so often and clearing his throat. Jane was absent, having elected to stay behind to look after Jeremy, and Pip had shuffled off somewhere on his own, mumbling an excuse. Pearl and Rayner stood together on the far side of the grave. Pearl mopped her eyes with a fragment of lace handkerchief and tossed a small bunch of garden flowers onto the coffin. Rayner stood with head bowed, gripping his peaked hat in his hands, his knuckles showing white beneath his skin. When the short ceremony ended, he looked up and met Meg's eyes for a few seconds. There was no mistaking the sadness or the silent entreaty in them, and she felt a tug of regret together with the desperate need to forgive him, but one look at the coffin in its lonely grave made her harden her heart. As long as the war went on and as long as the Germans occupied her home and the island, she knew that she could not, must not, let Rayner back into her life. She lowered her gaze and turned away, tucking her hand through her father's arm as they led the way down the path.

Pearl caught up with them as they reached the churchyard gate. 'Be brave, darling. I miss him too.'

'I know you do. You and your family were wonderful to Gerald when he was with you.' Meg bit her lip as tears threatened to flow again.

Pearl squeezed her hand. 'I'll see you soon.' She pointed at Rayner who had remained at the graveside, allowing everyone to leave ahead of him. 'Don't be too hard on him, Meg. You loved him once.'

Meg turned away. 'They killed my brother.'

Back at the house, the family gathered in the parlour for a cup of tea made from wild herbs and some biscuits. The tea was more like hot water without the addition of milk and sugar and the biscuits were like small paving stones, but everyone drank and nibbled politely; food was food and no one was going to quibble about the taste or texture.

'I can't make a speech,' Charles said, sinking down on the only armchair that remained in the room. 'I've lost a son whom I loved but didn't have the courage to acknowledge until it was almost too late, and that is something I am going to have to live with for the rest of my life.'

'Don't, Pa,' Meg said softly. 'You did what you

thought was right. Gerald understood that.'

'My boy. My son.' Marie gave way to a flood of tears.

Simone helped her to a chair. 'Don't, Mum.'

'I'm sorry.' Marie gulped and wiped her eyes on the back of her hand. 'I'm so sorry.'

'I wonder if you'd be as upset if anything happened to me?' Simone said with a bitter note creeping into her voice. 'No, I don't think so. Gerald was always the favourite. But then he was a Colivet and I'm just a LeFevre.'

'Stop it,' Meg said in a low voice. 'Don't you ever think of anyone other than yourself?'

'You've got your son,' Marie said, wiping her eyes on a handkerchief that Maud passed to her. 'You've got little Jeremy.'

Simone glanced at the baby cradled in Jane's arms. 'He's better off here. I can't look after a child. I never wanted to have a baby. I'm just not the maternal type.'

'Shame on you,' Jane cried, cuddling Jeremy and kissing his chubby cheek.

Meg studied Simone's face and realised with a sense of shock that this was not just another tantrum. 'What are you saying, Simone?'

'I've got a good job and a steady young man now. No, not a German, he's one of us. When the war is over, which Derek says will be soon, we're going to the mainland where he's got business contacts.'

'Who is this man?' Marie stared at her in astonishment. 'You've never mentioned him.'

'Derek Lussac. You don't know him.'

'I do.' Charles raised his head, showing a sudden

323

interest in the conversation. 'He's a damned black marketeer.'

Simone tossed her head. 'So what? You're not my father, Mr Colivet. You can't tell me what to do or not to do. Derek loves me and he's got money. We'll do very well in London. He says there'll be plenty of opportunities for an enterprising chap after the war.'

'But Jeremy,' Meg said, aghast. 'You can't just abandon him.'

'Can't I? I thought I already had.'

'You're not fit to have a child.' Jane covered the baby's ears as though Jeremy could understand what was being said.

'I won't argue with that,' Simone said with a careless shrug of her shoulders. 'And you've taken such a shine to the little chap it would seem cruel to take him away from you.'

'Simone, you can't do this,' Marie said in a shocked voice.

Charles reached out to hold her hand. 'Have you thought this through, Simone?'

She turned to face him, bristling with defiance. 'You've lost a son. I'm giving you mine. Jeremy will be better off brought up as a Colivet, and Derek isn't interested in kids.'

'You're a heartless hussy,' Maud said, shaking her head. 'The little chap will be much better off without you.'

Bertrand coughed behind his hand. 'Steady on, Maud, old girl.'

'I'm not arguing,' Simone said, reaching for her jacket. 'So it's settled then?'

Charles rose to his feet. 'I'll get the adoption

papers drawn up, if that's what you really want.'

'That's what I want.' Simone went to the window and looked out. 'Got to go. I don't suppose I'll be seeing much of you from now on.' She dropped a kiss on her mother's forehead. 'Bye, Mum. I'm sorry I've never been the sort of daughter you wanted, but then you had Gerald, didn't you? For a while at least.'

Meg met Simone's eyes and saw a brief reflection of the other Simone, the courageous girl who had risked her life helping the saboteurs and used her charms to extract information from the enemy. She was shocked that she could abandon her child but she knew instinctively that it was not as painless as Simone wanted them to believe. She held out her hand. 'Keep in touch when you can, and good luck.'

Simone met her eyes with a flicker of understanding. 'Thanks.' She shrugged herself into her jacket and hurried from the room.

Maud ran to the window and peered out into the hazy September sunlight. 'Would you believe it? He's down there waiting for her in a car.'

Jane craned her neck, peering over her mother's shoulder. 'Only a black marketeer could still afford to run a car, even a little one like that. That girl will come to no good, you'll see.'

Meg slipped quietly from the room. She left the house through the scullery door and walked until she came to the edge of the north woods, where she collapsed onto a broken stile. The hazy sun warmed the field of stubble where only recently she had helped Gerald harvest a crop of barley. The hedgerows were berried with red hawthorn and orange rosehips and there was already the faint hint of autumn chill in the late afternoon air. A mist crept slowly from the sea, curling like beckoning fingers through the trunks of the trees. She felt a deep sense of sadness and the gnawing pain of loss, not only for Gerald but for Rayner and the love that had blossomed in that far off May time and had withered now like the leaves that were falling softly all around her. The winter was coming with no sign of an end to the war despite the Allied victories that they heard of on Pip's crystal set.

As the autumn gave way to a bitterly cold start to the winter, survival became the only major factor of day-to-day life. Getting enough food to keep them alive and enough fuel to heat even a kettle of water became the main task of each long and dreary day. Rations were reduced and supplies of gas had ended in September with electricity due to be cut off at the end of the year. The family listened to the news quite openly on Pip's crystal set now. Nordhausen had been relocated. Meg neither knew nor cared where he had been sent. The soldiers and officers who remained were quieter now, their former arrogance dulled by hunger and their confidence sapped by reports of German defeats in Europe.

Clustered around the radio receiver every evening, Meg sat with the family listening to the newscaster telling of the terrible V-2 rockets bringing terror and death to London. It was a small comfort to know that Mother, Adele and her twin girls were safe in the heart of the Devonshire countryside, but Red Cross messages had long since stopped coming through and Meg could only hope and pray that all was well with them. Her father and Marie never mentioned Gerald but Meg knew that they grieved silently as she did, and that he was far from forgotten. In October they heard that the British had landed in Greece. In November news filtered through that the RAF had sunk the Germans' last major warship, the *Tirpitz*, and in December they heard that the Americans, under the command of General Patton, had reached the Siegfried Line.

Meg watched helplessly as her family suffered from cold and malnutrition. Then, just as morale had sunk to its lowest, the news came through on 7 December that the SS *Vega* had sailed from Lisbon laden with Red Cross parcels for the Channel Islands. Meg prayed that its journey would be fast; she had heard of several elderly neighbours who, on the brink of starvation, had died of cold, and she feared for her father whose already delicate state of health was steadily worsening. Meg missed Gerald more than she would have thought possible. Now she had no one to talk to, no one to share a joke with and no one to squabble with. Until now she had not realised how much she had relied on his quiet strength and dependability. She knew that she would have lost him anyway, had his escape from the island been successful, but at least she would have had the comfort of knowing that he was doing what he wanted to do, and that one day they might meet again. That was impossible now.

Meg was not looking forward to Christmas; no one in the house was in the mood to celebrate. There was no money to buy gifts, and even if there had been the shelves in the few shops that remained open were bare of goods. She was surprised and a little cheered to receive a message from Pearl, delivered by a ragged boy who claimed that he had been paid for his trouble with a pound of potatoes. Meg hurried to the kitchen and found a small turnip by way of a tip. She scribbled a hasty reply on the back of the note and handed it to the boy with a slice of bread that was to have been her own lunch. He crammed the food into his mouth like a ravenous dog, and scuttled off in the downpour of rain that was rapidly turning to sleet.

On Christmas Eve, Meg wrapped herself in as many clothes as she could pile on without losing the use of her arms and legs, crammed her feet into a pair of her mother's old suede boots that were two sizes too small and began the long walk to the Grange. She found the Tostevins huddled in the kitchen with Hannah and Buster. They wore their outdoor clothes and the room was in darkness as the gloom of the winter's afternoon settled on the beleaguered island. Wrapped in blankets, Pearl's parents dozed in their chairs on either side of the unlit range. Hannah was in the scullery and Meg could see through the open door that she was scrubbing mud off potatoes at the sink. Buster, a thin shadow of his former self, padded up to Meg and licked her hand. His eyes were warm and alive as usual but he moved slowly and his ribs showed through his black coat.

'Meg, darling, you're a heroine to walk here in this God-awful weather.' Pearl flung her arms around Meg and hugged her.

'Well it is Christmas, although you'd never think it,' Meg said with a resigned sign. 'I wish I had a present for you.'

'But I've got one for you,' Pearl said, smiling. She dragged Meg from the relative warmth of the kitchen into the freezing hallway. She opened the door and gave Meg a shove that sent her stumbling into the drawing room. The door closed behind her and, as her eyes became accustomed to the poor light she realised that she was not alone. Even if the room had been pitch dark, Meg would have recognised the man silhouetted against the grey light of the French windows.

'Rayner.' In a moment of near panic, Meg reached for the door handle.

'Don't go, Meg.'

She hesitated with her fingers curled around the cold brass doorknob, refusing to look at him. 'I have nothing to say to you.'

'At least hear me out.'

She turned her head slowly, but his face was in deep shadow. She shivered and her knees gave way beneath her. She sank down onto the sofa. 'Say what you've got to say and then go.'

He took a step closer, moving warily like a man approaching a timid wild animal. 'You mustn't blame Pearl. I begged her to arrange this meeting.'

'I don't blame her. I know how persuasive you can be.'

'All right, I'm everything you say I am. I won't argue if you'll just hear me out.'

'Go on, but it won't make any difference. I can't do this any more. It's too painful.'

'I was sent to a new posting at Fort Hommet without prior warning. There was no way that I could contact you, but don't think I didn't try.'

'It doesn't matter now,' Meg said dully. 'It's all in the past.'

'It isn't in the past if you still think I abandoned you deliberately. I was coming to see you when I learned that there was an escape attempt in progress. It was the first time I had been able to get any form of transport and I was on my way to Colivet Manor when I overheard the transmission on my driver's radio. Somehow I knew you were involved, don't ask me how, and I knew you were in danger.'

'Do you really expect me to believe that?'

He moved closer and this time he reached out to hold her hand. 'It's the truth. And I wouldn't have wished any harm to come to Gerald.'

The warmth from his fingers seeped into Meg's flesh and crawled treacherously towards the icicle that was her heart. Feeling herself weakening, she stared doggedly at their linked hands, refusing to meet his eyes. 'Maybe so.'

His grip tightened. 'It is so, and I had to see you and tell you to your beautiful, stubborn face that I still love you. I love you to distraction, Meg. I can't bear to be apart from you. Every minute I spend shut away in that damned fortress on the other side of the island is like torture. Just tell me that you still love me and I'll live off that until this wretched war is over and I can return as a free man and we can begin all over again.'

She was frightened now, but not of him. Her fear was of losing herself in a relationship that was doomed from the start. She had seen what misplaced love had done to her family and the unhappiness it had caused to so many. She drew her hand away. 'Nothing will ever be the same as it was.'

'Look me in the eyes and tell me that you don't love me.'

She shook her head and her hand flew to the base of her throat and the string of pearls that he had bought for her so long ago, in Oxford. 'Don't do this to me.'

With a swift movement he drew her hand away, exposing the delicate necklace. 'So, you don't love me? Then why do you wear the pearls I gave you?'

'What difference does it make?' She met his eyes at last and saw pain, doubt and then a darkening look of comprehension and molten desire that made her traitorous body cry out for his embrace. 'Don't look at me like that. It's not fair.'

He released her hand only to wrap his arms around her. His kiss was anything but gentle and she felt herself falling into the abyss of need and desire, but just as she was drowning in his embrace he drew away. 'So you don't feel anything for me at all?' There was barely disguised triumph in his voice. 'You do love me. Admit it, Meg.'

A loud rapping on the door brought her back to her senses. She struggled free and rose shakily to her feet. 'C-come in.'

Pearl stuck her head round the door. 'Rayner, your driver's at the door. You're wanted urgently back at the fort. Sorry.' She withdrew hastily.

331

He stood up, reaching for his peaked cap and gloves. 'I'll have to go, but you still haven't answered my question, Meg. Is it really all over between us?'

CHAPTER EIGHTEEN

The clock on the town church struck two and Meg glanced anxiously around her. If he had not come in five minutes she would know that yet again Rayner had been unable to get away from Fort Hommet. She recalled their last heart-wrenching goodbye on Christmas Eve, when she had finally capitulated. The bitterness that had poisoned her soul since Gerald's untimely death had been dissipated by the love that she had tried so hard to conquer. Standing outside the Tostevins' house in the softly falling snow, she had finally given way to her true feelings and admitted that she loved him. Ignoring the urgent entreaties of his driver, Rayner had swept her into his arms, regardless of passers-by who might see the German major and the girl from the island who were so obviously in love. They had arranged a time and place where, if humanly possible, they would meet once a week. Meg had known from the start that it was a vain hope but the alternative was to sit at home and wait, and she had done enough of that.

Bad weather had made the long walk into town impossible for the first three weeks and she had braved the rain and wind on the two following

Thursdays, but he had not come. Not knowing the reason for his absence was the worst thing. Meg paced up and down, clutching her coat around her and stamping her feet in an attempt to regain the feeling in them. Her teeth chattered uncontrollably and she was beginning to feel faint with hunger and exhaustion. She would have to make a move soon or collapse on the pavement. The church clock struck the quarter, and Meg was about to leave for home when she was overcome by a feeling of faintness. She stumbled against the railings, clutching at them and just saving herself from falling.

'Are you all right, dear?' An old woman, muffled like a ragbag, stopped and peered at her.

The mist cleared from Meg's eyes and she focused with difficulty on the pickled-walnut face of the old countrywoman. 'Yes, thanks.'

'Get yourself home, my girl. None of them are worth catching your death for.'

Meg watched as she hobbled painfully on her way. A German soldier, gaunt and hollow-eyed, was unashamedly poking through the contents of a dustbin. His uniform hung off him, making him look more like a scarecrow. So much for the master race, Meg thought wearily. But in her heart she knew that the Germans were suffering just as much from the privations as the islanders. If there was one thing that she had learned, it was that the enemy were human beings, with all their attendant failings and weaknesses.

Rayner would have come if he possibly could; she knew that. And she had not the strength now for the long walk home. The rain was falling in a steady, drenching downpour and she could feel the cold water trickling down her neck, soaking her to the skin. She put her head down and began to trudge back up the Pollet towards the steep incline of Berthelot Street. She had to keep stopping and leaning against the nearest wall while she regained her breath but she kept on doggedly, taking the shortest route towards the Grange and the safety of the Tostevins' house.

Pearl and Hannah stripped her naked in the chilly kitchen and scrubbed at her emaciated flesh with cotton towels until Meg felt that her skin was being sandpapered down to the bone. Buster, having been pushed away after his attempts to jump up at Meg and lick her face, was curled in a ball, eyeing the proceedings from the safety of his bed by the unlit range.

'Stand still,' Pearl said, as though she were speaking to a wayward three-year-old. 'Do you want to die of pneumonia?'

Meg tried to say something but she had lost control over her teeth, which clattered together like castanets. 'I don't know what you were thinking of, standing for hours in the rain,' Pearl said, towelling Meg's hair energetically. 'You make sure she's dry, Hannah, while I go and find some clothes for her.'

'Just look at you,' Hannah said, scrubbing at Meg's back. 'Thin as a rail and with about as much strength as a newborn baby.'

Meg closed her eyes and ears to Hannah's scolding and was glad when Pearl came back into the room carrying an armful of clothing.

'Sorry, darling,' Pearl said, chuckling. 'You

won't win any fashion contests but at least you'll be a bit warmer.'

Finally, dressed in a selection of Pearl's old clothes that were about six sizes too big for either of them now, Meg sat at the kitchen table watching Hannah as she opened a haybox and took out a steaming pan. 'I collected this from the communal kitchen,' she said, ladling a stream of soup into a mug and passing it to Meg. 'It's amazing how it keeps things hot. My mother used to make porridge in ours when I was a girl.'

Meg shook her head. 'No, this is your supper. I can't take your food.'

'Don't be a silly ass, Meg.' Pearl sat down opposite her and leaned her elbows on the table. 'You eat it and don't make a fuss. There's plenty of it even if it's only cabbage water.'

'And a turnip,' Hannah said, stowing the pot back amongst the hay and pressing the lid down. 'I swapped a few cabbage leaves for a turnip, so you eat up and be grateful, miss.'

The thin, tasteless liquid warmed Meg's stomach and she sipped it slowly, savouring it as if it had been the finest consommé.

'That's better,' Pearl said, nodding with approval. 'You've got a little colour in your cheeks. You looked like death when you fell through the door.'

Meg forced a weary smile. 'I'd been waiting by the town church for an hour. He didn't come.'

Buster let out a sharp bark just as the brass bell labelled *Front Door* jangled from its spring on the bell board. Hannah shuffled off to answer it, grumbling beneath her breath.

'She never changes,' Pearl said, smiling. 'It could be Hitler himself standing on the doorstep and Hannah would send him off with a flea in his ear.'

Buster bounded off up the passageway, the sound of his claws skittering across the tiled floor and his yelps of pleasure echoing throughout the house. Meg rose unsteadily to her feet as Rayner strode into the kitchen. He was closely followed by Hannah, protesting loudly as pools of water dripped off his sodden greatcoat.

'I thought you might be here,' he said, scooping Meg up in his arms regardless of his audience, and completely ignoring Buster who bounced up and down barking hysterically.

Meg gave herself up to the aching sweetness of a long-drawn-out kiss, winding her arms around his neck, barely conscious of the damp seeping through her borrowed clothing.

Pearl cleared her throat. 'We'll be in the drawing room if you need anything. Come on, Hannah. Grab the dog, will you?'

'Where were you?' Meg demanded when they eventually drew apart. 'I waited for hours.'

'Everything's changed now. We've got a new commander-in-chief. Regulations have been tightened up so that no one, not even officers, can get passes to come into town. I had to steal a motorcycle to get here and I'll probably be shot for desertion and misappropriating army equipment when I get back to Fort Hommet.'

Meg pushed him away. 'Don't joke. It's not funny.'

His smile faded and he gripped her by the shoulders. 'It's no joke, darling. Von Schmettow has

336

been replaced by Vice-Admiral Huffmeier. He's a fanatical Nazi who refuses to admit the possibility of defeat, but no matter how much he tries to whip the troops back into shape we all know that the Allies are advancing towards Berlin. The RAF have decimated Dresden. It's only a matter of time before Berlin falls.'

'I heard about Dresden, Rayner. You must be worried sick about your parents.'

His eyes clouded. 'I am, but there's no way I can find out if they're safe until I get back to Germany.'

'What are you saying?'

'I'm saying that it's only a matter of weeks, or maybe a couple of months, and it will all be over. We'll be repatriated – or possibly sent to camps, I don't know which, but it must be coming soon.'

'I've prayed so hard for the war to end, but I didn't think of how it would be.'

'I promise you I'll come back for you as soon as I can and then we'll be together for the rest of our lives.'

She drew away from him, cold fingers of fear clutching at her heart. 'That sounds like goodbye.'

'Huffmeier has forbidden all fraternisation with local women. We have to stop seeing each other. I won't risk putting you in unnecessary danger.'

'I'm not afraid. I will see you again no matter what.'

He stroked her cheek with the tip of his finger and his frown melted into a rueful smile. 'My brave and beautiful girl.'

Meg's throat constricted painfully. She could cope with hardship but his tender words brought hot tears to sting her eyes. If this was to be their last meeting, she was determined he would not take away a picture of her red-eyed and weeping. She covered a sniffle with a shaky laugh. 'Beautiful? Bundled up in Pearl's oldest clothes with tennis shoes two sizes too big on my feet and my hair hanging in rat's tails?'

He cupped her face in his hands and kissed her forehead, her eyelids and then her lips, smiling in a way that made her heart do a somersault. 'You will always be beautiful to me, my darling. And after the war, when we are together again we will make a pilgrimage to Oxford and stand on Folly Bridge to gaze down at the river which brought us together in the first place.'

The memory of that fateful afternoon and the way their bodies had entwined beneath the turgid waters of the River Thames made her shiver. 'My life belongs to you,' she whispered.

'That's right, and I will come back and claim you for my bride.' He kissed her long and hard. 'We will be together again. I swear it.'

Meg forced her bruised lips into a tremulous smile. 'There's always Folly Bridge.'

Rayner's eyes were suspiciously bright and he nodded. 'We'll meet there at midnight on the evening of the May Ball, and you will be wearing your golden ball gown.'

'I gave it away after Adele's engagement party.'

'Then I will buy you a new one.'

She smiled. 'This year, next year, sometime...'

'I know that rhyme. David used to do it with prune stones at breakfast in our digs. The land-lady had a passion for serving those nasty

338

shrivelled plums.'

Meg pulled away with a watery chuckle. 'How lovely and normal that all sounds. I'd almost forgotten what life was like then.'

'And it will be again.' He brushed Meg's forehead with a kiss. 'Now, I must take you home. That is if you don't mind riding pillion on a motorbike.'

'That's something I've always wanted to do. Like driving a Rolls – I don't suppose...'

'No. Definitely not. Driving a car is one thing, riding a motorcycle is quite another. I want you in one piece.'

Despite her gallant attempt at making light of things, Meg had to struggle to keep from bursting into tears as they parted outside the gates of Colivet Manor. The rain had stopped and the air was filled with the nutty scent of damp earth and wet leaves. It was almost dark, with just a faint greenish glow in the sky towards the west making it possible for Meg to see Rayner's face clearly as they said goodbye. They drew apart from a long, achingly tender kiss, and then, with one kick on the accelerator pedal, the motorcycle engine roared into life and Rayner rode away at speed. Meg stood in the lane and listened until the sound faded into the night and all she could hear was the sighing of the wind in the Spanish oaks. It seemed in those silent moments as though a vital part of her being had gone with him, leaving a mere shadow to walk through the gateway and up the drive to the house.

A rustling noise in the thicket of laurel just inside

the entrance made her stop and spin round, peering into the violet shadows. The hairs on the back of her neck prickled and she was conscious of her heart thudding hard against her ribs. There'd been no sentries posted on the gates for weeks now and it was getting dangerously close to curfew time. She took a pace forward and then stopped as a black shape emerged from the bushes and lunged at her. A hand clamped over her mouth and a terrifyingly familiar voice whispered in her ear.

'Meg, don't scream. It's me.'

Someone was slapping her face, calling her name. Meg opened her eyes and saw a man silhouetted against the darkening sky. Everything was hazy as she struggled to sit up and for some reason she could not quite grasp her attacker was helping her; she recognised the scent of him even as she knew his voice.

'Meg, it's me, Gerald. Please don't faint again.'

'But you're dead. We buried you.' She peered into his face as she tried to stand up, but was overcome by dizziness and she sank back onto the wet grass.

'Sit still for a minute and you'll be okay. I'm sorry I scared you.'

The world suddenly righted itself and she scrambled to her feet. 'Scared me?' she cried, pummelling him with her fists. 'You frightened the life out of me. You were dead.' She flung her arms around him, laughing and crying all at the same time.

'Sorry,' Gerald murmured, holding her in a rib-crunching hug.

Feeling his cheek wet against hers, Meg laid her

hands flat on his chest, pushing him far enough away to see his face. Shocked at the sight of tears rolling down his cheeks, she stood on tiptoe to kiss them away. 'You bloody idiot, Gerald. Have you any idea what we've all been through thinking you were dead and buried in the churchyard?'

He caught her by the wrists. 'Can we talk about this somewhere else?'

'Talk about it? We've all been to hell and back because of you. And you want to chat?'

'I'll explain everything, but if the Germans catch me I really will be dead.'

She shivered convulsively. 'Fine, but let's find somewhere a bit warmer. I'm freezing.'

'No one must know I'm here.'

She thought fast. 'There's only one place you'll be safe for tonight, but we've got to get inside the house without being seen.'

Meg closed her bedroom door and leaned against it, breathing a sigh of relief. 'That was a close one. I thought we'd had it when von Eschenberg came down the stairs.'

'Yes, thanks for shoving me into the broom cupboard. I've always wanted a mop handle rammed up my backside.'

'Think yourself lucky it was me who found you, and stop grumbling,' Meg said, raising a warning finger to her lips.

'Is he in his room?' Gerald perched on a stool next to Meg's bed.

'If you mean our father, then say so.'

'I still can't quite get my head round that. It's going to take time for me to forgive him for the way he treated Mum and me.'

'As a matter of fact, Pa is in his room. He's old and sick and has been ten times worse since he heard that you'd been killed.'

'There was no way I could get word to you.'

She sank down onto her bed. 'Tell me every-thing.'

'I was hit in the first volley of shots and the force knocked me overboard. That's the only reason I survived.'

'How did you get ashore? Were you badly hurt?'

'I took two hits in the chest but I didn't know that at the time. I couldn't feel anything except the waves trying to drag me under. I managed to kick off my boots and when I surfaced I couldn't see the boat – or anything at all, come to that. The current must have carried me round the point. I remember being thrown against some rocks and then nothing until I was being dragged out of the water. I thought the Germans had got me, but it must have been the Vaudins. I woke up three days later in their farmhouse loft with Simone bending over me, giving me a good telling off.'

'Simone?'

'Somehow they managed to fetch Dr Gallienne and Simone from the hospital. I wouldn't be here now if they hadn't patched me up. According to Simone my chest was like a colander and the bullets had gone straight through. I was just lucky they hadn't hit any major organs.'

'And have you been at the Vaudins' farm all this time? How could Simone let us go on thinking you were dead?'

'Don't blame her. I made her promise not to

tell anyone, not even Mum. She would have insisted on coming to see me and that would have put the Vaudins in danger.'

Meg considered this for a moment and unwillingly saw the sense of it; she nodded slowly. 'All right, I give you that. But if you're alive, who did we bury in a grave next to Eric?'

'It must have been Hugh. He was at the helm and Bob and I were rowing. He was only wearing an old guernsey and I lent him my jacket because he was cold. My papers were in the pocket.'

'But someone must have missed him by now?'

Gerald shook his head. 'His family evacuated to the mainland at the beginning of the war. He had no one close left on the island; that's why he risked so much.'

She reached out to touch his hand. 'And you, you fool. You risked your life and nearly lost it. Thank God you're safe.'

'Maybe it would have been better if I had been killed. It would have made things simpler all round.'

'Stop feeling sorry for yourself. Pa and Marie love you and they've been heartbroken thinking you were dead.'

He shot her a quick glance and then turned his head away. 'And you?'

'I love you too. I always have done but I just didn't know what sort of love it was. Now I do know. You're my brother, part of me, and nothing can change that.'

'I'm so ashamed of the way I behaved. My feelings for you weren't so innocent. D'you know how that makes me feel? Do you?'

Meg slid off the bed and gripped him by the shoulders, giving him a gentle shake. 'That was a lifetime ago. We didn't know the truth. You can't blame yourself for that.'

'No. I blame the man who calls himself my father.' Gerald met her eyes this time and Meg recoiled at the desperation and anger she read in their dark depths.

'You're tired,' she said, rising to her feet. 'You're still not fully recovered. I'm going downstairs to see if I can find something for you to eat. Rest on my bed until I come back and for God's sake keep quiet.'

She left the room silently and felt her way down the dark staircase. It was not late but the house was quiet. Unusually there was no sound emanating from the rooms used by the German officers. The darkness was suffocating and the silence eerie, but Meg was cold and ravenously hungry. She made her way slowly to the kitchen. The chill rose up from the tiled floor, nipping at her ankles like a bad-tempered terrier, but she was too hungry to care about mere physical discomfort. She found some milk in the larder, and a crust of bread, which she broke in two and shoved half of it into her mouth, chewing and almost choking on the sawdust-dry crumbs. She washed it down with a mouthful of the milk and put the rest in a cup for Gerald, with the remainder of the bread.

When she returned to her room she found him sleeping peacefully and she had not the heart to wake him. Curling up on the floor, she fell into an exhausted sleep.

Meg awakened at first light, cold, stiff and wondering why she was sleeping on the floor. Then it all came flooding back and she sat up, listening to Gerald's rhythmic breathing. He could not stay in her room and risk discovery by one of the family. She rested her chin on her knees, frowning. He had to be fed and he definitely needed to wash. The facilities in the Vaudins' attic obviously did not run to such luxuries as warm water and soap was almost impossible to obtain anyway. She wrinkled her nose, wondering if she could sneak him into Pa's bathroom. She could hear her father moving about restlessly in the next room and the solution came to her in an inspirational flash. She scrambled to her feet and tiptoed out of her room and into her father's.

'Pa. I need to talk to you.'

Ten minutes later Meg leaned over Gerald, shaking him by the shoulder. 'Wake up, sleepyhead.'

He opened his eyes and stared up at her, looking puzzled and then alarmed. She pushed him back amongst the pillows as he attempted to sit up. 'Don't say anything, just listen to me.'

'What?' Gerald cried in a hoarse whisper when she finished explaining her plan. 'You expect me to hide in the old man's room? I'd rather take my chances with the Jerries.'

She shrugged her shoulders. 'Go on then. If that's what you'd prefer. And we'll all end up in prison camps or shot.'

He struggled to a sitting position. 'I can't do it.'

'You can and you will. No one goes into his room, apart from your mother and me. His bathroom is the only one that you could use without being seen, and Marie can smuggle a little extra food upstairs. If anyone notices they'll just think that Pa is on the mend. Besides which, and he agrees with me, it will give you two time to get to know each other properly and sort out your differences.'

'You expect me to forgive the man who ruined my mother and refused to acknowledge me as his son?'

'I think you could try.'

'I don't have much choice, do I?'

'No,' Meg said, pulling the bedclothes off him. 'You don't. He's waiting to see you. Go now and remember that he's a sick man. Be kind to him, Gerald.'

When they were alone in the kitchen, Meg broke the news to Marie as gently as she knew how. She could only imagine the scene in her father's room when Marie, trembling and on the verge of tears, went upstairs with the breakfast tray.

Jane gave Meg a curious look as she hurried into the kitchen carrying Jeremy. 'And where were you last night? Were you out after curfew?'

'Of course not,' Meg said, opening the haybox and taking out the pot of barley porridge. 'I went to bed early. I had a headache.'

'Your bloke didn't turn up then?' Jane set Jeremy down on a chair and poured some milk into his beaker.

'I went to see Pearl. Pass me Jim's bowl, please.' Jane passed it to her, frowning. 'It's Jeremy, not Jim. And I don't believe you.'

'Suit yourself,' Meg said, blobbing some of the

346

gooey, grey mess into Jeremy's *Bunnikin* porringer.

'Now I know you were up to no good,' Jane said, taking the bowl from her. 'You can't fool me, Meg.'

There was no point in denying it and suddenly Meg felt too tired to keep up the deception. It would be better to admit that she had seen Rayner than to get into a conversation where she might let it slip that the real cause for her non-appearance at the evening meal was that Gerald had suddenly risen from the dead. 'All right! Since I'm unlikely to be able to see him again I admit it, I went to meet Rayner. Are you happy now? Or are you shocked and disgusted that I'm no better than the other Jerrybags?'

Jane picked up the spoon that Jeremy had flung on the floor, wiped it on her apron and gave it back to him. 'Naughty boy. Don't do it again.' She turned her head to look at Meg and her gaunt features cracked into a smile. 'Not me. I had my fling with a French fisherman, Pip's father, when I was just seventeen. Mummy and Daddy never really forgave me. They sent me to Jersey where very few people knew me. I stayed with an old aunt who employed a midwife to help at the birth, but the old hag didn't seem to know what she was doing. If I'd had proper medical care when he was born Pip might not have been the way he is, but I've never been sorry that I had him.'

'What happened to Pip's father?'

'He was handsome and charming but he omitted to tell me that he was married. He went back to his wife and children in France and I never saw him again.'

347

'How terribly sad,' Meg pushed her plate away. 'Give this to Jeremy, he's finished his already.'

Jane scraped the porridge into Jeremy's bowl and he spooned it greedily into his mouth, watching them with his huge, pansy-brown eyes. 'Ta,' he said, smacking his lips.

'Good boy,' Jane said, automatically. 'It was awful at the time, but I got over it. I hope you have better luck with your German. I liked him when he was here. He was a gentleman, not like some of them.'

By day, Meg went about her work on the farm, and in the evenings, after she had listened to the BBC news with Pip and Jane, Maud and Bertrand having gone to bed as soon as the light began to fade, she went to her father's room. In almost complete darkness she perched on the edge of the bed, and Gerald sat on a chair drawn up close so that they could converse in whispers without raising the suspicions of anyone who happened to pass the door.

By the end of March the Allies had crossed the Rhine and it seemed as if the whole world had declared war on Germany. As Meg had hoped, being sequestered in the one room had brought Charles and Gerald together as nothing else could have done. They read books that she smuggled in from the shelves that still lined the upper landings and had been ignored by the Germans as being of little use and no interest to them. They played chess, dominoes and card games and sometimes, as the evenings drew out, Meg joined them. Gerald might fume and fret outwardly at being

348

virtually imprisoned, but Meg could see that the two of them had formed a bond. They had developed a mutual understanding that would not have been possible in any other circumstances, and she was glad. Charles grew stronger, spending longer periods of time out of bed as the spring days grew warmer, but the fiction that he was a helpless invalid offered some protection to Gerald. Meg was careful to keep her father's slow recovery a secret from the rest of the household.

She walked into St Peter Port once a week, ostensibly to visit Pearl and make a fuss of Buster, but it was the desire to learn something of Rayner's fate that really motivated her. Not being able to see him and talk to him was the worst kind of torture, but she bore it as she had borne everything else during the long years of the occupation. If she could have disguised herself as a German soldier and walked into Fort Hommet, she would have done so, but the stronghold was on the far side of the island, and she had no means of getting there. She had not even the comfort of being able to stand outside the walls and imagine that he was only feet away from her.

Listening to the BBC on Pip's crystal set revealed the hideous secrets of the Nazi concentration camps, making Meg physically sick. The news of the death of Mussolini and the surrender of Italy was followed two days later by the fall of Berlin and the suicide of Hitler and his mistress, Eva Braun. While the family secretly rejoiced, von Eschenberg and Hauptmann Dressler huddled in their office apparently awaiting orders, and the soldiers quartered in the stables were unusually quiet.

At the beginning of May, rumours of liberation flew round the island, and, on the eighth, Meg gathered the whole family, including Marie, in her father's bedroom. Their astonishment on discovering that Gerald was very much alive was soon replaced by exclamations of delight, followed by the inevitable flood of questions. How had he escaped death? Who had saved him? And who was the unfortunate man they had buried in his stead? Everyone was talking at once until Pip raised his hand. 'Shut up, I've got London on the radio. Churchill's going to speak.'

Everyone was silent, hanging on to the great man's words. 'Hostilities will end officially, at one minute past midnight tonight, Tuesday the eighth of May, but in the interest of saving lives the cease-fire began yesterday, to be sounded all along the fronts – and our dear Channel Islands are also to be freed today.'

There was a moment of absolute quiet, and then everyone, even Charles, cheered loudly. Pip grabbed his mother round the waist and danced her round the room, Maud and Bertie clapped their hands and Marie hugged Gerald with tears running down her cheeks.

Meg took her father's hand and squeezed his fingers. She forced her lips into a smile. The war might be over for the Channel Islands, but her own personal battle was far from ended.

CHAPTER NINETEEN

The soldiers had left in a hurry, marched off by the British troops. Everything had happened so quickly that it was hard to grasp the fact that they had really gone. Meg recalled the fast-moving events as if they had occurred in a dream. Just a short time ago she had stood beside her father as Hauptmann Dressler and Major von Eschenberg left the house under armed escort. Beside the healthy, comparatively well-fed British troops, the Germans looked thin and gaunt; mere shadows of the men who had first invaded their home. Dressler had stopped and drawn himself up to his full height to look Charles in the eye. Meg knew that she'd always remember the mixed emotions that had flitted across his face. He had held his hand out to her father with a ghost of a smile. 'Goodbye, Herr Colivet. This is not how I expected it to end but it has been a privilege knowing you.'

For a moment Meg had thought her father would ignore the unspoken apology for five years of intimidation and virtual house arrest, but he had smiled and shaken the Hauptmann's hand. 'You will be as glad to return to your homeland as we are to have our island free again.'

It was all over now, and Meg made her way to the stables. She had only one thought and that was to find Rayner before he was transported back to Germany. She picked her way across piles of debris in the tack room and discovered her bicycle propped up against the wall. She breathed a sigh of relief on finding that it was in a reasonable condition, and she wheeled it out into the stable yard. It was almost impossible to believe that she was free to go anywhere she liked.

A constant stream of military vehicles clogged the narrow roads and lanes leading to town, but now they were filled with British troops. The soldiers leaned out to wave at Meg as she edged her bike between the trucks. Wolf whistles and teasing remarks accompanied her on her way and she acknowledged them with a smile, but she had only one thing on her mind as she free-wheeled down Le Val des Terres at breakneck speed. She arrived breathless and amazingly in one piece at the jetty. Abandoning her bicycle she pushed and shoved her way through the crowd. People had gathered to watch the dispirited men in grey uniforms as they prepared to board the vessels that would take them away from the island.

Meg waited all day without sight of Rayner. She returned the following morning, again without success. On the third day, when she had almost given up hope, she stood on the White Rock straining her eyes as a column of soldiers approached. The crowd pressed forward, some of them jeering and shaking their fists, other simply watching in grim silence. She recognised Rayner instantly as he brought up the rear in a group of officers from Fort Hommet. She had begun to elbow her way through the crowd when a scuffle broke out as a young girl flung herself at a young man at the head of the column, weeping and

352

throwing her arms around his neck.

There was a brief hush, broken by a shout of 'Jerrybag' which was taken up in a chant. A woman rushed forward and grabbed the girl by her hair, and it took the British soldiers a few minutes to break up the fight that ensued. A burly sergeant hoisted the kicking, hysterical girl over his shoulder and carried her to safety. Undaunted, Meg pressed forward as Rayner drew nearer. She called his name, waving frantically, and he turned his head. He had seen her, of that she was certain. She had but one thought in her mind and that was to get close enough to speak to him, but before she had a chance to move she was held back by a young private. 'I wouldn't do that, miss. You've seen what can happen.'

She opened her mouth to cry out to Rayner but the soldier raised his finger to his lips. 'Best be quiet, miss.' He jerked his head in the direction of the women screaming insults as they surrounded the army lorry where the girl had been taken for her own safety. Meg could do nothing but watch helplessly as Rayner marched past her. Their eyes met for a few precious seconds and then he was gone.

The soldier let her go with an apologetic grin. 'You all right, miss?'

She nodded wordlessly.

'He's not worth it, love. Find yourself a nice local chap.' He ambled off to help disperse the crowd.

Meg walked blindly to where she had left her bike and found it had been stolen. She was too numb to feel shocked or angry that someone could have taken her only means of transport. She

353

cared for nothing at that moment. She felt that her life was drifting out on the tide with the ship as it weighed anchor and sailed away. The sun beat down on her bare head and the hot pavements burned the soles of her feet but she felt nothing except the dull ache of despair as she trudged past the Albert Statue, making her way home.

She had reached the entrance to Castle Cornet when a painful stitch in her side caused her to stop and lean against the sea wall. Just as she was recovering, a car screeched to a halt at the edge of the pavement and Simone stuck her head out of the window, beckoning furiously. 'Get in.'

'What's the matter?'

Simone leapt out of the car and bundled Meg unceremoniously into the back seat before throwing herself in beside the driver. The driver put his foot down on the accelerator and the car shot forward.

Meg stared at the back of his sleek, dark head and realised slowly that it must be Simone's new man, Derek Lussac. 'What's going on?' she demanded. 'Why the hurry?'

Simone twisted round to face her. 'We're getting out on the next boat. We're not too popular round here, are we, sweetie-pie?'

Derek glanced at her and grinned. 'You can say that again, Toots.'

Meg lay back against the leather squabs and ran her hand over her eyes. 'I don't understand.'

'A Jerrybag and a black marketeer,' Simone said with an expressive wave of her hands. 'Come on, Meg, use your imagination. You saw what happened just now and it's going on all the time.

354

Any girl who's consorted with the Germans is a Jerrybag, and black marketeers might have been popular when people were desperate, but now they're public enemy number one.'

'Yes. People who were pleased enough to fork out for black market food have now turned self-righteous and want my blood,' Derek said, changing gears as the car struggled up the steep incline of Le Val des Terres. 'Ironic, isn't it? But that's life. Toots just wanted to say goodbye to her folks and the kid, and then we're off to London and the big time.'

'And you'd better keep quiet about your German,' Simone said. 'Or you'll end up the same as me.'

Meg laid her hand on Simone's shoulder. 'But you were helping the saboteurs and passing on information. You saved Gerald's life.'

'Try telling that to the mob. We're off to the mainland and we won't be coming back. That'll be best for everyone.'

There was almost a party atmosphere back at the manor. Meg found everyone congregated in the drawing room drinking the gin that Charles explained had been given to him by one of the British officers. Meg noted wryly that no one seemed bothered now about Derek's shady dealings. She doubted whether Rayner would be as welcome in the family. No matter what he had done, Derek was an islander and therefore one of them. His misdeeds were as nothing when compared to Rayner's misfortune of being born a foreigner and a German.

Simone held her arms out to Jeremy, but he

turned his head away and buried his face in Jane's shoulder.

'He doesn't understand,' Marie said sympathetically. 'He's too young.'

'You will tell him about me, won't you, Mum?' Simone's eyes filled with tears. 'I'll come back one day and see him. I'll send him presents on his birthday and at Christmas.'

'Oh, Simone, I wish you weren't going,' Marie said, mopping her eyes with a crumpled hanky. 'I'll miss you so much.'

Simone's mouth drooped at the corners. 'I haven't been a good daughter, Mum. I'm so sorry.'

Gerald wrapped his arms around both of them. 'Stop it, the pair of you. You'll have me crying next.' He turned to Derek. 'You take good care of her or you'll have me to deal with.'

Meg slipped from the room and went outside, taking deep breaths of air filled with the perfume of roses and the salty tang of the sea borne on a gentle breeze. However much her heart was aching, she knew she had no choice but to go on. She had taken responsibility for the running of the estate during the occupation and her father's recurrent bouts of illness. She could not abandon it now, and for the moment she was not needed in the house. She had said her goodbyes to Simone, and she was glad that they were parting as friends. She walked around the farm, assessing the damage with a fresh eye now that there was a chance of reclaiming the land that the Germans had laid to waste. It would take time, money and a huge effort, but there was nothing that could not be mended, except, she thought, the gaping hole in her heart. She had reached the north field when a gentle whinnying and the sound of horse's hooves on the baked earth made her turn to see Conker trotting towards her swishing his tail and whickering softly. She rubbed her cheek against his soft muzzle. Things might never be quite as they were before the occupation, but Mother would come home soon. She would take over the running of the house and restore order to chaos. Meg slipped her hand through Conker's halter and led him back towards the stables.

Muriel arrived home looking sleekly plump and vaguely disbelieving as Maud and Jane tried to explain what life had been like during the occupation.

'At least you weren't bombed,' Muriel said, gazing around the shabby drawing room with her lips pursed. 'You have no idea what it was like going to bed at night never knowing if a V-1 or a V-2 was going to fall out of the sky and kill you.'

'And we all thought that you, Adele and the twins were safe in the heart of Devon,' Charles said, smiling. 'It just goes to show how little we knew of the outside world when we were under the benevolent care of the Third Reich.'

Muriel shot him a suspicious glance. 'If that is meant to be sarcasm, Charles, then it's not funny.'

Meg stifled a giggle. Mother was back and on good form.

Maud and Bertrand huddled together in a corner, holding hands. 'I suppose you'll want us to move out directly?' Maud said, her bottom lip trembling.

357

Muriel eyed them thoughtfully and then, to Meg's amazement, she smiled. 'No need to worry about that yet. We'll see, shall we?'

Jane sniffed and scooped Jeremy up in her arms. 'It's time for your tea, my little man.' She carried him out of the room.

'I made a crystal set,' Pip said, breaking the awkward silence. 'We listened to the BBC news every night.'

'Are you an electrician?' Muriel eyed him with sudden interest.

He nodded. 'I'm good with my hands.'

'Then we will need you to help fix this place up. It all looks so dreadfully dilapidated and old-fashioned. You should see the Bartons' houses in London, the Home Counties and Devon. Mr Barton has had a lovely villa built for Frank and Adele close to their main home in Hampshire.'

'My dear, I think I ought to go to the office,' Charles said, rising stiffly from his chair.

'Yes, if you have to. I see nothing much has changed.' Muriel offered her cheek to receive his kiss. He obliged with a peck and hurried from the room. She sighed heavily. 'I expect everything will be left to me as usual. Meg, you're being very quiet. Have you nothing to say for yourself?'

'Welcome home, Mother,' Meg said, smiling.

'I returned not a moment too soon as far as I can see.' Muriel squared her shoulders with the air of a general about to face battle. 'I need to see Marie and discuss menus with her. Heaven knows we've suffered terribly from rationing on the mainland. The meals became so boring and predictable, but I suppose we were luckier than most. Pip, go and

358

fetch the wicker picnic hamper from the hall and take it to Marie. Mrs Barton's cook packed a few extras for you all when we heard that food was even scarcer over here than on the mainland.'

'Mother, you're an angel,' Meg cried, giving her a hug.

'Really? What did she send?' Bertrand's eyes brightened and he leapt to his feet. 'Is there any chocolate, or maybe a meat pie?'

'How do I know, Bertrand? I expect it's something delicious. The Bartons' cook can perform culinary miracles with very few ingredients.'

'We'll go and help Marie in the kitchen,' Maud volunteered, edging towards the doorway. 'Come on, Bertie.'

'Don't let that greedy pig Pip get to the food first.' He hurried after her, closing the door behind him.

'I've returned to a madhouse.' Muriel fanned herself with a lace handkerchief. 'I go away for a few years and when I come back I find the whole place crumbling about my ears, and dependent relatives popping up left, right and centre.'

'Yes, Mother. It's very trying.'

'But at least the house is still standing. I suppose that's a good thing even if you have let everything go to rack and ruin, Meg. Plymouth was virtually razed to the ground, you know, not to mention the East End of London, and I believe Coventry was very badly hit. You really were most fortunate to escape the bombing.'

Meg slipped her hand through her mother's arm. 'Come outside, Mother. I want to show you something.'

359

Muriel allowed herself to be led out of the house. When she saw the sad state of the stables and outbuildings it was only a sharp intake of breath that betrayed her innermost feelings. Ruthlessly, Meg dragged her on through the vegetable garden, across the wasteland that had been the pleasure gardens and down to the ruined summerhouse by the lake. 'Well, Mother? Do you still think we had an easy time of it?'

Muriel looked around her and with a slight shake of her head she raised her chin, meeting Meg's eyes with a look of pure steel. 'There must be some form of government compensation to pay for all this. Your father must look into it at once. We'll soon have everything back to normal. I'm here now, Meg. You've done your best, I'm sure, but this will take some organisation.'

Meg opened her mouth to protest and then closed it again. Mother had not changed during her five years' absence and she probably never would. She had never been able to resist a challenge and the one presented to her now was of epic proportions. Meg could only stand back and admire her mother's single-minded determination to whip the world around her into a manageable shape. But instinctively she also knew that she was being quietly but firmly relegated to her lowly position as the youngest daughter. Mother had taken charge.

'Come along, Meg,' Muriel said, stepping daintily over piles of rubble. 'This isn't the time to mope around. There's much to be done, starting right now.'

'Yes, Mother.'

'I must find Marie. I need to tell her that I was very sorry to hear about Eric. We'll never find another estate manager as good as he.'

Meg had to run to keep up with her as she marched across the cracked, sun-baked earth. 'Wait a moment. There's something I must tell you.' The thought of her mother sailing into the kitchen and coming face to face with Gerald filled her with alarm.

Muriel stopped and turned her head to look Meg in the eyes. 'I know all about Gerald masquerading as David. Charles told me in the car on the way home.'

The look in her mother's eyes confirmed Meg's suspicion. 'You've known about him all along, haven't you, Mother?'

Muriel replied with an expressive shrug of her shoulders. 'Your father and I have no secrets. Marriage isn't all about romance and passion, Meg. It's a question of give and take and mutual understanding. I won't pretend that it's been easy, but we came to a compromise many years ago and it's worked.'

'And you don't mind us knowing that Gerald is our brother?'

'He's chosen to keep the name LeFevre. I don't think there is any need to broadcast the details of his birth certificate, and I think that eventually, when I've had time to train him, he will make an excellent estate manager. David has never been interested in the farm.'

'You've seen David?'

'Of course I have. You may have been marooned here for the duration, but there is life outside the

361

island, you know.'

'Yes, Mother.'

Muriel walked on, stopping momentarily to make tut-tutting sounds when she came to the place where once her rose garden had been her pride and joy. She carried on, talking over her shoulder as she went. 'Did I tell you that he's engaged to a delightful girl called Sonia? No? Well he is, and her father is something high up in the RAF. David has decided that he wants to stay in the air force and make it his career. In that event, Gerald will be very useful indeed.'

Meg hurried after her. 'I suppose you've got my future planned as well?'

Muriel stopped again, this time to fling open the tack room door and poke her head inside. She wrinkled her nose. 'Someone has been using this place as a lavatory. It will have to be thoroughly disinfected.'

'Mother?'

'Of course I'm not going to interfere in your life, Meg. What a silly idea. But I think it might help you get over your crush on that German if you spent a few months in Oxford with Josie.'

'Mother!'

Muriel raised an eyebrow. 'I know all about Rayner Weiss. Adele told me in confidence about the May Ball, and your father mentioned that he'd turned up here as well. I'm not stupid, Meg. I can work these things out for myself.'

Feeling as though she were ten years old again, Meg stared at her mother in amazement. 'I don't want to go to Oxford. What would I do there?'

'I don't know. Study something or simply keep

Josie company. She's been very depressed since Paul ran off with the silly little ATS girl. Apparently the affair started before the war, but she was married. Then her husband got himself killed and she wept all over Paul Shelmerdine's broad shoulder. You know how susceptible men are.'

Struggling to cope with this shocking piece of news, Meg swallowed hard. 'I can't believe it. Aunt Josie and Uncle Paul seemed like a perfect couple. She absolutely adored him.'

'You have a lot to learn about men, my dear Meg. Anyway, Josie is expecting you as soon as we can book a passage. The change of air will do you good.'

The London planes were heavy with dusty summer foliage as the taxi pulled up outside Aunt Josie's house. Meg felt as if she had travelled back in time; everything looked exactly the same as it had six years ago. She paid the driver and he carried her cases up the red brick front steps just as Josie opened the front door.

'Meg, darling. How lovely to see you again.' She flung her arms around Meg's neck and kissed her cheek, enveloping her in a heady waft of Mitsouko. Tipping the cabby handsomely, despite Meg's protests that she had already done so, Josie waited while he hefted the suitcases into the hall. She closed the door on him, turning to Meg with a welcoming smile. 'You're so thin, but you look utterly gorgeous. Come into the drawing room and we'll have a drink.' Leading the way, Josie rang for the maid and almost instantly a large girl with thick legs and a sulky face barged into the room.

Meg suspected that she had been loitering in the hallway. Either that or she had a magic carpet secreted somewhere in the servants' quarters.

'Grace, will you take the suitcases up to the guest room, please?'

For a moment Meg thought that Grace was going to refuse, but she replied with a grunt and lumbered out of the room. She could be heard grumbling as she bumped the cases on each tread of the staircase.

'You just can't get good help nowadays,' Josie said, sighing. 'Girls don't want to go into service. They earn far more in factories than we can afford to pay them.' She went to the cocktail cabinet and poured a measure of gin into a glass. 'I'm having a snifter, Meg. How about you?'

Meg shook her head. 'No, it's a bit early for me, thanks, Aunt Josie.'

Josie added a splash of water and took her drink over to the sofa. She sat down, raising her glass to Meg. 'Here's how, darling. Now, tell me everything. I want to hear your story from the day you left us until – well, until today.' She curled her legs elegantly beneath her, listening quietly and sipping her drink. Meg gave her a graphic account of their life during the occupation, but she hesitated when it came to explaining about her relationship with Gerald.

Josie put her head on one side, smiling. 'Darling, you don't have to be tactful. I know all about my brother's peccadilloes.'

'You knew about his affair with Marie?'

'Of course I did. Don't forget I was just a child

at the time and living at home. Charles was a very naughty boy. He had an eye for a pretty face, but don't they all? Anyway, I have to give Muriel her due; she was an absolute brick about everything. We never really got on, you know. Too different, I suppose. But I did admire her for standing by Charles as she did, and for seeing that the boy had a good education. But then, Marie was an excellent cook and maybe Muriel thought that Gerald would be useful one day.' Josie pulled a face. 'I'm sorry, darling. That was extremely bitchy of me. I know I wouldn't have behaved so well in similar circumstances. Well, actually, I haven't, if it comes to that.' She broke off as Grace bounced into the room to announce that dinner was on the table. She left as suddenly as she had appeared, slamming the door behind her.

Josie raised her delicately pencilled eyebrows. 'Thank goodness we don't entertain nowadays. Grace would sound the death knell to any dinner party.' She uncurled herself in a sinuous, catlike movement and stood up. 'Let's eat, shall we?'

Meg stood up and brushed the creases out of her skirt. 'Aunt Josie, Mother told me about...'

'About Paul and the beastly little redhead? It's all history now. I'm completely over it. But please, Meg, don't call me aunt. It makes me feel old and ugly.'

'You're the most gorgeous woman I've ever met in my life and you don't look a day older than you did six years ago.'

'You're very sweet, Meg dear. But I know it's not true. Anyway, Paul's gone and he won't be coming back.' Josie gave her a brittle smile and led the way to the dining room.

Grace plonked a bowl of brown Windsor soup in front of them. 'Tureen's broke, missis. I had a bit of an accident.'

'Thank you, Grace. That will be all.' Josie waited until she had gone, shaking her head. 'I'll have to let her go, of course. Anyway, I can't really afford to keep her on.'

Meg tasted the soup. 'This is good.'

Josie poured wine into Meg's glass and filled her own, taking a mouthful and then refilling it to the brim. 'This is the last of Paul's wine cellar. It gives me a morbid satisfaction to think that I'm enjoying it and he isn't.'

Meg forced her lips into a smile, but she did not believe a word of it. She could sense Josie's pain was still raw, and worse still, she was obviously drinking far too much.

'Don't worry,' Josie said, refilling her glass for the second time. 'I'm not drowning my sorrows in drink, but it does help a bit. I'm divorcing him, you know.'

'I can't say I blame you, but are you sure that's what you want?'

'Listen to you, poppet. You sound like the sensible adult and I'm the gauche teenager. No, of course it isn't, but I don't have much choice. Paul is dotty about Pamela and he's asked me for a divorce, so what can I do? Anyway, I found out that she wasn't his first affair. It's amazing how people crawl out of the woodwork to tell you things you'd rather not hear when there's the hint of a scandal. Apparently most of those nights spent working late at the office had nothing to do with his career. Sorry, this is all very sordid.'

'You could fight for him.'

'Oh, my dear! You are so very young.'

'Well, I would. If you really love him go out and get him back.'

'And you'd do that, would you?'

'I most definitely would.'

'Maybe, but you're thinking about that handsome young German, aren't you? Not an unfaithful husband like mine.'

Meg felt the blood rush to her cheeks and she stared down at her empty plate. 'I don't think I'll ever see him again.' She could not bring herself to admit that Rayner was never far from her thoughts. Even now she had a letter in her pocket ready to post to the only address she had, which was his parents' home in Dresden. She had already sent two such missives but had not yet received a reply.

Josie was silent for a moment, sipping her wine. 'If he truly loves you, Meg, nothing will keep him away.' Then, as if being serious was too much for her, she chuckled mischievously. 'In the meantime, there's nothing as good for a broken heart as keeping occupied. You could go to college and study, or you could come and work for me in my little boutique.'

'Really? You've got a shop?'

'Boutique sounds better, darling. I invested most of the money that Paul gave me to salve his delicate conscience in the lease on Madame Elizabeth's dress shop. Do you remember it?'

'I'm not likely to forget.'

'Her husband was badly wounded in North

367

Africa and she sold up so that she could stay at home and look after him. I bought the stock and used my inimitable fashion sense to build up my clientele. It also helps to have rather well-off friends with lots of clothing coupons.'

'You're amazing, Josie.'

She threw back her head and laughed. 'I am, aren't I, darling. And tomorrow you can come and lend a hand. It will take your mind off that young man of yours.'

'I just wish I could find out where he is and if he's all right.'

'Maybe Walter would know.'

'Walter?'

'You remember Walter. The boys were insepar-able, as I recall. Anyway, poor Walter suffered a dreadful injury when he was clearing landmines in Normandy. He lost his right leg below the knee and he was discharged from the army over a year ago.'

'Poor Walter. How dreadful.'

'He's made a marvellous recovery, poor dear, and makes jokes about his peg leg. He's been terribly brave about the whole thing and now he's back in his old college finishing his degree.'

Meg felt a surge of renewed optimism. Walter had been close to Rayner. He had been planning to visit the family in Dresden before the outbreak of war put a stop to such things. If anyone knew how to contact Rayner, it would be Walter. 'Do you know where I can find him?'

'He comes to tea every Sunday afternoon and we have long talks. He's a dear boy and he's helped me enormously. He'll be delighted to see you,

Meg. He always had a soft spot for you.'

'I liked him too, but that's as far as it ever went.'

Josie shrugged and drained her glass. 'Well, who knows? Anyway, tomorrow I'll take you to my little shop and we'll find you something more suitable to wear than that frightful thing. Frankly, darling, it's only fit for the dustbin.'

'But I haven't any clothing coupons.'

'Not to worry. I have a nice line in second-hand gowns that I keep for special clients. No coupons needed, you just have to promise not to wear them where you'll meet any of my snooty friends.' Josie tapped the side of her nose and began to giggle. 'Oh dear, I'm quite blotto, sorry. I meant to keep sober tonight of all nights. Ring for Grace, will you, darling? I need some of Mrs Sparks' Woolton pie to sop up the alcohol.'

Madame Elizabeth's, now renamed simply Josephine, had changed almost beyond recognition. Josie had replaced the red floor covering and spindly gold chairs with coffee and cream carpet and stylish art deco armchairs in chocolate-brown leather that she had bought in a house sale. The fitting rooms were lined with floor-length mirrors and everywhere there were vases of fresh flowers and planters spilling over with ladder ferns and tradescantia. It soon became obvious to Meg that Josie was a shrewd business-woman, and, once inside her shop, she changed from the languid social butterfly into a hard-headed but charming saleswoman. She had lost none of her generosity though, and Meg was soon kitted out with a wardrobe that went beyond her wildest expectations.

'Can't have you letting the side down,' Josie said, standing back and critically appraising a slim-fitting dress in dove-grey moiré that Meg was modelling to great effect. 'That's very elegant. Just the sort of thing my assistant would wear.'

'I didn't think you had an assistant.'

'I have now, darling. And there goes the shop bell. Why don't you begin right away?'

It was fun. Meg had to admit that working with Josie was the most enjoyable thing she had done in years. Some of the clients were stuck-up and patronising but others were charming and a pleasure to serve. Meg had never thought of herself as being interested in fashion, but it was a welcome change from the hard physical labour of working on the farm, and she discovered another side to herself. The artistic and sensuous part of her personality that had never had a chance to develop now revelled in the touch of silk, satin and velvet. Her eyes feasted on the vibrant primary colours, the rainbow shades, and the subtle taupe and stark black and white. She wasn't a bad saleswoman either, she thought, as she danced around the shop after her first sale. She threw the handful of crisp pound notes into the air with a joyous whoop. She did not hear the shop bell in her excitement, but when she realised that someone was standing in the doorway she stopped cavorting and turned slowly, her hand automatically flying to smooth her hair back into the sleek pageboy style that Josie's hairdresser had expertly shaped.

'You haven't changed a bit,' Walter said, grinning. 'It's fantastic to see you again, Meg.'

'Walter.' Forgetting that she was supposed to behave with decorum, she rushed to his side and gave him a hug, almost knocking him off balance. 'I'm so sorry. I forgot about your...'

'My peg leg? Don't worry. I'm getting used to it.'

She moved away and bent down to retrieve the notes. She did not want him to see the tears of pity that threatened to spill down her cheeks. Poor Walter. Why did it have to happen to someone like him? She swallowed hard and went to the till to stash the notes away. 'Josie tells me you've helped her through a bad time.'

'And she's helped me too. She's a wonderful person, Meg, and that rotter of a husband of hers didn't deserve her.'

She shot him a curious look, wondering if there was more to his relationship with Josie than either of them acknowledged. She had suspected as much years ago, but had abandoned the idea as being ridiculous. Her aunt was gorgeous, but even though she was many years younger than Uncle Bertie and Pa, she must be at least ten or twelve years Walter's senior. 'You've seen a lot of Josie recently?' she said casually.

Leaning heavily on his walking stick, he made his way to the nearest chair and eased himself into it. 'We've supported each other through the bad times. I doubt if I'd have got through the first term back at Trinity if she hadn't alternately bullied and sweet-talked me into it. Anyway, that's enough about me. I want to hear everything that has happened to you. You must have had a terrible time.'

Meg cleared her throat. There was only one

question she wanted to ask him, but her mouth had gone dry and she struggled to find a way to bring Rayner's name into the conversation. She glanced at her wristwatch.

'It's lunch time,' Walter said, as if reading her thoughts. 'I'm sure Josie won't mind if I take you out for something to eat.'

'She went to buy flowers for the shop. She should be back soon.'

'Then I'll wait and perhaps we can all go together.'

Meg gave up trying to be subtle. 'Have you – I mean – I don't suppose you've heard from Rayner?'

'I have as a matter of fact. Had a letter only last week. Poor chap, he lost both his parents when Dresden was bombed.'

'I'm so sorry. How awful for him.' Meg sat down suddenly. 'But he wrote to you, Walter. Where is he?'

Walter leaned forward, his brow puckered into a worried frown. 'Are you okay, Meg? You've gone a funny colour.'

'Is he all right? Do you know where he is now?'

CHAPTER TWENTY

'Brazil?' Meg almost fell off her seat.

'Yes. Apparently there was nothing left for him in Dresden, and his uncle has always wanted him to help run the coffee plantation, so off he went.'

Meg's heart was doing a fandango inside her ribcage. She could not believe that Rayner would have done such a thing without letting her know. 'Have you still got the letter?'

Walter shook his head. 'I read it and then I burnt it. Ridiculous, I know, but quite honestly, I didn't want anyone to find me in possession of a letter from a German. Feelings still run high, you know.'

'But Rayner was your friend.'

'And still is, but some people might get the wrong idea.'

'That's appalling.'

'Yes, you're right, but I'm afraid that was my first reaction. I did write back though and wished him well.'

'Can you remember his address?'

'I can't and I didn't write it down either. Anyway, why the interest? I'd have thought after five years of living under German occupation you'd be glad to see the back of them all. Unless ...' He gave her a shrewd glance. 'He said that he'd sat out the war in Guernsey. Is there something going on between you two, Meg?'

She was about to deny it when the shop door opened and Josie breezed in with her arms full of flowers. Her face lit up when she saw Walter, and he struggled to his feet with a smile that convinced Meg that her suspicions were well founded. The air fairly crackled around them, and it was obvious that the only person on his mind was Josie.

'Let me take you both out to lunch,' he said, relieving Josie of several bunches of dahlias. He set them down on the bow-fronted bird's-eye maple desk that served as a counter.

'I'll get a vase and put them in water first,' Josie said, blowing him a kiss as she disappeared through the curtained archway.

All Meg wanted at this moment was to be left alone as she struggled to come to terms with the fact that Rayner had left Europe without bothering to contact her. He had written to Walter, but had not seen fit to send her so much as a postcard. Despite his promise to love her forever it looked as if it was all over between them. Perhaps the death of his parents in the bombing raid had been too much for him to bear. Her spirits plummeted to a new depth of despair, and the prospect of having lunch with two people who couldn't take their eyes off each other was even more depressing.

'Meg, come on,' Walter said cheerfully. 'We're ready to leave.'

Josie and Walter were standing in the doorway, waiting for her. She felt as if her lifeblood was draining away from an invisible internal wound, but she must put on a brave face. She had lived through the hardships and terrors of the occupation; she would live through this too. 'I'm coming.'

Josie's divorce came through just before Christmas. Walter had somewhat unwillingly decided that he would return to his parents' home for the vacation. On the day of his departure, Meg watched as he and Josie parted with self-conscious pecks on the cheek. It was obvious that their feelings for each other ran deep, but they both appeared to be in denial. Meg wondered when, if ever, they would admit that they were hopelessly in love. That evening, Josie had drunk far too much before, during and after dinner. She had fallen asleep on the sofa, but when her snoring became too much for Meg to bear, she shook her aunt awake. After giving her a much-needed lecture on the stupidity of drinking herself to an early death, Meg informed her that they were going to Guernsey for Christmas whether Josie liked it or not.

The manor house was a chaotic mix of adults and over-excited children. Meg was staggered to find that her mother had allowed Maud and Bertrand to stay on. Muriel appeared to tolerate them as if they were a pair of garden gnomes who were not much use and not very pretty, but served some indefinable purpose of their own. Everyone else had been slotted neatly into their places like silver cutlery in a mahogany canteen. Gerald seemed happy enough in his new job, taking over almost exactly where Eric had left off, but with the promise, so he told Meg with a pleased grin, that eventually he would inherit his fair share of the estate.

Jane was now well established in the nursery suite caring for Jeremy who also seemed to have been absorbed into the extended Colivet family; so much so that Meg wondered whether Simone had been another of her father's little mistakes and had nothing at all to do with Eric. She hastily pushed the idea to the back of her mind as being unworthy. Jeremy was not alone in the nursery as Adele and Frank had arrived a day or two earlier, bringing with them their twin daughters Amy and Lucy and their son, Francis, a noisy and demanding two-year-old.

Pip had been elevated from being the Guernsey joke to Muriel's devoted follower and handyman. Meg was compelled to inspect his work on the stables where, with the help of Billy and Joe, he had dismantled all the bunks erected by the German soldiers and taken down the partitions. They were now restoring the stalls to their former use.

Marie was still undisputed queen of the kitchen, and to Meg's surprise was now living in at the manor, having decided to let out her house in Hauteville. Meg suspected that her mother would not have sanctioned Marie's continued presence in the house had she not been such an excellent cook and therefore totally irreplaceable. Nevertheless, her admiration for her mother's stoic handling of the situation grew by the hour.

The drawing room had been cleaned and redecorated. The Aubusson carpet had been re-laid and Muriel's precious collection of porcelain figurines had been brought down from the attics. The silver-framed family photographs were now in their right places on top of the Steinway, which bore a few scars and cigarette burns but these had been polished almost out of existence. Meg sighed appreciatively; only Mother could have brought about this transformation in such a short time. It was good to be home but only for a visit; deep in her heart she knew that there was no real place for her here. She would always be welcome, she knew that, but Mother was the undisputed mistress of the house and there was no room for a rival, not even a much-loved daughter.

Her father had been delighted to see her and

Meg was pleased to see that he had gained weight and appeared to be much fitter. He had reopened his chambers in St Peter Port, attending daily, even if it was just an attempt to escape from Muriel's unrelenting campaign to restore Colivet Manor to its former glory. Meg realised, with a tinge of jealousy, which she quickly pushed to the back of her mind, that without her mother there to organise his life, the father she had always adored had been, despite his academic brilliance and personal charm, only half a man. His love for Marie had matured into an enduring and mutual friendship, which his wife accepted with surprisingly good grace. They were a ménage à trois in a way that might baffle anyone who did not understand their history.

Adele was happily rotund in the sixth month of her latest pregnancy, but still managed to wrap her devoted Frank around her little finger. Then there was David, who seemed just the same as ever, except for the deeply etched furrows on his forehead and the tracery of fine lines that radiated from the corners of his eyes. But the rigours of war had not blunted his boundless enthusiasm for life or his sense of fun, and he was obviously very much in love with Sonia. Meg realised within a few moments of meeting her brother's fiancée that this was the one and only girl as far as he was concerned, and she herself took an instant liking to Sonia. Even Adele and Mother, who on occasions in the past had behaved like a witches' coven and ganged up against David's former girlfriends, seemed unable to find anything in his fiancée to criticise. Meg sometimes caught them watching Sonia closely as if waiting to pounce on the tiniest of social blunders, but Sonia never seemed to make mistakes. She was so patently good-natured and eager to please that even Maud and Bertrand were charmed by her. The children rushed to greet her whenever she came into the room, sticking to her like burrs on a dog's coat, and had to be physically prised off when David wanted Sonia to himself.

The only person who seemed at all out of place was Josie. Meg sensed immediately that Mother and Josie, although they had greeted each other with hugs and kisses, deep down harboured a mutual dislike. Mother was too clever to show it in front of the family, but Josie seemed edgy and chain-smoked until Adele complained that it made her feel sick. After that Josie disappeared into the garden whenever she needed a cigarette, joining David and Sonia on the terrace.

Two days before Christmas, Gerald and Pip felled a twenty-foot pine tree and dragged it home on the cart drawn by a very elderly Sapphire, who was really retired from duty now but, as Gerald said, they harnessed her up occasionally to make her feel wanted. Meg and Sonia decorated the tree with the help of the twins and Jeremy, who stood on and crushed more of the glass balls than he managed to pass up to them and was eventually relegated to sorting the tinsel. Muriel was supervising activities without actually getting her hands dirty. Having given everyone their tasks for the day, she retired to the study with the *Morning Post*. Maud, Bertrand and Charles dozed by a roaring log fire in the drawing room. Marie and Jane were in the kitchen up to their elbows in flour and mincemeat, and Meg discovered David peeling potatoes in the scullery.

Taking off a floral print apron he tossed it at her. 'I've done my share of the chores for today. You can clear up for me, Meg.'

'You don't get out of the washing up that easily, David.' She hung the pinafore back on its peg. 'Anyway, I'm on child-minding duty in the hall. Come and see the tree. It's finished.'

He linked his hand through her arm as they left the kitchen and made their way to the entrance hall. 'How are you really, Meg?' David asked anxiously. 'Do you still miss the old Kraut?'

She patted him on the cheek. 'Like hell, if you must know. But I doubt if I'll ever see him again. I've just got to get on with my life.'

He stopped to give her a hug. 'Good for you. I only want you to be happy.'

In the hall, they stood side by side, admiring the tree. David turned to Jeremy who was chasing Amy with a sprig of holly. 'Are you supposed to be doing that?'

'It's fun making her squeal,' Jeremy said, grinning impishly.

David swooped on him and set him on his shoulders. 'There, now you can't get into any trouble, can you?'

Jeremy's response to this was to pull David's ears. 'I can see you with half a dozen kids, David,' Meg said, wistfully. Having a family of her own seemed a distant dream now.

'The more the merrier,' David said, tickling

Jeremy's bare legs and making him shout with laughter.

Sonia had been clearing up but she paused, smiling indulgently. 'Don't I get a say in this?'

'Of course not, darling. You're just the little woman.'

She tossed a pine cone at him, narrowly missing Jeremy, who screeched gleefully. 'Do it again, Auntie Sonia.'

David set him down on the floor. 'I think that's enough of that, young man. Why don't you go and find Auntie Jane and ask her for a mince pie?'

Lucy tugged at his sleeve. 'May we have one too, Uncle David?'

'Sure, poppet. You and Amy go with Jeremy.'

'I'll take them,' Sonia said, grasping Jeremy by the hand. She brushed David's cheek with her lips as she went past.

'Thank you, Auntie Sonia,' Lucy said sweetly.

David watched them walk away, shaking his head and smiling. 'What polite children. Addie must beat them with a stick every night.'

'Shut up and do something useful,' Meg said, thrusting an empty cardboard box at him. 'Help me finish the tidying up.'

He eyed her speculatively. 'And what about you, Meg? Are you really all right? About Rayner, I mean.'

'I'm okay.'

'You'll get over him eventually and find someone who deserves a splendid girl like you.'

'Have you heard from him recently?' She had made an effort to sound casual, but she could not quite control the telltale break in her voice.

'As a matter of fact I had a Christmas card from him a couple of weeks ago.'

Meg's fingers froze around a glass ball that had rolled beneath the tree. 'And?'

'He said he'd written to you many times, but you hadn't replied. He wanted to know if you'd met someone else.'

The glass ball shattered in Meg's grasp and she stared blankly at a pinprick of blood oozing from a small puncture wound. 'I didn't get any letters.'

David shrugged his shoulders. 'He must have sent them here. Ask Mother, maybe she's kept them for you.'

'Did he say anything else?'

'You're bleeding all over the floor, Meg. You'd better go and stick that finger under the tap.'

'Did he say anything else, David?'

'You know me, Meg. I can't be bothered with reading letters – or writing them come to that. As far as I can remember, it sounded as though he was settling down in Brazil, and wasn't thinking about returning to Europe. There can't be much left for him in Germany, after all.'

Wrapping her hanky around the cut on her finger, she pushed past him and went in search of her mother. She found her in the study, opening the post. 'Where are my letters, Mother?'

Muriel looked up, the paperknife poised over a deckle-edged envelope. 'What letters?'

'You know very well what letters. The ones postmarked Brazil.'

'I don't know what you mean.'

Meg thumped her good hand down on the

381

desk. 'Yes, you do.'

Muriel's eyes narrowed and her lips set in a thin line. 'As a matter of fact I burnt them. Your unfortunate liaison with the young German is best forgotten, Meg. He was quite unsuitable for you.'

'How dare you, Mother? How dare you interfere with my life? Those letters were addressed to me.'

Calmly, with eyes like shards of glass, Muriel stood up. 'That's quite enough of that, young lady. I can see Josie's influence here and I don't like it.'

'It's got nothing to do with Josie. I'm a grown woman not a schoolgirl and you've probably ruined my life.'

'Calm down, Meg. I won't have these tantrums in my house.'

Muriel's icy voice and hard eyes had their effect and Meg's anger crystallised into a hard ball inside her stomach. 'When I didn't reply to his letters he must have thought that I didn't love him any more, but nothing could be further from the truth. He may even have found someone else, and it's all your fault.'

'If he's found someone else already then he didn't think much of you in the first place and you've had a lucky escape.' Muriel held her hand out towards Meg with a conciliatory half-smile. 'Meg, I know what it's like to have a husband who cheats on you. I wouldn't want you to suffer the same thing.'

For a moment Meg hesitated, feeling like a child yearning for her mother's smile of forgiveness, but she was too angry to apologise. Anyway, she thought bitterly, why should she? She was not the one in the wrong. She took a step backwards,

382

shaking her head. 'It won't work on me, Mother. You may be able to make the rest of them do exactly what you want, but I've been through too much not to know my own mind.'

Muriel dropped her hand to her side. 'You've lost your mind, if you want my opinion. You've seen how the islanders feel about Jerrybags. You would be socially ostracised if you took up with a German.'

'There's not much danger of that, is there, since you decided to interfere. I'll never forgive you for this. Never.' Meg stalked out of the room, slamming the door behind her.

'Hey. Where's the fire?' Gerald grasped her by the shoulders as she cannoned into him.

'Let me go.'

His eyes searched her face. 'What's happened, Meg? Who's upset you?'

'I've got to get out of this house before I scream.' He hooked his arm around her shoulders. 'It's pouring with rain. You'll be soaked to the skin in minutes.'

She made for the front door. 'I don't care.'

Hurrying after her, he caught her by the arm. 'Wait a minute and I'll fetch our coats. I'm taking the car into town to collect your father from his chambers. Come with me and you can tell me all about it.'

Gerald drove in silence while Meg told him what her mother had done. 'So that's it,' she said finally. 'I stood up to her for the first time in my life, and now all I want to do is get the next boat back to the mainland.'

'Unless you can walk on water you'll have to wait until the Christmas holiday is over.'

'I'm so bloody angry. I feel I could run across the waves without sinking.'

'Well, at least wait until it stops raining.'

His expression was so comical that Meg found herself giggling, or was she crying? It felt much the same. She wiped her eyes on her sleeve. 'Oh, Gerald, I have missed you. I'm so glad that we're friends again.' She reached out and laid her hand on his as it rested on the gear stick.

'Me too. I never thought I'd be able to say that and mean it, but I do. Part of me will always love you, Meg, but I've grown used to the idea that you're my sister. It's an odd thing, but working on the estate and living in the manor house actually helps me to feel part of the family.'

'And you're happy with that?'

'I wasn't at first, but I am now. Give it time, Meg. Maybe you've got the wrong idea about Rayner. After all, he did write to you and you've no idea what those letters contained, so don't be too quick to jump to conclusions.'

'But both Walter and David said that he'd settled in Brazil.'

'He's too besotted with Sonia to get things straight. I'm sure you'll hear from Rayner again. Just give it time.' He brought the car to a halt and leaned across Meg to open the door. 'Hop out. I'll pick you up on the way back. That'll give you half an hour at least to have a girlie chat with Pearl.'

Meg realised that they had stopped outside the Tostevins' house. She kissed him on the cheek. 'You're the best friend and brother in the world.'

'I know it,' Gerald said, chuckling. 'Off you go.'

She climbed out of the car and waved as he drove off towards the town centre. She had a feeling of déjà vu as she walked down the path. It was exactly a year ago that she had arrived cold and distraught on Pearl's doorstep. There had been the same salty bite in the air then, and the monotonous swish of rain bouncing off glistening pavements. The electrically charged emotions of that afternoon in the Tostevins' bitterly cold parlour came flooding back, and her hand shook as she reached for the doorbell.

Pearl screamed with delight on seeing her. She dragged Meg down the hall to the drawing room where a coal fire burned in the grate. A small Christmas tree swathed in twinkling fairy lights stood on top of the piano. Buster cavorted around Meg, nuzzling her hand and whimpering with excitement. It was only then that she realised that they were not alone. A young man wearing naval uniform rose from a chair by the fireplace.

'Isn't it marvellous, Meg?' Pearl said, smiling happily. 'Teddy has come home on leave after all this time.' She held her hand out to him. 'You remember Meg, don't you, darling?'

'Of course I do,' Teddy said, slipping his arm around Pearl's waist. 'It's good to see you again, Meg.'

'You too, Teddy.' Meg forced her lips into a smile, but their happiness only seemed to make the hollow place in her heart grow larger.

'Pearl has been telling me about the terrible time you've had,' Teddy said sympathetically. 'You poor girls, what you must have been through.'

'It's all over now,' Pearl said, waving her left hand in front of Meg's face. 'Do you like my ring? Teddy bought it for me yesterday. I'm so happy I could burst.'

On the journey home, Meg sat in the back of the car barely speaking. Her father and Gerald chatted amicably about practical matters, and it was a relief that they did not expect her to join in. She felt strangely alienated from the people who had been so much a part of her life. None of them could fully understand her pain and loneliness. She would never know what Rayner had put in his letters, and by the same token he would be left wondering why she had not answered them. She could only hope that Gerald had been correct in his assumption that Rayner would try to contact her again. Buster snuggled up against her on the back seat and licked her hand as if he alone understood. Pearl had tried to persuade her to leave him with them, but Gerald had promised to look after him while Meg was away from home. She felt that if she lost Buster now, she would have lost everything she loved. She knew it was irrational, but his mere presence was a comfort.

Muriel met them in the hall. She gave Meg the all too familiar Gorgon look, with her pencilled eyebrows raised. It was a challenge, and Meg knew that in a battle with her mother she would be the loser.

'Sorry, Mother.'

Charles glanced at her in surprise. 'What are you sorry for now, Meg?'

Muriel took him by the arm. 'Nothing, dear. It

was a silly misunderstanding, but it's all forgotten now. Meg, go and find everyone and bring them into the drawing room for drinks. It is Christmas after all.'

For the next few days, Meg made a huge effort to appear happily normal and she joined in everything from the Christmas morning church service to parlour games on Boxing Day. She tried to enjoy the long walks over the frosty fields with Buster and the children gambolling on ahead, but somehow no matter how much effort she put into each day, she could not shrug off the feeling of alienation. The war years were too fresh in her memory to be blotted out by her rumbustious family who, much as she loved them all, had no understanding of the torment she was enduring. She kept up the unarmed truce with her mother, but Meg knew that she had overstepped the mark by openly defying her, and she could not forgive her for destroying Rayner's letters.

It was only with Josie and Gerald that Meg felt really comfortable. But she discovered to her dismay that Josie was bolstering her spirits with frequent nips from the gin bottle hidden in her bedroom.

'You can't go on like this, Josie,' Meg said when she found a second empty bottle lying on the floor by the bed.

Josie lay sprawled on her green satin eiderdown, fully dressed with her lipstick smeared and her mascara running down her cheeks like tears painted on a clown's face. She squinted up at Meg with bloodshot eyes. 'Just a little Dutch courage, that's all, darling.'

Meg tossed the bottle into the wastepaper basket. She perched on the edge of the bed. 'Josie, this is damned ridiculous. When we get back to Oxford the first thing you're going to do is to tell Walter how you feel about him.'

Josie raised herself on one elbow. 'Meg, I couldn't.'

'You must. Unless you want to drink yourself to death.'

'He's a mere boy and I'm almost forty. Everyone will say I'm cradle-snatching.'

'Who cares? And anyway, he's twenty-eight if he's a day. It's obvious that you're both crazy about each other and he needs someone like you. You need him. So where's the problem?'

Josie winced. 'Please don't shout, Meg. My head aches.'

'I'll stop if you promise to tell him how you feel.'

'All right. I promise.'

Christmas was over and it was time for the family who were returning to the mainland to leave for the ferry terminal. Meg was able to lose herself in the confusion of tearful goodbyes, hugs and kisses and promises to keep in touch. She brushed her lips against her mother's scented cheek, sensing the undercurrent of disapproval. It was quite different when her father held her in a fond embrace, and there were tears in his eyes as he begged her to come home soon.

Gerald held her for a moment and then kissed her on both cheeks. 'Good luck,' he said softly. 'Write to him and tell him what happened. Give him a chance to make things right, but remember that I'll be here for you if you ever need me.'

Meg threw her arms around his neck and gave him a hug. 'You'll always be special to me. Take care of yourself and don't let Pip tease Buster.'

Billy had already left driving the farm truck piled high with their luggage, and the family were clambering for places in the three waiting taxis. When they finally drove off in convoy, Meg craned her neck to catch one last glimpse of Gerald standing on the steps, holding Buster by the collar, waving frantically. She sat back and closed her eyes. She had secretly telephoned Walter at his home in Wiltshire. If he was not on the quay at Weymouth waiting for Josie with a huge bouquet of flowers and the courage to tell her he loved her, then she would wash her hands of them both.

The winter months gradually gave way to spring and Meg concentrated on managing the boutique, leaving Josie free to concentrate on buying stock and doing the rounds of her well-to-do friends to persuade them to part with their unwanted gowns. Business was brisk and Meg worked hard, resolutely pushing all thoughts of Rayner to the back of her mind. Although the strategy succeeded reasonably well during the busy daylight hours, it failed miserably at night. He invaded her dreams, causing her to awaken in the early hours and making further sleep impossible. She often crept downstairs to the kitchen at four in the morning to make herself a pot of tea. As the mornings grew lighter and the weather warmer she would take her tea into the garden to watch the sunrise and listen to the warbling notes of the dawn chorus.

Josie and Walter were now officially a couple. Meg had the satisfaction, as well as the occasional stab of jealousy, of seeing them unashamedly together. Walter had given notice at his digs in January and moved in with Josie. At times Meg found their obvious happiness almost unbearable and she was glad to escape to the shop. There was only so much she could take of walking into the drawing room and finding them wrapped in a passionate embrace, or seeing them wandering hand in hand amongst the daffodils and cherry blossom in the garden.

When the finals results were posted, Walter telephoned the shop immediately telling Meg that he had graduated with honours. With the money that his father had promised him if he did well, he intended to go out straight away to buy Josie an engagement ring. When Meg returned home at lunchtime, Josie was sporting the solitaire diamond as though it were the Koh-i-noor. Walter said ruefully that he could not afford the magnifying glass needed to appreciate the stone fully.

When they were alone for a moment, Josie confided in Meg that she had hidden away all the expensive jewellery that Paul had given her during their marriage, but that Walter's ring meant more to her than the Crown jewels. Meg hugged her and congratulated Walter as he came back into the room with a bottle of champagne and three glasses balanced precariously on a tray. She was happy for them, but, as soon as she could without looking too obvious, she slipped away and walked back to the shop to open up for the afternoon.

She was seated behind the desk, not really thinking about anything in particular, when the doorbell jangled and she looked up with her practised smile. 'Good afternoon.'

'Hello. I wish to buy a dress for the evenings.' The woman spoke with an attractive hint of a foreign accent. She was young and strikingly beautiful in a dark exotic way that would make anyone turn and stare at her. It was as if a bird of paradise had suddenly walked into the shop making everything around her seem pale and dull by comparison. Meg settled her client in one of the armchairs and went through to the stockroom to bring out an armful of dresses, hanging them on a gilded dress rack.

'You may like something here. If not, I have more I can show you.' Meg selected a bronze satin dress and held it up so that the material caught the light. 'Is this what you had in mind, or would you like something a bit less formal?'

'I like that very much.'

Meg couldn't help staring and thinking that she had never seen such large, lustrous eyes. They were so dark that the iris and the pupil seemed to merge into one.

'I am on my honeymoon. We only stop briefly in Oxford and then we go on to London. My husband has business there.'

'This gown wouldn't be out of place anywhere in London. If you would care to step into the fitting room?'

There was no need to flatter this customer. Her figure was perfect and the dress could have been

391

made for her. Meg stood back and waited for her decision.

'I like it very much and I think my husband will too. But I would like to try that one as well.' She pointed to a gown in gold and rose shot silk, quite similar to the one which Meg had worn at the May Ball.

'Yes, of course.' Meg helped her to take off the bronze satin gown and slipped outside to hang it on the rack. When she stepped back into the cubicle it was as if the last six years had melted away and she was staring at herself in the gold creation. Taking a deep breath, she forced a smile. 'That looks lovely too, madam.'

'The choice is difficult. You have so many beautiful things.'

'I'm very flattered that you decided to buy here instead of in London.'

'I was advised to come here. Rayner said there is no other place to buy gowns.'

Meg's fingers froze into talons and her heart kicked like a mule against her ribs, momentarily robbing her of speech. Her eyes misted and she had to struggle against a primitive desire to claw the perfect back exposed by the low-cut evening dress.

Blissfully unaware of the storm of emotion she had raised, the woman smiled. 'I am torn. The choice is painful.'

'They both suit you perfectly.' Meg's tongue seemed to have swollen to twice its size and threatened to choke her. 'Have you come from far away?'

'I'm Brazilian and my husband is German. But

perhaps I should not say so. I don't think you English like the Germans too much now.' Her laugh was melodious, like the tinkling of a wind chime. She allowed the gown to slide to the floor, exposing her voluptuous curves. 'I must take them both.'

'And your name, madam?'

'Luiza.' She gave a self-conscious giggle. 'I am not yet used to my married name. Luiza Weiss.'

CHAPTER TWENTY-ONE

Meg burst in through the front door, almost knocking Walter over in her hurry.

'Meg, you're home early.'

She pushed past him and headed for the stairs.

'Wait, please. I've got something to tell you.'

'I don't want to know.' She stormed upstairs to her bedroom, hurling herself down upon the bed and wrapping the pillow around her head. She did not cry; there were no tears left. She had lived through the most traumatic period of the war and had coped with everything that had been thrown at her, but this was the ultimate betrayal by the man she loved more than life itself. It was something she had feared but had never really thought would happen. If he had truly loved her, Rayner would have come looking for her. Nothing would have kept him away. He would not have sailed off to Brazil leaving her to face the world alone.

Luiza Weiss. The name echoed in her mind; a

death knell to hope and happiness. How could any man resist Luiza with her beautiful face and perfect body, all curves like a modern-day Venus, made for love and loving. Meg groaned out loud and stuffed the sheet into her mouth.

She must have fallen asleep, as it was growing dark and someone was sitting on the edge of the bed, calling her name. Meg opened her eyes and found herself looking into Josie's worried face.

'I didn't mean to wake you, but I was worried.'

'Go away.'

'I will, but I've brought you some supper on a tray. You should try to eat something, Meg dear.'

'I'm not hungry.'

'What happened to upset you like this?'

'I don't want to talk about it.'

Josie was silent for a moment. 'I don't understand. How did you know? Walter says he didn't get a chance to tell you.'

'Tell me what?' Meg turned her face towards the wall. Her head ached and there was a nasty taste in her mouth. She wanted to be alone.

'That Rayner came to the house today.'

Meg jackknifed into a sitting position. 'What?'

'He asked after you. Walter told him that you were here in Oxford.'

'He can go to hell.'

'Meg, darling, this isn't like you. Do you understand what I'm saying?'

She drew her knees up to her chest, wrapping her arms around her legs. 'He's married, Josie. His bloody wife came to the shop today to buy evening dresses. They're on their honeymoon.'

Josie's eyes opened wide and her mouth formed

a perfect circle. She shook her head. 'He didn't say anything about that to Walter.'

'He wouldn't, would he? But it's true, she told me so herself.'

'But Walter said...'

'Leave me alone. I don't want to talk about it.' Meg buried her face in the mound of bedclothes covering her knees, but she felt awful the moment Josie closed the door softly behind her. Poor Josie, it wasn't her fault. Talk about shooting the messenger. She flung off the blankets and swung her legs over the side of the bed. She felt suffocated and she needed air. She went over to the window and opened it, leaning out and breathing deeply. Why did he have to bring his bride here of all places? Had he done it deliberately to wound her? A small remnant of common sense told her that Rayner could have had no idea that she was in Oxford, but she thrust it aside. Once she started to be reasonable she would begin to forgive him and make excuses for his callous behaviour. There was no excuse for what he had done, none at all. Maybe he had come asking after her in order to salve his own conscience.

She paced up and down, her bare feet moving silently across the soft contours of the Chinese carpet. She stopped for a moment to stare angrily at the evening gown hanging outside the wardrobe. Josie had persuaded her that she ought to attend the May Ball as it would do her good to go out and mingle with young people instead of staying in night after night, listening to the wireless or with her head stuck in a novel. She had actually worked up some enthusiasm for the outing, but now everything was ruined. Rayner's timing couldn't have been worse, she thought bitterly, fingering the blue slipper satin. Their pledge to meet on the Folly Bridge now seemed ridiculous and farcical. Would he tell the woman he had married about her? Meg shook her head, of course he wouldn't. She was in his past now. The truth was that Luiza was his future and the truth hurt like hell.

When Meg woke up next morning her head ached miserably and she felt ill. Instead of rising early as she normally did on a working day, she lay in bed with her eyes closed until Josie put her head round the door.

'Are you feeling better this morning?'

'I feel awful.'

Josie came in with a rush and sat down on the side of the bed, laying her cool hand on Meg's forehead. 'You don't look well, darling, and you feel awfully hot. Maybe I should call the doctor.'

'I'm all right. Please don't fuss.'

Josie pursed her lips and frowned. 'You didn't eat your supper. Would you like some breakfast?'

'No.' Meg bit her lip. It wasn't Josie's fault. 'Sorry, I mean no thanks. I'm not hungry.'

Josie stood up, looking at Meg with sympathetic eyes and a furrowed brow. 'You've had a shock, darling. Better stay in bed for today. I'll manage the shop.'

'Weren't you going to the wholesalers in London today?'

'That can wait. It's more important that you get well.'

Meg raised herself on her elbow. Her head was thumping and she felt sick but she was not going to hide away. 'A couple of aspirin and I'll be fine. You go to London as you planned.'

'Are you sure?'

'Absolutely. In fact I've a good mind to go and see Rayner and tell him to his face that I think he's a cheating bastard.'

'Darling, that's not like you.'

Rising from her bed, Meg reached for her housecoat, taking care to move slowly so that the demons with picks that were hammering at her temples were not disturbed. 'I'm going down-stairs to take something for my headache and then I'll go to work.'

Josie followed her. 'Take your tablets and then I've got a better idea. We'll shut the shop for the day. After all, it is early closing, and I doubt if I'll go bankrupt losing a morning's takings.'

Meg paused on the wide oak staircase. 'Are you sure?'

Josie nodded and suddenly, as if she couldn't hold it back any longer, she chuckled excitedly. 'You can come to London with me and help choose my wedding outfit.'

'You're getting married?' Meg missed a step and only saved herself from falling by clutching the banister rail.

'It was supposed to be a secret until the day. We want to get married very quietly in the register office.'

'And you weren't going to tell me?'

'Of course we were, but we don't want a fuss.'

'And when is the wedding?'

397

Josie pulled a face and giggled. 'The morning after the May Ball.'

'But that's the day after tomorrow.'

'I know. It's fun, isn't it?'

'Josie, you're an incurable romantic.'

Josie's smile faded. 'I'm sorry, Meg. I'm being totally selfish.'

'Nonsense,' Meg said with a lift of her chin. 'To hell with Rayner Weiss, I say. We've got a wedding to organise and we'll go to London and buy you a dress that will make Walter's head spin.'

Rayner had been trying to reach her by phone all day, so Walter told Meg when she and Josie eventually returned from London, laden with the results of their shopping. He handed her a phone number where Rayner could be reached. Meg tore it up and went to bed. Next day Josie insisted that Meg was not needed at the boutique. Meg argued at first and then, relieved to have time to herself, she agreed reluctantly, promising to spend the day quietly preparing the shop accounts for the accountant.

The telephone rang several times but Meg ignored it. She shut herself in Paul's old study and applied herself to the books, finishing late in the afternoon and then luxuriating in a hot bath until Walter and Josie returned home in time to change for the ball.

Meg lay on her bed with her wet hair wrapped in a towel and her eyes closed. She could hear Josie's excited chatter and peals of laughter and Walter's deeper tones as they splashed around in the bath together. They sounded like a couple of children getting ready for a party, and Meg's intention of excusing herself from accompanying them to the ball suddenly seemed selfish. Reluctantly she raised herself, did her hair and makeup and slipped the cool satin gown over her head. She smoothed the material down over her slim hips and flat stomach, smiling a little as she remembered the last time she had dressed for a May Ball in this very room. Coming from a sheltered background, she had been little more than a child then; a girl on the brink of her adult life. She sighed. She was no longer that girl. She was a woman tried by love and war. She squared her shoulders. No man was going to get the better of Marguerite Colivet. She was not going to mope for her lost love or give in to despair. The war might be over but her personal battle had just begun.

It was a quarter to midnight and the ball was in full swing. Walter and Josie had done their best to include her in their celebrations but Meg was struggling to enjoy herself. Everyone around her was paired off, dancing, flirting, drinking champagne and having a wonderful time. She did her best to join in, but the ice-cold feeling in the pit of her stomach had grown worse as the evening wore on, and no matter how much champagne she drank it did not seem to have achieved the desired effect. She sat quietly watching Walter and Josie waltzing together, totally lost in a world of their own. Suddenly she could stand it no longer, and she scribbled a note on a paper napkin telling them that her headache had returned and that she was going home. Like a modern

Cinderella, she left the party and ran the few hundred yards to where she had parked Josie's little Austin Seven. She had insisted on driving them as it gave her the chance of an early escape. She gathered her dress into a bunch above her knees, settled herself down in the driver's seat, pulled out the choke, switched on the engine and pressed the starter button. The car coughed and spluttered and the engine purred into life on the second attempt; Meg thrust it into reverse and as it shot backwards there was a loud hiss and she felt the front nearside wheel deflate with a bump. She climbed out of the car and prodded the flat tyre with the toe of her satin slipper. There was no one about to offer help. She had not thought to bring money for a taxi, and she did not want to drag Walter away from the ball and spoil his evening. There was only one thing for it. She bundled her skirts up around her waist and kicked off her dancing shoes. She had learnt how to change a tyre, but she had never done it in the dark and certainly not in a long gown. It took her nearly an hour as the wheel nuts were tight and it needed a huge effort to loosen each one, but eventually she secured the spare wheel and wiped her hands on the travel rug that Josie always kept neatly folded on the back seat. Her dress was streaked with oil and her hands and forearms were covered in dirt and grease, but she climbed back into the car and started the engine.

She had intended to go straight home, but on an impulse she turned the car in the opposite direction. When she reached St Aldates she turned right into Thames Street and drew the Austin to a shuddering halt. She shivered in spite of the warm evening. Suddenly the most important thing in the world was to be on Folly Bridge at midnight. She knew that Rayner would not come; he would be too busy making love to the beautiful, sexy Luiza. All Meg knew was that she had to be there. There was no logical reason for it; she just knew it was something she must do, if only to lay a ghost. She picked up her skirts and ran towards Folly Bridge like a lemming about to leap over a cliff.

The silence of the night was unbroken, apart from the gentle sound of the river lapping against the stanchions of the bridge and the tip-tapping of her high heels on the pavement. There was no one in sight and she stopped in the middle of the bridge, leaning against the parapet. A faint breeze rustled the drooping branches of the willows as they dipped their fronds into the oily darkness of the water. The fruity damp earth smell of the riverbank and water meadows took Meg back to the day when they had punted downstream. She might have drowned if Rayner had not dived in to save her. But he was not here now and if she were to throw herself into that tempting swirl of watery oblivion he would know nothing about it until he read it in the morning newspaper.

'Are you all right, miss?'

She spun round and found herself staring at the buttoned tunic of a policeman.

'I didn't mean to startle you.' His face looked ghostly in the pale light of the street lamps. 'It's not a good idea for a young woman to be out alone this late at night.'

Meg licked her dry lips and leaned her back

against the parapet, realising suddenly what an odd sight she must look. 'Thanks but I'm fine, constable. I just needed some fresh air.'

He took a step forward, advancing warily as if she might fling herself over the edge at any moment. 'Come along, miss. I know it's high jinks time at the colleges but don't you think you'd be better off at home?'

Suddenly the whole thing seemed so ridiculous that Meg wanted to giggle. 'Oh no, you've got the wrong idea. I wasn't going to do anything stupid.'

'If you say so, miss. But I suggest you get yourself off home. Things will seem better in the morning.' He stood with his thumbs tucked in his belt and his feet planted squarely apart, watching her.

She backed away towards the street where she had parked Josie's car. 'Yes, you're right, officer. I'm going home.'

Poor man, she thought as she hurried towards the spot where she had parked the car, he really thought I was going to jump.

'I've brought you a cup of tea, Meg.'

Meg screwed her face against the light and squinted at the clock on her bedside table. 'Oh, my God. I've overslept. Why didn't you wake me earlier?'

Josie put the tea tray on the table and smiled. 'Don't worry. You've plenty of time to get ready. The ceremony isn't until eleven thirty. I've run your bath, so have a nice long soak.'

Meg sat up and stretched. 'I ought to be rushing around looking after you, you're the bride.'

'Never mind that. I'm all ready except for

putting on my dress.' Josie headed for the door but she paused, looking anxious. 'You will be all right, won't you, darling?'

'Don't worry about me. This is your day.'

'The taxi will be here at ten past eleven.'

'I'll be ready in time.'

Meg had to scrub her skin with a loofah and a pumice stone to get rid of the last traces of oil on her hands and arms, but less than an hour later, she was combing her hair into a shining pageboy bob and adding a touch of rose pink lipstick to her pale lips.

'Meg. Are you ready?' Josie's voice floated up from the hall.

'Coming.' Meg snatched up the confection of turquoise silk and feathers. The colour was a perfect match to her fashionable gown, which fitted tightly at the waist and then flared out in an elegant swirl to mid-calf length. She was pinning the hat to her head as she ran downstairs.

'Walter's gone on ahead,' Josie said, struggling to set her own hat at the correct angle and looking to Meg for help.

Meg adjusted it with a twitch of her fingers and handed Josie her bouquet of white lilies and trailing stephanotis. 'You look gorgeous.'

'Oh God. I'm so nervous.'

'You'll be fine. You look absolutely wonderful, Josie. Like a young girl.'

'Darling, I feel ridiculous. Everyone will say I'm cradle-snatching.'

'Don't talk rot. Walter is a mature man who's lived through all the horrors of war and is coping bravely with his disability, which you helped him to conquer. And anyway, he's dotty about you.'

Josie began to pace the room. 'I can't do it, Meg. The family will never speak to me again, and Walter's parents are going to be so furious with him for going behind their backs.'

Meg ran to the window as she heard the sound of a car pulling up outside. 'The taxi's here.'

'I can't do it. You'll have to go and tell Walter.'

'I'm not telling Walter anything of the sort.' She moved swiftly to Josie's side and gave her a hug. 'You'll be fine. Everything will be absolutely wonderful.'

They were only a couple of minutes late arriving at the register office. Walter was already seated in one of the red plush chairs and he stood up as Josie entered the room. Meg came to a sudden halt as she recognised the man standing at his side. Looking incredibly nervous and unforgivably handsome, Rayner met her eyes with an attempt at a smile.

She would have bolted back into the vestibule but the registrar, apparently unaware of any undercurrents, closed the door firmly and went to his position behind the desk. 'I have another wedding in twenty minutes,' he said apologetically. 'I don't want to rush the proceedings, but I suggest we begin straight away.'

Meg felt her legs about to give way beneath her and sank onto the seat beside Josie, turning her face resolutely away so that she would not have to look at Rayner. She barely heard the words of the short ceremony. She refused to look at him when they signed their names as witnesses and she moved away hastily, making for the door.

They emerged from the gloom of the vestibule into the dazzling sunshine outside. Another wedding party had just arrived and this time there seemed to be dozens of guests, all dressed in their best and chattering excitedly. Walter held on to Josie's arm as they edged through the crowd to where their taxi was waiting.

Rayner was at her side and Meg stole a glance at him. 'What are you doing here?' she murmured in an undertone.

'Walter asked me to be a witness.'

'Well, you've done your bit. I hope you're not thinking of coming in the taxi with us.'

Walter handed Josie into the back seat of the taxi and he turned to them with a warning frown. 'Don't spoil Josie's day.'

Meg opened her mouth to protest, but she saw Josie's anxious face peering out of the window and she knew she was trapped.

'Sit next to Josie,' Walter said, giving her a gentle nudge towards the open door. 'I'll find it easier to cope in the front seat.'

It was a waking nightmare for Meg as she sat between Josie and Rayner. The cloying perfume of the lilies could not blot out the sensual scent of the man, and it plunged her into a maelstrom of emotion. She could feel the warmth of his thigh burning into her flesh but his body was stiff and tense. They might as well have been total strangers.

The taxi ride only lasted a few minutes but to Meg it seemed like an eternity. When they decanted themselves onto the pavement outside the Mitre Hotel, she was tempted to walk away, but she knew that such an action would ruin Josie's day and that was unthinkable. Bracing her shoulders, Meg followed the bride and groom into the hotel, walking just a little ahead of Rayner but deeply conscious of his presence. Inwardly she seethed with indignation and bewilderment. She could not understand why he had agreed to be Walter's best man when he knew that she would be present at the wedding. It seemed like a cruel joke in which they had all colluded, but Josie was never knowingly unkind and Walter would cross the street rather than have an argument with anyone. Puzzled, hurt and angry, Meg followed silently as the maître d'hôtel led them through the crowded restaurant to a table in a quiet corner, which was fragrant with the scent from the white lilies and roses that surrounded a delicately iced wedding cake.

As they took their seats, Meg noticed that there were two more places set at the table and she was just trying to work this out when Rayner and Walter rose to their feet. She twisted round in her chair and almost fell off it as she saw Luiza walking towards them with a beaming smile on her lovely face. 'Rayner, we're late and it's all my fault.' On seeing Meg she threw up her hands with a throaty chuckle. 'But I know you. You are the kind lady who helped me choose the lovely gowns.'

Meg leapt to her feet but Rayner slipped his arm around her shoulders before she had a chance to speak. 'Meg, may I introduce my cousin Georg and his wife Luiza.'

Stunned and barely taking in the information, Meg nodded and found herself automatically chanting 'How do you do' in a prim little voice that sounded as if it came from someone else.

Georg grasped Meg's hand in a grip that almost welded her fingers together, and his Nordic blue eyes were disturbingly similar to Rayner's. 'This is a pleasure, Meg. We have heard so much about you.'

She found herself returning his smile. She was saved from replying by the soft hiss of a champagne cork leaving the bottle, and the waiter began to fill their glasses. There was nothing she could do without drawing attention to herself. She sat down, and Rayner took his seat next to her.

Walter stood up and raised his glass. 'Here's to my beautiful bride and to you all for joining us on this wonderful day.'

'This is so exciting,' Luiza said happily. 'Georg and I were married just two weeks ago. This is our honeymoon, and now we are here to share your wedding day. I hope you will be as happy as we are, Josie and Walter.'

Meg turned her head to look Rayner fully in the face for the first time. 'Three on a honeymoon. How Continental.'

'Meg.' Josie cast her an agonised glance.

'Continental?' Luiza frowned and then laughed. 'You are joking, of course. It is the English sense of humour.'

'It is a business trip really,' Georg said earnestly. 'We are going to London. We have new markets to open up for our coffee. It was a practical solution, yes?'

'Very practical.' Meg gave Rayner what she hoped was a withering look. He had put her in an invidious position and she was not ready to forgive him yet, maybe ever. She was uncomfortably aware that people were staring at them. The sound of German accents must inevitably be unwelcome and out of place in a quiet Oxford hotel. She could see by the covert looks from people at the adjoining table that feelings were still running high after the horrors of the war. She was even more concerned when Rayner stood up, pushing his chair back. 'Excuse us for a moment. There are one or two things I have to say to Meg that won't wait.' He seized her by the wrist and before she had a chance to protest she found herself being propelled through the maze of chairs and tables. With her nerves already on edge, she was even more agitated by the sudden silence in the room as people watched them leave the restaurant. 'What are you doing?' she hissed. 'We can't just walk out before the meal has even started.'

'They will understand.' He thrust a door open and ushered her into the hotel lounge. The room was empty except for an elderly couple seated in armchairs by the window drinking coffee and studying the daily papers. Rayner pushed Meg onto the nearest sofa and sat down beside her, grasping both her hands so that she would have had to fight to free herself. 'I've had enough of this. You are going to listen to me whether you like it or not.'

'How dare you drag me away from the table and how dare you assume that I want to listen to what you have to say?' She clenched her hands into fists but his fingers held her like bands of steel. A quick glance at the determined set of his jaw was enough to convince her that a struggle would look undignified, and it would be a waste of time.

'Whatever you're thinking of me is entirely wrong. I tried to contact you. I wrote you dozens of letters and never received a reply. I wrote to Walter and to David asking them to explain things to you, but it seems they got it all wrong.'

Meg met his eyes reluctantly and she knew that he was telling the truth, but all the pain of the last few months had etched itself into her soul. Part of her wanted to believe him while the other half of her brain warned her to be wary. 'I didn't receive your letters. My mother destroyed them.'

'I knew there had to be a good reason why you didn't reply.'

'Then why didn't you take your honeymooners to Guernsey? You couldn't have known that I was in Oxford.'

'I telephoned your home when we arrived in England. Gerald told me you were here.'

'You could have phoned Josie's house.'

'I did, several times, but there was no answer, and when I did get hold of Walter you wouldn't speak to me.'

Meg struggled with the logic of all this. She wanted to stay angry, but she felt herself slipping back under his old magic spell no matter how hard she fought against it. 'Why did you send Luiza to Josie's shop? What was I supposed to think?'

He released his grip on her wrists and slid his hands up her bare forearms to hold her by the shoulders. His eyes softened and his lips curved into his charming, crooked smile. 'You thought she was my wife?'

'Of course I did, you fool. Luiza turns up in the shop and says she is Mrs Weiss and she mentions you by name. What else was I supposed to think?'

'There never has been and never will be anyone else for me but you, my dearest Meg. How could you imagine that I'd fall out of love with you and marry someone else in such a short space of time?'

'Luiza is gorgeous.'

'Yes, and my cousin adores her but she is not you. I love you and only you.' He cupped her face in his hands and punctuated his words with swift, hard kisses that forced her lips open and left her desperate for more.

'But you sent her to Josie's boutique to buy a dress like the one I wore all those years ago. What was that all about?'

'I had no idea then that Josie owned the shop. As I recall it was Madame Elizabeth's.'

'And the dress?'

'Come with me.' He stood up and helped Meg to her feet. Holding her hand, he led her through the lounge, into the foyer and up the ancient staircase to the first floor. Walking on ahead through the narrow passage with its crazily sloping floor, he stopped outside a room and unlocked the door.

Meg hesitated on the threshold, taking in the quaint room with its latticed windows, chintz curtains and four-poster bed.

'Come in, please.' Rayner opened the wardrobe and lifted out a box that she instantly recognised. He thrust it into her hands. 'Take a look inside.'

She lifted the lid but already she knew that it contained the gown that she herself had packed in layers of white tissue paper. She raised her head. 'The dress?'

Rayner nodded. 'I asked Luiza to find me a golden gown just like the one you wore to the May Ball.'

She lifted the shimmering garment from its wrappings and held it against her. Suddenly her eyes were full of tears. 'It fitted Luiza, but I can't wear this. I'm too thin.'

He swept her into his arms, crushing the dress between them. His mouth sought hers in a hot, ruthlessly demanding and passionate kiss that swept Meg into a dizzying spiral of delight and the dawning of happiness.

'It was just a token,' he said, looking deep into her eyes. 'A reminder of how we met. Wear it for me now, Meg.'

She laughed shakily. If he let her go she had no doubt that her knees would buckle beneath her. 'It would fall off. I haven't got Luiza's curves.'

He nuzzled her neck. 'You're perfect as you are. I don't mind if it falls to the floor. I want you desperately, Meg.'

She felt his hot breath at the base of her neck and the thrill of his lips as they moved hungrily down to the swell of her breasts where her buttons had somehow come undone. The four-poster bed was only inches away and her head swam treacherously as her body cried out for him.

'We mustn't. This is madness.'

'Do you want me to stop?'

'No, but we can't do this to Josie and Walter. It's their big day. We have to return to the dining room.'

'You can't go down to the restaurant like that.'

411

Rayner grinned and began to button up her dress. 'What would they think if they saw us now?' he added softly.

She laughed and wriggled free. 'We must go back to the party, or I'll never be able to look Josie in the eye again.'

'All right. If you insist, but we'll continue this conversation later.'

When the last drop of champagne had been drunk and everyone had kissed the bride and shaken Walter's hand until he complained that it was in danger of falling off, they stood on the pavement outside the hotel while the bride and groom prepared to climb into the taxi that would take them to the station. Josie flung her arms around Meg. 'I'm glad it's worked out for you, darling. But do think carefully before you commit yourself to a man who was once the enemy.'

'It's not like that,' Meg said softly. 'I love him, and I've always loved him.'

Josie kissed her on the cheek. 'Follow your heart then, Meg.'

Walter took Josie by the hand. 'Come along, Mrs Howe. We've got a train to catch.' He helped her into the waiting cab. 'Good luck, old boy,' he said, addressing himself to Rayner, who was standing close behind Meg. 'Take care of her; she's a wonderful girl.'

'I know that very well,' Rayner said, smiling.

'What a happy day this has turned out to be.' Luiza wiped her eyes on a handkerchief, waving frantically as the taxi drove off.

Rayner had his arm firmly clasped around

412

Meg's waist. 'It's not over yet.'

She dug him in the ribs as Georg cast them a puzzled glance.

'We are going sightseeing,' Luiza said. 'Will you join us?'

'No, thanks. You two need time on your own,' Rayner said gently. 'And we have a long-standing appointment to keep, haven't we, Meg?'

They walked, hand in hand, along the High Street and down St Aldate's towards Folly Bridge.

Meg stopped in the middle, gazing into the water below. 'Why didn't you come last night?'

He took her hands in his and kissed them. 'But I did. I waited for an hour. Where were you?'

Looking into his eyes she wondered how she could ever have thought they were cold. They were like blue sapphires, filled with light and warm with love. She threw back her head and laughed. 'Josie's car had a puncture. It took me an hour to change the wheel, and then I ran here covered in oil and dirt but there was no sign of you. I almost got arrested for attempted suicide.'

It was Rayner's turn to laugh now, and Meg thought it was the most wonderful sound she had ever heard. There had been so little opportunity or reason for laughter during the war and now everything was so different; so wonderful.

'We're blocking the footpath,' Rayner said, taking her by the hand and starting back the way they had just come. 'There are two things I want to do urgently.'

'What?' Meg had to raise her voice to make herself heard above the traffic noise. 'What two things?'

413

He stopped and wrapped his arms around her. 'First we must find a jeweller's shop and I will buy you the biggest diamond engagement ring they have in stock.'

'But I don't like diamonds,' Meg protested, chuckling. 'And you haven't asked me to marry you yet.'

'All right, then.' Rayner went down on one knee in the middle of the pavement. 'Marguerite Colivet, I love you with all my heart. Will you marry me?'

Someone applauded and passers-by stopped to watch them, openly amused. It seemed to Meg then that the old saying was true. All the world loves a lover, and whatever problems the future might hold their feelings for each other would transcend them all.

'Get up, you crazy man. Of course I'll marry you.'

'And will you come with me to Brazil and help me run my part of the business?'

She traced the outline of his face with the tip of her forefinger. 'With all my heart.'

He sprang to his feet and gave her a long and passionate kiss.

'Meg, really,' he said, laughing at her protests. 'Everyone is looking at you.'

She giggled and slipped her hand through his arm as they walked on. 'All right. I give in, but I'd rather have a sapphire than a diamond. What was the second thing?'

'Put the gold dress on when we get back to the hotel and then I'll show you.'

The publishers hope that this book has given you enjoyable reading. Large Print Books are especially designed to be as easy to see and hold as possible. If you wish a complete list of our books please ask at your local library or write directly to:

Magna Large Print Books
Magna House, Long Preston,
Skipton, North Yorkshire.
BD23 4ND

This Large Print Book for the partially sighted, who cannot read normal print, is published under the auspices of

THE ULVERSCROFT FOUNDATION